the PRIVILEGE of the SWORD

the PRIVILEGE of the SWORD

Ellen Kushner

Small Beer Press
Northampton, MA

Copyright © 2006 by Ellen Kushner. All rights reserved. Published simultaneously in trade paperback by Bantam Spectra.
www.ellenkushner.com

Small Beer Press
176 Prospect Avenue
Northampton, MA 01060
www.smallbeerpress.com
info@smallbeerpress.com

Distributed to the trade by SCB Distributors.

ISBN-13: 978-1-931520-20-1
ISBN-10: 1-931520-20-8

First edition 1 2 3 4 5 6 7 8 9 0

Printed on 50# Natures Naturale 50% Recycled Paper by Thomson-Shore of Dexter, MI.
Text set in Goudy Oldstyle.
Cover illustration © Corbis: Detail Showing Hand on Ornate Sword Hilt from "Portrait of Charles IX of France" by Francois Clouet.
Endpapers illustrated by Marc Peltzer.
Book design by Glen Edelstein.

This book is
for Delia
and always was

Small pow'r the word has,
And can afford us
Not half so much privilege as
The sword does.

—Anon., "The Dominion of the Sword" (1658)

If the old fantastical Duke of dark corners
had been at home, he had lived. . . .
The Duke yet would have dark deeds darkly answered.

—Shakespeare, *Measure for Measure*, IV.iii; III.ii

All the same, he had no manners then, and he has no
manners now, and he never will have any manners.

—Rudyard Kipling, "How the Rhinoceros Got His Skin"

What a gruesome way to treat one's niece.

—James Thurber, *The Thirteen Clocks*

the PRIVILEGE of the SWORD

Part I

TREMONTAINE

chapter I

N O ONE SENDS FOR A NIECE THEY'VE NEVER SEEN before just to annoy her family and ruin her life. That, at least, is what I thought. This was before I had ever been to the city. I had never been in a duel, or held a sword myself. I had never kissed anyone, or had anyone try to kill me, or worn a velvet cloak. I had certainly never met my uncle the Mad Duke. Once I met him, much was explained.

O N THE DAY WE RECEIVED MY UNCLE'S LETTER, I was in the pantry counting our stock of silverware. Laden with lists, I joined my mother in the sunny parlor over the gardens where she was hemming kerchiefs. We did these things ourselves these days. Outside, I could hear the crows cawing in the hills, and the sheep bleating over them. I wasn't looking at her; my eyes were on the papers before me, and I was worrying about the spoons, which needed polishing, but we might have to sell them, so why bother now?

"Three hundred and thirteen spoons," I said, consulting the lists. "We're short three spoons from last time, Mother."

She did not reply. I looked up. My mother was staring out the window and gnawing on one end of her silky hair. I wish I had hair like that; mine curls, in all the wrong ways. "Do you think," she said at last, "that we should have that tree taken down?"

"We're doing silver inventory," I said sternly, "and we're short."

"Are you sure you have the right list? When did we count them last?"

"Gregory's Coming-of-Age party, I think. My hands smelt of polish all through dinner. And he never even thanked me for it, the pig."

"Oh, Katherine."

My mother has a way of saying my name as though it were an entire speech. This one included *When will you* and *How silly* and *I couldn't do without you* all at once. But I wasn't in the mood to hear it. While it must be done and there is no sense shirking, counting silver is not my favorite chore, although it ranks above fine needlework and making jam.

"I bet no one likes Greg there in the city, either, unless he's learned to be nicer to people."

There was a sudden jerky movement as she set her sewing down. I waited to be chastised. The silence became frightening. I looked to see that her hands were clutching the work down in her lap, regardless of what that was doing to the linen. She was holding her head very high, which was a mistake, because the moment I looked I knew from the set of her mouth and the wideness of her eyes that she was trying not to cry. Softly I put down my papers and knelt at her side, nestling in her skirts where I felt safe. "I'm sorry, Mama," I said, stroking the fabric. "I didn't mean it."

My mother twisted her finger in a lock of my hair. "Katie . . ." She breathed a long sigh. "I've had a letter from my brother."

My breath caught. "Oh, no! Is it the lawsuit? Are we ruined?"

"Quite the contrary." But she didn't smile. The line that had appeared between her brows last year only got deeper. "No, it's an invitation. To Tremontaine House."

My uncle the Mad Duke had never invited us to visit him. It wouldn't be decent. Everyone knew how he lived. But that wasn't the point. The point was that almost since I was born, he had been out to ruin us. It was utterly ridiculous: when he had just inherited vast riches from their grandmother, the Duchess Tremontaine, along with the title, he started dickering over the bit of land my mother had gotten from their parents for her dowry—or rather, his lawyers did. The points were all so obscure that only the lawyers seemed to understand them, and no one my father hired could ever get the better of them. We didn't lose the land; we just kept having to sink more and more money into lawyers, while the land my uncle was contesting went into a trust that made it unavailable to us, along with its revenues, which made it even harder to pay the lawyers. . . .

I was quite small, but I remember how awful it always was when the letters came, heavy with their alarming seals. There would be an hour or two of perfect, dreadful stillness, and then everything would explode. My father would shout all sorts of things at my mother about her mad family, and why couldn't she control them all, he might as well have married the goosegirl for all the good she did him! And she would cry it wasn't her fault her brother was mad, and why didn't he ask her parents what was wrong with the contract instead of badgering her, and hadn't she done her duty by him? I heard quite a lot of this because when the shouting started she would clutch me to her, and when it was over she and I would often sneak off to the pantry and steal a pot of jam and eat it under the stairs. At the dinner table my father would quarrel with my older brothers about the cost of Greg's horses or Seb's tutors, or what they should plant in the south reach, or what to do about tenants poaching rabbits. I was glad I was too young for him to pay much attention to; only sometimes he would take my face in his big hands and look at me hard, as if he were trying to find out which side of the family I favored. "You're a sensible girl," he'd say hopefully. "You're a help to your mother, aren't you?" Well, I tried to be.

Father died suddenly when I was eleven. Things got much quieter then. And just as suddenly, the lawsuits stopped as well. It was as if the Mad Duke Tremontaine had forgotten all about us.

Then, about a year ago, just when we had begun to stop counting every copper, the letters started coming again, with their heavy seals. It seemed the lawsuit was back.

My brother Sebastian begged to be allowed to go to the city to study law at University, but Seb was needed at home; he was much too clever about land and farming and things. Instead Gregory, who was Lord Talbert now, went to the city to find us new lawyers, and take his place on the Council of Lords. It was expensive having him there, and we were once again without the revenue from my mother's portion. If we didn't sell the spoons, we were going to have to sell some of my father's land, and everyone knows once you start chipping away at your estate, you're pretty much done for.

And now here was the Mad Duke, actually inviting us to the city to be his guests at Tremontaine House. My mother looked troubled, but I knew such an invitation could mean only one thing: an end to the horrible lawsuits, the awful letters. Surely all was forgiven and forgotten. We would go to town and take our place amongst the nobility there at last, with parties and dancing and music and jewels and clothes—I threw my arms around my mother's waist, and hugged her warmly. "Oh, Mama! I knew no one could stay angry with you forever. I am so happy for you!"

But she pulled away from me. "Don't be. The entire thing is ridiculous. It's out of the question."

"But—don't you wish to see your brother again? If I hadn't seen Greg or Seb for twenty years, I'd at least be curious."

"I know what Davey's like." She twisted the handkerchief in her hand. "He hasn't changed a bit. He fought with our parents all the time . . ." She stroked my hair. "You don't know how lucky you are, Kitty, to have such a kind and loving family. I know Papa was sometimes harsh, but he did care for all of us. And you and I have always been the best of friends, haven't we?"

I nodded.

"Davey and I were like that. Friends. Good friends, together against the world. We made up games, and protected each other. But people grow up, don't they? You can't stay a child forever. When my parents chose a husband for me, we were—he was—well, Davey just didn't understand that things must change."

"He hated Papa, didn't he?"

"He was only a boy; what did he know? Charles was a neighbor, not some stranger. My parents trusted him and knew he'd take good care of me. Of course I shed a few tears; I was a young girl, afraid to leave my home for the first time. My brother, though—well, he simply could not understand that, in the end, one has a duty to one's family. He never did, and he never will."

She was going to ruin that cloth, but I didn't want to stop her flow of words. A lot had happened in our family that no one had ever explained to me.

"And now it's the same thing all over again!" she cried, ripping the hem without seeing it. "Just when we thought things were about to get better, he went and made them worse, much worse, to please himself and hurt the rest of us. Just the same as now."

She started stabbing at the kerchief with her needle. "How?" I breathed, hoping to still her hands, hoping to keep the words coming. "How is it the same?"

"The duchess," my mother said, her lips tight. She wasn't even seeing me, I could tell; her eyes were on an invisible past when everything had gone wrong before I was born. "Our grandmother, the noble Duchess Tremontaine. Who didn't even come to my wedding; she still wasn't speaking to our mother. But she invited my brother to the city, to stay with her at Tremontaine House. It was his big chance—our big chance—to reconcile with her, to make something of himself. And what did he do? He ran away."

"Where?"

"To University." She bit a thread in half. "Right there in the city, right under the duchess's very nose. Mother was beside herself. Gregory had just been born, and I had to leave him here all alone with your father and the servants to go and tend to her. You know what she was like." I nodded; Grandmother Campion had been terrifying. "Next we heard, he'd run away from University as well, gone to live in some city slum. We were sure he was dead. But he wasn't dead. He was bringing more shame on us by carrying on with a notorious swordsman. It all came out when the duchess found him. I suppose he amused her, because a few years later she died, naming him her heir! Mother wrote him a long letter, and sent him some things, but he never replied."

"Go and see him," I urged her poetically. "Who knows but that he may yet relent, and remember the days of his youth, when you were the best of friends?"

"Katherine Samantha." She looked away from the past, and directly at me. "You have not been listening to what I've been telling you. It's you he wishes to see."

"Me! But—but— Why?"

She shook her head. "Oh, it's too ridiculous even to contemplate."

"Mother." I took both her hands in mine. "You cannot say that and expect me to go on counting silver as if nothing had happened. It is impossible. What does he want to see me about?"

"He says he wants to make a swordsman of you."

I laughed—well, I snorted, actually. If I'd had anything in my mouth, it would have flown across the room. That sort of laugh.

"Just so," she said. "You go live with him and study the sword, and in return he'll not only drop the lawsuits, he'll pay off all our debts, and—well, he's prepared to be very generous."

I began to see, or thought I did. "He wants me to come to the city. To Tremontaine House," I breathed. "To make our fortune."

She said, "Of course, the thing is impossible."

"But Mother," I said, "what about my duty to my family?"

chapter II

"YOU HAVE NO USE FOR GIRLS. YOU TOLD ME SO YOUR-self."

In a fine room in the Mad Duke Tremontaine's house, a fat and messy young woman sprawled on a velvet chaise longue, one hand buried in a bowl of summer strawberries. Across the room, the Mad Duke examined the back of his chimneypiece for cracks. "Utter incompetents," he grumbled. "They wouldn't know wood-bore from a tick on their dog's ass."

She stuck to the subject. "Neither would girls."

"I *do* have no use for girls. Not that way; not with ones I'm related to, anyway." He popped out of the fireplace to leer briefly, but getting no response went back and continued, "You should be grateful. Or, as the only respectable female of my acquaintance, you are the one I would have to impose upon to escort my niece to dances and things when she gets here."

The homely woman, whose name was Flavia, but whom everyone thought of as That Ugly Girl of the Duke's, put a large berry in her mouth, wiped her fingers on the velvet of the chaise and talked around it. "Any titled lady whose husband owes you money would be delighted to take your niece in hand, if only to show you how it's done properly and try to instill some gratitude in you." She licked juice off her lips. "You know, I've been meaning to ask you: why do you talk so much, when half of what you say is utter crap?"

"To keep you on your toes," he answered promptly. "How would you like it if everything I said suddenly started making sense? It would only confuse you."

Unfolding his long body from the guts of the fireplace, the duke thrust his ruffled cuffs under his fat friend's nose for inspection. "Would you say these are dirty?"

"*Dirty* is not the word I would use." She stared at the lace. "That implies that somewhere under the carbon there exists white linen in its original state. But I think an alchemical transformation has been effected here."

"At last!" He lunged for the bellpull. "I shall have to document it." His fingers left black smudges on the embroidered fabric. "You will be amazed to learn that I, too, have read Fayerweather. You have, as usual, completely bollixed his concept of Original State: it has nothing to do with alchemy."

"Did I quote Fayerweather?"

"No. You eviscerated him, and threw his carcass to the geese."

The duke's summons was answered by a stocky boy. Everything about him was middling: his height, weight, color and curl of hair, skin, ears, even his deportment, caught as it was in the middle between a boy's awkwardness and a young man's strength. His arms were a little long, but that was all.

"Isn't he wonderful?" the duke asked fondly.

The Ugly Girl threw a strawberry at the boy, which he failed to catch; nor did he run after it to pick it up when it rolled into a corner. "Dear one," she said to the duke, "you could surround yourself with much prettier company than those present."

"I do," he replied. "But they have a tendency to think too highly of themselves. So I get rid of them. Over and over and over and over," he sighed. "Marcus," he told the boy, "get me a clean shirt."

"Yes, my lord."

The duke pulled the one he was wearing over his head. "And have this one examined—the cuffs—for alchemical transformation."

"Yes, my—" The boy's face bent and broke into a laugh. "Do you mean it?"

The duke tilted his head to one side. "Hmm. Do I? I'm not sure. It was *her* idea. *Do* I mean it?"

The Ugly Girl rolled onto her back, gazing nearsightedly at the elaborate blur of the sculpted ceiling above her. "You never mean anything."

When the boy had left the room, she said approvingly, "He's got brains. It's funny how you can always tell."

"Like calling to like." It was as close to a compliment as the duke ever came; she wisely ignored it. "Well, as you pointed out, I hardly chose him for his beauty."

"I'm surprised you chose him at all. He lacks the aura of great wickedness, or great innocence. You like extremes."

"I do." The duke helped himself to the strawberries; they were his, after all. He ate them one at a time, in the manner of one who is not used to plenty.

Making sure that her fingers were well licked and dried, the Ugly Girl went to take a book from the pile on the mantelpiece. She sat by the window reading her treatise on mathematics, ignoring the duke as he received and donned his new shirt, received and interviewed an informant (who was not offered strawberries), received and made fun of a small but very ugly lamp meant as a bribe and finally went back to his fireplace excavations.

Then she lifted her head and announced, "I have thought of and discarded many conceivable reasons for you to have sent for your niece. It therefore remains that your reason is inconceivable."

"To any but me, of course."

She waited an appreciable amount of time before giving in and asking, "May one hear it?"

"I intend to make a swordsman of her."

The Ugly Girl slammed the book shut. "That tears it. That is idiotic. Possibly the stupidest thing that I have ever heard you say."

"Not at all." The duke could appear quite elegant when he chose to. He did so now, lounging in his wide shirtsleeves against the ornate mantel. "I must have protection. Someone I can trust. Of course I have a lot of hired guards—but I am paying them. And I do not like the constant company of strangers."

"You could hire handsome ones. They need not be strangers long."

"I do not think," drawled the duke at his most stickily aristocratic, "that that is very appealing. And yet—I must constantly be protected from the sudden sword-thrust, the irrevocable challenge. There are so many people around who imagine their lives would be miraculously improved by my removal. So: who better to fulfill the protective function than family?"

"Surely you have nephews?"

"Whole flotillas of them. So what?"

Not being the sort to throw a book, she pounded her fist on her cushion. "*So what*, indeed! Not content to find freaks, you must create them as well?"

The duke did not try, ever, to hide his contented smile. "I do not make the rules," he said creamily. "This annoys me, and so I comfort myself by breaking them. She is my favorite sister's—my only sister's—youngest child. I shall ensure that she has a distinctive and useful trade to follow, should the family fortunes fail. Or should the Good Marriage that is every noble's daughter's ambition prove elusive or less than satisfactory. A distinctive and a useful trade . . . it is, alas, too late for her older brothers to learn anything, really. And, anyway, I think one sword in the family is enough, don't you?"

"Crap," she said. "Utter crap. You must really hate your sister a lot."

I HAD ALWAYS KNOWN I MUST GO TO THE CITY, BECAUSE that is where one goes to make one's fortune these days. Men go there to take their seat on the Council of Lords and meet influential people; girls go to make a brilliant match with a man of property and excellent family. We had scraped together the funds to send my eldest brother, but apart from writing the occasional letter complaining about the food, the streets, the weather and the people, Gregory didn't seem to be doing much. I wasn't surprised. Greg always lacked dash.

I, on the other hand, while not quite pretty, look very nice when I get dressed up, and neighbors at parties have been known to admire my dancing. I always remember the steps, and never tread on toes or bump into others. Before my uncle's letter came, I had often tried to encourage my mother to send me to town to try my luck at finding a good match. But no matter how I begged and reasoned, it always ended with her saying, "Kitty, you're too young," which was ridiculous, since she was married herself at fifteen. If I explained that a dazzling City Season was completely different from one's mother picking a convenient neighbor, she'd say, "Well, but what man would have you with your portion tied up in a lawsuit?"

"A very rich one, of course, who cares nothing for my sad estate! I will enchant him. He will love me for my winning ways. And for my connections. I'm very well connected, aren't I? Your brother's still a duke, even if he is mad and dissolute. That counts, you said."

"But think how much more enchanting you will be when you have reached your full height, and gotten all willowy and elegant, dressed up in long gowns with real lace—"

"And a train! I must have a train, for staircases, mustn't I, Mother? And a peacock feather fan, and shoes with glittery buckles and a velvet cape." I knew that was all I needed to break anyone's heart. Let me appear on the right staircase just once in a velvet cape, and I was a made woman.

Now I was headed for one of the most glorious houses in the city, at the invitation of Duke Tremontaine himself. The lawsuit would be withdrawn, my dowry restored, if not, indeed, doubled. I was sure he had a staircase.

So there I was in the carriage, hurtling toward the city, my expectations high. The letter had included all sorts of bizarre rules I was to follow once I got there, like not writing or receiving any letters from family for six months, but that wasn't forever. I had no doubt that I was doing the right thing, and that all would be well. My uncle might have quarreled with the rest of the family, but he'd never met me. Of course I would have to prove myself to him at first; that's why he had set up the rules. I was going to be tested for courage, for endurance, for loyalty and other virtues. Once I had demonstrated my worthiness, I would be revealed to the world in my true guise and reap the rewards. The masked ball would turn to wedding feast, the silly comedy to glorious romance with myself as heroine. First disguise, then revelation. That was how it worked. What else could the story possibly be?

It was not at all the way I had ever planned to go to the city, but at least I was going. If my mad uncle wanted me to learn to use a sword, fine, as long as I would also attend balls and meet eligible men. The important thing was, he was inviting me to join his household. The Duke Tremontaine wanted me by his side, and the world was open to me.

chapter III

A YOUNG GIRL STEPS OUT OF A TRAVELING CAR-
riage into a courtyard already in shadow. But all above
her, the house's high windows glitter with the last
golden rays of the sun.

She is wrapped in a simple grey wool traveling cloak. As she
looks up at the house's glorious facade of honey-colored stone
and many-paned glass, she furls a corner of the cloak like a ballgown, and slowly pivots in place.

M Y UNCLE THE MAD DUKE LOOKED ME UP AND
down.

"You aren't very tall," he said.

Beyond his face I could see his back reflected in the convex mirror over the fireplace, so that he swallowed up the room.

"No, sir."

It was a delicious room, painted blue and white with touches
of gold; very modern, very airy, filled with pictures on the walls

and curios scattered on little tables that seemed to have no other purpose but to hold them. Tall glass doors opened onto gardens overlooking the river.

He said, "This is Tremontaine House. It is very elegant. I inherited it from my grandmother, the last duchess." When he mentioned her, the planes of his face hardened in distaste. I recognized the expression from many family dinners of our own. My uncle's face kept turning familiar, as though I'd known him all my life. A tilt of the head, a flick of the eye—I knew him—and then it was gone, and I was confronting a fearsome stranger. He had my mother's long brown hair, which looked very odd. I thought only students had long hair. He'd been a student once, but surely that was long ago.

"But you need not dress for dinner," the duke said. "Nor for much of anything, really." He drifted off, his attention caught by a china statuette on a little table. I had never been so effortlessly ignored; it was as if I'd disappeared, as if his attention could only hold one thing at a time. He picked the china up, and brought it close to his eye to examine its gilded curlicues in the light.

"I did bring nice dresses," I said. He'd almost beggared us, but he needn't think I could not dress for dinner.

"Did you?" my uncle asked idly. "Why?"

"Why?" I repeated. "To—well, to wear." His attention returned to the statue in his hands. The duke had very long, graceful hands; just the sort I've always wanted, only bigger, and studded with jeweled rings: a whole fortune, riding on one hand. This ill-mannered, well-dressed man, the monster of the family stories, was like nothing I'd ever seen before. I had no idea what he was going to do next—and, I reminded myself, I mustn't anger him. The family fortunes were at stake. But how to make him like me? I should try being more modest, and display maidenly virtue.

"I'm sure they're not in style," I said humbly, "but I could make my dresses over, if someone will show me. I do know how to sew, although I'm not very accomplished."

He finally turned his head and looked at me. "Oh, I wouldn't worry about that. Dresses. You won't be needing any."

Finally! I thought. I'd been right about one thing: the duke was going to dip into his coffers to provide me with a whole new wardrobe. I remembered my manners and said, "Thank you. That's very generous of you."

His long mouth quirked in a half-smile. "We'll see about that. Anyhow, I've arranged for your training to begin tomorrow. You will be living here at Tremontaine House for a while. I don't like it here. I'll be at the Riverside house. Unless I change my mind. I've got you a ladies' maid, and a teacher . . . and there are books and things. You won't be bored." He paused, and added coolly, "And if anyone tries to bother you—just tell them I've said not to."

I was gone again; I could see it on his face. He subsided into an armchair. How was I going to charm him with my winning ways if he wouldn't even look at me? Of no use now, the pretty speeches I'd planned in the carriage mile after mile. I stared at the elegant figure. It didn't seem rude, since by his lights I wasn't there at all. The duke had ivory-pale skin, long brown hair and long, thinly-lidded eyes and a long, rather pointed nose. He was perfectly real: I could see the fine lines in the corners of his eyes and mouth, hear him breathe, feel him shift his weight when he moved. But he was still like something in a dream. My uncle the Mad Duke.

He looked up, surprised to find me still there. "I should think," he said, in a slow, drawling purr, "that you would want to go to your room now . . ." It was one of the most unpleasant things an adult had ever said to me, awash in surprised scorn: " . . . after the carriage ride, and having to talk to me."

I risked a smile, in case he was joking. But he did not smile back.

"I don't know where it is," I finally said.

He waved one arm through the air. "Neither do I. Looking over the river, I think: it might smell a bit in summer, but the view is better." He reached out and found a bellpull. "What was your name, again?"

If he hadn't seemed simply not to care, I might have lost my temper. Still: "Campion," I said icily. "Like yours. It's Katherine Samantha Campion Talbert, in full."

He was seeing me again. The duke leaned toward me. His eyes were green, fringed with dark lashes. For the first time, his face was edged with humor. "I have been the Duke Tremontaine for something like fifteen years now," my uncle said. I didn't see what he found funny about that. "Do you know what my real name is?"

It seemed important to know it. As if, by knowing it, I might prove to him that I was real. Put all his names together, and I might come to some understanding that would tell me what he wanted.

I stared back at him. As if we were mirrors of each other, I felt curiosity, and fear, and excitement—and did not know whether those feelings were his, or my own.

"I know two of them," I said. *Campion,* and the one my mother had called him. "Three, if you count Tremontaine. I can ask my mother for the rest."

"No, you can't. Not for six months, anyway." The duke swung himself round in the chair, hooking his long legs over one arm in the graceless sprawl of a child settling down with a book. "Don't you read your contracts before you sign them?"

"I couldn't sign. I'm not of age."

"Ah, of course. Your family took care of all that for you." He swung back around to face me, with an expression on his face that made me feel cold all over. "Do you understand the terms?" he demanded. "Did she even tell you? Or did they just send you here like some sacrificial goat to buy me off?"

I met his fierce gaze, although I hated doing it. "I know about the swords," I told him, "and the six months. I have to do what you say, and wear the clothes you give me. Of course they told me. I'm not a goat."

"Good." He swung away, satisfied.

A very handsome man with short blond curls and a snub nose came into the room. He walked right past me without a glance, and leaned over my uncle's chair. He leaned down farther and farther, and my uncle reached up one arm and put it behind the man's head, and pulled him down farther still.

There was no mistaking the meaning of that kiss. This was one, just one of the many reasons my uncle the Mad Duke was not considered fit to know. I could not stop looking.

And I saw the beautiful man as he came up for air cast me a triumphant glance.

He murmured to the duke so I could hear, "Having truck with serving girls, this time?" I tugged at my dress to smooth it. It was not cheap cloth by any means, even if it was plain.

The duke hauled himself up in the chair to a level nearer dignity. "I am dismayed, Alcuin," he said in that unpleasantly smooth voice, "that you do not immediately note the resemblance. This is my niece, my only sister's youngest and dearest child. She will be staying here awhile, so you had better keep a civil tongue around her, or you will not be."

"I *beg* your pardon," said the beautiful Alcuin. "I see it now, of course—a certain, ah, cruelty about the mouth. . . ."

It took all my self-control to keep from wiping my mouth. The duke said, "Alcuin, you're not very bright. You're just nice to look at. I suggest you play your strongest suit."

The beautiful man dropped his eyes like a maiden. "Certainly, sir, if it pleases you. Will you be my master at cards, as in other things?"

"Always," said the duke dryly; "and I'm doing you a favor." Then they started kissing again.

I went and yanked the bellpull myself. Whatever it produced next, it could not be worse than Alcuin.

A boy slipped into the room like a shadow. He nodded at me, but addressed the busy duke: "My lord. Fleming asked me to remind you that your guests will begin arriving in two hours' time, and do you really want to wear the blue velvet tonight when it's this warm?"

My uncle disentangled himself from Alcuin. "Guests? What guests?"

"I knew Your Grace would say that," the boy answered with perfect equanimity. I wanted to laugh, and I thought he did, too. "You invited the poet Almaviva to read his new work here tonight. And you've invited a great many people who don't like poetry, and a sprinkle of ones who do. It's not really a fair fight."

"Oh." My uncle turned to me. "Do you like poetry, Lady Katherine?"

"Some," I managed to answer.

"Then you must swell the ranks of the believers. Can you drink?"

"*What?*"

"Can you drink a great deal of wine without behaving like an idiot?"

"Certainly," I lied.

"Good. Then go have a bath and all that. Don't rush: it'll be hours before they all get here so we can eat. Marcus, tell me, did Betty ever show up?" he asked the boy.

"Oh, yes: she's in the kitchen, practicing her curtsey."

"Well, she can practice it up here. I expect," my uncle said to me, "your room will be wherever they've put your bags. Someone will know."

B ETTY PRACTICING HER CURTSEY WAS A TERRIBLE sight to see. She had each separate move in the right sequence, but getting them to flow together seemed beyond her skill. She tugged her skirts out to each side of her. She crooked her knees. She came perilously near the ground. Then she did it again. And again; but it was never very convincing. Short and fat with middle age and scarlet with embarrassment, she resembled a quaking beet-pudding about to collapse in on itself.

"My lady," she stammered, "forgive me—there's a right way to do these things, I know—and I'll begin as I mean to go on, just the way you like it . . ."

"Thank you," I said, in an agony of impatience; "yes, thank you."

But she kept right on going: "You'll get satisfaction from me this time, my lady, and no messing about with the master, not this time, not this one, bless his boots—"

Finally I gave up and just said it: "Please, could you show me my room?"

"Of course," she panted, nearly worn out with curtseys; "that's what I'm here for, isn't it?" I handed her my cloak, in hopes it would steady her. "Of course," she said. "Of course, my lady."

She didn't look as if she could balance much more than the

traveling cloak. I picked up my other small things myself. "My room," I repeated. "Please."

"Yes, well, it's a great big house, this one, isn't it? So many doors you don't know where you are—not like the Riverside house, well, that one's big too, but different; here everything looks the same . . ."

My heart misgave me as I followed her up the sweeping staircase (it was, in fact, the Perfect Staircase of my dreams, but I was too busy handling Betty to notice. Poor woman, I thought; trying to make a good impression and not quite equipped for it! I had considerable sympathy for her, after what I'd just been through).

"Now I know it's this way," she repeated as we rounded the same corridor a third time. But at last the door stood open to the right place.

There were my trunks in the corner, looking especially shabby in the glory that was my room at Tremontaine House. A huge bed with gauzy curtains, just right for the time of year; a painted wardrobe set off perfectly against the pale butter-yellow of the walls; prettily framed pictures and vases of flowers . . . and the whole reflected in the curly gilded mirror that hung over the marble fireplace.

Betty looked at the room, looked at me, attempted another curtsey and fell flat on her bum. When I leaned over to help her up, I found that my sympathy had been misplaced. Her breath smelt like a drover's on payday.

It was too much. My rich uncle had hired me a drunkard, a slovenly woman from who knows where, to serve as my first very-own lady's maid!

I looked at her red, babbling face, at my bags, at all of it reflected in the mirror (including my own shocked face and travel-frizzled hair) and burst into miserable tears.

"There now, my lady." And the creature had her arms around me. "There now." I let her hold me while I sobbed my heart out on the drunkard's warm breast.

M Y ROOM DID INDEED LOOK OUT ONTO THE RIVER, and into the hills beyond, where the sun was finally setting. That morning it had found me waking in a strange inn on the road, surrounded by strangers. What a long day it had been! I leaned as far as I could over the balcony—*my* balcony—drinking in the sight. For natural beauty, the view from my room was not a patch on the rolling hills of home, the long vistas and sudden curves. No one could get lost in *these* hills, or tired walking along that river. But still they seemed far more exciting. And below me stretched a shadowy garden, suggestive of hedges and statues and paths one could, perhaps, get lost in. I watched as it all went blue and cold, and stars began to come out in the distance.

My huge white bed seemed to glow with its own light. I lay on its downy luxury, just for a moment—and woke to pitch darkness, and a thud against my bedroom door, and footsteps in the hall, and laughter.

Wide awake, I pulled an overdress on over my wrinkled chemise, and peeked out into the hall. A candle on a stand flared in the draft from my door. A man and a woman, whispering and laughing, were running down the hall toward its light, their inky shadows smeared out along the carpet behind them. I turned the other way, toward the stairs, where most of the noise was coming from. There were laughter and shouts, and the strains of string music flowed remarkably placid under the revelers. The party was in full cry.

I had no idea where Betty was, or how to get her to help me dress. I struck light to a candle, and picked out a green overdress that had covered deficiencies in the past; unplaited and combed out my hair, and knotted it up with a couple of pins, and clasped my coral necklace around my neck. My dove-grey slippers were nowhere in evidence, so I had to wear the apple-green, even though they did not match the dress. But I have noticed that, in large crowds, no one looks at anyone else's feet. I'd be all right if I could just get down the staircase unseen.

I paused at the top of the stairs to examine the scene below. People were spread out across the great hall; they looked like badly arranged pieces on its gameboard squares of black and white marble. They seemed to be just the spillover from the crowded receiving rooms beyond the double-doors.

I did my best to drift inobtrusively down the stairs. I was terribly hungry; there might be food beyond the doors. The people all looked very grand—*gaudy*, my mother would have said—in rich fabrics and jewels and lace and ruffles. Bobbing amongst them was a dyed ostrich feather, elegantly curled over a sleek, dark head, almost like a little hat. The head turned to me, and suddenly I was looking right into the eyes of a girl my own age. She darted forward, and seized my hands in hers.

"Isn't this *fun?*" she said. Her cheeks were pink, her blue eyes sparkled, and she wore a very good pair of pearl earrings.

"I've only just arrived. I came today, from the country."

"And already you're invited to all the wickedest parties! But I can tell that you are very, very good; I can always tell about people—aren't you just a little bit terrified, being *here?*" She gave a theatrical shudder. "Of course, the old duchess had exquisite taste; that's really why I wanted to come, to see the house, you know. Although the duke's parties are events all their own—the ones at Tremontaine House—not the Other Place—we wouldn't go *there*, of course." My new friend flashed a smile at the whole room. "Isn't it *grand?*"

I could not really see much for all the people. I noticed a cunning little pair of diamond buckles flashing by on someone's feet—or maybe they were paste, I couldn't tell. I wished I had a pair.

"Oh, yes!" I breathed.

She put her arm around my waist. "I just know we are going to be the best of friends. Where is your escort? I came with my brother Robert—the truth is," she pulled me a little closer in; "I made him bring me. He didn't want to. He said it wasn't any place for me. But I said if he did not I would tell our parents the true reason he needed the advance on his allowance. *He* told them he'd given the money to a poor friend who needed it—they encourage us to be generous—but I knew it was really because he'd spent it all on a duel over Lavinia Perry, which is silly, because she's almost a cousin. I wouldn't fall in love with a cousin, would you?"

"Oh, no!"

I had been in the city only a few hours, and already I had a friend—someone whose brother hired swordsmen, and who admired me for getting into dangerous parties. I felt very happy as she circled my waist with her arm. My new friend was shorter than I; the feather tickled my cheek.

"So...you're just up from the country. This must all seem very strange to you—although one wouldn't know it, you have such natural grace. And of course you will be at all the dances. I'm sure to see you there—we will have such fun, searching out beaux together!" She was leading me out of the press, to a corner where we could be fully absorbed in each other.

"Do you know, I've already received flowers from—an admirer!"

I clutched her arm. "Oh, *who*? Is he here?"

"No, not here; this isn't the sort of place he would be seen at. I shall get a dreadful scolding from him if he hears about it." She tossed her head, looking pleased. "But next week...Will you be at the Godwins' ball?"

"I—don't know. I don't believe we've been invited yet."

My elegant friend said, "But I feel sure that Lydia Godwin would dote on you, if only she knew you as I do! I shall speak to her. She is such a dear friend of mine. Perhaps you could come in our party, with your brother. Or was it your cousin?"

"Cousin?"

"With your escort—the one who brought you here."

"Oh. It's my—uncle."

"Oh." She frowned briefly but prettily. "Not one of those boring old married men who only comes to parties to play cards?"

"No, I—don't think he's married. I mean, he isn't. He's very elegant."

"Perhaps you'll introduce us." She pulled away for a moment, to fish in her beaded reticule for a little engraved card. "You must call on me tomorrow." She laughed happily, indicating the throng of revelers: "Not too early, of course!" I had no idea what time it really was. Close to midnight, surely. No one at this party would be up early tomorrow.

I pocketed the card. "I will come, if it's not being a bother," I said shyly, picturing a disaster, with no one home. But she squeezed my hand in hers. "Yes, yes, you must! Then you can meet my brother Robert in decent circumstances—maybe even turn his head away from the Perry chit!"

Was that all it took to get beaux—just meeting friends' brothers? This was going to be easier than I'd thought! I said, "I have no card, not yet—we don't need them at home, everyone knows everyone else. But let me introduce myself—"

"No, let me. It's much more decent," a voice announced from above. "This is my niece, the Lady Katherine Samantha Campion Talbert." My friend was staring, rather pale, over my head, at the tall duke dressed in black. He turned all the pink and silver and powder blue and turquoise in the room to sugar candy. Even my friend's delicious feather looked addled. He said, "And you're a Fitz-Levi. I can tell by the nose."

She sank down in a very lovely curtsey, with her head bowed to hide her flaming cheeks. "My Lord Duke."

My uncle looked down at the feather. "Fitz-Levi...hmmm... I don't remember inviting you. Marcus will know—" His eyes scanned the room, presumably for the boy Marcus. From what I had seen this afternoon, the duke didn't remember having invited anyone. But I could hardly tell her so at this moment. She flashed me a haunted look, pressed my hand once more and fled. By the time my uncle looked down again, she was gone.

He looked curiously at me, as though I had performed a conjuring trick.

"What happened?"

"You frightened her," I told him.

He shrugged. "Well. At least you're still here. Let's get something to eat. Are you hungry?"

I was ravenous. "Yes, please. But—why did you say that, about her nose?"

"What about her nose?"

"You said she was ugly."

"Did I?" He considered for a moment. "I suppose I did. I'd better make her an apology, then. I'll have Marcus send her some flowers."

"Don't!" I exclaimed quickly. "You'll get her in trouble."

He looked at me again with great curiosity. "What do you care?"

All the while he had been maneuvering us out of the hall and off to a side room where tables were spread with food and drink.

"By the way," he said absently, "those shoes don't match that gown."

He handed me a plate piled with strawberries, bonbons, smoked fish and asparagus.

"Ah!" he said. "Finally. Someone to talk to."

The duke was looking with great delight at a large, ugly woman coming toward us across the room. Her complexion was muddy; her hair was chopped like badly mown hay, and of the same rough color and texture. It was hard to tell how old she was; older than I, and younger than Tremontaine, I would guess. Under her shapeless dress, her big body looked thick and without contours. She couldn't be a serving maid; any of them would take pains to present a better appearance. He had terrified my friend with the lovely feather, but was smiling warmly at this troll-like apparition. The corners of his eyes crinkled, which is how you can tell whether someone is really smiling, or just curving their lips.

The ugly woman stumped up to us. "Is this the niece?"

"This is Lady Katherine. She's not very tall, but I think she'll grow."

"How do you do?" I said to her, trying to restore myself to my rightful place in the situation.

"Hello," she said to me. She nodded to the room. "What do you think?"

It was not a question I, or anyone else, could answer. She didn't seem to realize it. I reached for the safety of the commonplace: "It's very nice."

"Oh." The ugly woman nodded, as if that told her all she needed to know about me. She seized a bonbon from my plate and bit it in half. "*Ig*," she objected. "Peppermint." She began to drop the other half back onto my plate, realized what she was doing just in time before she did it and cast about for somewhere else to bestow the offending morsel.

My uncle the Mad Duke was watching her, vastly diverted, and not offering to help. I realized I was watching her with the same fascination. It was not right. "How was the poetry?" I asked.

"Brilliant." "Awful," they said at the same time.

"It depends on your perspective."

"It depends on your brains."

"The most discerning brain could find nothing to catch and hold on to in those babblings."

"What—the articulation of the *soul* holds no interest for you?"

"As a matter of fact, it doesn't."

I wished I had not missed the poetry. I had thought a great deal about my soul in the past year.

"One wonders, then," the duke said to her, "why you are here at all, since you don't like poetry, and you don't know how to dress for a party."

"I come, of course, for the food. Here." She held out her hand, with the squashed and sticky half a bonbon. I could actually watch him making up his mind whether or not to take it. From his sleeve the duke pulled out a clean handkerchief. He pincered the candy in its folds, and turned to a passing gentleman who, at the touch of the duke's hand on his arm, stopped with a pleased expression.

"Furnival," the duke said engagingly, "I was wondering if you could take care of this for me?"

He didn't even watch to see what the man did with it.

"Have you seen Marcus?" he asked his ugly friend.

"Yes, he was stopping some people in the Violet Room from climbing the curtains."

"What for?"

"They were not professionals."

"Oh."

I could see my uncle the Mad Duke eyeing the asparagus on my plate. To forestall them making any further inroads on my supper, I picked up a green spear myself, and ate it as best I could without a fork. It suddenly occurred to me that asparagus was not in season.

I ate another. I realized that my nerves were partly hunger. I couldn't remember the last thing I'd eaten; maybe some bread on the road. I had a vision of it always being like this: a house without rules, without regular meals, one that came alive only when it was full of guests, a house whose inmates had to inhabit the party world just to get something to eat. Impossible—or so I hoped. But it was even harder to imagine the mundane, us sitting down to dinner together and discussing the events of the day: what lands needed grazing, what room airing out and what servants correcting— I was suddenly brutally homesick. As if I'd eaten something tainted, I would gladly have sicked up this whole new life to get back the old. *Stop it,* I told myself sternly. I would not cry. Not here, not now—not at all. This was the world I'd wanted: the city, the parties, the glitter and gallants, fine clothes and rare company.

It would be better in the morning.

The Mad Duke had drifted off to make someone else's life miserable. The ugly woman was gone in his wake like a seagull following a ship to scoop up what amusement he let fall.

I filled another plate, made myself small in the folds of a curtain, ate resolutely, and then found myself so tired there was nothing to do but wend my way back up the impressive stairs. My new friend was nowhere in sight; she'd probably gotten her brother Robert to take her home. I felt the little square of cardboard in my pocket, reassuring like a talisman. By some miracle, I found the door to my own room. The noises of the party roared around me like the sea.

chapter IV

I N THE MORNING, THERE WAS CHOCOLATE.

Betty seemed recovered from the previous day's excesses. She must not have been working the party. The tray barely rattled as she set it down by the bed, and a heavenly rich scent filled the room.

I got up at once to engage with the little pot of bitter chocolate, set out with an entire jug of hot cream, as much sugar as I should care to put into it and, oh, the loveliest china cup to mix it in! I wished my mother were there to share it with me. I poured slowly, watching the cream swirl in the cup. It made the confusions and indignities of last night seem a little more worth it; I felt even better when Betty said, "And your new clothes have come, too."

The chocolate was marvelous, but I gulped it down, assuring myself, There will be more again tomorrow, and tomorrow, and again the day after that. I was eager to get to the brown paper parcels piled at the foot of the bed. I unknotted the string myself, being careful to put it by to be used again. Fine white linen, some heavier blue; a little lace, good . . . no silk, no velvet, but maybe I would be fitted for ballgowns later. I shook out the blue: it was a tight, short linen jacket. Not a fashion I'd seen before; maybe a riding coat? It had a skirt to match—no, it was breeches. Breeches that buttoned up on either side, with a flap in the front.

I frowned. "Betty, are you sure these are for me?"

"Oh, yes, my lady. The duke sent them."

"But they're men's clothes. I can't put these on."

"Oh, don't worry about that." She chuckled. "I've helped a few fellows in and out of those, to be sure. I can dress you up all right and tight."

"But—but I can't wear these!"

"Why not, dearie?"

"They're not—they've got—"

She unrolled stockings, white neck-cloths still in need of ironing, vests and jackets with heavy buttons and shirts with loose sleeves.

"See? They're made specially to your measure sent before-hand, my dear; they'll fit a treat."

I could hardly bear to touch them. It wasn't that I'd never handled men's things before; I've mended my brothers' often enough. But these were for me. I was to dress myself in what men wear. Stockings, neck-cloths, vests and jackets, with heavy but-tons and loose sleeves—they were all wrong.

I said as calmly as I could, "They're very nice things. But I will not wear them today. Please take out my blue flowered gown, and the yellow petticoat—"

"Oh, no, my lady. You're to put these on right away, and go to your lesson."

"Lesson?" I said sharply, remembering things like sketching and arithmetic, the lessons I'd had at home until we had to let my governess go, but doubting that was what she meant.

"Yes, that's right; a proper swordmaster coming all the way to Tremontaine House, just to teach you."

I felt my bargain closing in on me, tighter than neck-cloths and hard-buttoned jackets.

"Not today—surely not today, not yet—"

But of course it was today. He had told me it was. The duke owned me now, and I had agreed to it, weeks ago.

"I shall wear them in the house," I said firmly, "if it pleases him. For my lessons." But that, I secretly promised myself, was all.

So I let her pull the shirt over my head— clean, crisp linen that would have made the loveliest chemise!—and then the breeches—the buttons pulling closed flaps that were all that stood between me and the world, and nothing to hide my legs from anyone's eyes but the short hang of the jacket and the coarse stockings that revealed in outline everything they covered. The jacket buttoned tightly; it was well tailored, flattening my breasts and clinging around my arms. Men's clothing gripped me in places I did not want, showed me in ways I could not like, claimed me with strange bindings and unbindings.

I stood trembling, like a young horse being broken to saddle, as Betty's fingers did the final buttons up. I would not look in the mirror. I couldn't bear to see myself transformed into something neither boy nor girl. Was this what my uncle wanted? I hoped he would be satisfied, then!

Betty drew out a blue velvet ribbon, smiling conspiratorially as if it were a sugar cake. It was for my hair, to tie it back in a queue. I let her do it: wearing my hair unbound was not going to change me back.

"Now you're all ready for your lesson. I'll show you the practice-room, and by the time you're done, I'll have all these nice things tidied up and put away."

I had left my last night's party gown spread out upon the chair. Before she could collect it, I snatched from its pocket the pasteboard card my friend had given me, and stowed it well away in my jacket, a little piece of comfort nestling there.

When I moved, no swing of petticoats surrounded me. I had lost the protection of full skirts, the support of boned bodice. There was nothing for my hands to hide in. I felt the air on my legs as I moved. Cloth covered my skin, but still I was naked, exposed. Anyone could look at me, and see almost all of me!

A plum-colored cape peeked out of the brown paper; in desperation, I seized it and wrapped it around myself. At least it covered my knees.

"No, no, my lady, you won't need to be going out of doors, His Grace has had a whole room made over, just for your practice."

But I clutched the cape tight around myself. And so we ventured through the halls of Tremontaine House, Betty uncertain, as always, of where we were going, and I doing all I could to keep from looking in mirrors. It wasn't easy. Frames were all over the gilded corridors, startling on walls and sudden turns; sometimes the frames contained still, painted pictures, and sometimes glass reflecting a window, a staircase or my own pale face. But even when I didn't look, I knew. I was dressed as a man. I was wearing men's clothes. They were like men's eyes looking at me; like men's eyes touching me. The cape came to just below my knees; if I'd let go of it, it would have swirled very nicely; it was well cut and full. But I held it tightly, like a blanket wrapped against the cold.

Betty kept up a frantic babble which I barely took in: she was grateful to the duke, unworthy of the position, knew a thing or two about ladies and never would mess with their husbands now, no, not if you forced her at swordspoint—

"Here." At last she stopped. "It's the double-doors with the wet rabbits on them." Well, it was a reasonable description of the artfully painted woodland storm scene. Before she could fling them open, I knocked.

"Yes!" a man shouted. "Hurry up!"

He was standing in the middle of the huge, sunlit room. A thickset, muscled man, half-clothed, wearing only breeches and an open-collared shirt. He had a full black beard and bristling mustaches, like nothing I'd ever seen.

"How? How?" he demanded. "You are cold, you wear your bed-blanket?"

My fingers unclenched from the folds of the cloak. I let it fall to the floor. The man nodded curtly at me, and then at a rack of real swords.

"Pick one up. And I will show you how you do it wrong."

His voice was so strange; I could barely recognize the words, the way they trilled and sang high and low in unexpected ways. "Come! Come! Venturus does not like to keep him waiting. Venturus have many many students are beg him for instruction. He must tell them, 'No, no, I am not for you, I must be for the Mad Duke whose little boy does not even know to pick up the sword!'"

"I'm not a boy," I said.

He shot me a look. "No? You are a rabbit? You have furry paws? Then pick me a sword!"

I grabbed the closest one.

He stood to one side, hands on his hips. "Good." He nodded. "Oh, very good." I began to feel a little less cold. "Very good—*if you are chopping up chicken!*" he thundered. "How you think you are defend yourself when you are need to change lines, eh?"

I had no idea what he was talking about. And I was too afraid to tell him that this was not the way you hold a knife to chop up chickens.

"Lines, change lines—shift the tip by you shift the wrist!"

I tried to, but the sword's weight pulled against me until I turned the hilt in my hand; then I could move my fingers to direct the point better. He wouldn't like that. I stared at the tip, refusing to look at him.

"Yes," Venturus said. "Now you are see. You see—but you do not see!" With a sword in his hand, he suddenly struck my own blade so hard that my hand stung. My sword went flying.

"Ha!" he shouted triumphantly. I didn't see that disarming a beginner was such a triumph. "Don't grip so tight like you mama's tit. Hold gentle, gentle—like you are hold a baby child, or a dog that bite."

I tried not to laugh at the picture. When I held the sword more loosely, it flexed in my hand. "Ye-e-es," he hissed contentedly. "Now you see."

I smiled and, feeling not quite foolish, struck a swordsman's pose.

Venturus screamed as if he had been lashed. "*Wha-a-at* you think you do with you legs? You arms? Do I give you permission to do that thing? I would not. I could not! No student of Venturus ever look like *this*." His imitation of my pose looked like a rag doll strung with wires.

In a small voice I said, "I'm sorry." I hate being made fun of.

"You know you sorry! Stupid duke-boy! Now you practice: practice holding, only holding. You like you kill someone now—maybe you kill Venturus, yes—but first, you hold! Ha!"

The weird foreigner flung a cloak around his shoulders.

"Where are you going?" I asked.

"I go see other students, students know how to listen to
Venturus. You study to hold. Maybe tomorrow, I show how not to
stand. Ha!"

And with a swirl of his cloak, he was gone.

I held the sword. Even after the door closed, I was not at all
sure Master Venturus would not suddenly reappear through it, his
mustaches bristling.

In my hand the sword looked solid and workmanlike, like a
rolling pin, or the handle of a hoe. Then I looked down the entire length of it and saw how narrow the steel was, how shiny. It
had no purpose but distance and death.

I wondered what my mother would say, and found no answer.
For the first time in my life, I wished I could be holding a sewing
needle instead; suddenly that instrument of torture seemed small
and comfortable and harmless. My arm ached, no matter how I
turned the sword. I decided to put it away, and go back to my
room and change into the sort of girl who might ask a housekeeper if she needed help with the mending.

In the wardrobe, my new clothes were neatly hung and
folded. I looked behind them for my old gowns, and found
nothing. Nothing in the chest, nothing hung out to air; nothing remained of all my skirts and bodices and petticoats and
stockings, carefully chosen and mended and packed a few days
before.

I did not bother trying to find Betty. I knew what had happened. I knew, and I was not having it. This was one contest the
Mad Duke would not win.

The card in my pocket read: ARTEMISIA FITZ-LEVI, BLACKBURN
HOUSE. I would be seen on the street in these ridiculous clothes once
only. Grimly clutching my cloak around me, I set out through the
gates of Tremontaine House to find my friend.

I T WAS NOT LONG BEFORE LADY ARTEMISIA FITZ-LEVI BE-
gan to tire of the antics of her new pet. The parrot was a bit too
clever—she had expected a sort of colorful talking doll, not some-

thing with a mind of its own. The parrot preferred fruit to cakes, earlobes to fingers and velvet to the bottom of its cage. It liked women better than men; when her cousin Lucius Perry came to call, it flew at him, and she had to get her maid to take it downstairs, where, no doubt, it would amuse the house staff far more than it did her, though it had not been acquired for that purpose.

"You look decorative," she approved her cousin Lucius. Artemisia thought that the right amount of lace always complimented a man's appearance. Of course, with his slender build, dark hair and blue eyes, Lucius had good material to work with.

"And you look exhausted." Lord Lucius Perry, lounging in her windowseat, gazed longingly at the fragile cinnamon wafers that lay just at the edge of his reach on an equally fragile painted table. "Out dancing your slippers to ribbons again, coz? What gallant has caught your eye this time?"

In strictest confidence she was perishing to tell him about the duke's party last night, but he went on without waiting for an answer, "And where is your reprobate brother? Robert promised me a bout of tennis today; is he out already paying court to his last night's conquests, or still sleeping them off?"

Artemisia smiled patiently at him. He was a cousin, so not worth much more, and a younger son at that. "Do I look awful, Lucius? Have I got rings under my eyes? I bathed them in cucumber water, but I'm not sure it's done any good—and I particularly don't want Mama to know what I've been doing," she hinted broadly.

Lucius did not even pretend to be interested. "Nothing awful, I hope. You don't want to get yourself talked about, Artemisia, not when your prospects are so good this year."

"Of course nothing awful! What do you take me for? You're a fine one to lecture me, Lucius, indeed you are. I understand you were once up to all sorts of mischief Mama won't even tell me about."

"That's just it," he drawled; "I've reformed."

"Well, it's made you uncommon dull."

"Do you think so?" He smiled just a little; his eyelashes fluttered over his cheeks as he extended one languid finger toward the plate—but his cousin was impervious to that particular sort of innuendo.

"Honestly, Lucius, you are the laziest man I ever met! Lean

over and take your own biscuit, don't expect me to get up and pass them to you when you're this close to the table!"

Lucius Perry leaned back, instead, bathing his fine-boned face in a slanting patch of sun. All he could see through his eyelids was a rich, comforting red; if his cousin stopped talking for a minute, he might fall asleep.

No, he wouldn't: a knocking on the front door and a flurry of feet below heralded the approach of another visitor. "Artemisia," he said, not bothering to open his eyes, "you want to be careful. You're pretty, the family's good, your father's generous and you've got a nice voice. I wouldn't be surprised if someone offered for you before the year turns. Just don't compete with Robert in daring: city ballrooms are not exactly the same as climbing trees and jumping out of haylofts back home."

She drew herself up proudly. "Thank you for the advice, cousin. As if I don't know how to behave in town! I like it here, a great deal better than in the country. As far as I'm concerned, I'd be happy to call this home for the rest of my life, and I hope I marry a man who thinks so, too: someone with style and a bit of dash like Robert, not a dullard like you, who thinks an exciting day is playing tennis and calling on relatives, and an exciting evening is staying home and reading a book or whatever it is you do with yourself—anyhow, I didn't see *you* at Tremontaine House last night!"

"Tremontaine House?" Lucius Perry abandoned his lassitude. "You don't want anything to do with those people, cousin."

She tossed her head, and her curls bounced. "And why not, pray? I am not the Country Filly you seem to think me, cousin. I know how to handle myself in Society."

"Do you?" He was leaning forward, his blue eyes dark and full on her.

She squelched the humiliating recollection of her host putting her to flight. "Certainly. There's nothing so terrifying at Tremontaine House"—she laughed brightly—"except perhaps for the Mad Duke himself, of course. He's quite rude, isn't he? I don't know what all those people see in him, really."

"No, you wouldn't. That is why he's dangerous." His smile was now consciously charming. "Of course you understand Society, cousin: you are one of its brightest ornaments. But the

Duke Tremontaine is outside Society. Even he agrees that that is where he belongs. And he encourages others—not, of course, that you could be so encouraged—but those around him, to, ah, to explore those outposts as well."

"Well, they all seemed perfectly normal to me: the usual sort of Ball and Salon types, just both in one place, that's all. It's hardly—"

Her curls splashed her neck as she turned her head toward the commotion downstairs: a clatter in the marble hall of booted feet, a shrill cry.

"Perhaps it's Robert," Lucius drawled, "with a new conquest."

Someone was running upstairs—two someones. The first was the footman, who opened the door to the sitting room just wide enough to announce breathlessly, "A—female, my lady, who will see you, she says, though I did—"

"From the party," a girl's voice insisted shrilly. "Tell her Katherine, Lady Katherine Talbert—only I don't have a card—from Tremontaine House."

Lucius dealt his cousin a jaded look.

The footman threw open the door. "Lady Katherine."

There stood the oddest figure Lady Artemisia had ever seen outside the theatre; worse than the theatre, really, because there the actresses in boys' roles at least made some attempt to trim their hair, hide their figures and adopt a manly bearing. This was so clearly a girl, small and round, her long hair messily escaping from a ribbon in frizzy tendrils. Only her clothes were a perfect copy of a man's, in every detail.

Artemisia Fitz-Levi put a hand over her mouth. She knew it was rude, but she couldn't help it, the laughter just came squeezing out. The girl stared at her. Her face went pale, then red.

"From Tremontaine House," said Lucius smugly. "Well: you see my point."

Katherine Talbert spun on the heel of her ridiculous boots, and ran clattering out the hall and down the stairs.

~

N O ONE WOULD HAVE LOOKED TWICE AT THE BOY IF he had not been running frantically through a very sedate section of the Hill, where running generally meant some kind of trouble.

"Hey, there!" A hand shot out, bringing the figure to a skittering stop. Philibert, Lord Davenant, was not an observing sort of man; he saw a boy's face because he expected to see a boy's face, and the estimable Lord Davenant was one who liked the world to be compassed by order and decorum. This boy's long hair, therefore, meant University, and few scholars belonged on the Hill. Furthermore, the boy had been crying and seemed terrified at being apprehended.

"Aha," said Lord Davenant. "What's your hurry? Something in your pockets, maybe?" He thrust a hand into one of them, keeping a grip on the boy's wrist.

"Help!" shrilled the boy. "Let go of me!" He tried to wriggle out of the older man's grasp. "How dare you?"

"Little rat!" Davenant surveyed him, half-amused. "Shall I call the Watch, or just thrash you myself?"

The boy wiped his nose with his free arm. "If you were a gentleman," he said suddenly, "you would escort me back to Tremontaine House."

"Oh." Abruptly Lord Davenant dropped the wrist as if afraid of contagion. "So you're that kind of rat, are you?"

"What do you mean?"

"Go on, get off with you." Davenant's views on Tremontaine were well known in Council. The last thing he wanted was to be seen accosting one of the Mad Duke's fancy boys on the open street. "There's your direction, go on."

The boy drew himself up and walked away shakily.

⌒

I HAD FORGOTTEN THE WAY AND HAD ONLY A DIM RECOLlection of what Tremontaine House looked like from the street. All the walls of all the great houses looked the same, and all their black and gold-tipped gates. I tried to walk as if I knew where I was going.

"Hello, Lady Katherine."

Standing before me was a boy about my age. He was plainly

dressed, with a plain, ordinary face. It took me a moment to recognize the duke's servant, the valuable Marcus, the boy who knew where everything was. He said, "I'm heading back to Tremontaine House, if you'd like to come with me."

I followed him in silence. He had never introduced himself, and he didn't do so now, just talked to me as if we had always known each other.

"It's a nice day, isn't it? Betty thought you'd run away, but I guessed you might just have gone for a walk; you wouldn't want to get her in trouble by disappearing or something. You should try exploring the House gardens," he chatted amicably, "they're very interesting. Paths, and statues and fountains and things, though I think they've turned the fountains off for the season. The gardeners dig up the flowers all the time and put new ones in. They grow them in a big glass house. It's quite a production. You can have flowers put in your room, if you like. Want me to order them for you?"

The front hall of Tremontaine House was cool and white and empty. Gone the bustle and striving of last night; in their place was a spooky sweet serenity.

"Where is the duke?" I asked.

"Gone. Everyone's gone to the Riverside house."

"Everyone? But I—"

"Oh, not you. You're staying here."

"Alone?" Panic sharpened my voice.

"Not really. There's a whole staff lives here. He comes and goes, you see. He likes to have things ready for him always, here. They'll take care of you. Just tell Betty what you need."

"Are—are you staying here?" I hated myself for wanting a particular answer, but at least he was a friendly face.

"No. I go where he goes."

"When will you—will he—be back?"

"Whenever he feels like it. The Riverside house is warmer in winter; this one's better in summer. In between, like now…" Marcus shrugged.

"Is it far out in the country?"

"Is what far?"

"Riverside."

The boy laughed, as if I'd told him a joke on purpose. Then he shook his head. "Riverside? It's right here in the city. The other end of the city, the old bit, near the docks. Riverside's an island in the river. It's nothing special, really. I wouldn't live there. But he likes it."

"Is it a nice house?"

"It's an odd house." Again, the shrug. "He likes it."

"Well," I said, and something struck me. "Then, while he is there, I am the mistress of this house?"

"Why would you be?"

I'd never met such a rude servant. But then, this wasn't a normal household. I explained carefully to him, "Well, most houses have a master and a mistress. If the lord is unmarried, it's a sister, or a daughter, most often, who takes over the duty. So it stands to reason—" Marcus continued to look at me patiently, waiting for me to begin making sense. It put me off. "It stands to reason that, as the duke's niece, I would— In his absence I would be—"

"He left no instructions about that," Marcus told me gravely. "I could ask him, if you like, but..."

He didn't have to complete the thought. I had had quite enough of the Mad Duke's notice already. "Well, then," I said airily, looking around the huge front hall, "with no duties, I shall be a lady of leisure."

"If you're all right," he said, "I'd better be getting back."

Marcus did not bow as he left me. Only after he was gone did I realize that he had not seemed to notice the strangeness of my clothing, and that, while I was with him, neither had I.

⁓

IN MY BEAUTIFUL ROOM OVER THE RIVER, I SAT IN A delicate armchair working out just how miserable I could be. My visit to Artemisia's had been a disappointment. But then, probably she hadn't recognized me without my gown, and that terrible man with her had started being snide before I could explain. I'd just have to watch and wait for another chance. Artemisia had spoken last night of eternal friendship. Surely, once she knew what my uncle had done to me, my friend would help me to find some decent clothes and make sure I met decent people. I could not escape Tremontaine House entirely. I must do what I had to do to please the duke; after all, my family's fortune depended on it. But surely I wasn't meant to be a prisoner here!

I took a deep breath, and comforted myself opening a pretty box that contained beautifully ironed handkerchiefs. It wasn't going to be so bad, was it? Alone in one of the loveliest houses in the city, with no Mad Duke popping out from behind doors to torment me. No onerous duties, no housework whatsoever, as far as I could tell. Stupid clothes and pointless lessons, of course. But Master Venturus hadn't said anything about my killing people; he seemed to just want me to look nice with a sword. Like dance lessons; I could do that.

I looked in the charming gilded writing desk to see if it contained notepaper. There was none. I would have to tell Betty to get me some so that I could write to Artemisia, and to my mother. No, wait, that was in the bargain, too: no family letters for six months, and no visits, either. My brother Gregory had lodgings somewhere in the city, but he was not permitted anywhere near me. It was probably just as well. Gregory is very earnest, like our father; although he had been in the city for several months, the Mad Duke had never invited him to visit, and I could see why, now. Gregory believes in rules, so he would probably not try to sneak around and find me, even though my mother probably wished he would. I could write to her, anyway... but the thought of page after page of letters piling up unread over the weeks just made me feel worse.

How was she getting on without me? I worried. She was probably doing everything wrong, even though I'd left her a list—forgetting to air the winter linens, not keeping the tables waxed, letting the kitchen maids fight over the boot boy.... And who was going to comb her hair out so it didn't hurt, and match her embroidery silks, and remind her to take her tonic?

The house was doubtless going to wrack and ruin in my absence, and here I was, a useless creature being asked to take up useless skills I wasn't even any good at and never would be! And all for some mad whim of my mad uncle, who couldn't even be bothered to say good-bye to me when he left me alone in a strange house.

My boots made a satisfying thump as I stomped downstairs to look for a library where there might be paper. Or maybe I could find a genealogy that would tell me all of my stupid uncle's mysterious names, so I could impress him if ever I saw him again. At last I found it, a grand room laced floor to ceiling with more books than I'd ever seen in my life. They looked very dull: *On the Causes of Nature, The Tyrant's Dialogue,* that sort of thing. Most of the bindings were chased and stamped with gold, making the outsides far more appealing than the insides. Lost in the wealth of volumes, at last I found a lavish book called *Geographical Exotica* and settled into a window seat to examine pictures and descriptions of distant places I only half-believed existed. In the margin of a page about the island of Kyros, someone had written, *Where the honey comes from!* The book said it was an island of thyme, in which the bees sang all day.

chapter V

IN A WARM AND RICHLY FURNISHED ROOM IN RIVERSIDE, the smell of candles and food and bodies and wine wove a net of security and comfort around a group of men who usually settled for less. They were as happy as they were ever likely to be, with bellies nearly full, and no brakes upon the conversation.

"Pass Soliman the meat," the Duke Tremontaine commanded. "He can't discuss our animal nature until he becomes one with it!"

With his plate well stacked, the philosopher started up again. "All I was saying, with Dorimund's permission, is that training is the antithesis of nature. It must be. If shunning what is called vice were natural, as shunning cold or the pain of a fire is, then we would not need to be counseled against it!"

Taking a drink, an older, bearded man said, "I see you have no children, Sol. You must pull their hands back from the fire a hundred times, or risk losing them to it."

"Experience," another asserted. "Experience is the teacher there. 'The burnt hand shuns the fire' and all that. There is a difference between experience and training."

"Abstract thinking is what we're talking about. The fruits of vice are not immediately apparent, as the pain of fire is."

The duke leaned forward across the table. Like the scholars he was dressed in black, only his was studded with jet and dark embroidery. "The 'fruits of vice,'" he said, "are open to debate. They are not empirical, like a burnt finger. They may be abstract, Dorimund, but—" He stopped when the boy Marcus appeared at his side. "Yes, what?"

"A woman," Marcus murmured, "has come to the West door."

"Bugger the woman," the duke snarled. "Make her wait."

His servant showed him a ring. "She said you gave her this."

The duke's eyes widened slightly. "And so I did. I didn't think she'd show. I had better—" He pulled himself up from the table, bowing to his guests. "Gentlemen. I'll catch the rest of this later, or when Soliman publishes his controversial theories to the disgust of all right-thinking people, an effort I will be delighted to finance. Sol, stop eating, you look all round and rosy and harmless; people will feel silly hissing someone on the street who looks like a cradle doll."

To the laughter of his guests he left the table, ducking between hanging cloths, following Marcus through an arched door and down two small flights of steps, each one a different width, one turning to the left and another to the right.

⌒

THE CLOAKED WOMAN STARTED WHEN HE ENTERED. She had not expected a door behind the paneling. The duke shrugged. "It's quicker. I didn't want you to wait. I was afraid you'd lose your nerve."

Her voice was only a little breathy. "It's quite steeled, thank you."

Abruptly he caught her hand in his. "But you're cold."

"Chilly. I often am before a performance."

"I'm not a demanding audience."

"I've heard otherwise."

His smile was slow and personal, oddly charming. "And you the celebrated Black Rose. Well, I am honored."

"The honor is mine, my Lord of Tremontaine." She took a strand of his long hair between her fingers, put it to her lips.

The duke closed his eyes for a moment. Then he twined thumb and forefinger about her wrist. "Not just yet," he said. "There is the matter of your intriguing friend, first."

She stood quite still. "He's not all that intriguing."

"I find him so."

"You don't have to sleep with him."

"Neither do you, really, but you choose to do so." She drew breath to speak, but he put his fingers lightly on her lips. "Lord Davenant is becoming an important man, closely allied to the new Crescent Chancellor. Prestige, money, adventure . . . It's your game; I won't tell you how to play it. I'm just delighted you're going to play it with me, too."

She raised her own hand to his to caress the backs of his fingers on her lips. Abruptly he turned away, businesslike. "I asked you for evidence of his latest clever scheme. Now, let's see it. Even flat on my back—or yours—I can tell a real document from a fake one."

The actress reached into the folds of her cloak. He stepped back a pace, because it might always be a dagger. But she produced a real document, hung with seals and ribbons, very official.

"Nice," the duke said, examining it. "Very nice. This will more than do. Marcus—" Without looking behind him, he handed it to his servant. "Arthur knows what to do with this. Tell him to make two copies and return the original"—he looked the woman in the eyes—"how soon, do you think?"

"Soon. I'll be missed if I'm not back tonight."

"Can't you tell him your rehearsal ran late?"

"I already have."

The actress was trembling. The duke drew her into the crook of his arm, and slipped his ring back onto her finger. "Keep it."

"I'll probably sell it."

"That's all right." The man in black pulled her against his chest. "I don't give things away with an eye on their future."

The Black Rose turned in his arms, a tall woman who still came only to his chin. Her mouth sought his skin above the embroidered collar. "You're very generous."

"Am I? You don't have to sleep with me, either, but if it—"

"Prestige," she murmured into his throat, "money, adventure."

"—if it makes it any easier, I can give you—"

She kissed him, and he was silent.

They left through the door he had come in. Like a young man squiring a debutante through crowded seats at a ball, the Mad Duke escorted her through the mad halls of his house, from the secret room to a bedroom hung with red curtains, already warmed by a fire.

B UT THAT WAS NOT WHERE MARCUS FOUND HIM TWO hours later—more than two hours, for it took him a while to locate his master, after the woman had been shown the door. The Duke Tremontaine was alone in a room empty of furniture. He was hunched over a dying paper fire in an elaborately carved fireplace. His unbound hair swept the ashes. The room was cold and dark, but for the red glow of the last of the embers.

Marcus knew which floorboard creaked.

"I need more wood," the duke said without turning around. "I'm cold."

"There's a fire in your bedroom."

A shudder passed through Tremontaine. "No. I won't go back there."

"Shall I get blankets for you?"

"Yes. No—I can't sleep in this room. Not here."

"If you'd let me move a bed in, or even a couch..."

Tremontaine wore nothing but a velvet robe. It twisted around his long limbs when he turned to look up at his servant. "No, Marcus. There will not be any bed in here ever again."

"All right. What if I make a fire in the library? You could have some blankets in there, and read for the rest of the night."

"Where are my guests, my scholars?"

"They've all gone to bed, or gone home. Shall I wake one up for you?"

The duke shook his head, and noticed his hair. He tucked most of it into his collar. "No, you go to bed. I'll...I'll be along."

"I think you'll like the library," coaxed Marcus doggedly. "There are cushions, and rugs, and nice heavy curtains. And plenty of books."

"I know what's in the library," the duke snarled, sounding a bit more like himself.

Marcus held out his hands, and the tall man took them; to-gether, they pulled him to his feet.

chapter VI

I T WAS ALL RIGHT DURING THE DAY. BUT AT NIGHT, stripped down to my boy's shirt, tucked in the great bed in the empty house in a city of strangers, I wanted my mother! We always shared our woes and tried to help each other. I wished she knew how brave I was being, but there was no way to tell her about any of it, and what could she do, anyway? I cried very quietly, not liking to hear myself.

In the morning, I let the chocolate console me, and let Betty do up all my clothes with her able fingers. She didn't smell of drink—yet. I left half the chocolate for her.

My new clothes were not so hard to move in today. They seemed looser, more welcoming, less restrictive.

Master Venturus was waiting for me in the wet rabbit room. He was practicing against a wall, and didn't seem to see me when I came in.

"Good morning!" I said, to show I wasn't afraid this time.

"Yes," he said, still crouching and springing with sword in hand. "Why aren't you practice?"

"I will if you like."

"You get up, you practice. You eat, you practice. You go to bed, you practice—first." He turned at last to face me. "Otherwise, no good. No point." He looked me over. "No blanket today? Not so cold? Very good. Now you show Venturus you hold."

I held. Then I stood—wrong, of course, at first, and then right, so perfectly, I was told, that I must not move, and did not, and thought I was going to die of the ache in my arm holding the sword and my legs holding the stance, a gradual ache that became pain that sharpened to agony.

"Strike!" Venturus shouted suddenly.

I sprang forward, heedless of form, just to release the pain— and nearly fell over. My sword clanged from my hand to the floor.

"Not so good." My master's exaggerated sympathy failed to cover his smugness. "Not so good, ha? You practice, practice, practice, then no pain, no hurt, you strike—strike like snake. Ha! Now pick up sword." He hissed. "Tsss! No thumb on blade! Stupid. Rust, dust, all kinds of blick. You polish, make good."

It was worse than polishing silver. The blade's shiny metal darkened the moment my finger touched it. And those edges could be sharp, too, though the tip was blunted. Venturus gave me lime powder and oil and a soft leather cloth. For once, I was glad of my breeches; it would have been hard to do in skirts.

Venturus waited 'til I was done. Then he said, "I go. What you do now?"

I looked out to the garden. It was raining. "I practice," I said.

"Good." To my surprise, he added, "Not too long, first day. Then make bath, good soak with—tss!—how you call, good salts—then wine. After." On his way out the door, he paused and whirled back to me: "No-wine-no-sword!"

"I beg your pardon?"

"You no drink with sword! Drink is ruin sword."

With a swirl of his cloak, he was gone.

⁓

THE MORE TIME I SPENT IN TREMONTAINE HOUSE, the more beautiful I found it. I couldn't understand why my uncle the Mad Duke didn't like it here. Maybe it was just too good

for him and he knew it. Everything about the house was perfect:
the colors carefully chosen, the furniture balanced in form and size
to every room; even the views out the tall windows were as lovely
as pictures. I would find myself just looking at the way the lines of
a room's molding met the ceiling. Sometimes they joined in car-
ven leaves, edged with just a little gold; sometimes faces peered
amongst them; sometimes there were patterned jags, hard edges
that almost made blocks of letters, like words you couldn't quite
read.

Each room was filled with treasures. I made myself choose a
favorite in each one: the game was that I could save only one
thing from each room, and what would it be? In one it was a tiny
ivory carving of balls within balls, each one moving separately
but never touching. In another I was hard put to choose between
a painted fan mounted on a stand and a little china calf with the
most winning expression! I was surprised at how many of the
things I found were ladies' things. I remembered the duke my uncle saying with some distaste, "It's very elegant. I inherited it
from my grandmother." His grandmother had been Duchess
Tremontaine before him; that much I knew. Perhaps it was her
very own armchair that I loved to sit in, in my room above the
river, my feet tucked up under me as I watched the colors change
over the hills.

I liked to visit the dining room with the long windows and
mirrors, even though I never ate in there. At the center of the
enormous table, there was a serving epergne as large as a baby's
cradle, made out of silver. Branches twisted around it, ending in
oak leaves on which sweets might be placed; the middle was a
large dish supported by silver deer that grazed or glanced up
around it, amongst life-sized silver walnuts that were half as big as
the deer were. Sometimes I patted or stroked the deer, although I
knew it would make the silver tarnish faster. But it was folly to
leave silver out like that in the air, anyway. A girl came in once a
week to polish it; I came upon her one day and offered to help,
but she would not let me. If the servants found me odd, they
didn't say so. They were very polite and always called me Lady
Katherine. Of course, they must be accustomed to behavior far

odder than mine. And you couldn't know where they themselves had come from—though, as my mother had taught me, it would be the height of rudeness to ask. It's different in the country, where we know everybody for miles around. It seemed like a waste to keep on polishing the thing, but I was not invited to give advice on housekeeping. I began to realize just how much money my uncle the duke had at his disposal, and was fascinated by what he chose and did not choose to spend it on. I wondered whether the Riverside house were as richly furnished, or even more so.

And I wondered what was in my uncle's private rooms, here in Tremontaine House. I knew which ones they were: at the other end of the house from mine, a large suite that overlooked both the river and the courtyard. He could watch the sunset, and he could see visitors arriving. Once I stood outside the door, wondering if it was locked, and what I would do if it wasn't. He'd never know if I looked in, would he? But what would I see if I did? Next time he makes me really angry, I promised myself, I'll sneak in and look at everything, no matter what. Behind me, the portrait of a sad young woman gazed mournfully at me, as if to warn me of the perils of intrusion.

Portraits spattered the walls of Tremontaine House: large and small, square and round, dark and bright. In our house in the country there were portraits, too, but they were all my father's forebears. This was my mother's family. I tried to figure out which of the painted people looked familiar, and who was related to whom. When I couldn't guess, I'd make it up. The young man with the sour face and riding crop in the upstairs narrow hall was pining for the stiff young woman holding a rose in the little salon. But she was betrothed from birth to a red-faced bedroom man with a goblet. I could tell they would never be happy. I considered having the young man break his neck in a riding accident just to make sure everyone was good and miserable. I even wrote a poem for the young lady beginning *Ah, never shall I see thy shining face once more*, but all I could think of for next was *When I stand looking out the garden door*, and even though it did rhyme I knew it wasn't really poetry.

But the pictures also discomfited me: after looking at them long enough I would begin to wonder who these people truly were, and what order they had come in. Was the old man the son of the pretty young girl, or her father, or her husband? Or had he died before she was born? My painted forebears could not speak to answer, and no one in Tremontaine House could tell me who they were.

In the mirrored salon was one portrait that always pleased me. The painting was vivid and bright, not so old-fashioned as the rest: a woman in a pretty dress, with curls so fair as to be almost silver. It was a wonderful, lively painting. She was looking just past my shoulder as if someone was coming in the door behind me and she was sharing a joke with them, laughing as if she wanted a secret teased out of her. Her eyes glistened, and the pale grey satin of her dress did, too; even her jewels looked real, until you got close enough to see that it was only bits of paint: streaks of white over rose swirling to red, and such. Behind her, I was almost sure I recognized the lawn of Tremontaine House itself, sweeping down to the river. People were playing flamingo on the grass. I decided we had nearly the same nose. I wondered if, when I had the right gown, I might get the same artist to paint my portrait, too, and if I might look even half as lovely as the lady in grey.

ARTEMISIA FITZ-LEVI'S MOTHER DID NOT THINK MUCH of her choice of gowns for the evening's festivities, and was busy telling her so. "A supper-party, my dear, is not a ball," she said. "Even if there is dancing after, you want something a little more... restrained."

"But Mama," Artemisia argued, "the green silk was most particularly admired by the Duke of Hartsholt at the Hetleys'! And you said his taste is impeccable."

"So it is, my dear—and don't think he won't notice if you wear it again! Do you want to look as if you are courting his favor? And Hartsholt a married man... no, no, it would never do."

Artemisia pouted. "Don't be ridiculous, Mama. No one

would think that. Besides, I wanted to wear the tourmalines Papa gave me, and they suit it perfectly."

"So they do, my love, and you shall wear them at the next possible occasion. But not the green, not so soon after you've worn it once. Do you want people to think you don't have enough gowns?"

That worked, where nothing else had. "What about the yellow?" Artemisia asked hopefully. The yellow dress was the result of an argument her mother had lost, with a bodice cut down to there, and enough flounces to trim a cake.

"Don't you think it might hurt Lydia's feelings, since it is her party and she looks so peaky in yellow?"

"Mama, you are an angel of kindness!" Artemisia flung her arms around her mother's neck. "How could I be so unfeeling? I know—I shall write to my dear Lydia." Artemisia settled in a ruffle of dressing gown at her escritoire. "I'll see what she's wearing. If it's white or cream or ecru, I'll wear mine, too."

"Now why," her mother said dryly, "did we not think of that before?"

And Lady Fitz-Levi went to scribble off a note to Lydia's mother, so that Dorrie could take them both at once, and return with the correct response.

⟶

MASTER VENTURUS CONTINUED COMING EVERY DAY. Every day Betty laid out my sturdy practice clothes, and every day I dutifully put them on and went to the practice room to meet him. And every day after he'd left I'd practice for an hour or more. What else was there for me to do with my time? I could hold the sword without my arms aching for quite a while now, and my legs could hold their position without trembling, at least until Venturus was gone. I learned how to hold, how to stand, even how to strike—if aiming at a spot in the air can be accounted striking. It was all a bit dull, really, this training to be a swordsman. Venturus talked, and I repeated drills for him, and he talked some more, and finally he left and I did them again and again, until it was time for my bath.

I didn't even notice the morning I woke up with no ache in my muscles at all. Betty did, though; *sprightly*, she called me, and I went down to my lesson feeling very pleased with myself for being sprightly instead of sluggish and dull. Venturus retaliated with a whole new set of moves for me to learn: parries and ripostes, with no particular purpose that I could see except to make me turn my wrist in funny ways and feel like even more of a useless idiot. He would never even show me how to do them properly, just talked talked talked until I got it right, it seemed, only to stop his voice. I began to wonder if he was ever going to teach me to fight for real.

So it was a great startlement to me, the day he stood waiting for me stripped to his breeches and shirt, holding a powerful sword with an intricately woven basket. It was not a practice sword. It had an edge, a real one.

I drew in a deep breath. Guard, feint, parry, riposte...I could do this. I would have to, to keep that evil blade from me. Venturus had thrown his jacket over the rack of practice swords. He smelt sweaty, as if he'd been drilling already. But when I went to pick up a weapon, he stopped me. "No. You no sword. You stand."

His sharp steel tip directed me to the center of the room. I stood there at the guard, miming a sword in my hand.

"No guard!" my strange teacher corrected. "You standing stand."

I stood still, my arms at my sides. He raised the sword in one swift motion. I flinched.

"Stand."

I said carefully, "I think that you are going to hurt me. I can't just stand here without—"

"Good. Good you think. No laughing sword. Laughing sword is death sword." He smiled, showing large yellow teeth. "But Venturus not to hurt. No hurt if stand, no move. No-o-o move." I didn't move. Slowly, but perfectly steadily, the sword was swinging in a great arc towards me. I watched it come. I thought as hard as I could about how much practice it must have taken for Venturus to be able to keep it at that steady rate, without wavering.

The blade stopped at the cloth of my shirtsleeve.

"No-o-o move."

I did not move. He swung it suddenly to my knee, and I would have jumped except that I was afraid he'd hit me by accident then.

Venturus stepped back a pace. "Good."

So quickly I had no time to be frightened, he had the tip at my neck. Without appearing to change his stance, Venturus extended his arm a crucial fraction simply by tightening his muscles, and the metal pressed into my skin. I knew it did not break through, although I felt it all the way down to the small of my back. I did not swallow until he'd taken it away.

"Yess," he said in his satisfied hiss. He was not even winded. "Now you see."

"See what?" I demanded hotly. When I lose my temper, I'm afraid it's gone. "See you are the biggest show-off in the world, or see you nearly scared me out of a year's growth?"

He lowered his blade and twirled it at his side in a very show-offy way. "Hmm," he observed to the air around him, "little scared duke-boy gets anger."

"Yes, I get angry when I'm scared—what do you want me to do, cry?"

"Anger," Venturus said, "is enemy to sword. Many angry men killed by sword."

"Is that so?"

Venturus made a tour of the room, working the sword in flashy patterns so that I had to keep well away. "Fear," he observed to the air, "is enemy to sword. And fear to sword is friend. You see now?"

"No."

"No? Why not? You have eyes, but you no see. I teach and teach, but you no learn. Why you no learn, silly duke-boy?"

I took a deep breath. "I see one thing," I said, "and that's that I'll never be any good at this. And you know what? That's just fine with me, because it was never my idea in the first place, remember? So why don't you just go ahead and tell my uncle that I have too bad a temper and I'm too scared and stupid ever to be a decent swordsman, and then we can all go home!"

He turned to me with real hardness in his eyes. The sword

was down at his side, but for the first time, the man truly frightened me. "Do not sharpen your tongue on Venturus," he growled. "Do not command like to some servant." His nostrils flared as he breathed deeply. "I go now, yes? This no day for sword."

I stood very still as he put on his shirt and jacket, picked up his sword-belt and weapon and left. *"Do you ever even take a bath?"* I shouted to the door once it had closed behind him.

chapter VII

A S THE CLOUDLESS SKY ABOVE THE RIVER FADED
from blue to grey to green before settling into another
deeper, darker blue that set off the evening star to perfection, the curtains of Godwin House were drawn against the
night chill and the vapors of the river.

Scented candles were lit in the music room, which turned
warm, hazy and dreamlike amongst their fumes, the vases of flowers and the perfumed men and women in their whispering satin.

The young Lady Lydia Godwin had assembled a group of
friends for a dinner—or, rather, her mother had assembled them
for her from a slightly longer list of Lydia's. Since her first ball,
Lydia was now allowed a certain number of small gatherings,
carefully monitored and chaperoned.

After a dinner of eleven dishes and much innuendo, all Lydia
wanted to do was to disappear into a corner with her closest friends
to discuss the preceding events: looks and comments, dresses and
ornaments, jokes and compliments. Instead, she must play the
hostess and restrict herself to the occasional glance across the room
at Artemisia Fitz-Levi when anything particularly struck her.

It wasn't so easy to catch Lady Artemisia's eye. Her attention was occupied by a nobleman in mulberry silk who seemed always to be speaking earnestly to her.

Artemisia could not be certain of whether Lord Terence Monteith was a bore or not. He had good clothes and good jewels, and a very pleasant face. The Godwins had invited him and he was unmarried, so clearly he had prospects. But nothing he was saying interested her. Which was odd, because he was not, as is usual with men, demanding that she listen to him. He was asking her opinion of things, and hanging on her every word. It was just that she had no opinion on the things he asked her. She hadn't spent a lot of time thinking about whether musicians who played on the street should be required to have licenses, or livestock entering the city be inspected for disease. It was, of course, flattering that he wanted to know. "Really?" he kept saying. "Do you think so? And what about...?" until she was taxed for invention. In fact, it was beginning to feel a bit too much like a lesson she hadn't prepared for, which made her cross. She was not, after all, in the schoolroom any longer. Artemisia tossed her curls. "Lord Terence," she said, "how charming to find a man who thinks a woman knows more than just fashion and poetry!" hoping that at least he'd want to ask her about those.

His eyes never left her face. "What perfect teeth you have," Lord Terence said, confirming her suspicion that he was, in fact, a bore and, having no conversation of his own, had simply been asking her to provide it while he stared at her.

Lydia's parents came in then with a handful of their own friends who had been dining elsewhere. Artemisia had to restrain herself from dropping a schoolgirl's curtsey to Michael, Lord Godwin, and his lady, now that she was a young lady herself.

The eddy of newcomers should have been enough to detach her from Lord Terence, but the young nobleman was nothing if not persistent. In a moment he would ask if he might call on her, and she would have to say yes, or she would hear about it from her mother. She looked desperately for Lydia to signal for aid, but the daughter of the house was being dutiful with one of her parents' guests: a tall, dark-haired man with a distinguished air.

"Old people," Artemisia murmured daringly to Terence, no longer caring what he thought of her, "why must they insinuate themselves and spoil the party?"

Sure enough, her suitor drew back a little shocked. "That is Lord Ferris," he said, "the new Crescent Chancellor himself! Really, I wonder that Lady Godwin will have him here, now that he has taken her husband's place as head of the Council of Lords; but I suppose they are used to these ups and downs in politics. I have already taken my seat in Council, of course, but I've spoken only once or twice, on minor matters...."

"About cattle?" she asked piquantly, "or fish?"

Lord Terence missed the mockery completely, and was about to tell her which, when suddenly Artemisia made the mistake of catching Lydia's eye, and burst into helpless laughter.

Lord Ferris turned his whole head to look at her. His left eye was covered with a black velvet patch. "Hmm," he said to Lydia. "Possibly the first person ever to find Terence Monteith at all amusing. Pray introduce me to your friend."

"Do you mean *Artemisia?*" Lydia could have bitten her own tongue for sounding like a schoolgirl. But the Crescent Chancellor smiled at her in such a way as to indicate a complete understanding of what a complicated task it was for a young woman to play hostess at her own dinner party; indeed, he made her feel, just for a moment, as though running a party of eligible young people and running the Council of Lords were not such entirely different tasks.

"With pleasure," Lydia said smoothly. Lord Ferris must be older than her father, but unlike her father, he took the trouble to treat a young girl like a proper lady, not someone who still ate in the nursery with her little brothers. His hair was very black, with just a little silver, and his hands were finely shaped, ornamented with heavy, tasteful gold rings. The eyepatch only gave him an air of mystery. She felt tremendously grown-up when he offered her his arm and guided her across the floor to where Artemisia Fitz-Levi stood, with Terence Monteith gawking beside her.

Lord Ferris was, after all, a widower; and if Terence had had the sort of mind that observed the world around him, he would have known to exactly what purpose Lady Godwin had invited the Crescent Chancellor to stop in at her daughter's party.

⁓

AVING SAID I WOULD NOT CRY, I WAS HONOR BOUND not to. After Venturus left, though, I was ready to cry or spit.

I stalked down to the library. It was a soothing room, quiet and well proportioned, with cozy chairs and an excellent view. But to my annoyance, the duke's librarian was there. He was a dreamy man who hardly seemed to exist, and usually he did not notice that I did. He catalogued and rearranged, making faces at things no one else knew the meanings of, like flakes on the outside of books and notes on the inside of them. He saw me come in, this time, and said, "Good day, Lady Katherine. Can I help you with your studies? Or are you looking for some more, ah, feminine diversion?" To this day, I don't think he noticed I never wore a dress.

"Yes," I said poisonously; "what have you got that's really feminine in here?"

The librarian's face took on a worried look, as though if he couldn't find the right thing, he'd have to kill himself forthwith. "Ah, nature," he said nervously, "I believe is suitable for young ladies. The late duchess had many rare volumes of plants and animals—and though the classification of birds as animals is still in dispute by Doctors Milton and Melrose, I have put the bird books over here."

I settled myself in a cushioned window seat with a big illustrated volume. The pictures were bigger than live birds are, and you could see all the details. But it was hard to concentrate after my fight with Venturus, with the librarian there muttering to himself. I looked up and saw him pry a little worn leather volume out from between two grand tomes on a shelf. He flipped it open, then dropped the little book on a table as though it had a contagious disease, making disapproving noises all the while. When he left to wash his hands, I pounced on it.

"*The Swordsman Whose Name Was Not Death*, by a Lady of Quality." Opposite the title page was a woodcut of a man in old-fashioned clothes bowing to a lady, one hand on the sword at his side.

I opened to the first page. Many hours later, when the sun went down and I couldn't see the words, I had only gotten to the part where Lady Stella discovers she is with child, and runs away to her cousin in the country so that Fabian does not know it is his, which would ruin his concentration as he prepares for his duel against his great enemy in the University clock tower— although I was fairly certain even then that he would win it, but Mangrove would get away somehow, which he did.

I wrapped the book in my handkerchief and took it to my room. It wasn't stealing, because the duke's book was still in the duke's house, and it had looked to me like the librarian was just going to throw it out anyway.

I wasn't sure how Fabian got to be such a great swordsman when he never seemed to practice, but I admired the way he could fight up and down stairs, and how he lived by the swords-man's code but still was so clever about not killing Lady Stella al-though he was bound to. He took money for his work, but no one could make him do a thing that he despised, or harm the inno-cent. His word and his sword were his honor, everyone knew it, and they all respected him, even Mangrove, who hated him.

I tucked the book under my pillow, determined not to open it again 'til morning. But after supper I put a fresh candle in the holder, and settled down to find out who won the fight in the clock tower, and what became of Stella's baby. I cried so hard I had to get up and hunt for a fresh handkerchief. Even when I'd snuffed the candle I lay with my eyes open, thinking of swords-men in dark cloaks, their perfect form, their steady hands and clear, unwavering eyes.

The next day I finished the book and immediately started it over again.

When the librarian appeared I asked him if there were any more books about swordsmen. He gave me *Lives of the Heroic Swordsmen*, which didn't mention Fabian or Mangrove, but did have some interesting people in it, like Black Mark of Ariston, who had fought one-armed after his great battle; and Harling Ober, who never refused a challenge, and had carried the sword at the wedding of my great-grandmother, Diane, Duchess Tremontaine. Ober had learned his art by sneaking up to a dangerous rooftop and peeking down at the great swordsman Rampiere, who had refused to teach him. I supposed that I was lucky to have Master Venturus. But my teacher failed to show for my next lesson. Perhaps he had quit, insulted. Perhaps he was staying away just to try and teach me respect. And perhaps he was preparing more mockery about a little scared duke-boy who could not learn the sword. I was all dressed for practice, so I practiced by myself. I wondered how I would fare if I were set upon by king's guards (if we still had a king), or had to fight with one foot on water, the other on the shore. I thought that I would like a cloak as black as night, and a jeweled pin to bind up my hair.

chapter VIII

H AVING SOWN DISSENT AT A MEETING OF THE
Council of Lords that morning, and being in the
process of acquiring a new coat that afternoon,
the Duke Tremontaine was in excellent spirits. He stood in a
sun-washed room in his Riverside house, permitting one of his
secretaries to read him the latest set of letters received and
logged, while he simultaneously dictated responses, tried to hold
still for the tailor and entertained a friend.

The duke's chief secretary, a balding young man named
Arthur Ghent, removed the tapes from another roll of papers
and shook them out. "These are the ones addressed to 'the
Duke of Riverside,'" he explained. "I've passed the requests
for money on to Teddy; he'll work from your list and include it
in the month's report for you to approve. What's left are
from people I've never heard of that maybe you have: the usual
litany of complaints and suggestions." He shook out a ragtag
batch of correspondence written on anything that could hold a
sentence, from the backs of old bills to leaves torn from books.
"Hmm..." He observed the writing on note after note. "Same

hand, same hand, same hand...popular scribe. I wonder who it is?"

"Here, let me see." The duke stretched out his hand for the papers, opening up the seam the tailor had just carefully pinned. "Yes . . . I know him. Another University man—like you, Arthur, but not so fortunate as to have secured an important secretarial post. First he tried verse, then plays, then drink, which brought him to scribing letters for the less fortunate in Riverside. Let's see . . . what is on the mind of the less fortunate these days?" The duke scanned a few lines of one, then another. "They don't like the tearing down of ruins—too bad. They like the new gutters—I should think so. Sam Bonner fell in one of them and twisted his foot and wants reparation. Bonner . . . is he still alive? He was already pickled when I was a boy." He held the letter out to his secretary. "No reparation, bad precedent. No, wait—where's he writing from?" The duke scanned the bottom of the sheet. "'At Old Madge's off Parmeter Street.' God, he's living in a cellar. Send him something; send him some wine. But no money." Ghent made a note on the back of Bonner's letter.

"It's a joke, you know." The Ugly Girl was sitting in the corner, watching the sun move across the patterned carpet. "This 'Duke of Riverside' business. It isn't your real title. You derive no income from Riverside; it's just your toy."

"That's what you think." The duke eased his long arms out of the coat for the tailor.

"You're wasting your time on all this. The world will always be full of drunks and liars and people down on their luck who never had any to begin with."

"Stick to your field, and let me amuse myself with my particular corner of it. Not so tight," he told the tailor, who nodded, his mouth full of pins. "I must have my hobbies. I don't ride, I don't dance, I don't race, and I don't collect objects of virtue."

She snorted at that. "I still say it's a waste of time. You'd do better to apply yourself to your mathematics."

Because he was in a good mood, he did not attack her. "But I am so useful. I am useful all the time. Today I managed to scuttle an appalling suggestion from an appalling nobleman who thinks he knows something about how this state should be run, and has managed to convince far too many people that he is right. It's just the beginning, of course: Davenant won't stop there; oh, no. He and his very good friend the Crescent Chancellor have a bright new tax plan in mind. One doesn't go after the Crescent like that, so I have started a rumor campaign against Davenant on the street, and called his allies into question with a plethora of minutiae in Council. It will take them days to get over it, by which time I have every reason to believe his mistress will be abandoning him for one of his supporters, which will make him do something stupid." The duke preened. "It is so nice to have work to do that is both useful and amusing."

The Ugly Girl grinned. "All right. I take it back. You are an ornament to society."

"I will be when this jacket gets done. You," he told the tailor, as he eased the duke back into it, "are nothing short of brilliant. I shall be the only man in the city able both to move his arms above his head and look well composed. I'll have another in blue—a different blue, I mean. Lighter. Silk. For when it's hot."

The tailor said, "I will have cloth samples sent for my lord to choose from." He nodded at his assistant, who stood against the wall trying to be invisible, to make invisible note of the duke's request.

"Ahem," said Arthur Ghent. "You said you'd decide today about the Talbert money. For your sister."

"Did I? I thought we'd set the whole thing in motion the day my niece arrived."

"You said not to. You said to wait."

"Did I?" the duke said again. "Well, I suppose I was worried that she'd bolt. She hasn't bolted, has she?"

"No, my lord," said Ghent's assistant. "Still at Tremontaine House, studying with Venturus."

"Well, then. Send the family the big sum, everything they asked for, as a loan against releasing their entire disputed property at the end of the six months."

"How complicated," Flavia said.

"It wasn't my idea; it's what I have lawyers for."

Arthur Ghent finished his notes and picked up another sheaf of papers, on better paper, some of it scented. "These are this week's invitations. Marlowe wants you to listen to his new so-prano—"

"No. It's his mistress. She howls."

"Lord Fitz-Levi wants you for cards Wednesday—"

"On the Hill? No."

"Right. But you've turned him down twice now."

"Invite him to the next thing he can be invited to. Not the wife, though, just him."

"Right." He made a note. "Private theatricals at the, ah," he took a deep breath and said it: "the Gentlemen's League of Self-Pleasure."

The duke crowed. "Never! Tell them I am decadent, not des-perate." The secretary's hand wavered above the inkwell. "Never mind," his master said mercifully. "Don't answer."

"Thank you, sir. Now, this is a grateful letter from the Orphans' Asylum, thanking you for the beds and the new roof and inviting you to their Harvest Pageant, where the children will sing, dance and recite."

"Regrets." The duke grimaced. "Just regrets. Ignore the other nonsense."

The Ugly Girl swung her foot under her. "You founded the place. Why don't you want to go?"

"I don't like children," the duke replied.

"Then why put out all that money to preserve them?"

"Because it is wrong to let them die." The duke shook the foam of lace at his cuffs, each flower and petal and leaf twisted thread upon thread by the fingers of an artist. "I did nothing to deserve this. I got it all because I had a grandmother with lots of money who left it to me. Before that I lived in two rooms in Riverside. I saw what happened to the products of a moment's pleasure. Other people do not deserve to starve or to be fucked before they know what the word means, just because they have no one."

The beautiful Alcuin had wandered in to hear his final

words. He placed a proprietary hand on Tremontaine's silk-covered shoulder. "No one? Then you must get them someone."

"Sometimes," the duke drawled without looking up, "I am almost sure I do not deserve *you*."

Alcuin fiddled with the fall of lace on Tremontaine's collar. "I wish you would not speak that way."

The duke's secretary glanced over at the Ugly Girl. She caught his look and smirked back.

"The nobility of this city have no right to live the way they do," the Duke Tremontaine returned to his observations. "When they undid the monarchy, they revoked the traditional magical rights, not just of kings, but of themselves. They thus have no real right to rule, nor to hold land and profit by others' labors on it. It's odd that nobody's realized that. Though I suppose if anyone tried to say so, he'd be challenged or locked away somewhere, depending on his rank and his lucidity. The Court of Honor, you see, exists not just to legalize noble assassinations but to ensure that only a court of nobles ever has the right to judge a noble's deeds. A neat system, although I believe the privilege of the sword, as they call it, is beginning to show signs of fraying and wear."

"Is that so?" Flavia asked, drawing him out, amused—he did love to lecture—and he obliged:

"Most challenges are fought as pure entertainment. Your swordsman gets a scratch, or *his* does, and you're done for the day. The two nobles who called challenge on each other know what the fight was about, and usually their friends do as well, and everyone respects the outcome. Nobody asks swordsmen to die anymore just to prove a point of honor. Accidents or infection happen, of course, but as long as your man doesn't expire on the spot, nobody's bothered.

"But the darker side still exists, the practical origin of those little skirmishes. A noble can still hire a swordsman to challenge a nobleman without giving him time to find a professional proxy for himself. Even with all the protocols of formal challenge, at the end of the fight, unless he's amazingly lucky, you've got one dead nobleman. Does privilege of the sword extend to the swordsman who did it? Certainly, as long as he can prove he was in a noble's employ. The privilege belongs to them, after all. But to determine this, the matter is brought before the Court of Honor. That's where the real fun begins. The rules of the Court of Honor are arcane, the judgments colorful and highly personal... it's a perfect charade. I've been through it"—he shuddered— "I know. There's more honesty in Riverside, where all the privilege is about who's stronger and madder and meaner."

"What about your noble *women*? What's their privilege?"

He held up his arm to test the stretch of the sleeve again. The tailor nodded. "A woman's honor is still the property of her male relatives, according to the Court."

"Naturally."

"Noblewomen have been known to hire swordsmen when they felt a point needed to be made. But it's considered unlady-like these days, as I understand it."

"And your niece?"

"What about her?"

"Will she, as a noblewoman, be fighting her own battles on her own behalf, or will she have to hire a man to do it?"

The duke smiled. "Well, that is the question, isn't it? She seems like a peaceable enough child. We'll just have to wait and see."

Cautiously, the tailor eased the duke out of his new jacket, and handed it to the assistant to fold. The duke watched with interest. "I think you fold things better than my valet," he said. "How would you like a new job?" The assistant turned bright red with the inability to answer. "You should seize your moments," the duke told him; "they may not come again. This is why it's so hard for tradesmen to advance in this city," he explained to the room at large: "timidity, lack of initiative; that, and the refusal of nobles to let them marry their daughters. You see," he told Flavia, as if their conversation had never been interrupted, "the nobles are going nowhere. The people who've actually done something to get the comforts they enjoy are the ones who are worth something: the merchants and craftsmen—not to mention the farmers, though you can't get rich off little patches of land, you have to have lots of it, and get others to work it for you— You didn't know that, I suppose?"

"I'm not a historian, or an agrarianist. Go on, though; I'm fascinated."

"If the nobles had any sense, they'd marry into families who knew how to fold things properly, instead of working so hard to marry back into each other."

"The trouble with you," the Ugly Girl said, "is that you think you know just what everyone should do, don't you?"

The Mad Duke smiled at her. His face was bright and sharp, smooth and glittering. "Yes," he said, "I do."

"And what," she said, "if you're wrong?"

"And what," he said, "if I'm not?"

W HEN MY NEXT LESSON CAME, I WAS READY. "MASTER Venturus," I told him, "I deeply regret any unpleasantness between us." I'd never said anything like that before; I'd copied it from a speech of Mangrove's, the lying villain, because although he was at core a rotten being, no one could fault him for style. (I did, however, leave out the bit about passion overwhelming, because it did not suit.) "I hope you will forgive me, and consent to teach me as before."

The foreigner frowned. "Venturus is here, no? Why else here but to teach? You think he come to drink chocolate and pass the biscuit?"

So that was all right. We did the standing-still exercise with his serious blade again. But this time I remembered that, however weird he was, Venturus was a master swordsman. He wouldn't hurt me unless he wanted to. I admired his form. He was in perfect control of his body, the sword an extension of it; he could repeat the same move precisely, and he did, without wavering. Once I'd realized that, I started to enjoy the illusion of danger, the way his blade hissed past my cheek, tickled my sleeve.

"Good!" he said. "Because this time, you know no angry. You know no fear. You trust Venturus. But you not always fight Venturus. So you learn you trust you skin. Know where man's sword is all times. Know how close, how far."

This time the sword came from above. My whole scalp

prickled with the sensation as it came at me. I felt the blade in my hair, like a leaf that had fallen, or a bug.

I knew when it was gone, before I even looked to see. It was not only that I no longer felt it, or that I saw him move. Or, I suppose, it was both of those things, and another I can't quite explain. Anyway, the sword was gone, and nothing in my body or Venturus's said it was coming at me. It was the oddest thing. I unclenched the hand at my side.

"Now you try," he said, standing perfectly still.

I retrieved a practice sword, harmless and dull; but before I could swing he was out of my reach, his sword up and guarding against me.

"You no say 'No move,'" he taunted, like a child. I felt a slow flush of anger. "Venturus always move," he grinned, "no matter you say." But then he turned to display a bulky figure behind him, swathed in a cloak. Theatrically, he whipped the cloak off to reveal a straw man. "So *here* this your partner to practice. He no listen, but he no move!"

I swung my blade at the straw figure, and was proud when I stopped the sword just short of it without wavering much. I targeted another point on it, and again I made it. I'd almost forgotten my teacher was there, when he said, "How? How? This you practice you chopping down trees? No!" But I did not fear his roaring. In fact, I thought he sounded amused. "Is practice now. Once again with the guard, the feint, the parry—but this time, when you strike—hit home!"

In guard, I glared at the straw man. If he tried a direct cut I would do—thus—and counter with—thus—feinting so that he changed his line—and I plunged the sword home into his heart! The tip went in so deep it was almost out the other side. I looked at it half in shame, half in satisfaction.

"How?" Venturus roared again. "What trickery is this? These are not patterns Venturus teach you, this mummery-flummery dancing about! Venturus is no dance-master. You think you partner is some girl-doll to play with, you make up you move? Why you laugh?"

The very last doll I loved was a china-faced lady with painted blue eyes. I used to dress Fifi in stylish gowns made from my mother's old dress scraps.

"Again," he said. "You show you move, just like I teach."

What sort of costume would I dress this huge straw doll in? Perhaps Betty would help me make a sweeping cloak as black as night. Using the patterns of attack and defense that he had taught me, in just the right order I had practiced many times, I stabbed Huge Fifi right through the heart.

Venturus nodded. "See, now, when you follow Venturus teaching, see how sweet she is?" He almost sounded coaxing. "See, how swift and clean is the stroke? The pure attack? The sureness of the thing that there is?"

I grinned at him. It did work, after all. "Good!" he cried. "I go now. You follow teaching, is good. No follow, no practice, you hear me?" I nodded. "Bad habits ruin sword. Practice practice practice ... now!"

I waited 'til he was gone; then I stared hard at Fifi. The straw head was just a featureless orb. Could I find somewhere a wig with inky curls? "You," I said, "may live to regret this day. Or, if not this day, the day that you met me. They are much the same. For two entered by that window, but only one of us shall leave by it. Have at you!"

⌒

I T WAS AN AWFUL, AWFUL DAY. ARTEMISIA COULDN'T SAY why, but it was. Her new dress had been delivered, and when she tried it on, she was convinced that the blue, so becoming in the shop, made her look like a frump, or an old lady. She actually cried over that, until Dorrie, her maid, in despair went and fetched her mother, who swore that it became her better than Lady Hetley's rose taffeta, which she had so much admired at Jane's barge party. Artemisia sniffled and allowed Dorrie to pin some ecru lace to the collar, and thought perhaps that did help. As she stared at herself in the mirror, she realized she had a spot coming out on her chin. Her gasp of horror was interrupted by her brother Robert storming into the room, calling, "Mother! Mother, I've been all over the house looking for you. Kirk says I cannot have the carriage, because Artemisia wants it to pay calls."

"Indeed she does," Lady Fitz-Levi said, "and doesn't she look like a picture?"

Her brother bit back a nasty comment about what kind of picture his sister made. "It is intolerable, Mother. I told you two days ago I needed the carriage to go out to the races today."

"Why don't you ride there, dear?"

"Mother, no one rides to the races! Where is Artie going, anyway, just across the street or something? Why can't she walk?"

"Oh, it's all right for *me* to get splashed with mud, is it?" Artemisia cried. "You pig, Robert! Well, it hardly matters, does it, since I have nothing to wear and I'm the ugliest thing in creation. Take your carriage, then—I just won't go. I'm never going anywhere again. And get out of my room, you pig."

Lady Fitz-Levi motioned Robert to follow her out into the hall.

"What on earth has gotten into her? She used to like going to parties."

"You must be patient," their mother explained. "She is a bit under the weather today. She did not receive an invitation to the Galings' musical luncheon, and she particularly wanted one, because a certain—ah, gentleman said he would be there."

"Oh really? Who?"

"Never you mind." His mother put a finger to her cheek. "The less said on that front, the better."

"Come on, Mother, maybe I know him."

"I'm not sure you do—he is a rather plodding young man, not for your set at all."

"If he's plodding, what does she see in him?"

"My concern is what he sees in her. He was starstruck, moonstruck, and paid her all sorts of compliments at the Montague ball. Trust Helena Montague to invite half the city, even ineligibles. I made the mistake of telling Mia not to take him seriously, so of course now she is making a meal of it. I would have done better to keep my mouth shut. Don't *ever* have a daughter."

Robert laughed. "I shall have several, and send them to you for advice. But maybe a dull, plodding sort of fellow is just what Artie needs to settle down and be happy with."

"Don't be patronizing, Robert. Dull is not what your sister needs. And most particularly, not dull and poor with romantic connections." Robert raised his eyebrows. His mother nodded. "Gregory Talbert. Yes. The most unmarriageable young noble in the city."

"*And* Tremontaine's oldest nephew. Who's to say there's not a duchy in his future?"

"Tremontaine, for one. There's a feud between the families. The duke has the privilege of naming his heir, and I doubt it will be any of his sister's children."

"What about the daughter, that girl he had brought here?"

His mother pressed her lips together. "You don't see her at any of the parties for the young ladies, do you?" She did not mention, even to Robert, that she had already intercepted one letter from the Lady Katherine to Artemisia, frantic and flowery and badly spelt, hinting at dire fates and desperate measures. She profoundly hoped that there would be no others. "Whatever the duke means to do with her, it can't be anything decent."

"The brother seems a solid enough fellow.... Don't worry, Mama, when I see him I'll try to warn him off."

"Thank you, Robbie. I know I can trust both my children to do the right thing. Anything you can do to help your sister right now ... you see, you cannot underestimate the importance of her always being in her best looks and spirits at this particular time."

"Oh, she's always a huge hit. I don't see what the fuss is about."

"Robbie." His mother sighed. "Darling. May I speak to you as an adult?" He drew himself up. "All right. Listen. What happens to Artemisia this Season or the next will determine the course of her entire life from now on. She is on display, everything about her: her clothes, her hair, her teeth, her laugh, her voice ... so that some gentleman can choose whether he wants to make her the mistress of his household and the mother of his heirs. Think of it as—oh, I don't know, as a horse that has only one race to win. If she marries well, she will be comfortable and happy. If she makes a poor choice, or fails to attract a worthy man, the rest of her life will be a misery. I know you young people think that, ah, physical attraction is enough. But when you're forty and the parent of a brood, if your spouse is poor or poor of judgment, believe me, there is no romance there."

She leaned forward confidentially. "Now, you and I know what a tremendous success Artemisia is, once she gets out there. You know no one has anything but good to say about our darling—and you'd tell me if they did, wouldn't you, Robbie, dear? But a woman alone, in her boudoir, well, she suffers certain anxieties. So you see, we all need to be very kind and helpful to her, right now. You understand that, darling, don't you?"

"If it will help get her married and out of the house, I shall do everything in my power," her brother said devoutly. And though his mother said he didn't mean it, and that there was no friend like a sister to see you through life's ups and down, he rather thought he did, and left, nearly colliding with the footman coming up the stairs with flowers for his sister.

Dorrie brought them in to her, hoping her mistress would be cheered by them. And indeed, Artemisia's face brightened when she saw the fine bouquet of roses and freesias. If a Certain Person had sent them, it would make up for everything, and she might hope again. With trembling hands (and with her mother standing by), she unfurled the note from the center of the bouquet. She could imagine already the soft words from one whose eye had caught hers, whose hand had gently caressed hers, and whose heart, perhaps, might someday win her.

"Oh no!" she shrieked. The note was signed *Terence Monteith.*

She cast herself upon the bed, sobbing, "I *hate* Terence Monteith! I hate everyone! It's all a disaster! Everybody hates me. Oh, leave me alone!"

In the end, they had to put her to bed with tea and a little brandy. Had Robert only been a little more patient, he might have had the carriage, after all.

Artemisia curled up with her favorite book, and cried, and wondered whether any man would ever love her enough to risk his soul's honor for her sake, and why swordsmen were so *boring* these days.

chapter IX

M Y UNCLE'S SERVANT MARCUS HAD BEEN RIGHT:
the gardens of Tremontaine House were beautiful,
and beautifully tended, delightful and various.
There were well-kempt paths and carefully clipped bushes punc-
tuated by classical sculptures. Some of their stories I knew; other
figures were quite obscure, but seemed to be involved in unlikely
couplings. Perhaps they were a joke, or came from books only my
brothers were allowed to read. There were also arcs and swirls of
flowers and leafy plants of different heights and colors, set
throughout with benches and bowers, though no one ever was
sitting in them. And long grassy alleys ran down to the river. The
more I practiced my sword, the more I felt like running down
them, especially as the last of summer began to take on the bite of
autumn.

In my boy's clothes I could hurtle along the banks and slopes
without pausing to think about my skirts. Stone walls were easy
to get over. I never had to go around, and even falling down
never meant a torn hem or ruffle. I did tear a sleeve once, but
that was a piece of foolishness, stretching my arms out over my

head and rolling all the way down the grass to the river landing. The duke's barge floated there, wrapped in canvas. I wondered when I'd get to ride in it. I mended the sleeve myself as best I could, but it showed. When Betty took it away from me I thought she was angry and might tell the duke, but she only had it mended by a real tailor, good as new.

If my family had had the money for lessons, I might have learned to sketch and paint well enough to portray the gardens. If Artemisia had been a true friend to me, I might have invited her by now to do just that, for I was sure she had all the accomplishments. If ever I saw my uncle the Mad Duke again, perhaps I would ask him why I could not have a drawing master, in addition to Master Venturus? I could not spend every minute on swordplay. Why should he mind if I learned watercolors or something nice in my spare time?

Certainly I was not failing in my lessons. Venturus watched carefully as I strove against my straw doll, Fifi. He gave me pointers, and I began to realize that despite the bluster, his advice was always solid. I couldn't help giving Fifi a personality and clever countermoves to go with it—one day, when Venturus was being unpleasant about a failed move of mine, I said, "But what else am I to do when Fif—when my opponent comes at me with a high disarm?"

"Here." The swordmaster took a weapon from the rack. "I show." He came at me with a high disarm, which I failed to disengage and pass under until he showed me how. And, so simply, that was how we started sparring together.

I came to know the bright blade, first as something like a dance-partner as we rehearsed our patterned strokes and counters, parries and ripostes, and then as an unexpected visitor, to be anticipated in a half-breath, and turned as brusquely away.

The hardest part was looking in my teacher's eyes as I fought, but this he said I must do, although it felt horribly bold and immodest.

"No watch sword," he rasped, "watch man. Man is mind of sword."

As often as we sparred, my teacher grumbled that I was a waste of his time. "I fall asleep practicing you, duke-boy. Other students of Venturus learn on each other. You all alone with straw man and me, too much alone. Lucky have great teacher, very lucky he be practicing you. Why you crazy father make you live alone?"

"He's not my father," I said automatically for what was surely the hundredth time. "I'm not a boy."

"Venturus not fight with no girls." He raised his sword high, and pointed it downwards to signal a pause in the bout, so he could attack me with his temper. "You got no respect for teacher, you! Other students beg Venturus for lessons. You *argue* him. Ha!"

In the end, always we went back to practice, all morning now. I liked the feel of my teacher giving way on the floor before me, even if it was only an exercise. But I thought I deserved a chance at watercolors, too.

⁓

THE DUKE'S LOVER SAID, "I WISH YOU WOULD MAKE UP your mind."

He shivered as the duke ran a cold finger down his back. "My mind is quite made up. The problem is, you don't like the way it's gone."

"I want to stay here in Riverside."

"And so do I. But not tonight. My poet must have dignity. He'll have more standing on the Hill."

"The whole city knows what you are. Which house you do it in hardly makes a difference."

The duke said, "You don't like my ideas, you don't like my choices . . . the truth is, you don't like me very much, Alcuin, do you?"

"Of course I do, I love you."

"It's all right. I don't like you much, either."

"Why do you keep me, then?"

"Who said anything about keeping you?"

Alcuin bent his beautiful head over the duke's manicured hand, sweeping it with his lips. "Please . . ." And Tremontaine did not push him away.

When the duke slept, though, Alcuin dressed, and scribbled a little note and propped it on the duke's dressing table, and ordered up a carriage to take him to the Hill. In the duke's bedroom, the curtains were always drawn; his lover was almost surprised to find that outside it was daylight.

They knew him at Tremontaine House, and he still wore their master's ring. They let him in, and nobody followed him through the corridors to the duke's apartments. There he looked for papers, any papers that might serve his needs and embarrass his lover, but he could not find what he wanted there, any more than he had in Riverside. He proceeded to the library and opened the likeliest books, but all that they contained were words. He had expected the room to be empty, and started violently when he heard the crackle of paper.

It was only a boy, pretty and well dressed, with astonishingly long hair—a student, then—sitting in the window seat with a book. As he prided himself on his ability to deal with any situation, Alcuin bowed to him. It was not, after all, as though he had been doing anything but looking at books. That was what one did in a library. He'd just have to wait for privacy for the desk to divulge its contents.

The boy got up hurriedly, shoving the book under a cushion. "Oh!" he said. "Is my uncle back?"

Alcuin stared. "And who is your uncle?"

"The duke, I mean," the boy stammered. "You're—you're Alcuin, aren't you?"

The man smiled, not unflattered to be known. "You've come early for the party, child." He moved in a little closer. Yes, you could see the family resemblance if you looked hard, though it was mostly in the tone of the skin, the setting of the eyes.

"Were you looking for something in here? Perhaps I could help you." This boy's lineaments were soft and round where the duke's were sharp-cut. In fact—

"No!" Alcuin snapped. "You keep out of my affairs." He should have recognized her sooner. Those silly clothes confused him.

The duke's niece boldly faced him, looking at him with a direct gaze he found disconcerting.

"There is no call to be so angry," she said. "When will my uncle be back?"

"I—" But he could not say he did not know. "Soon. In time for his party. Will you be performing the comic theatricals?"

He had the satisfaction of seeing her blush. But she stood her ground, and so the library was closed to him for now.

He returned to the duke's own chambers upstairs, which he found now occupied by their master in a snarling foul humor, attended by his boy, Marcus.

He was preparing to leave them when the duke said, "Stay out of the way tonight, Alcuin."

"Why? Are you afraid I'll draw attention from your precious poet?"

"I'm afraid you'll bore them to death. Nobody wants to hear your opinion on meter and verse. It is all too painfully obvious that you start thinking of these things only after other people have begun to talk about them."

"You're screwing your poet, too, aren't you?"

"If I am, you'll still have nothing interesting to say."

Alcuin went off to kick his valet, who surely had arrived by now.

"And stay out of my papers," Tremontaine said to the closed door behind him.

⁓

I HAD NOT ACTUALLY BEEN INVITED TO THE DUKE'S party, but I was sure that was an oversight. I lived here, after all. And it would be a literary party, the servants said, not some debauched revelry, so there was no reason for me not to attend.

Except for one thing. My clothes.

"You have perfectly nice clothes, my lady," Betty said grumpily, "lovely ones the duke had made for you special." She was grumpy because the house staff were all busy getting ready for the influx of guests, and no one was listening to her stories of past mistakes. She'd gotten into the wine already, and it was making her stubborn. No matter how hard I explained to her that it was out of the question for me to appear before my fellow nobles dressed so outlandishly, she refused to listen. Clearly nothing short of a direct order from the duke himself would persuade her to retrieve even my meanest old gown out of wherever she'd hidden them all. I decided to go get that order from him myself.

I knew where the duke's room was. I marched right up to it and readied myself to knock.

The door opened, and a boy slipped out. It was Marcus, the servant about my age. He stood between me and the door, his back tightly to it, as if shielding it from me, or me from it.

"I just wanted to—" I began, but he held up his hand and looked concerned. "I wouldn't," he said. "Not right now."

"But it's—"

He shook his head. "Honestly. Trust me. Later. There's about to be an explosion." The door shuddered behind him. "And I have to go and get egg whites. Later." He fled down the hall one way, and I went back the other, sighing. So much for the party, then.

With the kitchen in chaos, it was easy to sneak in and supply myself with provender. I shut myself in my room to wait the evening out. I heard carriages arriving, names being called, people laughing. There was a long silence as they left the main hall for dinner; not a huge party, then. I ate apples and biscuits, watching the ever-glorious sunset over the river. As I lit a candle, I heard servants passing in the main hall below, lighting the many candelabra. It occurred to me, then, that I might easily watch undetected from the shadows at the top of the stairs.

It was just like when I was a child, sneaking out to the banisters to watch the grownups at my parents' parties. People had begun to mill about the hall's great gameboard, few enough at first that I could discern individual voices, fragments of conversation:

"...Godwin doing here? I thought..."

"...well, in poetry, if nothing else..."

"...not if you held a candle to my feet!"

"Bernhard! Never knew you liked poetry."

"I don't. Wait and see."

"...I knew he was pretty, but my god!"

"I doubt he'll last much longer. But consider, my dear..."

As I got to the top of the stairs, the horrible Alcuin came

staggering up them from the hall. Even I could see that he was
very drunk, his eyes and feet unsteady, his lovely face slack with
incomprehension. He was without his coat, and his shirt was
loose. His hair was weirdly spiky, as if he'd gotten egg whites in it.

I stepped aside. He seemed to be reaching for the banister, but
he grabbed my wrist instead, leaning hard, as if he would have fallen
without me. He did not look happy to see me. "Tremontaine," he
slurred. "Another one." The weight of his grip was pulling me
down. I couldn't shake him off. There were people downstairs in the
hall just below us; I could get help if I needed it. But I would rather
not let them know I was there. "Another Bitch Duchess."

Stupidly, I laughed. "I'm not anyone."

He pulled me to him. Amazing, how someone so beautifully
made could be so loathsome. He began calling me names. I
protested, "I haven't done anything to you. Stop it. Leave me
alone." It was as though he couldn't hear me. If I screamed,
everyone would come running, but it would be so embarrassing. I
brought my heel down, hard, on his foot.

Alcuin howled, but no one heard it because of the uproar
that began downstairs: ladies' shrieks mingled with cries of delight; more laughter, and shouts to come look. Alcuin staggered
down the hall to throw up, and I raced to the railing to see.

Two men were standing in the middle of the hall with drawn
swords. Crouched, they began to circle each other, taking each
other's measure. There were no tips on their blades. The sharp
steel was pointed at each other's faces. This was it, then: real
swordsmen, my first swordfight! I clutched the railing, looking
down, half afraid of being seen, but more afraid to miss it.

Right under me, people were edged against the wall to
watch. Their voices drifted up: "Not a chance . . . The dark one's
got the reach."

"But look at that arm."

"Fifty on the dark one—what's his name? Anyone know his
name?"

"You know who it *isn't*."

"Fifty, done."

Both swordsmen looked decent to me. One dark, one fair,

and the fair one seemed edgy. *Fear hurts sword.* But was he really nervous, or just cautious? He seemed alert to everything, every possible move. That could be to his advantage. The dark one had a lot of force. He might overspend that, though.

"Who else is game? Hurry up, before they're through."

There was a clash of weapons. Were they trying each other's mettle, or just making noise to get attention? Steel on steel rang out like a pure bell, long and long in the Great Hall.

"Nice form, there. Good job."

"And twenty more!"

I saw my uncle the duke, his arm around the shoulders of a rather pale young man who was clutching a bundle of papers. In the ringing silence the young man squeaked, "This is ridiculous. I am sure there was no insult intended."

The fighters began circling again.

"But a moment ago, you were sure there was," the duke said.

"I should not have said so."

The dark one made a feint, which the other backed off from.

"In real life, my sweet poet," the duke said as the swordsmen circled, "words can never be undone."

"But these men—to fight over such a thing—it's ridiculous."

"You are my guest," the duke said smoothly. "Your poetry was challenged in my house. It's lucky there were swordsmen here to take up the matter. Look out for Finch, the blond one; he's defending your verse's virtue."

A guest shouted, "All right, boys, let's go, let's see some action!"

The dark man's point was steady, pointed at Finch's chest.

"Let's have it!" a man's voice cried. "I've got money on this, let's go!"

Finch pressed suddenly forward, too quickly. It was a flashy move designed to startle your opponent and go right through his defenses, but it only works if you make them think you're doing something else, and he didn't take the time. Finch's opponent had no trouble blocking the blow. He parried and thrust home.

"Blood!" a guest called, and others took it up: *Blood! First blood!*

Finch staggered back. A dark stain spread on his white shirt. His opponent stood very still, his sword lowered. There was silence in the hall.

The duke said to the poet, "You've lost. Or, rather, Finch has lost in your person. It comes to the same thing. Unless you want them to go past First Blood to the Death? There's still a chance—"

"No," said the poet.

Finch dropped his sword then, and pressed the free hand to his side. The winning swordsman bowed to the duke.

I gripped the stair rail. I wanted to make them do it over again, do it right this time; but it wasn't an exercise. I wasn't sure what it was.

Finch sat down and put his head between his knees. Servants passed through the circle with bandages and water for him.

"Well, that's it, then," the duke announced loudly, and, just as loudly to the poet, "I'm afraid you will have to leave."

"But—why?"

"Your poetry turns out to be awful. I wouldn't have thought it, but there it is. Finch is bleeding."

The poet laughed uncertainly. "I see. Very amusing. But it's not real; you can't take it seriously."

The duke just looked at him. "My dear. Here on the Hill, I'm afraid we take it very seriously. A nobleman of the city brought your poetry's virtue into question—'Duller than a rainy Tuesday and twice as long' was the way you put it, Bernhard, I believe? A challenge was issued. There was a duel, and the swordsman defending the honor of your verse was defeated."

"But—one man sticking another with a sword cannot change my poetry from good to bad just like that."

"The duel is the ultimate arbiter of truth. Where men's judgment may be called into question, the opinion of the sword always holds fast." Half the room was listening to him, amused; the rest were settling debts or debating the fight. If these people didn't stop laughing and gambling soon, I wasn't going to be able to stand it. "If you stayed—well, you could stay. If you like. But it gives license for people to be very rude to you. I don't think you would enjoy it. No, really, you had better go."

They brought the poet his cloak and hat. My uncle saw him

to the door himself; as they passed beneath the stairs, I saw his ringed hands pass the poet a small heavy purse.

I wondered if the poet would think it had been worth it.

"Bernhard!" the tall duke turned and shouted into the crowd. "That was not very nice."

"You are ungracious." A large well-dressed man detached himself from the throng. "I thought you would enjoy a good fight better than whining poetry."

"*You . . . thought?*" An invisible wind had blown the duke from hot to cold. The room itself felt chilly, and the guests were still. "Let me ask you, Bernhard: do you *think* the Lords Justiciar would be pleased to hear that you called formal challenge on some poor scribbling fool who, as far as they are concerned, has no honor to defend?"

Lord Bernhard had the sort of heavy face that turns red with any emotion. "Hardly a matter for the Court of Honor, I would have thought."

"Or did you mean the challenge for me, here in my own house?"

"I had not known you for such a traditionalist, Tremontaine," Bernhard said, earning a laugh from some of them. "Although," he went on, "I suppose the purity of swordsmen is a passion of yours, isn't it, my lord?"

The laughter stopped. The duke spoke quietly, but I had no trouble hearing him. "Bernhard. Let me do a little thinking for you. You are in my house. Finch is not my only sword. If I call challenge on you this very moment, who will come forward to fight on your behalf?"

Bernhard forced a laugh.

A nice-looking man in blue said, "Tremontaine, really; you know the world. The Court doesn't attend to such trivia. And I am sure Bernhard meant no insult to you or to your house."

I would have done whatever he suggested; even the duke shrugged mildly. "I am not insulted, Godwin. When I am, Bernhard, I'll send you formal notice. I just wanted to point out that this fight was not strictly legal. And since Tremontaine sits on the Court of Honor (when I have a mind to), I could invoke the Lords Justiciar to attend to such 'trivia.'" He turned to the room, holding up his hands as if he were in a play: "Good heavens; if I, a known scoffer and reprobate, am the only one left willing to uphold the ancient forms, what hope is there for any of us? Who else are we planning to extend the privilege of the sword to?"

There was an embarrassed silence. My uncle let it last a long time before he said cheerfully, "Oh, well. Now that you have taken our original entertainment from us, Bernhard, I'm afraid I must ask you to supply the lack. What can you do?"

"I?" The man was bright red.

"Can you fight? Well, of course not. You do breed dogs, but nobody wants to watch that—not unless they're a member of your Gentlemen's Self-Pleasure League." I heard a woman shriek with embarrassed laughter. "Heavens, Bernhard, what *can* you do? Surely you can . . . read. Yes, I think you had better read to us. Something of my lady," he bowed to a serious-looking woman, "my lady Evaine's choosing. If you will follow me to the library, we'll find many excellent volumes there. You can regale us with . . . poetry, I think, don't you, my lady?"

And so, one by one, the party and its guests passed out of my sight. Of the two swordsmen no sign remained. Not even a smear of blood marked the black-and-white patterned floor of the hall of Tremontaine House. Instead there were fragments of flowers, a dropped fan, half a pastry, several buttons, a comb and a broken glass.

I took off my clothes and got into bed. I felt the hard lump of the book under my pillow, *The Swordsman Whose Name Was Not Death.* How could I sleep with that thing sticking into my head? There was not a grain of truth in it, none. Swordplay was two fools hacking at each other with razors until one of them was hurt. I took the book out and hurled it across the room.

chapter X

Tremontaine House was quiet the next morn-
ing, not because it was uninhabited, but because its occu-
pants were mostly asleep. Everything wet or edible had
already been cleared away; everything valuable had been cleaned.

Only one large, high-ceilinged room had its curtains pulled
back to let in the long cheerful ribbons of morning sunlight.
Outside the tall windows, a garden beckoned. But the muscular
black-bearded man stood with his back to it. Occasionally he
would spin around as if to challenge the view, stamping one foot
on the floor to make the decorated ceiling ring, then turn again
towards the door. Once he sprang from a crouch and leapt almost the length of the room. He hummed disapproval into his
mustache. He inspected the rack of glittering swords, first overall,
then blade by blade, looking for rust spots or fingerprints. As he
found none, he permitted himself a smile.

Because he heard the door open, and saw who it was reflected
in a blade, he did not turn around to look at the girl dressed in
sober blue-grey linen. When she had shut the door behind her,
then he turned, and let her see the smile.

"Clean blades," he said. "Very good."

"Thank you."

"Well? You are a statue? Pick up sword!"

The girl fixed on his face the steady gaze that he had taught her. "I will not fight today."

"How, not fight? You will not fight? Maybe we will play at dice, then, ah? Or learn the dance? *Booger*, you will not fight!"

She did not smile. "No. I will not be going on with these lessons."

"What lessons, then?" He thrust a finger in her face like a dagger. "You have some other lessons? Your mad father think you are too good now for Venturus, that you will learn more better from some street-puke swordsboy indeed? Ha!"

"Ha," she repeated tonelessly. "Do you know, Master, you sound like a jealous lover?"

"*Do you know . . .*" he mimicked. He took a step back, with a little bow. "But who have we here? Is it not some fine-aired lady, indeed? This lady I do not know, though she wear the britches."

"I will be sure that you are properly paid," she went on. "I am certain that there is money here for that. And your other students will no doubt be glad of your time."

"But this is grave." He stopped his posturing and met her gaze with one of his own. "This is no girlish humor, I think."

She dropped her eyes. "No. It is not."

"Why you no wish fight?"

She turned away. "You wouldn't understand."

"Ha. Girlish humor after all. You are in love?"

She spun in quick riposte. "Certainly not! Love? I shall never be in love, if people always think it makes you stupid! No, I'll tell you what it is—" And it was her turn to lean in to him, her face closer to his than a swordsman would normally allow— "I've seen them. Real ones. Last night, at the party here. Two swordsmen. A duel. It was disgusting."

"Blood. A mess. Now you are afraid—"

"I am *not* afraid. I see twice as much blood every month. It was the duel— I told you you wouldn't understand."

"I am not paid to understand you humors." He'd pulled a blade from the rack and began circling her with it. "You not afraid, ha?"

"No, I'm not. But I will *not* be made a show of."

"A show, ha?" He jabbed at her with the padded tip, feinted and jabbed again. "Just a show?"

"That's all any of it is, a show for people to laugh at. It was a *game* to them, that's all, just some stupid game! They place *bets*— stop that."

"Bets?" He was forcing her back a pace, two paces, now that she had begun to take notice of his blade.

"Bets on the outcome—two perfectly good— Ouch!" Her back was to the rack; he'd jabbed her in the shoulder. "Perfectly good swordsmen, nothing wrong with them, but they were doing it for—"

"Money? You think men should not fight for money, little girl?" He backed off, making midgelike circles with the tip of his blade. "Men without nice dukes should beg they money in streets, before fight they for pay?"

"He's not paying *me*," she said tightly. "I don't know what *your* fee is, but he's not paying me. I'm supposed to do it for free, to make a show of myself to amuse—to amuse—" The swordmaster feinted high, low, elaborate little spirals of disengage and riposte up and down his target, annoying as summer flies. "I said, stop that."

"What for? No peoples looking here. Just us, little boy duchess."

The sword was in her hand, and she attacked. Venturus fell back before her. She tried to kill him, despite the blunted tips, and he fought with a grin splitting his beard. She went for the eyes, the throat, but he was quick in his defense. Around and around the room they went, and he let her tire herself out with every trick she knew. He waited until she began to slow, and then Venturus stepped in with one perfect thrust.

She flung her blade into the corner. It rattled and clanged.

"Not too sad a fight," said Master Venturus. "Now we will stop for awhile. Good day, Lady Katherine."

And she was alone, sweating, in the practice room with the wet rabbits on the door.

⌒

I WAS AWAKENED EARLY THE NEXT MORNING IN THE COLD grey light. The fire had not yet warmed the room any. Betty was bustling about, folding clothes and putting them in a trunk. "Come," said Betty, "hurry up, dear. My lord says you're to travel. The carriage waits."

There was no point in arguing with her. If he said travel, travel I must. I let her button me into my chilly traveling clothes topped with long boots, hat, heavy cloak. A mist was on the river.

Into the carriage with bread, a hot flask and blankets. Betty waving to me; a cluck of the coachman, a creaking of gates and Tremontaine House was behind me. The city passed away like a series of pictures; then, for the first time in many weeks, I was in the open country. The sun was coming up, a golden haze of warmth. Wrapped in the blankets, I dozed, woke to a stop for the horses, stretched my legs and sat the rest of the afternoon, watching as unfamiliar countrysides of fields of golden wheat gave way to streams and cows and orchards. When the shadows started to stretch across the road, they stopped the coach to consult with me.

"Shall we push on to Highcombe tonight, my lady? It will be dark. But there's a nice little inn not far along, if you'd rather stop for the night."

It was all one to me. But I knew when I was being suggested to. We stopped at the nice little inn, and I got a good dinner and a reasonable bed. I did not ask the coachman or the groom what Highcombe was, could not think of a way to do it that would not betray the fact that I had no idea what was going on. Until they had named our destination, I had dared to think that perhaps I was going home—a failure, maybe, but going home, still. A trunk of my belongings was lashed up behind us; wherever I was being sent, it was not for a brief visit.

The next morning we rose again early, and by the time the sun shone watery above in a cloudy midmorning, the carriage was rolling through the gates of a lodge and down a graveled alley lined with tall trees. I caught glimpses of a great stone house, three times the size of my old one. But instead of rounding the drive to its front steps, we suddenly went off the path and began bumping over the grass to the other side of the house. We pulled up before a little cottage tacked onto the wall, with its own wooden door painted a cozy blue.

I stood in the damp grass and smelt earth and apples crossing with hay and horses. It wasn't quite the smell of home, but it wasn't city, either. Stretching away from the blue door across from the lawn (now beribboned with the silver marks of our carriage wheels) was an apple orchard in one direction and fields in another. A stream cut through them both. The fields were silvery with long, wet grass; it had rained here in the night, and clouds still lingered. Coming across the fields I saw a man with a staff, his head uncovered.

"There he is," said the coachman, and hailed him: "Master!"

Fine drops of mist ornamented the man's dark hair. He raised his head and leapt the stream, and came to us.

The footman spoke. "The duke's greetings, Master. He presents his niece, the Lady Katherine. She will be studying with you, he says. And we've brought you some things from the city."

"Thank you," said the man. "You can put them inside."

The blue door was not locked. I stood looking at my new tutor and wondered what I would be studying. He had the earth-caked hands of a gardener, well-shaped fingers squared off at the tips. His face was unshaven but not yet bearded. He did not seem to mind my staring, though his own gaze was less direct. I felt he was looking past me.

"Are you Janine's daughter?" he asked.

"You know my mother!"

"No. But Alec's spoken of her."

"Who's Alec?"

The man smiled. "The duke."

Another name. "You're his friend? Is this Highcombe?"

"Yes, it's his house. One of them. I live here."

The men had finished their deliveries. Even my trunk was stowed inside. "Will that be all, sir? Will you need anything else?"

"Thank you. Nothing else, if you've brought everything I asked for."

"All in the chest, according to my list. The spoons are wrapped in the linen. We can wait if you like, but our orders are to return to town as soon as convenient."

"That's all right, then. Thank you; good-bye."

I did not feel melancholy or afraid as the Tremontaine carriage pulled away, leaving me in a strange place with a strange man. Indeed, I could hardly wait for them to go, so I could find out what would happen next.

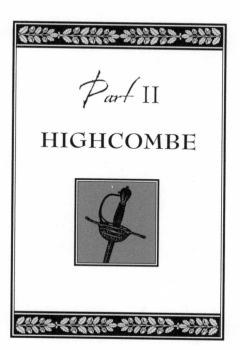

Part II

HIGHCOMBE

chapter I

WHAT HAPPENED NEXT WAS THAT HE ATTACKED me. His staff swung up and I ducked, my hands over my head.

The staff hovered in midair, brushing the edge of my cloak.

"You haven't been studying long," he said.

"Not very," I agreed, adding, "You aren't supposed to do that. You didn't call for my guard, or issue a challenge, or anything!"

"Sword against staff is tricky," he observed. "But you didn't even reach for your blade."

"I'm not wearing one."

"Even then. You aren't in the habit, and that's dangerous. Go put one on right now, and then we can get you fed and rested."

None of my baggage was long enough to contain a sword. I followed him through the blue door, into the little cottage.

"Climb that narrow flight of stairs," my host said. "At the top, in the corner of the room, left of the window, you'll find a chest with blades wrapped in oilcloth."

I had to open the shutters before I could see anything. It was a very plain bedroom. The chest was plain as well, but what was inside it made my breath catch. From the protective cloth I un-wrapped long gleaming blades of extraordinary beauty, with hilts both plain and intricate. I'd never seen anything like them. Everything about them was sharp, including the tips. One, with a dragon's head on the pommel, looked just like the sort of thing Fabian would carry, or someone in *Lives of the Heroic Swordsmen*.

I called downstairs, "May I choose any one I want?"

"No." His voice was firm but amused. "Try the twisted basket hilt; it's probably closest to the right weight for you."

I stood at the top of the stairs. They were horribly steep, not much more than a pitched ladder, really. If I slipped or stumbled, the sharp edges in my hand could turn against me.

"Had I better find a scabbard?" I asked nervously.

"Bottom of the same chest. Leather, and not too gaudy, youngling."

Getting the long sword into the soft scabbard was a bit like getting a bootie onto a baby's foot: neither was very interested in helping, though in the end they fit together just fine. I came care-fully down the steep stairs.

"Don't I need something to stick it in? I've got a belt, but there's a hanging thing, too, isn't there?"

"Oh, dear," the man sighed. "He wasn't thinking, was he?"

Whether he meant the duke or Venturus was all one to me; I was just glad he didn't think it was my fault. Reaching for his staff, the man rose suddenly, and I jumped, clutching the sword to myself. To my surprise, "I'm sorry," the man said. "I'll try to move more slowly, until you learn me better. I was just going to get you a hanger."

He stood closer to me than Venturus ever had, fitting the sword's hanger on my belt, and the sword in with it. His fingers were steady and sure, like a stableman's harnessing a horse; he didn't even have to look, and I felt his breath warm across my hair. When he moved away, there was a part attached to me that had not been there before. It moved when I moved, like a cat's tail—though without any of its grace!

He put a loaf of bread on the table, and a block of yellow cheese. When I sat on the bench I had to move the sword out of the way to keep from sitting on it, which wasn't as easy as you'd think. I looked to see if the man was laughing at me, but he was cutting bread. It was good bread, and the cheese was good, too.

"What about a knife?" he asked. "Did he give you a knife, at least?"

"I—I have a penknife." It had been a New Year's gift from my brother.

"No sword, no knife... Use this." He handed me his. It was well worn and rather ugly, with a plain wooden handle, but the blade very bright and thin with repeated grinding.

"I couldn't take your knife," I began to demur politely, but he interrupted, "I've got more. One with a dragon's head, one like a falcon... I won't miss this one. Don't lose it, though; wear it on your belt." He caught my moment of hesitation as if it were a ball I'd thrown. "—In a sheath, of course. Oh, dear."

When he got up from the table I jumped and fumbled for my sword, which took the bench up and over with it. This time, he did laugh. He sounded so helpless, as if I'd just crippled him by telling a brilliant joke very well, that I laughed, too.

"Never mind," he said when he could speak again. "You're just going to give yourself a stomachache. Learn to walk with it, first, and then we'll see about defending yourself."

I was so horribly grateful that I had to stand up for my pride. "I can fight. I fought Master Venturus."

"Did you? Who won?"

"He did," I mumbled.

"Good. Then it was a real fight." He put the bread and cheese back in the cupboard. I swept up the crumbs. "There's milk in a pitcher in the stream," he said, "and sometimes beer, when they remember. Well water's in the courtyard—it's a bit of a haul, so I keep a bucket by the door. Don't drink from the stream; the cows step in it. It's all right for washing. You can go off exploring now if you'd like; you must be cramped from the ride. Just don't go in the field with the bull. Oh, and I'd stay clear of the village; I don't think they're ready for you."

I concluded regretfully that he was right, which was a shame, since they could probably tell me all about him. But I knew our own villagers. They would not warmly receive a girl dressed as a tumbler, and I bet the Highcombe folk wouldn't either. So I followed the stream into the woods instead, and found a little waterfall and a blackberry thicket with plenty of berries left, and an empty bird's nest floating in the water.

I came back as the shadows were long across the fields, my favorite time of day. The man was standing in front of the cottage, wearing nothing but a shirt over his breeches, sword in hand. I waved, but he didn't wave back; instead he turned and did something like a dance that wasn't, because the sword was flashing about in a determined manner, and when he stopped, you had the impression that he had won. I took a deep breath and went forward.

"Are you ready?" the swordsman asked.

"Wait—" I fumbled, and wrestled my sword out of its sheath. I was on guard, and so was he. And then things were happening very fast. He'd move, and I'd find his blade within my guard, and I'd think of the parry I should have made if only I'd seen him coming in time, but by then he'd struck again somewhere else. After a bit of this, at least I was ready to do *something* when he moved, even if half the time it was something that left me poking into thin air while he came at me again. Of course I never came anywhere within his guard; I only had to think about it for him to be right where I wanted to attack. As if he were weaving a fence around himself with his steel.

At last he stepped back and put up his blade, and I saw it just in time to keep from making a fool of myself by trying to skewer him.

"I take it," he said, "you've never killed anyone."

"Oh, dear no!"

"Just checking." He turned and went in the house. He wasn't even panting. I went and washed my face in the stream. And then went in to supper, which was vegetables boiling on the hearth. And bread and cheese.

But on the plain wooden table were a pair of candlesticks, silver dragons supporting the candles with their mouths. At each of our places was a wineglass flecked with gold, whose stem was a twisting dolphin.

"How beautiful!" The words escaped me. He held his glass by the stem, stroking the fragile curves familiarly. I could almost feel the cool, smooth glass just by watching him.

The vegetables needed seasoning, but I was hungry enough

not to care. When I finished eating, suddenly I was so tired I could have put my head right in my empty plate.

"Sleep upstairs," he said. "I'll help you carry your things."

I wrestled myself and my gear gingerly up the narrow stairs, holding the candle.

"Don't worry," he said. "There's a pot under the bed; you don't have to risk breaking your neck in the dark."

I grinned, then considered that since there seemed to be no house servants I'd have to empty the thing myself. Not down the ladder-stairs, please! Maybe out the window. There were two: a large one with shutters, and a little round one over the bed. It glowed red with sunset, like stained glass.

He reached out and shuttered the window. As with everything else he did, his movements were economical and practiced. Suddenly my heart started to beat very hard. This was his bedroom. Did he know I was not a boy? He did know, didn't he? I could sleep in my clothes. I had a knife, but I'd better not try it. I remembered his hands on my belt, his breath in my hair, the sharp tip of his blade dancing around me. Maybe it would be all right. He was so quiet.

"Take the belt off," he said, "sword and dagger all at once, and try not to drop them. Hang the whole thing on that hook, then you can put it right on in the morning."

With cold fingers I complied. Of course I dropped the whole kit on the floor: the sword pulled one way, the dagger another, slipping along the belt. It was hopeless.

"Never mind." He smiled. "Good night."

He was on the stairs before I had the wit or the breath to object politely, "But where will you sleep?"

"I've got a pallet by the fire. It's fine. I get up during the night; this way I won't disturb you."

I heard an owl cry once, and then I was asleep.

⁓

DRESSING THE NEXT MORNING, I FOUND A TINY RIP IN the sleeve of my jacket, as if it had caught on something sharp like a nail. Betty hadn't packed me any needle and thread;

it was my turn to mutter, "Oh, dear." The swordsman apologized. "That was me, I'm afraid." He seemed annoyed. "I'm sorry; I didn't mean to touch you at all."

He had caught my jacket once in the entire bout with naked blades. I didn't think Master Venturus could do that well. Maybe he could. Fabian certainly could; he could even put out a candle flame. Maybe everyone could but me, even those showmen dueling at the duke's party.

"Let's go find some practice weapons," the man suggested. "I don't want to tip my good steel, and you're bound to knock it about some at first."

That was when I found out there was another door to the house. It was next to the hearth, and I hadn't even noticed: a piece of the wall with a handle and hinges. We passed from the modest cottage into the marble grandeur of the great house at Highcombe, like moving from one dream to another. A great hall with ceilings twice as high as the entire cottage. Useless, decorative space, and everywhere there was furniture shrouded in sheets, tall windows shuttered.

"Does he come here ever?" I wondered aloud.

"Oh, sometimes. He doesn't like the country much."

We found the old armory, full of antique weapons and country things like boar spears. My teacher picked us out some old, blunt practice swords, and we started back through the hall.

Suddenly, he grinned at me. "Hey!" he cried. "On your guard!"

I raised my sword, and he retreated before me. "Don't worry," he called, "I'll keep falling back—just come on!"

And so I advanced on him, all the way down the long gallery, driving the master swordsman back with my clumsy tipped blade, sweeping past the portraits and landscapes, the swathes of sheeting, the covered mirrors, over the polished parquet.

He fetched up against a door, his face bright with laughter, and spread his arms open to me. I sighted my spot, to the left of his breastbone, and lunged—but he deflected the point with the tiniest of motions and my sword jarred in my hand.

"You want to relax your grip," he said, "but that was good: a nice, clean attack." He was laughing, looking back down the length of the hall. "God, I've wanted to do that ever since I got here! Thank you."

As the doorlatch behind him clicked, he spun, weapon raised. The woman coming through the doorway screamed and dropped her tray. He jumped back, and I chased after the rolling silver goblets while he said, "I'm so sorry," and she gasped, "Oh, sir! Oh, sir!"

It was awkward having no apron to collect them in. Boys don't need aprons, do they?

"This is my new student," he said, and to me, "Marita is the housekeeper." I was grateful to him for not revealing me as the duke's niece; it would have been all over the countryside by nightfall. As it was, she just looked hard at me, registered my sex and decided not to do anything about it. Then she took her silver and curtseyed. "I'm sorry to disturb you, sir," she said, for all the world as though he were some nobleman, and not the tenant of a tacked-on two-room cottage. "Is everything in order?"

"Yes—no, wait, we need, what was it? Needle and thread."

She curtseyed again.

I suppose being able to kill people was enough to make them very polite to you, but I couldn't help wondering. "Are you a lord?" I asked when she was gone.

"Me?" His smile flashed white. "Hardly."

And that was all. He dressed very plainly, he wore no rings. He did not speak like a countryman. But neither did he sound educated, and there were no books where he lived. Nothing but swords, and precious things.

"I expect you have killed a great many people," I said at dinner in my best grown-up conversation voice.

"Yes, I have."

"Is it hard?"

He looked out past me. His eyes were unusual: blue, almost violet, like the heart of a candleflame. "Killing them instantly is hard. You want a blow to the heart, which is tricky, or through the windpipe, or through the eye to the brain, but people don't like to see that." I began to be sorry I asked. I put down my food. "Disabling them is easiest; they may die later, from infection or loss of blood. It's less satisfying. But it takes a lot of force to kill with one blow. You'd be surprised. I'm not sure you've got the strength yet. Even to pierce a lung...I could give you some exercises. Did you mean dueling, or street fighting?"

"Neither," I whispered. "I don't want to kill anyone."

"Then put your sword away," he said mildly, "or you will be killed." I shot a look up at him, but he merely looked interested.

"I don't want it," I blurted. "I never wanted any of this!"

"Really?" He considered me with his head tilted. "Then what do you want?"

I thought of gowns and balls, and of sewing and housekeeping, and of swordsmen and towers. . . . Nowhere could I see myself. "Nothing! I wish I was dead!"

He did not mean to laugh, but I could hear the stifled breath. "How old are you?"

"Fifteen. And a bit."

"Hmm. When I was sixteen I left home and went to the city. I didn't know what I wanted, either. But things kept happening to me. It was interesting, and I found I could manage."

"That's different. You're a man. And you could fight."

"So you're a woman. And you will be able to fight. Are you sure you wouldn't like to reconsider?"

"Reconsider what?" I said rudely, deep in my own misery. "It's not as though I have a choice."

"Well," he said, "I suppose that's true. Do you have any idea why he's doing this?"

"None," I said. "Because of my father. He hates us."

"I think he hated his own parents more. I think he thinks that if your mother had known how to fight, they couldn't have forced her to marry if she didn't want to."

I stared at the man across from me. "Did he tell you that?"

"No. I figured it out."

"They didn't force her. She wanted to get married. No one's going to want to marry me."

"So what? You can have lovers."

I nearly yelped with shock. What did he think I was? "I'll clean up," I said instead.

Before going to bed, I opened his sword chest. The weapons were so finely crafted, they looked like settings for jewels. I

touched the tip of one, gently, so that it did not break the skin.
The oil from my finger's tip would be enough to darken and cor-
rode the steel. I pictured the shining metal covered with blood.
Keeping cloth between my hands and the blade, I examined the
dragon's head sword. Near the hilt, a fleck of red. I rubbed at it.
Rust. I should clean it, or tell him it was still there. Carefully, I
wiped away the bit that I had touched.

H E WAS GONE WHEN I GOT UP THE NEXT MORNING.
He'd left plates and crumbs on the table and walked away.
I helped myself to breakfast, then began to rearrange things—not
on purpose, but piece by piece, as I got ideas on where they would
look nice. I set the dolphin glasses to catch the sun, made the jam
and oil and honey pots line up in order of size and even angled the
benches so we'd each have more room to sit. I did it all wearing
my sword, too. Nothing had been moved in a long time; there
were marks everywhere on floor and shelf, and so I swept and
dusted as well. When I finished, it looked quite nice: a tidy room,
glowing in the autumn sun.

I was drinking cold tea when the swordsman came in. His
face was bright, his cloak thrown back, as if he'd been for a good
long walk.

"Hello," I said politely. "Would you like some tea?"

"Yes." He smiled. He didn't say anything about the room. He
walked forward and smashed into the bench, landing hard on the
table, and sent my cup flying. I shouted, "Are you all right?"

"Yes." The swordsman got up slowly. "I just didn't see it.
Have you moved things?" I'm afraid all I could do was stand and
gape. "Because it would be better if you didn't."

He could see, I knew he could! I remembered the way he'd
shown me around, the sure way he cut the bread and dished
things up. . . . My skin crawled when I thought of our duel with
the bare-tipped swords, and his annoyance at having grazed my
sleeve just once.

"I'm sorry," I managed to whisper. "I won't anymore."

He brushed himself off, found the bench and righted it and

walked around the table, touching it, seeming to see it with the edges of his eyes.

I glanced over at the glasses, the pots.

"Shall I show you the rest?"

"No, I'll find them. I just wasn't expecting it."

"I'm sorry. I could move things back—"

"No, I'll take care of it."

I had to know, and was afraid to ask. I watched him touch things and look at them. He never held them up in front of his face, but somewhere to the side, or even above. Sometimes he'd find them and touch them first, and never seem to see them at all. It was as if his hands and his eyes were not connected: one knew the world one way, the other another one, and to make them speak to each other was an act of deliberation.

"Lady Katherine." He did not like being watched. "You might take this time to practice. We will duel this afternoon."

I should have been quiet, obeyed the dismissal in his voice, been a good child, kept the unspoken agreement between us that neither would ask anything uninvited, or come too close. But I was frightened now. Nothing was as I'd thought. I had power over him, to move things and make him crash into them, to hurt him by shifting a bench, and he had power over my every breath and I didn't even know who he was—

"Are you blind?" I demanded.

"Almost."

"But then how . . . ?"

"Hold your hands up in front of your eyes. No, a little further than that. Now, can you see?"

"Yes— No—I can see around them, but not . . ."

"That's exactly it. It takes some getting used to."

"What happened to you?"

"Nothing. It just came on me."

"Were you a swordsman?"

"I am a swordsman if I am anything."

"But if you can't see—"

"I can see what I have to."

"Did you work for the duke? Were you his swordsman?"

Surprisingly, the man smiled. "I suppose you could say I was his. And I certainly am working for him now: I've never been anyone's tutor before. It will be interesting to see what you can learn."

This time, I took his unspoken direction. "I'd better go practice, then."

Outside, I closed my eyes and hurled myself against the weight of the sword, the quickness of my own breathing, the slowness of my feet, the brightness of the day.

chapter II

As the Duke Tremontaine had predicted, there was chaos in the Council of Lords, and some of it could be laid at his door. The apportioning of new land taxes had been all but decided upon, and penalties for noncompliance laid out strictly but fairly. The unfortunate lack of rain in the south did not excuse a poor harvest; the nobles whose lands were the country's breadbasket would just have to extend themselves in some other way—lumber, perhaps. It was unfair that the northern nobles were expected to provide more than their share of wood for shipbuilding, at a time when trade was so profitable and the river so low that in places you could barely bring the northern lumber down at all. But foreign grain was cheap this year, and shipping lucrative. And if the river was impassable, roads could be widened and improved—roads that happened to pass through the lands of the ambitious Philibert, Lord Davenant, and his political affiliates. They were powerful men; they served their country well, as had their fathers before them. What harm in a little profit for their faithful service, when the benefit to all was so clear to any but the most pig-headed of councilors?

But when copies of a certain document—a private agreement between Davenant and a foreign shipper, misleadingly worded so as possibly to be mistaken for a treaty between two countries—began to circulate, it threw the motives of all his associates, these noble councilors, into question. The original of the document was never found, of course, and no one could ascertain where the copies had come from; but it was enough to throw the coalition into disorder, their opponents into a rash of aggressive realignments and their tax proposals into brightly fluttering shreds. If that wasn't enough, that same Lord Davenant was suddenly burdened with a faithless actress mistress, an angry well-placed wife and a chief lieutenant who'd acquired one and, some said, the other, as well.

While no one could say exactly how or why, many of the coalition thought their troubles stemmed once again from indiscretions on the part of the Mad Duke, who always seemed to know more about the city than anyone could remember having told him. Nor did he scruple to disseminate his knowledge where a true gentleman would have kept his mouth shut. There was no use challenging him again; his swordsmen were as likely to win as not. The sword loved Alec Campion, it seemed, and always had.

The Crescent Chancellor, leader of the Council of Lords and head of the Inner Council, decided to go and speak to the Duke Tremontaine. Anthony Deverin, Lord Ferris, had not visited the Riverside district in many years—not since his days as Dragon Chancellor, when the future duke had been a callow and obnoxious boy known only as Alec, and Deverin, already Lord Ferris, a rising star.* Diane, Duchess Tremontaine, had taken Ferris under her wing and tutored him in statecraft. When he tried to outsmart her in that shadowy arena, she smoothly engineered his downfall, sending her young kinsman to Council to do the deed. Everyone knew, after all, that the beautiful duchess never meddled in politics.

His punishment, an ambassadorship to the icy and barbaric lands of Arkenvelt, wasn't a death sentence, though, and Ferris liked to think Diane had retained enough feeling for him to send

---

*See *Swordspoint*.

him where he might succeed if he had the nerve and the brains, not to mention the endurance. The rewards of frozen Arkenvelt did include access to some of the world's finest fur trading, and when his exile was over Ferris returned home with enough wealth in his pockets to reestablish himself in style. He frequented the right gatherings, married the right woman with the right connections, who died leaving him a small country estate and a good house in the city. He resumed his family seat on the Council of Lords, and there combined sense with statecraft in such perfect accord that, a mere ten years after his return, he was elected head of that august body of noblemen. It was in that capacity, now, that he paid a visit to Diane's heir and successor, whom he disliked as much as ever.

At the time of his last visit to the little island between the river's banks, Riverside had been no one's domain: a warren of criminals and swordsmen living in abandoned houses. But the Mad Duke in his fancy now occupied it, in more ways than one. Ferris was aware that once he crossed the Bridge, he trod the duke's territory. The City Watch still gave wide berth to the unsavory district, but it was honeycombed with Tremontaine's people. So the Crescent Chancellor traveled in semi-state, with both guards and swordsmen, that no one there might mistake his person.

Lord Ferris had never been invited to Tremontaine's Riverside house, and knew he was not welcome. Nevertheless his horses were stabled, his escort refreshed with courteous efficiency, and he was ushered into the ducal presence in very little time. It was not a house he himself would have chosen to live in: old-fashioned small rooms, dark paneling, heavy curtains . . . nothing shocking, though. Ferris felt almost disappointed. If there were indeed the pornographic frescos, instruments of torture, naked serving girls and other items popular opinion had decorated the duke's house with, they were not on public view.

The duke himself was sitting in an upholstered chair eating crackers and cheese and slices of apple. He was wearing a brocade robe, and possibly not much else. His hair was tousled, imperfectly caught back in a black velvet ribbon.

He bit a cracker and shrugged. "Sorry. I get hungry."

Lord Ferris refused the offer of any refreshment. If he'd roused the duke from carnal pleasures so be it, but he would be heard. "Tremontaine," he said, "I'll not take much of your time. I come from the Council on my own initiative, to ask you to reconsider your stand on the new tax laws."

"Stand? I have no stand."

"Of course not," Lord Ferris said with mild irony. "You never do. Like your grandmother, the late duchess, you have no interest in politics."

The duke smiled. "Exactly like." One of the late duchess's secret protégés, Lord Ferris knew the worth of that statement better than most. "It's a family tradition."

"And it is by pure accident that you have managed to bring down a coalition that was months a-building to make some honest change—"

"Honest change? Honest? Has someone altered the definition of the word while my back was turned, or have you recently developed a sense of humor?"

Lord Ferris pressed his lips together tightly. He endured these little sallies in the open Council Hall, as His Lordship of Tremontaine sporadically descended upon their proceedings. But there was no audience here to snicker appreciatively.

"Oh, Campion," Ferris sighed. "Your grandmother was no friend to chaos. I wonder what she was thinking of when she made you her heir."

"Perhaps," the duke said around a mouthful of apple, "she thought I would reform."

Ferris flashed him a look. In these, his later years, he had even less patience with people pretending to be stupid. But he only said, "I do not think it."

"Nor do I," the younger man said frankly. "Perhaps she did not care what happened to the state, once she was dead. Maybe she wanted to bring it down after her."

From a low, polished table, Ferris bent to pick up one of the little glass birds she had collected. He held it gently. "Oh, no, not she."

"Or she thought you and Godwin and all her other fancy boys would rise to the occasion. As indeed you do. She trained you well. The Council bears her stamp, I bear her title and every-one is happy."

Carefully, Ferris put the bird down. "There is something else I thought . . . " his drawl had become almost as long as the duke's, a relic of both their youths " . . . when I heard you had inherited after all. I wondered if she had not intended all along for your ex-quisite swordsman, St Vier, to direct the duchy. One so admired his balance. And you did seem inseparable, back then." He looked lazily at a spot over the duke's head. "Yet you did separate. Perhaps that was the flaw in her reasoning."

The duke scrutinized his pearl-handled fruit knife as though he had forgotten just what it was for. Finally, he applied it care-fully to the skin of his apple.

"It is interesting how one idolizes the departed," the duke mused. "You admire the late duchess now, but I remember you calling her some very ugly names when she had you exiled to Arkenvelt over the matter of your misuse of my exquisite swords-man. I did think then, my lord, that you had learned that St Vier cannot be used against Tremontaine."

Ferris heard the message and noted it for further study. He had been wondering if the swordsman was still alive. It appeared he might be. *Alive, but not in play.* He chose to ignore the dig at his own past disgrace; it was, after all, Tremontaine who had brought him to the political exile he had spent years and a small fortune to return from, and there was no reason for either of them to have forgotten it. "I remember," the Crescent Chancellor added, "how very much in demand he was in his heyday, your swordsman. He killed with one blow to the heart."

"If he liked you. As you may also remember, he was not al-ways so merciful." The duke gathered the folds of his poisonous green-and-black robe around him. "And now, if you will excuse me, there's someone waiting for me."

Lord Ferris did not bow, but said tightly, "We must all excuse you. Constantly. I trust we will see you no more this season in Council?"

The duke cocked his head. "Now, why should you think that?"

Lord Ferris opened his mouth to make a double-edged rejoin-der, and closed it again, suddenly sick of the whole thing, and not at all sure of keeping his temper—another provocation he very much resented from the duke. "You disappoint me," Ferris said heavily. "You could be more, much more."

"I don't think the city would take much more of me."

"It would if you put your position to good use!" This was the speech Ferris had come planning to make, but it came pouring out of him untempered. "You have opinions, everyone knows you do; why will you not come and debate them in open Council with the rest of us? Statecraft and policy take time. They take patience and forethought and, yes, even compromise. They are not toys—we are not toys—to be picked up and put down at your whim, because you cannot stay the long course that it would take to effect real change. You are not stupid, you must surely know that. You find no one worthy of your vision, you do not wish to be a reliable ally? Fine. But at least be a reliable opponent, instead of shifting like a weathercock, blown by the wind of your fancy."

The duke paused and looked at him with real surprise. "Ferris," he said, "I am not a boy any longer. I don't particularly care if I disappoint you or not. Save your pompous sermonizing for the young fools who want to impress you and run the country into the ground with self-serving tax schemes."

Many years ago, Lord Ferris had lost his left eye. He turned the patch to the duke, a black velvet gaze that often unnerved people. "Someday," he said, "you will regret the loss of that swordsman."

Which was not at all what he had intended to say. Before his temper could drive him to further indiscretion, Lord Ferris turned and left the room. His own swordsmen and guards stood ranked to escort him; and in the shadows of the corridors of the Riverside house, he fancied he saw the shapes of others, watching.

⌒

THE DUKE TREMONTAINE THREW HIS FRUIT KNIFE AT the wall, where its point stuck, quivering, due to luck or the fury of the blow.

Then he went into the adjoining room, where the Ugly Girl was sitting on his bed reading, fully dressed.

"God, you're a pig when you wake up," she observed.

"He should not have come so early."

"Early!" she snorted. "It's after noon. Though you'd never know it; in your room, it is eternal twilight." She reached for one of the red velvet curtains, but he barked, "Stop. I like it this way."

"Come down to the library," she suggested, "where there's plenty of light, and quit hoarding books in your room. What else have you got in that pile?"

"Poetry," he said sweetly. "And pornography. Nothing to please your maiden eyes."

"Crap. You've got Merle's *Antithesis*, and after you swore you'd let me read it first."

"I will let you read it first. I was saving it to give to you on a special occasion."

"Like when you've been really annoying?"

"Just so. Where else are you going to get a copy of a banned book?"

She extended herself across the bed and snatched it from the pile. "For a noble and a libertine, you're not so bad. Want to go downstairs and work on Coverley's Last Theorem?"

"No," he drawled; "I want to stay here and smoke something."

The fat woman shrugged. "Suit yourself. But when I solve it without you, don't expect any credit for helping."

"I am going to have visions."

"Some people," she said, "have no idea how to enjoy themselves."

But the duke opened a cabinet by his bed, and began sorting through his collection of little vials. "*You're* all right," he said to the door closing behind her. "Without poetry or pornography, it's unlikely that anyone will ever strike you through the heart."

Soon he began to feel better.

chapter III

I LEARNED THE SWORD FROM HIM, BUT I LEARNED more. I learned to be quiet in the wood, and how to breathe so no deer could hear me. I learned how to gut a fresh-caught fish, and how to rob a beehive of its honeycomb. I learned to know where my feet were at all times, and how to make the sword I wore a part of myself, so that when my teacher took a sudden swipe at me, my hand was no longer empty, and I was not defenseless.

I rediscovered skills I'd had as a child: climbing trees, knocking down nuts, skipping stones across a pond.

And I learned him well enough that it became harder for him to surprise me with a sudden attack. I could sense the stillness of his impending motion, and I was ready.

I raided the great house's kitchen gardens for herbs, and made a little plot by our door so that I would not have to go so far to make our food taste like something. As the harvest came in, the house staff left us baskets of good ripe squash and tomatoes and leeks and chard. I was going to miss the sweet green peas I ate by the handful that were already gone by. I dried bunches of thyme and sage, and brought indoors a little pot of rosemary I hoped would last out the winter.

There was always enough butter and cream and cheese, since there were more than enough cows. And suddenly, as the night air turned cold and the day sky burned a bright and gallant blue, the world was full of apples. The air smelt of them, sharp and crisp, then underlaid with the sweet rot of groundfall. One day the orchard was infested with children, filling their baskets with them for cider. The next week, pigs were rootling for what was left.

On one of the last warmish nights of autumn we sat by the stream, grilling trout stuffed with fennel over a fire of apple wood. The stars were thick as spilled salt above us.

He pulled his cloak around him and poked the fire with his staff. "There were apple trees where I grew up. I used to collect fallen wood for my mother. And steal the lord's apples, with his sons."

"Were you caught?"

"Chased, not caught. He was a nice man. He understood boys get hungry. He liked my mother; used to lend her books and things."

"Did your father die?"

"I never had one, not in the usual way of things. My mother ran away with him when she was young, but she decided she didn't like him after all. By then she was stuck with me, but I guess she didn't mind. She used to show me bat skeletons and teach me the names of plants."

My mother seemed so far away she hardly seemed worth mentioning. And mine never had any bat skeletons. "She sounds a bit...unusual."

"Yes, I figured that out later."

"Did she teach you to fight?"

"Oh, no. I learnt from a swordsman. No, she couldn't do anything practical, really."

We'd eaten all we wanted to eat, but were in no mood to leave the fire.

"It's too bad neither of us can sing," my teacher said. "The nights are getting longer. Can you recite anything?"

Poetry? I thought in panic. "Just schoolroom things: 'The Maid Forlorn,' 'The King's Run,' that sort of thing."

"Can I hear them?"

He was always amazing me by not knowing the most common things. "Well, if you like."

But he stopped me halfway through "The Maid Forlorn." "Do you think that could really happen?"

I sucked fish off my fingers. "A girl believing everything a man tells her? Probably. Some people are very gullible."

I heard him smile. "True. But—are you supposed to admire her as well as feel sorry for her? Or just to think, *I'll never do anything that stupid?*"

I'd never considered it. "You know," I said, "I think the point is she's in love with him, even though she isn't supposed to be. That's what makes her stupid, really. It's not to say she isn't clever with other things. She might have been very good at sums or geography or something, beforehand."

"So they made you learn this as a lesson not to fall in love with unsuitable men?"

I drew myself up. I did not like having my upbringing criticized, even by him. "I learnt this," I said, "because it is *poetry.* Girls are supposed to know poetry. It is the inner beauty of the soul made art."

"I take it she dies at the end."

"She wants to die. She's been betrayed. She's lost her *honor.*"
He made a dismissive noise. "Well, what do you want her to *do?*"
I demanded. "Go off somewhere and open a *shop?*"

"Well, why not?"

"Because then it wouldn't be *poetry.*"

"How's 'The King's Run'?"

"It's heroic. The young king dies, but it's for the land."

"I thought nobles hated the kings."

"We overthrew the bad ones," I explained, drawing on my schoolroom lessons of a lifetime ago. "There used to be better ones, before, in the really olden days. Those are the poetry ones."

He leaned forward. "Look, I've been wondering about that. People have written books of history, haven't they? We might find a few in the library here."

"I could read to you."

"Yes, I'd like that."

I thought, and then said, "Your mother, she never taught you to read, did she?"

"It didn't seem important, then. You know how it is."

Well, I did know. Learning things was hard, and people were always trying to teach you things you didn't want to know. If I had a daughter, I'd never make her sew or cook if she didn't want to. But she'd have to learn to read and keep accounts. "History books?" I asked. I suspected they'd be dull. But maybe I'd find other books in the Highcombe library, good ones, like travel or adventure. "Could we send for more from the city?"

"I'll tell them, next time someone comes. Do you know how long you'll be staying?"

It was the first time he had asked.

"I don't know. I don't think anyone does. Maybe he has forgotten about me."

"I don't think so. He'll forget you for a few days, ignore you for a month, but he won't forget forever."

I had stopped thinking that the duke might send for me and drag me off to yet another life. I did not want to go.

I smothered the fire, while my master waited under the stars. He wouldn't let me touch him to guide him in, but walked straight over the field, his staff before him to intercept surprises.

In the dark, my teacher saw almost nothing. But he liked the night. He would go out for walks, and return at dawn to sleep. Sometimes I'd wake to hear him practicing, stomps and shuffles and whipcracks of steel, broken rhythms in the night. The first time it happened I crept, frightened, to the top of the stairs with a candle. My master was below, in the dark empty room. He was nearly naked, sweating, spinning and dodging with blade in hand, like someone battling a nightmare. My little flame flung his shadow wild against the wall.

If he heard me he did nothing, just kept on with the attack, high and low, behind and before. I watched him do things I did not know a swordsman could do. I began to see the design, the opponent's moves that his were counter to. I could never give

him a fight like that. Neither, I was sure now, could the swordsmen I'd seen at the duke's party.

I knew when the death came, a blow straight through the
heart. In the pale rays of my candleflame, finally he turned to
look up to where I sat. "I'm sorry," he said. "I wasn't thinking
about you. I'll try to be more quiet when you're asleep."

"Can you see in the dark?"

"Not at all. But night sounds completely different."

He was quiet and I was quiet, listening. There was no bird-
song, only the distant calls of hunting owls, and skitterings of
small things in the brush. I almost felt I could hear the daytime
creatures breathing their slow sleep in the night.

"May I practice with you?"

"I have the advantage."

"I know. But you do anyway. It would be interesting."

He wiped his chest with a towel. "Not tonight, I think.
Another time, without a candle, yes."

And I did that, once the days grew so short there was no light
left after supper; standing so still, in the shadowed dark, waiting
for him to move out of shadow or for one of the shadows to become him. We practiced with sticks. I never felt him move until
he struck. Over and over, until I wanted to cry. My every attack
beat off by one of his.

"Listen," he'd say. "Be still."

I closed my eyes. I stood still until my arms and legs ached.
Then I heard him move.

I cracked him right in the head, and then I had to be sorry
and get a cold cloth to put on it.

"Next time," he grinned, "you'll find the target. Although...
in a street fight you'd be fine."

"No one," I said, "stands like a block of ice in the middle of
the street after dark."

"You'll be surprised, when you get to the city, just what people will do."

"Tell me about the city, then."

The master shrugged. "It's crowded. It smells. There are lots
of things to buy."

I snorted. "I've been there," I said. "I know all that." But I didn't know the city, not really. I'd only passed through in a carriage, and spent my days in the duke's house on the Hill. "Did you like it?" I asked.

"It was interesting." He always said that about things another person would have strong feelings about. I knew there was a long story in him about the city and that he was hiding it from me.

"I expect I will have a house there someday," I said breezily. "Perhaps you will come visit."

"No. I would not like to go there now." But his calm, sure voice was quiet; he sounded as though perhaps he would.

I repented of my relentlessness. "Does your head hurt very much?"

"Not very much. Help me roll out the bedding."

The master staggered as he bent over to pull the pallet out. I had to make him sit down. "Oof!" he said, as I spread his bed on the floor. "It wasn't such a bad knock. It's funny; I was always sure I'd never live to be twenty-five. This all comes as a surprise, this business of after."

I had lit a candle, being unable to find things in the dark as he could. In the rich light he looked pale, fine-drawn, neither young nor old. I wanted to give him a strong dose of poppy and make him tell me things before he fell asleep.

I heated some wine on the hearth instead. Twenty-five seemed terrifically old to me. I couldn't imagine the time it would take to get there, let alone get past it. When I was twenty-five, my whole life would be decided. I'd probably be married, with children; at least, I hoped so. Unless I was killed by a sword, the way he had planned to be.

I put the wine into his hands. He drank it all, but did not ask for more. He wasn't going to tell me anything. I should have known.

chapter IV

I T WAS ONLY A LIGHT FEVER. ARTEMISIA FITZ-LEVI had managed to hide it from her family and was now on her way to the Halliday ball, dressed and decorated and dazzling. In the chill of the winter carriage, it was a positive benefit that she felt so hot. The Hallidays were important, their ball was always one of the best of season, and she was not going to miss it.

When she emerged into the ballroom, her eyes glittering, her face flushed, heads turned to admire her. Young men asked her to dance, asked if they could fetch her a cooling drink. She laughed and flirted with her fan, feeling her head floating high above them all, knowing that she could keep going forever, since if she stopped or sat down for a moment she would collapse. She accepted the dances, accepted the drinks, accepted the compliments and the jealous or inquiring looks of the other nobles' daughters who were also there to attract a husband of worth.

Seeing that she needed no coaching, Artemisia's mother had already gone off to find the card tables, her father to find a convivial crew to drink with and observe the gathered beauties. Her particular friend, Lydia Godwin, was traversing the floor with the scion of the house of Lindley, and seemed to be enchanted by the boy. Artemisia looked around for the next arm to take, the next eye to catch. She was relieved not to see the Mad Duke's nephew, Greg Talbert, anywhere; he had turned out to be a bore after all, despite his ardent admiration and exotic connections. She knew better, now; weeks of experience had taught her that flowery phrases and passionate glances were a minnow a handful. Every man was full of them; it was what came next that mattered. Her eyes darted anxiously. If no one approached her again soon, she would have to make for the haven of Lydia, Lindley or no Lindley; it was beyond impossible for her to stand in the middle of the floor looking as if she had no one to talk to. She bent her head down, carefully adjusted a curl by winding her dark tress around and around her jeweled finger. When she looked up, she was surprised to find her cousin Lucius bearing down on her.

"Cousin!" Lucius Perry kissed her cheek. "My friend Dav has begged for an introduction to the beauty of the evening."

She thought dear Lucius had had more than a little to drink; that accounted for the rose of his cheeks as well as the fulsomeness of his speech. But young Lord Petrus Davenant was a likely-looking man, with a jaunty eye and nice hair.

"Must all your friends beg you for favors, Lucius?" she teased. "You should be more generous!"

"You note," her cousin said to Lord Petrus, "she does not demur at being called a beauty!"

"That is because I know how free men are with their compliments, when they cost them nothing."

"Philosophy." She felt a strange shiver when the back of Davenant's hand swept her wrist as if by accident. She was wearing demi-sleeves, whose lace fell to just halfway down her forearm. The ruffles of his cuff had fallen back, exposing a broad hand tufted with wiry hair. "You did not tell me your cousin was one of those learned ladies, Perry."

"Oh, I assure you, my lord, I never pick up a book except to throw it at my maid!"

Lord Petrus said, "A learned man is merely a bore, a learned woman an abomination."

She tapped his sleeve with her fan. "You must not be cruel to learned ladies, for I fear they are so because they lack the power to charm and to delight."

"Only the fair are free to know nothing, then," observed Lucius Perry, and, bowing, "You will excuse me?"

His place was taken by Lord Terence Monteith, a man who managed to bore without being learned; but he seemed content to stare at her charms while Davenant attempted to delight her with his conversation.

The flashing jewels and fluttering fan, the rippling laughter and high-flung head were attracting other men. Artemisia Fitz-Levi found herself at the heart of a clutch of eligibles, saying anything that came into her head because it all elicited laughter and compliments from well-dressed, well-tended, well-jeweled men.

"The country!" she cried in response to Davenant's friend Galing. "Don't speak to me of the country! It is well enough for those who live to be milked two times a day!"

There was an edge to the laughter that surprised her; she must have said something really clever without realizing.

"I know some who do!" said Davenant.

"Well, don't we all?"

"What does any of us know, compared to the wit and wisdom of this most excellent lady?" a voice said warmly.

The young men's hilarity flattened out, and they turned like flowers in the sun in the direction of the speaker.

It was the older nobleman from the Godwin dinner who had so admired her spirit and told her so. Lord Ferris, the Crescent Chancellor of the Council of Lords, tall, commanding, still dark-haired despite his years, and dressed with elegant simplicity.

All the men were looking at Lord Ferris, but he was looking at her.

Artemisia felt her cheeks burning. She smiled brilliantly at him, tried to think of something to say that was clever and high-hearted, but her invulnerable feeling of a moment ago was suddenly gone. Her giddiness resolved into dizziness, and she reached out one arm. The crowd parted, and Ferris was miraculously at her side, giving her the support she needed.

"A breath of air, perhaps, my lady?"

"Oh, no—no, thank you. If I might just sit down for a moment. . . ."

"Of course." He kept up a stream of easy chatter as he guided her off the floor, past people and through them, keeping her on his right side, where he might see her with his good eye: "These endless parties are exhausting—not any given one, to be sure, for all must be equally delightful, but in the aggregate they are enough to send anyone reeling."

"Oh, but I love parties!" Artemisia rallied.

"Because you are such an ornament to them," he said smoothly, "as the jewel must love its setting, or the, ah, the pearls in your ear must love the place that shows them off to such advantage."

His voice was low and silky in her ear. She wondered if he should be speaking to her so; but he was a great nobleman, and more than old enough to know how things should be conducted properly in society.

She tried to say something pertinent. "What can jewels know of love?"

"Indeed." Lord Ferris seated her in an alcove. "They are love's servants, and not the thing itself. A wise lady, to know the difference." He seized a drink from a passing footman and offered it to her. "So you do not love the country, Lady Artemisia?"

"I had rather live in this city than anywhere else on earth."

"Not everyone agrees with you. But I do. No, I cannot see you buried in the country, raising herbs and children, and waiting for your husband or your eldest son to come home from Council with bolts of cloth and news of how new taxes will affect the estate. . . ."

She shuddered.

"Just so. You must adorn our ballrooms here for many years to come, I think."

Artemisia smiled. "Thank you, my lord."

She wanted to hear more, only her head was pounding so. He must have noticed something. "Will you permit me to fetch your shawl?" he asked, and she answered, "Oh, no, it is so very warm. I promised Lord Terence a dance, but I do not think that I could bear it now."

"You must be protected," the Crescent Chancellor said, "from such as Lord Terence, to be sure. Ah! Here is your mother. Lady Fitz-Levi is your surest bulwark. Madam, your daughter has given so much of her charm and beauty for the delight of the company, I fear she has little strength left to sustain herself."

"Curious," said her mother; "dear Artemisia is so seldom tired or weak. I assure you, my lord, she has never given us a moment's worry."

I N THE CARRIAGE, HER MOTHER HUGGED HER AND THEN shook her. "What do you mean, languishing in front of Lord Ferris like that? Do you want to get a reputation as a vaporish miss? No man wants a sickly wife!"

"No, Mama," she said, too tired and ill to try to explain how well the rest of the evening had gone. Her mother would surely hear of it from the other girls' mothers. "But he said I was a jewel and an ornament, Mama."

"He is a man of very good address," said Lady Fitz-Levi. "He married late, but Ferris has always had a way with women."

"I did not know that he was married, Mama."

"She died, poor thing, and his heir with her. Sickly, both of them. So you see where that gets you, miss!"

But her mama was pleased enough when the flowers began to arrive the next morning: lilies from Petrus Davenant, chrysanthemums from an anonymous admirer, more mums from Terence Monteith, even a bunch of carnations from her cousin Lucius. And from Lord Ferris, a great bunch of white roses.

chapter V

THE COLD ENCLOSED AND ENFOLDED US. DAYS WERE short; when they were fair the sun was sharp and clear, the earth hard and sparkly with frost, and I dressed in layers of clothes and set out across the fields, to race back again before early sunset stained the sky violet. I dredged up old nursery games and riddles to amuse us by the fire, and we burned a wealth of beeswax candles keeping up with our reading. Highcombe was well endowed with history books. Some of them weren't bad. I learned a lot about the habits and practices of my noble ancestors that no one had seen fit to teach me before. There was a lot more to history than dates: you had taxes and alliances and trade and secrets, and the wicked ways of certain kings. My teacher was particularly fascinated with battles. We spent hours and stacks of twigs, pebbles and candle-ends setting up and replaying the Battle of Pommerey. I was more interested in travel, though, and so we also learned about the wonders and marvels of foreign lands.

"It's never cold in Chartil," I suggested, "even in the winter, and all the noblemen are swordsmen, too. Let's go there."

"It would be summer by the time we got there," he said. "I understand, their summers, you can cook an egg on a rooftop."

"Well, how about one of the Cycladian Islands? Here's one, Kyros: 'the climate temperate, and so too its handsome inhabitants, who take their industry and pleasant mien from the humming of the bees that do perpetually labor and sing in the great banks of thyme and olive orchards to make that honey which is renowned throughout the world, as its sands are for whiteness.'"

"Promising. But it sounds a bit like poetry; not reliable. How about the place with the two-headed beasts that uproot trees with their tusks?"

"And red flowers big as cottages? You think that's reliable?"

"There's only one way to find out."

But we didn't really want to go far from the fire.

We practiced, of course. I practiced my footwork up and down the house's long gallery, but my favorite drill was a kind of game where we'd sit at either end of the cottage hearth, using nothing but our arms, working out flashy and subtle wristwork. There was a pile of nuts in the middle. Every touch was one nut to the victor, and every flinch, start or attempt to use the legs was a forfeit of two. I was lucky if I had any by the end of a bout. He could sometimes be tricked into moving too soon; I kept the first one I ever won off of him by feinting.

The tiny staff that kept Highcombe in order for its owner kept us well supplied with food and comforts. But if before I had secretly envied the grandeur of its halls and chambers, wishing we might occupy them ourselves, now I was reluctant to venture into those icy caverns.

As the winter dragged on, night and day alike seemed grey and steely and unwelcoming. I missed the snow we had back home. Around Highcombe it never got deep enough to be much fun.

I couldn't stay indoors all the time, though. And I liked looking at the patterns the bare branches made against the sky, the cracks of ice on the path, the dried grass frozen in the field. Sometimes just before nightfall the sky would clear. There was that one night I caught the most glorious sunset at the top of the rise, and ran all the way back to the cottage against the shadows.

The smoke from our chimney was heavy. When I came indoors, I found him sitting by a fire going so strong that the room was really hot.

The master's face was golden. "Put more logs on," he said; "really pile them high. It's Year's End tonight."

"Is it?" I thought of the famous city Last Night parties I would be missing. The notion of all that glitter and noise made my head ache. Sparks shot up as I dumped the new logs on the blaze. "I should have baked a cake, or something."

"No; I think a fire is just right to celebrate the Sun's return. When I was a boy, we built bonfires and threw all sorts of things on them."

"Oh! They did that down in our village, but we were never allowed to go." I pitched another log on in remembrance. It was so hot, we had to move away from the hearth, and I stripped down to jacket and shirt. "We had a big fire at home, and threw our naughtiness and regrets onto it."

The master smiled into his past. "Yes, bonfires, and people got very drunk and danced; that's probably why you weren't allowed."

I watched and let the flames dance for me. Year's End, and another year begun. In spring, I would dig out some beds. Maybe when the roads cleared, I would ride out to see my mother, and get some seeds from home. We could have little baby carrots in July.

"Listen!"

Carriage wheels rumbled on the drive. I grasped the leg of his chair without meaning to. Oh, please, I thought, oh please don't let it be anyone coming here. Please don't let them find us. The carriage swept on up the drive toward the main house. We both sat very still, listening.

"Maybe it's someone come to pay a Last Night call on the duke," I offered.

"They'd know he's not in residence."

"Maybe—maybe he told them he would be."

The master smiled, slowly, to himself. He knew my uncle. "Maybe he did."

Over the crackle of the fire we heard shouts and whoops of laughter, then doors slamming, and then nothing at all.

"In the main house."

"What if it's thieves?" I gasped.

"I doubt it, making that racket. Still..." He took up his sword. But nothing happened. No more sounds from the house.

"Should we go look?" I said.

He said, "Just wait."

My teacher slipped his jacket off, and sat with his sword in his shirtsleeves before the blazing hearth.

Next to the hearth, the doorlatch clicked. It was someone from the house who had a key. The swordsman's hand tightened on the hilt; then I saw him sit back.

"Hello," said the man in the doorway. "I've brought us some fish." He had a large basket on either arm. "And some very good wine, and cakes, and smoked goose, and candied fruit and anise wafers. I hope you're hungry. I am."

"Hello." The master was smiling at my uncle as though the sun had risen early. "Come in. Sit down. Have something to eat."

My uncle the Mad Duke edged his way in, cumbered with baskets and parcels. He dumped everything onto the table. His eyes were on the master; but he never came near him, as though the man were a fire that burned too hot for him to approach.

I couldn't believe it. Of all the people who had to come here on this night of all nights, why did it have to be him? Why didn't he warn us he was coming? Why didn't he ask me how I was? I'd almost rather it were burglars after all. I busied myself unwrapping things, opening jars and unfolding layers of paper. The duke said nothing 'til I took out my knife to cut a knotted string.

"Here," he said, "I've brought you something."

He reached into his coat, produced a slender bundle. "Happy New Year. A little early."

Oh, no. Should I have been stitching him some slippers or something? I hadn't made anything for anyone, hadn't even thought about them. Well, it was too late now. I unwrapped the duke's present.

It was a dagger in a glorious sheath of chased leather. The

grip was twisted to look like vines, and the blade, when I pulled it, was bright and damascened, chased with a pattern of leaves.

"She likes it," the duke said to my master.

"She does."

"What have you been teaching her, then; useful things?"

"Very. She'll do all right."

The duke and my teacher seemed to know one another so well, they could leave half the words out and still have perfect understanding. I had to pretend not to hear them. Everything they said was for each other. I busied myself with putting the new knife on my belt. They were talking about me, though; that was something. I rather hoped the master would praise my progress at swordplay, but he did not, or not that I could hear.

The duke shook out his long hair, and cast aside scarves and overcoat. "It's hot in here. Good. It was cold on the road."

"A sudden whim?"

"Just so. My friends were bored, and decided they wanted a country party."

"Friends? What friends?"

"Oh, Davenant, Hetley, young Galing... They've taken to following me around. Their lives are so dull. I said I was coming here for Year's End, and they insisted on coming too. I don't know; I think they must have been drunk or something."

"Oh, Alec." The swordsman sounded very amused. "What have you done now?"

"Well, they *would* come. But I seem to have lost them."

"Lost them?"

"Somewhere in the Great Hall. It was so dark in there."

"You left them in the hall. In the dark. My dear, did you forget to tell them that the staff always goes home for the White Days? Or did you just forget?"

"Is that why it was so cold?" My teacher made a noise. "Oh, well, they'll find wood. And somewhere to sleep—God knows there's plenty of rooms in this pile."

He really *was* mad, I thought. But my teacher was laughing.

"Here." The duke had gotten a bottle of wine open. He found the dolphin glasses, and a cup for me. "Don't drink too much; wait 'til it warms up a bit, it tastes better." But already

Tremontaine's wine exhaled the tang of summer raspberries, and the savor of sun on apple wood.

He busied himself with plates and spoons like any footman. "Cherries? No, you don't like them—good, more for me—try the cheese, it's got something odd in it; oh damn, the fish is squashed, but here, have a bite...."

I had forgotten food could taste this good, with layers of flavor and texture. The lovely wine washed it all down with waves of richness, and then there was sweet wine for the wafers and the fruit and the cakes, which were not squashed but retained the shapes of flowers, with sugar leaves and marzipan bees and another wine for them, as well.

"And how is your honey?" I heard the duke ask.

"If you think I can eat any honey after all this—"

"No, no, I was just being polite. About your bees."

"I'll tell them you asked after them, next time I see them."

That thought of the master conveying the duke's compliments to his bees made me giggle, which made me cough, so I drank more wine. I don't always like wine, but this was wonderful stuff, what the duke gave me.

"Let's see, you've got your bees, and what—do you garden now? Or fish?"

"Oh, now, fishing...where's the challenge in that?"

I let out a whoop at the picture: the master would be holding the one sword, and a bright gold fish the other, and they'd bow to each other and then they'd...I thought I would never stop laughing. It would be better to go outside and get a breath of fresh air, but the only door I could find was right next to the fire, and that was no good. The other side of that door was grey and cold, nowhere to travel on such a night.

The hearth was heaped with red and golden coals, now, like a pile of roses. I wondered what it would be like to lie down in it. What kind of creature would I have to be, to lie in the fire and not feel it? I began to see little beings, flickering white hot in the spaces between embers. They winked and danced and sometimes seemed to sing. I watched them for a long time, as the fire grew darker and they slept, or departed for hotter fires.

The men were talking, ignoring me; they didn't see what I saw. Stories that burned themselves into my eyes, that faded away as the fire died and the year ended. I turned to tell them, and found that the room was spinning.

The room was spinning. I lay down on the master's pallet, because I was too dizzy to make it all the way up the stairs. It was very quiet, lying down, and dark. I must have slept; then voices began weaving their way into my dreams, words that were about to have meanings, but then they changed before I could follow them. Voices I knew, but sounding all wrong. I knew where I was, safe at Highcombe, but it didn't make any sense because my uncle the Mad Duke was here.

"What about *her?*" I dreamed them saying it.

"She's asleep."

I opened my eyes to show I was not asleep, but all I could see was red fire; I was still in the heart of the fire.

"Why did you come?"

"Do you wish I hadn't?"

"No, of course not."

"Come to me," my mad uncle purred.

"Like this?"

"No. In the dark." The hiss of silk. The fire went black. "Perfectly in the dark. Come to me now...."

Silence. Long silence, and I was asleep again, only someone was being hurt, I heard them crying out; I struggled, but I could not free myself from the blankets to help them.

Then the crash of a log falling, and a whisper: "I love you."

"Liar! If you did, then you'd come back."

The swordsman's voice was low but clear, the voice I knew from hours of practice: "You know I would if I could."

"You can. You *must!*"

"I can't, Alec. Not like this."

"It wouldn't matter. I could make it not matter—"

"No, you could not. Not even you, my lord."

If I had had a sword, I could have stopped the voices, and the noise; but I had left it outside in the snow, the blade was turning to diamonds.

"You only stay here to feel sorry for yourself."

"Is that so?"

A muffled sound, then, "Don't, you're hurting me."

"I know." The swordsman, cool and detached. "If I kept on, I could kill you."

"But you'd miss me then."

"I miss you now. You aren't happy, you know."

"I would be, if you were there."

"No."

"Your pride, that's all that's holding you, just pride—"

"If you like."

"But I can undo that with my hands alone. . . ."

"Your hands. Your voice. You can, my lord. You do." A hissing of fire. "But only because there is something left of me to be undone. Be sensible, Alec. Just for a moment. What is there for me to do there, now, in the city?"

"What do you do here?"

"Here. Here . . . before you sent me this little diversion . . . I walk. I practice. It's quiet. Trees. Nobody bothers me."

"It's the people, then."

"Why do you stay there yourself? They only make you crazy. I saw what it was doing to you."

"I hate the country."

"Because you can't shock it. Or annoy it. Oh, Alec . . ." he sighed.

"What?"

"I don't know. I love you."

"I do not think so. Do you even think of me, when I am not right here pressed against you?"

"I think of you. I try not to."

"And is that difficult? Or is it easy here, not to think of me?" A hiss of breath, a cry of pain. "Is that what the country is for? So you can forget me? I give you a house to live in and safety, all so you can never think of me? Well, I think of you. I think of you a lot. Almost always, in fact. Do you know what my days are really like, Richard? My days, and my nights. Shall I tell you?"

"Shh, I know. Don't you think I know? I can feel it, feel it all over you. There, and there, and there— They are making you one of them after all. All that excess to no purpose."

"Shut up. You're never there, what do you know?"

"I know you. Be still, Alec, don't..."

"You've done this to me. I wish I could kill you, but I'm already dead. I'm dead, and everyone else is a ghost. I sleep with everyone I can find—I plunge myself into flesh like buckets of cream, and I am always starving. My mouth is open, but nothing gets in. You are the only one that's real. How do you do that, Richard? If you killed me, would I be real, too?"

"If I really killed you, you would be really dead. Please don't start that."

"Ah," said the duke coldly. "*Please*. Yes. Let's have you do some pleading for once. Because I'm tired of it. I'm sick of begging. I am not supposed to beg, certainly not to beg you. Do you know who I am? Sometimes I wonder if you understand how different things are now. I am not a ragged student who needs to be protected from tavern bullies. I am Tremontaine. I hold the power, the lands, the money. I hold Riverside, for one, and more of the city. I hold them, and I would burn them to the ground for you, Richard, I would kill them all and leave nothing—"

"So we could walk in a ruined city?"

"If that's what you want."

"Oh, my dear idiot. Then stay. Just stay here, with me. There's nothing to ruin, here."

"No, there isn't." The duke's voice, thin and flat, mud gone to ice. "Is that it? Have you simply lost your edge?"

A sigh. "Do you think I have?"

"You don't want challenge. How could you take one up, as you are?"

"I don't need that sort of challenge now."

"They would be looking at you there." The voice was honed like cold iron. "Looking at you, and you not know it. That's the challenge you can't take up. It's not their swords that vex you, it's their eyes. Isn't it? Not that they might kill you—you'd probably welcome that. But they might see you first, and know."

"Does it give you pleasure, my lord, to think that?"

"It is, believe me, one of my more comfortable theories. What else is there? That it bores you, our city where we were together? That you don't mind if I drop in from time to time, but really I bore you, too?"

"That is not so."

"Oh, then it's yes, you love me, yes, you want me, but not all that much? Not enough to risk being seen first, unknowing? Yes, you still love me, but in the end I'm not worth it to you. You'd kill for me, but you wouldn't give up an ounce of your pride. I'm not worth that to you, in the end, am I?"

"Hush, Alec, hush."

"Leave me alone. I want brandy."

"That's not what you want. Come here."

"I'm not your lackey. I don't come and go at your command."

"Please, then. Please come to me."

"I hate this." The low voice shook the room with misery. "I can't stand it."

"Come to me. That's better. Yes. You smell of smoke—ash—you've been in a tavern. Your hair—ah!—you washed it at home. Chypre. Something else—citron—barber—fish on your hands, your fingertips—walnuts—bitter—"

And I was dreaming of all those things and more, dreaming them thrown onto a fire that consumed but did not consume them, that fed but was never satisfied. The old sun was devoured by the new, and gave its strength to light a new year, in the course of a long night whose dawn seemed never to come.

My uncle shook me awake. "Get your things. We're going."

He stood a long way above me. I saw him filmed with grey, as though the whole air of the cottage were thick with the ash of last night's bonfire.

I tried to find my feet, but they were tangled in the blankets. I raised myself on my arms. They shook under me.

"She's ill."

"She's just hung over." He pulled my arm. "Come on."

I was standing up. The master put a cup of water in my hands, and lifted them to my mouth. I drank. My throat hurt.

"Alec," he said. "You drugged her."

"I didn't poison her. I just didn't want her bothering us. If she's sick, I'll take her to a doctor back in town. Come on."

I could see where my feet went if I thought about it.

"What about your guests?"

"They'll find their own way home. They can walk into Highcombe village."

The master laughed. "You're leaving them, are you? I wonder if they've made a bonfire of your furniture."

"There's plenty of furniture." The duke gripped my arm. "Come on."

"You're leaving? Now?"

"We're leaving. Come on."

The carriage was cold. The drowsy footmen piled us with rugs. My uncle chewed on his thumb and said nothing. We bumped across the frozen rutted drive. The further we went, the more I shivered. He took out a flask of brandy, placed it against my teeth. I was crying, I think. I drank. I slept.

I woke up coughing. The carriage was swimming with sweet, heavy fumes. But I was warm. My uncle held me in his cloak. I watched the pipe rise to his lips, and felt his breath expand and collapse against me. Again, and again, like a cradle rocking.

His breaths were forming curls around me. "Richard," he said. "Richard."

Part III

RIVERSIDE

chapter I

I LAY IN A CAVE OF DEEPEST BLUE, STAR-SPANGLED with silver crowns. I was explaining to Betty that I must not sleep in Tremontaine's bed; I could sleep on the floor next to the master. But every time I tried to explain something especially important, she'd make me drink a bitter potion. It was annoying, because it made it impossible for me to get up and practice, and at one point I was quite sure that the villainous Mangrove was coming to Highcombe, and if I didn't defeat him he would set it on fire. I was very hot and very cold and my eyes ached. I was very tired, too. Eventually I slept without trying to explain anything.

When I woke up I was thirsty, but my starry cave had become only curtains: silk velvet with silver embroidery, hung around a heavy, old-fashioned bed of dark wood. I pulled back a velvet corner.

Sunlight sifted in through the narrow windows of the room. The walls were paneled with dark wood, hung with old tapestries. I heard a chair scrape; a boy appeared in the gap in the bedcurtains, one finger in a book.

"You stir," he said. "I was told to give you this if you stirred."
He handed me a cool goblet. I drank; it was not bitter.

"I'm Marcus," he said. "I work for the duke."

I remembered him from my first days in the city; a boy about
my age, with brown hair and brown eyes. His voice was deeper
than I remembered.

"You took ill on the road," Marcus said. "But your fever's broken. Now, I expect you'll be bored."

"I'm tired," I said. "How did you get here?"

"Where?"

"Isn't this Highcombe?"

"No. You're back in the city. The oldest part of the city, actually; you're in the Riverside house."

"Oh." I realized that the ride in the smoky carriage had been
real, and the feast at Year's End, too, all those dreams were real—
which meant that my master was gone, and Highcombe was
gone, and even if I could find my way back there, nothing would
be as it had been.

I didn't even have the strength to care if I cried or not.
Marcus kindly dropped the bedcurtains closed so I could do it in
private.

⁓

BEING SURROUNDED BY FLOWERS IN ARTEMISIA'S ROOM
should have been enough for the two girls, but it was only the
prelude to the important task of passing judgment on their senders.
The man who was under discussion now would have been horrified
to hear that his considerable bouquet was being subjected to a very
knowing scrutiny. But then, the girls had been reading aloud to
each other while they sewed—so that their mamas would not say
they did nothing but waste time together—and it had affected their
outlook, not to mention their speech patterns.

"Armand Lindley," Lydia Godwin sighed. "I like him very
much, but in all honesty, he isn't a bit like Fabian."

"That's all right," said her friend; "you aren't a bit like Stella."

Lydia looked crossly at Artemisia Fitz-Levi. No one likes being told that they do not resemble the heroine of their favorite

novel, and while it was true that Lydia was unlikely to become pregnant by a swordsman of dubious reputation, like any young girl she liked to think that she could attract one to commit folly for her sake.

But Artemisia was smiling cheerfully, and offering her more of her favorite biscuits, which both of them knew were bad for their complexions, so Lydia decided not to take offense.

"He does have melting eyes." Lydia returned to her current obsession. "Like Fabian's trusted Tyrian, now I think on it."

"I wonder if he is as steady."

"I begin to doubt it." Lydia tossed her head. Artemisia greatly admired her pearl drops. The earrings were Godwin heirlooms, and perhaps should not have been worn on an afternoon visit, but Lydia was so proud of them that she wore them whenever she could. "Oh, Mi, what shall I do? I was sure, when he sent those flowers the next morning, that he had enjoyed the dance as much as I did! He pressed my hand, as well."

"Many men send flowers; but when they press your hand, what else are you to think? No, he loves you, it's sure."

"But then why did he not call yesterday? I made certain he knew I would be at home! No, no man who sends flowers and then fails to call can be said to be in love."

"What kind of flowers were they?"

"Roses, I told you."

"Roses . . . all roses, or mixed?"

"Roses with carnations. White and red."

"Mixed, that's bad. Though white and red is good. It could mean your complexion, or even heart and soul. Was there a note?"

"Of course." Lydia slipped it from her reticule. "Here, see what you think."

"'To the most adorable of all the Godwins,'" her friend read. "'With the fond admiration of her devoted Armand Lindley.'"

Lydia shrieked and fell back on the sofa cushions. "*Fond! Devoted!* Oh, Artemisia, I shall perish! How dare he so trifle with my heart?"

"What I wonder about is *adorable*," the other girl considered. "*Fond* and *devoted* are well enough, true, but is *adorable* what a lover says? It sounds—forgive me, Lydia—rather *papa*-ish for a lover."

Lydia fished a handkerchief from the reticule as she began to sniffle. "Oh, no. I cannot bear for him to mean it so."

"Of course, it might mean something else entirely, my sweet."

"I do think it must. After all, he is not old enough for a papa. And," she twinkled, "I do not feel at all daughterly when Armand leads me onto the dance floor. In fact, it makes me feel quite like Stella. After the ball."

"'I was a girl before tonight,'" Artemisia quoted with half-closed eyes; "'I am a woman now.'"

"Yes," Lydia breathed. "I fear I must have him or die. But how can I let him know, when he does not come to see me?"

"I expect he is delayed on business, or ill. Only think, there may be a letter waiting for you at home right now."

Lydia jumped up. "Oh, do you think?"

Artemisia patted her hand and pulled her friend to her on the window seat. "Very likely. You must tell me the moment you hear from him!"

"Oh, yes! But—what if Papa does not let me answer him?"

"Why should he not? If you may receive Lindley's flowers and visits..."

"Well, a letter is more serious, you know. Of course I show all mine to Papa and Mama—"

"*All* of them, Lydie?" her friend teased.

"Well..." she admitted, "yes."

"Even the ones that might be, say, hidden in a bunch of flowers?" Artemisia wriggled with pleasure. "Those are the very best."

"My maid is instructed to shake them out before she gives them to me. It is because of Papa's position. Now that he is to assume the post of Raven Chancellor and be back in the Inner Council, we must be very careful again."

"What a good girl you are, to be sure. We should all strive to imitate you. But what possible objection to your suitor can Lord Godwin have? Armand Lindley will most likely inherit the estate and become Lord Horn after his uncle's death. I think it a very good match indeed."

"Of course it is. But I have heard Papa say that all the Horns have evil tempers and goatish dispositions...."

"He cannot mean Lord Armand! He is thinking of someone else. Have you told him how you feel?"

Lydia blushed. "I dare not tell Papa. He has a very poor opinion of all young men. Why, just the other day he said at breakfast to Mama, quite loudly, so I could hear, 'The thought of any of them coming near our Lydia chills my blood. I know what they're made of. Perhaps we'd better'—oh, Mi, it was so awful—'Perhaps we'd better lock her in a tower until she is old and ugly!'"

Artemisia shrieked and hugged her. "He cannot mean it! What did your mama say?"

"She just gave him a look and sighed, 'Oh, Michael,' the way she does. Perhaps they had one of their little talks together; they left the table shortly thereafter, and I did not see them again until past noon, when he was much better-tempered."

"I am sure she will set him right. Your mama is such an angel."

"As are you, dear Artemisia."

⌒

DAYS PASSED. I ATE AND DRANK AND SLEPT. I CRIED A lot, and my head ached and I missed my mother; kind and careful as she was, Betty did not have the cool hands and sweet voice I loved when I was ill. I tried not to think about it, and I tried not to cry when Betty was there. It wasn't her fault, any of it.

As soon as I could stand up by myself, I went to the window to look out. The window was made up of little squares. The glass was thick and greenish; the little square panes had circles in them. The murky view was of snow and the corner of a roof. I didn't think much of Riverside so far.

When Betty saw that I was well enough to get up by myself, she made me try on all my clothes so she could have them altered. I had gotten taller, thinner in some places and thicker in others. There were new clothes for me in the wardrobe, town suits for winter: one bottle-green fustian with gold piping, one a deep blue wool with threads woven into it that made it almost crimson in the light. I supposed the new clothes meant the duke was pleased with me. But I didn't believe they meant I would be going back to Highcombe any time soon. So I didn't much care.

At first I was only well enough to sit up and walk about for a few hours each day. The rest of the time I was amazingly tired, and, as there was nothing to keep me from sleeping, I slept. Betty sat with me and told me servants' gossip about the household: Cook was a dear, but the steward down here, Master Osborne, thought altogether too highly of himself! If she had been drinking before she came in, she never drank while she was with me. As I thought I was doing her good, I tried to keep her by me. I heard all about Riverside, too, and so I found out at last who my master at Highcombe really was.

Of course I should have known. Even I had heard of St Vier, the greatest swordsman of our time, some said of any.

Everyone knew that he had dueled in the streets of Riverside and killed men in taverns and alleys to protect and amuse a mysterious runaway student, who later became the Duke Tremontaine.

"You wanted to watch out," Betty reminisced, "when those two were around. Riverside then wasn't like Riverside now: you had to be clever to live here, or stupid, or brave. We lived by our wits in those days, and took our luck where we could find it."

"Did you know them then?"

"Not know them like you'd *know* them, exactly," she slurred. I waited for her to untangle herself. "But I saw the pair of them, along with everyone else. Hard to miss. *Him* towering like a raggedy scarecrow in that flapping black scholar's gown, and the sword always quiet next to him, sweet as honey, and poison with it. Taverns would quiet when those two came in. Where would the fight be, and how would it start? Sometimes there wasn't a fight at all, and sometimes the night ended in blood. Real blood, not like now. But that was Riverside in those days. You didn't care so much how you died, as long as you did it well."

No one knew where St Vier had gone, not even Betty; some said he'd been killed in a fight—or poisoned, because he couldn't be killed by steel. Some said he'd found another lover, far away, where even the duke couldn't touch him, unless it was that the duke had killed him when he'd learned of it. Betty had also heard that St Vier had been wooed away by the Empress of Cham, to rule at her side in her palace over the sea. But she didn't believe that.

The man at Highcombe had not seemed like a legend to me, not while I was there with him. It was hard to imagine my teacher here, in this house, in the city, doing the things Betty said he had done. But back when it was different? When Riverside was the forest he'd stalked through, and he a young man who thought he would not live to be twenty-five?

At least it explained why I could never even come close to winning a fight with him.

⌢

THE ONE THING BETTY COULD NOT DO WAS READ TO me; like the swordsman, she had never learned how. The duke's Riverside house boasted a large library, but it seemed to be heavily stocked with modern, scholarly works.

"Ask the boy," Betty said. "That Marcus. He goes where he likes, goes back and forth. Does what he likes, too. Yesterday Cook caught him eating cream from the pot, bold as you please. Complained to His Grace, but duke said he's a growing boy, let him alone. You're growing, too, but you don't take liberties. Better brought-up, you are."

I wasn't sure how I felt about being compared, even favorably, to a Riverside servant. But I only said, "He's the duke's man, not mine. Why should he do anything for me?"

"If you didn't still look like something the cat dragged in, my lady, I'd say he'd taken a fancy to you, always hanging around here when he should be off keeping His Grace from jumping off roofs and his other fool nonsense. Not that I'm complaining; working for Tremontaine is being in Seventh Heaven next to... but never mind about that. Just tell that boy what you need; you'll see."

So I asked Marcus to send to the Hill for picture books and lighter matter.

He brought them to me himself: a book of birds, and one of poisonous plants, some poetry, an illustrated geography called *Customs of Many Lands*, and, tucked in amongst them, a surprisingly familiar little worn volume of soft leather.

I did not thank him for it, nor ask him how he had found it, just slipped it directly under my pillow to examine when I was alone.

It was my very own copy of *The Swordsman Whose Name Was Not Death*. I recognized the stain on the third page, where I had dripped apricot juice. I opened the book at random, expecting now to find it silly stuff. But it opened to Stella's escape from the city, right after she's lost the child and thinks Fabian's betrayed her, with Mangrove hot on her heels. No one could find that silly.

Stella wants to despair, but Tyrian won't let her. *You have done tonight,* he says, *what ten thousand men could not. Now show your great enemies what one woman alone can do.*

I am not alone, she says, and is about to make Tyrian very happy indeed when the hunting cats appear on the rooftops.

I did not read the book straight through. I read my favorite parts, and then the bits between them. Fabian still never practiced. Stella still nearly ruined everything by keeping secrets from those she should have trusted. But it didn't seem to matter. If anything, I knew now that people were even stranger and more unpredictable than that, and that when we don't know the truth about someone, we will make it up ourselves.

⌒

A FEW DAYS LATER, MARCUS BROUGHT ME THE SWORD. "From one of the country estates," he said, "for you, along with a big bag of fresh game, which is a good thing, I can tell you: I am getting awfully tired of fish."

It was the basket-hilted sword I had practiced with at Highcombe. One of his, one of my master's swords, mine now. I slipped it on a belt, along with the twisted dagger the duke had given me. The weight settled comfortably on my hips, one balancing the other.

"I'm going out," I told Marcus. He looked me over and nodded.

I was lightheaded in the bright day, and did not go far. Snow crumbled under my feet—I was glad my boots were of the best— and wind cut through from both sides of the river. Everything in Riverside was timber and stone and plaster: old houses with crumbling fronts, some missing windows, some set with coats of arms, their stone worn away like melting butter over the centuries. The houses were clustered up against one another as if they were afraid to let in too much sky, as if to be sure nothing would grow there. Still, there were weeds frozen in the cracks between the cobbles of those streets so narrow no carriage could pass through.

I felt someone following me. I'm not sure how, but I had learned the feel of a stalk now. I looked for the nearest tree, found the corner of a house, stepped behind it and drew the untipped sword.

It was a boy, younger than me—or at least smaller. He had no sword, no coat either. "Pal," he rasped, looking past the blade right at me. "Hey, pal, you got any money?"

I would have given him some if I had any. But I was not carrying a purse. I shook my head. The rake of his eyes up and down, from my thick boots to fur collar and hat, showed what he thought of that.

"Help me out," he whined; "I won't hurt ya."

I shook my head again, helpless, but I started to sheathe my sword. He fumbled in his shirt and pulled out a knife, flat-bladed and worn.

"Give me what you've got."

"No." *For death, you want the heart, the throat, the eye. . . .* I was not going to kill this boy. I would not. This was awful; there was no challenge here, no rules, no purpose but survival. I moved, he yelped, there was blood on the snow. I was fairly sure I'd only touched his hand. But he was gone before I could really see.

"Nice work." It was a woman's voice. She stepped out from the shadows of the house across from me, holding the edges of a tatty green velvet cloak heavily lined. Her red hair was dyed so bright she looked like a holly bush. "You really know how to use your blade. How about a drink for you?"

I felt so tired I couldn't answer. I nodded, followed her. "You new here?" Her voice was a pleasant purr. She moved through the streets with confidence, barely even looking to avoid ruts and puddles. "You a foreigner? Can't you speak? A drink, definitely, and then you can tell me all about yourself."

I realized, suddenly, what she wanted of me, what she thought was going on. I stopped in the grey patch of light between the darker shadows of the houses. "I'm a girl," I said. "I'm the Duke Tremontaine's niece."

"Is that a fact?" She squinted into my face, and shook her head. "He gets crazier every year." The red-haired woman shrugged. "Well, you tell him Ginnie says hello. Ginnie; he'll know who you mean."

I was going to tell him nothing of the kind. So far, I had not seen my uncle, and I was just as glad to keep it that way.

"Well, good-bye," I said, "and thank you for the—for the offer—"

"You should buy *me* one, young Tremontaine."

"When I have money, I will," I said lamely.

"Doesn't he give you any, your rich uncle?" Ginnie snorted. "You make him pay you what you're worth. He can afford it."

⁓

OUTSIDE TREMONTAINE'S RIVERSIDE HOUSE THE SNOW was wet and trampled with horse and cart tracks. It wasn't really one house; it was a twisting series of them, distinguished from the others around it by well-kept facades: the stone pointed, the shutters painted, the slate roofs and the gutters in perfect trim. I had made the mistake, when I left, of not looking behind me to note which door I'd come out of. Now I had to choose one at random, or rather, apply to one, for the doors of the duke's Riverside house were gated and guarded. Luckily, they had orders to admit me.

I passed into a stone hall hung with tapestry, a huge fireplace

and dark stairs carpeted in red. It looked like the right one; I remembered the tapestry. Up the stairs and down a hallway with
windows that seemed a bit narrower than mine. I had decided
that I was in fact lost when I heard voices: lots of people laughing, like a party. I knocked. Getting no answer, I opened the door.

The room was full of naked people.

"Shut the door, it's cold!"

My uncle the Mad Duke strode amongst them in a very beautiful dressing gown. He saw me.

"Ah! You're up. Good."

He had a bottle of brandy in one hand, and began tipping it
down the throat of an upside down man with his knees hooked
around the bedpost. There wasn't a stitch on him; if I had ever
wondered how accurate the classical statues in the gardens of
Tremontaine house were, I certainly knew now.

I started to back out.

"Don't you want a drink?" drawled the duke. "Everyone else
does."

I heard my own voice, quiet and still. "I am not like everyone
else."

The upside down people wriggled and laughed, reaching for
him and for each other. I was terrified that they would soon reach
for me.

"Bravo." He swigged on the bottle, just out of their reach.
"Bravo, Lady Katherine."

There was no one between me and the door. "Oh, by the
way," I told Tremontaine, doubtful of just how much longer he'd
still be standing to hear anything, "Ginnie says hello."

"Does she indeed?" The duke looked hard at me, swaying.
"She always wants what's mine. Miserable cow. You tell Ginnie
Vandall the moment she touches you, her pension's gone; I don't
pay her to meddle in my affairs—"

That was all I heard before my hand closed on the safety of
the doorlatch. I didn't understand, and I didn't want to.

chapter II

I T WOULD HAVE BEEN CHURLISH, WHEN LYDIA GOD-
win received an offer of marriage from Lord Armand Lindley,
for her dear friend Artemisia to be anything but delighted
at her friend's good fortune. With the Godwin and Lindley families' glowing approval, they were quickly betrothed and a wedding date set for the spring. But Lady Artemisia had always
believed she herself would be the first to capture a husband, and
she had to be careful not to think of that while congratulating
Lydia and listening to her endless plans for the future. Of course,
Lydia vowed a hundred times a day that even marriage to the
sweetest man alive would never alter her eternal bond with her
dearest Mi.

So said Lydia as they sat together in Artemisia's window seat,
dark and fair curls bent over the scraps of ribbon she had brought
so that her friend could help her decide what colors she should trim
the table with for her betrothal dinner. But the young lady was sen-
sitive enough to note when her friend began to tire of the details of
her upcoming nuptials, and she leaned back in the window seat
and said encouragingly, "Now come, tell me about your suitors."

Artemisia crunched a biscuit. "What suitors?" If she could not be a blushing betrothed, it would be best to take on the air of someone much wearied with the follies of courtship. "It is all very tedious. I go to dances, I receive flowers, but there is no one who touches my heart."

"But surely there must be *one*—what about Greg Talbert? He is poor, but of ancient lineage and utterly mad for you."

"Oh, him." Artemisia rolled her eyes in what she trusted was a jaded way. "Last week's news, my dear. All talk, no action."

Her friend hissed in delighted horror. "You don't mean that!"

Artemisia lowered her eyelids. She had seen Lady Hetley doing that, and thought it looked very sophisticated. "Do I not?"

"Well, then, what about Lord Ferris? He's certainly been paying you marked attention."

Artemisia shrieked. "As a *lover*? But he is so *old*!" She recollected her sophistication and smiled wryly. "He has polish, I'll give him that. And he's sent the most adorable roses—here, smell."

"Mmm, lovely." Lydia buried her face in the blossoms. "Expensive, too. Well, then—Terence Monteith?"

"Snowdrops." Her friend gestured.

"Even so . . . it's clear he's vastly taken with you."

She yawned. "Oh, he's pretty enough, but a terrible bore. Besides, what are the Monteiths? He is only a second son; what can he offer a wife? He'll be back to the country as soon as he's found one, to manage his brother's estate. I want a city life, and jewels, and gowns. How I envy you your Lindley, dearest!"

Lydia blushed. "Hardly mine. But I would not care were Armand as poor as a goatherd. I think I could live with him anywhere, if I could just feel his strong arm around me, and look into his eyes and know he loves me."

"There." Artemisia sighed. "That is true love. I believe it has made a woman of you already, Lydia, indeed I do. Your eyes—yes, there is a grave beauty in them that was never there before." She took her friend's face in her hands. "How I envy you!"

"Oh, dearest Mi."

Lady Artemisia's maid interrupted these girlish confidences with the news that her father required her immediate presence in the morning room. And so the friends were forced to part, with mutual assurance of future consultations.

~

THE MORNING ROOM CONTAINED BOTH FITZ-LEVI parents. Artemisia made her curtseys, and wondered frantically what she might have done wrong this time. They could not possibly have found out about the parrot. If they had, she'd kill her maid, truly she would.

"Daughter," her papa said, "there's very good news for you." Not the parrot, then. Maybe her dress bill had been lower than she thought, or the shoemaker had lost her receipts. "Anthony Deverin, Lord Ferris, Crescent Chancellor of the Council of Lords, has asked our permission to pay his addresses to you, and if you agree, we'll begin the thing at once."

Artemisia felt the room grow exceedingly hot, and the next thing she knew, she was sitting on the couch, smelling spirits of hartshorne.

"There, Fitz," her mother said, "I knew you'd make a botch of it." Lady Fitz-Levi took her hand. "Listen, child, one of the most important nobles in the city wants to make you the mother of his heirs and mistress of his establishment. There's not a girl in town but will be sick with envy. (Nor a mother, neither, I'll warrant!) You let him pay his court to you, and we'll make certain Lord Ferris makes a very decent settlement and allowance on you: all the dresses you want, shoes, jewels, gloves—and the houses, of course, furnished to your liking. Your dowry is nothing to sneeze at, and we mean you to live properly. You'll be one of the first ladies of the city, right after Lady Godwin, what do you think of that?" Artemisia managed to smile. "Lording it even over your friend Lydia and the rest of that family, how's that, then?"

Artemisia drew in what felt like her first full breath of air. "Yes, Mama. Thank you, Mama."

Her father leaned over the back of the couch. "How about a kiss for your dear papa, then? Pretty chit, I don't know how he could resist you— Of course, he couldn't, could he? Ha ha!"

Her father smelt of whiskey and barber's scent. Lord Ferris, she thought, was possibly even older. But contrary to her father's cozy sloppiness, Ferris was lean and fastidious; elegant, even. He was always dressed to the fashion, and knew exactly what to say.

Her mother picked up a flat box from the sideboard and brandished it in front of her. "He left you a gift, miss, and not only flowers this time."

Artemisia took the box and opened it.

A necklace nestled in the velvet folds: a delicate collar, designed just right for a young girl's daily wear, in the very latest style. But the twisted web was gold, the dangling jewels sapphires.

For the most exquisite woman in the city, the note with it said, *with the heart of Anthony Deverin, Lord Ferris.*

Artemisia breathed in her gilded fate. She wondered what Lydia would say.

chapter III

E VEN WHEN I WAS HEALTHY AGAIN, MY UNCLE'S
manservant still came to see me. Marcus liked to read, it
seemed. He brought me a book of poems and wondered
if we might discuss them.

"It's a new movement," he said. "The scholars are all mad for
it; they think it mixes sentiment with science."

I did try. The new poetry seemed to have a lot to do
with spheres: the motions of the heavens and the motions of
the heart. But I'd never learned much about the motions of the
heavens, except by observation. I thought of the glittering
night skies at Highcombe, the keen air and the silence by the
fire. I looked at the words on the page, and felt too defeated to
keep at it.

Nothing was said about sword lessons, so I practiced on my
own. The hall outside my room was long and no one much
seemed to come there; after a while, Betty got used to checking
before she turned the corner. I began not only to drill, but to con-
struct opponents in my mind and fight my shadow self.
Sometimes their style was like the master's, as he was the best I

knew. I wondered what it would be like to fight Venturus now. Sometimes I played that game, and then I always won.

I went out a lot, wrapped in coat and scarf and hat. Most people made Ginnie's mistake, calling me "sir" because they could see nothing of me but clothes and sword. I did not have cause to draw it again; with the duke's men so thick about the place, Riverside was not what it had been in the master's day. There were guards and footmen and messengers in livery, but not all the duke's people wore the Tremontaine silver and green. On the streets I recognized men I had seen in the house, and knew they were about Tremontaine's business. Just what that business was I only got inklings of from Betty; it was all a lot of names I didn't recognize, and money, and veiled threats, and threats enforced. When I mentioned Ginnie to her, Betty said, "Poor thing. You stay away from that Ginnie Vandall. She knows how to make herself useful, but not to you." I didn't ask her any more; none of it made sense, anyway. It was all my uncle the duke's business, not mine.

⁓

MARCUS BROUGHT ME A GOLD-CHASED CLASP. "What's this?"

"It's for your hair. If you're going to go around with hair like a student, you should at least do what they do, and tie it back."

It was too rich to be a gift from Marcus. "Is it one of *his?*"

"He won't miss it."

"I don't want it."

Marcus grinned. "I thought you might say that." He fished a bit of crumpled black ribbon from his pocket. "Here. Try this."

Without looking in a mirror, I pulled the hair back from my face and tied it.

"Where are you going, anyway, Kate?"

"I don't know. Out."

"You could get lost down here."

"I've been out. I always find my way back. It's not as though everyone doesn't know where this place is."

"True." He went over to the windows, started scraping

patterns in the frost with his fingernail. "Last year, the river froze solid and we skated under the bridge."

"I can skate. We skate on the duck pond, at home."

"That's right, you're from the country. I've only been once. Hated it."

"Why?"

He frowned. "Too noisy."

I had to laugh. "Riverside's not noisy?"

"Well . . ." Marcus scraped spirals around spirals. "But the noise here is—it's only people. You know where you are."

I said, "They never sleep. I hear them at all hours of the night. I woke up, went to my window last night, and there were men staggering by with torches."

Marcus shrugged. "The duke gives parties. It's different, here, from on the Hill. Especially in winter. The rooms here are smaller. Do you want to see?"

"Explore the house? I thought— I thought I was supposed to keep out of his way."

"Did you?" He turned his plain face and brown, open gaze to me. "I don't have any orders."

He did it a little too well. I thought suddenly, Oh, you do too have orders. The duke's personal servant wouldn't be spending free time with me because he wanted to. I wondered, was he supposed to find out if I was mad or vengeful? To keep me distracted? To cheer me up?

"Show me your room," I commanded. "You've been in mine. Now show me yours."

A hundred years ago, when I was a girl at home, I would never have invaded a servant's privacy. But in the Mad Duke's house, who Marcus was and what I was were not so clearly delineated. And if Marcus was spying on me, I wanted some parity.

"If you like." My rudeness did not seem to bother him. But he was used to my uncle's whimsies.

Some of the halls were white and new; others were strings of little old chambers, paneled in worm-eaten wood. As we passed from house to house what was under our feet changed, too: some floors were stone, some wood, some tile. There were steps and doorways to mark the passages, but you had to watch for the sudden shifts. The sounds of the street were muffled here, and there were closed doors everywhere. Once, though, we burst into the light of a gallery which ran the length of a courtyard in which people were drawing water from an old stone well.

I was fairly certain that Marcus was taking me the long way round to his quarters. I couldn't blame him.

In a hall with diamond-paned windows, he stopped at a tall dark door.

"Here."

I had expected a small room under the eaves, or at least at the top of the simplest of stairs, whitewashed and minimally furnished. Marcus's room was larger than mine. The walls were polished oak, hung with contemporary landscapes and a couple of maps. There was a row of books, and a jet-and-ivory shesh set on a table by the window seat. The bed was new, as well, with good woolen hangings and a huge feather quilt, puffed almost to perfect symmetry at the corners.

I couldn't say any of the things I was thinking.

There were thick cushions on the window seat. Marcus plopped himself down on one, utterly comfortable. The richness of the room did not embarrass him, nor my conjectures about his special status with the duke. Which could, of course, be wrong—

"Do you play shesh?" he asked.

"Only a little. I know the moves, but I'm not very good."

"Sit down," he said. "You'll get better if you play more."

I sat. He put a black and a white peon in either fist, and I picked for color and first move, and then we started to play. He watched me carefully, like a swordsman. It made me nervous, but I pretended to ignore it.

A blow on heavy wood made the sheshmen shiver. Through thickness of wall I heard a scream. I'd missed the other door to the room—bad observation, always dangerous, my master reminded me. Marcus just sat there, swinging his foot. He wasn't pretending not to hear, but his only response was a little smile. There was a shout, and yet another crash on the other side of the door.

"I've got the room next to his," he explained.

"Really?"

"In case he needs anything."

It sounded as though someone had just dropped a sheet of glass. I put my hand on my knife, I couldn't help it. "Do you think he might—need anything now?"

Marcus shook his head. "Naw. It's just Raffaela. She gets mad when he lies on the floor and laughs at her. Then she starts throwing things, and then *he* does." I jumped as another one hit. "I wish he wouldn't. He's always sorry afterward. He doesn't really like things to get broken."

You wouldn't guess from the sound of it. "I thought he didn't like women," I ventured.

Marcus righted a shesh piece that had fallen over. "At this point, I'm not sure he can really tell the difference."

"Oh." They were making a lot of noise. "Doesn't he ever *stop?*"

"Not since you came back. He's been taking a lot of stuff, smoke and all, plus drinking. I have the feeling," Marcus said, carefully positioning a piece in the exact middle of its square, "that he did not really have a very nice time at Highcombe."

Now I understood. That was why he was sticking so close to me. Marcus wanted to know what had happened to the duke.

"I don't know," I said truthfully. "I was asleep through most of it. And I got sick."

Marcus nodded. "So did you know he'd brought young Davenant and two friends down with him for Year's End? Brought them, and abandoned them there in the Great Hall. Dark and freezing. No fire, no food, no beds, no light. They had to find their own way back to town." He shrugged. "Of course, they should have known better than to go with him. Probably they did. That seems to be what draws them. Now Davenant's father has sent him a nasty letter, and Galing's lawyer is requesting damages. Which is very stupid; it'll be all over town how the duke made fools of them. People do talk."

Something was beginning to make sense to me. "Is that why he does it?" I asked slowly. "Because no matter how badly he behaves, no matter what he does, he always gets other people to be worse? Or to feel as if they were?"

Marcus looked at me as though I were suddenly more inter-

esting than the sheshmen. "I think so. But something at
Highcombe made *him* feel bad. I didn't think it was Petrus
Davenant."

I thought of the duke's face, lit by a tentative wonder and by
the Year's End fire.

"No. I don't think it was."

"*Marcus!*" It was the duke shouting. "Marcus—show the lady
out!"

"Oh, no." Marcus shook himself. "Not me. Last time I took
hold of that one, she got me. She scratches. I'm calling the
guards; they're dressed for it."

I sat alone in the middle of the sun-drenched room. Pointless
to try to ignore what I could hear clearly enough: the woman
screaming, "*Bastard! Bastard! I hate you!*" and the old wall shud-
dering as something struck it. I stood by the door, wondering how
tiny a crack I could make opening it, but not quite willing to do it
for fear of what I would see. "*I'm not some nobody, you know!
Who's good enough for you, bastard, if I'm not?*"

I closed my eyes, listening in the dark as my master had
taught me. The duke tripped over something, fell hard and
cursed.

I thought suddenly, I'm training to be his guard. Should I
rush in there? Would I be expected to stand watch over these—
proceedings, someday? I snorted. What could I do with his discarded mistresses, skewer them from a standing thrust?

Then Marcus arrived with real guards, and I heard how it
went. Definitely a job for someone else.

At last the next room was quiet, and Marcus sat back down
on the window seat.

"Is she beautiful?" I asked.

"She's a singer. Famous, I think. Anyway, he heard her at a
party, and next thing you know ... !"

"What happened to Alcuin?"

"Who? Oh, him. Gone. Right after you, actually. He was a
piece of work."

Marcus took a pear from a bowl, and handed me another. We
ate in silence, then I said, "Let's go out."

Marcus shook his head. "Can't. He might need me."

I looked around at the luxurious room with its many diversions. "Do you want me to stay?" I tried not to let my reluctance show. "We could finish the game."

But to my boundless relief, he said, "No, better not. There'll be a lot of cleaning up to do."

"Don't the chambermaids . . . ?"

"That's not what I meant. You go on, Kate. Have you tried the pies at Martha's yet?"

I felt myself dismissed, but was not sad to go.

⁓

Lady Artemisia Fitz-Levi, intended bride of Anthony Deverin, Lord Ferris, sat alone in her window seat with papers spread all over her lap, drawing up lists for her betrothal party. Her mother had tried to help her, and she had chased her mother out, certain she could do a better job herself. But it was harder than it looked, these questions of seating and decorating and precedence.

She was relieved when Dorrie told her Lucius Perry was at the door, and she admitted her cousin at once. He leaned over to kiss her cheek. "Congratulations, my lady! You've taken the prize, and no mistake. Everyone is pleased as the devil." He looked at her strained face. "But how are you?"

"Taxed," she said. "Lucius, I used to think all our friends were so agreeable, but here's Petrus Davenant and Albright Galing barely speaking to each other."

"Betrothal has sobered you up, I see." He sank gracefully into the chair by the window. "How sweet of you to be worrying about two unattached young men."

"Well, they used to be attached to each other, everyone knows that. And I wanted to invite them both to my betrothal party, as they're so amusing, but now if one of them is in the room, the other leaves it."

"Oh." Lucius Perry fiddled with his cuff. "That."

"Are you going to tell me, or are you just going to work at that buttonhole until you ruin it?"

"It doesn't matter," he said. "If you invite only one it must be Petrus Davenant, because his father is an associate of Lord Ferris, and if you invite Alb Galing, old Davenant won't come."

"I know that, goose. I just want to know why."

"Because Dav's father is going around telling everyone Alb corrupted his son."

"The hypocrite!"

"Not because they were 'attached,' but because the attachment led Dav to everyone's favorite opponent of all that is good and decent, the Mad Duke Tremontaine."

"Oh."

"Yes, oh. It all came to a head when the Mad Duke dumped them both in the country at Year's End, leaving them to get home by themselves."

"My mother would say it served them right. I should think Dav's father would be pleased."

"My dear Artemisia, try to see the full picture. It's political as well as personal: Lord Davenant and the duke are adversaries in Council, and Petrus Davenant knew it perfectly well when he took up with him." Artemisia gave him what she hoped was a knowing eye, but Lucius Perry was looking out the window. "It's the old story: boy comes to city, boy disobliges family, family hears about it, ructions ensue. Dav was lucky to have someone else to blame."

"Dear me!" Artemisia leaned forward in a rustle of striped taffeta, her papers forgotten. "I imagine Albright Galing doesn't think so. Is this politics? I suppose I am going to have to learn all about it, if I am to run Lord Ferris's household, and throw parties and all. Now...explain to me again just who hates who, and why?"

⟨⟩

A S THE WINTER WENT ON, MARCUS AND I WORKED on our shesh. I was never going to beat him, but at least we could have a good game, now. If letting someone else get ahead is cheating, he cheated: sometimes I'd feel him watching me as I went move after move in the direction I'd planned, and just when I was congratulating myself, he'd swoop down with something that confounded all my strategies. I didn't mind, though. It was only a game. I had a real dueling partner, now: a sober young swordsman named Phillip Drake, who turned out also to have studied with Venturus.

Phillip demanded that I practice even more. He showed me no mercy in our bouts, and was always very happy to point out what I'd done wrong and what I might do to improve on it. When I did well, he only asked for more. As there was little else for me to do with my time, I practiced hard between lessons. I grew less and less tired at the end of our grueling bouts, and Phillip Drake had less and less to criticize. He said I had a long way to go, still, before he'd be happy contemplating me actually dueling a real opponent— "You're not as good as all that yet," he'd say; "but every once in a while, you do something..."

I did not tell him St Vier had been my other teacher, but he usually knew when I was departing from the ways of Venturus. When I broke through his guard, he'd stop, whistle, shake his head and say, "Well, it works, I guess. It isn't stylish, but it works."

⌒

BECAUSE I WAS OFTEN WITH MARCUS I DID SEE MORE of the duke, who required him to be close by where he could find him. And so I saw my uncle drunk and otherwise incapacitated, and I also saw him doing very normal things like going over accounts and dictating letters and approving dinner menus and ordering new curtains. He never spoke to me of Highcombe, or of swordplay, or much else. He tended to treat me like some friend of Marcus's who had dropped in for a visit and might as well make herself useful while she was there. I helped Marcus to run errands, and began to learn my way around the house and around the city. I also took his lead on when to disappear; there were certain moments in Tremontaine's life, and certain visitors to the Riverside house, that no one was invited to witness.

We were sitting in the hallway outside a very splendid room hung in shades of azure and violet silk. That room always gave the impression of dusk, like twilight over a mountainside. We sat out in a sunlit embrasure, waiting for Marcus to be called for, and played knucklebones; Marcus didn't seem to know it was only a game for girls and was quite good at it.

A slightly built man with sleek black hair and fashionable clothes brushed softly past us on his way to the twilit room. Despite his finery, he moved like someone who knew how not to be noticed; he looked like a very stylish otter, swimming through the halls. So I looked hard at him, seeing the nice rings, the soft shoes, the very fine velvet and very wrinkled linen and the hair a little long, clearly tended to stay just that way. Hands that he held very still, even while he waited at the door to be admitted. I looked, and it occurred to me that I had seen him somewhere else, if only I could remember where.

"Who's that?" I whispered to Marcus.

"Who do you think?" When the young man had safely closed the door behind him, Marcus elaborated, "It's one of his fancy-boys. From Glinley's."

"Glinley's what?"

Marcus cleaned dirt from under his fingernail, saying casually, "Glinley's Establishment of Try-and-Guess. . . . Well, why would you know, a nice girl like you? It's the finest brothel in Riverside. That fellow comes here once a week to pay a little visit. They won't be long." I stared at the door. "I like the way he looks harmless, don't you? But my dear, he is riddled with vice. He takes money for engaging in sexual congress with strangers. Are you shocked? Say you are shocked, Katie."

"Shut up, Marcus," I said automatically; but then, because I really did want to hear more, "I *am* shocked, I guess. But not be-cause of that. I don't think he's really a—one of those brothel people. He's a nobleman. I've seen him before."

"Re-eally? Where?"

His drawl made me giggle. "You can't imagine who you sound like."

"What do you mean?"

But I did not have to answer him, because the door opened and the young man stepped out, his linen a little less disheveled. His back to us, his hand on the doorframe, he bowed into the room and said one word: "Tremontaine."

Then I knew where I'd seen him.

I clutched Marcus's sleeve, but said nothing because the man was turning towards us as he closed the door. I lowered my head and busied myself picking up knucklebones so he would not see and recognize me. He had laughed at me at my friend Artemisia's, when I went to her for help. Maybe it was his fault she'd never answered my letter. Maybe he was her brother, or one of her beaux. If so, she had no idea what he truly was.

It was Marcus who spoke up, bold as brass. In the duke's house, he feared nothing. "Do you need help, sir, finding the way out?"

"I know the way," he said mildly.

"Can I summon you a chair?"

The man's voice smiled. "I'll walk, thank you."

He turned down the hall away from us. As soon as he turned a corner, *"What's his name?"* I hissed in my friend's ear.

"I don't know it. Shall we ask the duke?"

"No! I'm going to follow him."

"You're *what?* Why? Katie, whatever is the matter with you? Why are we whispering?"

"I'll tell you later."

I noted which corridor the man turned down, and left the house by another door where I could see him leave and catch his direction. Marcus was right behind me. I gave him a Go *back!* glare, but he just grinned.

Our man crossed the Bridge into the lower city. It was a warm day for winter and the city stank. But dipping and dodging the people and puddles behind the mysterious man sent me back to the stalks with the master, the green green fields and trees, the silver sky, the cool wind's breathing and the musky deer waiting. It was strange to be in both at the same time. We left the docks behind, heading for the newer part of the city. The wider streets, more light, more air, made it harder to stay in the shadows, but there were more people and distractions to hide amongst.

Our young man went quickly. He seemed used to walking, and he knew his route well. He never checked behind him, and he did not stop to look at anything or to shop. Marcus stayed just behind me, only sometimes reaching out a hand to caution when

I started to move forward too fast. It was hard not to be distracted by the shops with their displays and tantalizing smells; here was a part of the city I'd never seen before, and I liked it very much. We seemed to be heading toward the Hill, though; perhaps he was leading us to his noble family's house, and then what? Maybe even back to Artemisia's...? But, no. He turned down a side street full of pretty little houses and gardens.

Marcus and I fell back on the quiet street, and sank into a doorway when our quarry stopped suddenly before a little gate. He had the key. We watched him slide it from inside his jacket, look up and down the street, then turn it in the lock, and slip like an afterthought through the gate and into the house.

We shot down an alley around the back. There was a garden wall, with a fruit tree limb hanging tantalizingly overhead. "Boost me up. I think I can—" But the tree branch wouldn't hold me, and I tumbled ingloriously back to earth, smudged with whitewash from the wall.

"You have to go over the *top*," Marcus said, uncharacteristically dancing with impatience. "Country girl, climbing trees. Anyone can see you've never tried to break into a house before."

"Don't come all Riverside with me," I growled. "You never have either, and I've skinned my palm." He produced a clean handkerchief. "Do you want to try again?"

"Not now," he said. "Maybe at night would be more..."

"Discreet?"

"Just so."

We noted the house, and started back downhill.

"That was fun," said Marcus, brushing whitewash off his knees. "Now are you going to tell me why we did it?"

"Marcus...do you remember that day, my first day on the Hill when you found me all lost and took me back home? I'd gone to see a girl I met at the duke's party, a girl my age who was there on a dare or something. When I went to visit her, *that man* was there, sitting in her day room. He said something nasty about Tremontaine House, I remember now."

"Did he? What a nerve. He's been coming there since last year, at least. And I don't see signs of him finding it especially nasty."

"Perhaps we ought to warn her. If he's a relative, or he's even courting her...don't you think she'd need to know he's doing this?"

"Living in a house near the Hill? It's not an outrage, that."

"First of all, we aren't sure he lives here, he's just got a key. Second, you know that's not what I meant. If I were betrothed to someone who worked at Glinley's, I'd want to know it!"

He said, "Oh, I'm sure it won't come to that. Your uncle's weird, but he's not that weird." I ignored this. "Is your friend betrothed to him?"

"She's *something* to him, or he wouldn't have been with her that day. Maybe he's her brother, I don't know. But I think it's important. You're sure," I demanded, "about Glinley's?"

"Oh, yes."

"But are you sure about what he does there? Maybe he just does—other business."

"There is no other business at Glinley's." Marcus was smug. "I'm sure."

"But why would he work there if he didn't have to?"

"Maybe he does have to. Or maybe he's just bored," Marcus said airily, sounding more like the duke than ever, "and too lazy to relieve it any other way."

"Lazy? You think that's lazy?"

"Of course. Or he would take the trouble to learn something new. As we have. Everyone already knows how to copulate."

We had to be quiet while some people passed us: other servants, carrying baskets and looking harried.

"Well, why would he go all the way down to Riverside to do it?" I persisted.

"Glinley's," Marcus explained importantly, "is a very particular establishment. It is expensive, and caters to specialized tastes."

I did not know what he meant, but I wasn't going to tell him that. "Then I'm surprised the duke doesn't live there," I said tartly.

"He doesn't need to. He's part owner. Our man was bringing him his share of the take."

I drew breath hissing in between my teeth. "That's disgusting." We were passing into the part of the city with all the lovely shops in it. "Marcus," I said suddenly, "do you have any money on you?"

"A little. Why?"

"Could we go in somewhere and eat cakes? And drink chocolate?"

"We could."

"Well, I want to."

He said, "People are going to take you for an actress."

I looked down at my legs, encased in breeches and high boots. "As long as they let actresses drink chocolate, I don't mind."

We found a place called the Blue Parrot where they served us excellent cakes. When we'd eaten and drunk all we could afford, we went to the Ramble by the river and watched children running races with hobbyhorses. Then we were hungry again, and bought gingerbread with some coins I found in the bottom of my jacket pocket. We watched a trained dog jump through hoops, and heard a fiddler playing "Maiden's Fancy," and whistled it all the way home.

The duke met us on the stairs of the Riverside house. He looked sober and displeased. "Do you have any idea what time it is? No, I suppose you were off courting murder and mayhem, and couldn't be bothered to wonder whether any was occurring at home."

"We went out for gingerbread." I offered him the bag. He took a piece and ate it.

"Well, I've been calling all over for you," he said, licking powdered cinnamon off his fingers. "I can't find my—" For the first time, he looked fully at Marcus. "Why is there dirt on your knees?"

Marcus looked down. "I dropped my money. When we were buying the gingerbread. I had to pick it up."

"Oh? And did Lady Katherine drop hers, too?"

My own breeches had a smear of whitewash from the wall we'd climbed, plus mud from where I fell. "I was helping."

"Nice try." The duke was smiling with the pleasure undoing a knotty problem gave him. "But a couple more questions, asked of you independently, and your whole story would unravel. You see—" he crouched down so he wasn't towering over us—"it's not street dirt, for one thing; it's whitewash and garden mud. Your palms are scratched. And this is Robertson gingerbread, with the cinnamon, and that is not sold on the street."

I felt at once very annoyed, and thrilled with the sort of challenge that a good swordfight gave me. "Some boys knocked us down and ran off."

Amused, the duke's eyes glowed green deep behind his crinkled features. "The gingerbread bag was closed at the time? And where did they push you down?"

"On the West Bank," Marcus said, "by the river."

The duke unfolded himself back up to his full height. "It is very annoying, I know," he drawled, "to have to account for all your time to someone older than you are. Very annoying. But I take care to be an annoying person."

"I give you my word," I said earnestly, as I had heard my brothers do when they'd been caught out, "we didn't do anything—"

"Gingerbread," Marcus overrode me coolly. "Katie told you."

Tremontaine's hand flashed out and gripped his shoulder. The sudden movement had sent my hand to my swordhilt; I admired my friend's ability not to flinch. "Marcus," he said, "I had a visitor this afternoon. You offered to fetch him a chair, and then you disappeared."

"He didn't want the chair. If you heard me asking, you heard what he said back."

"Katherine, please take your hand from your sword. It's a bad habit to get into; it makes people think you're about to start a fight."

I saw Marcus press his lips against the sharp grip on his shoulder. But I took my hand from my hilt; I did, indeed, know better than that.

"Do you know this man's name?"

"No," I said, and the duke lessened his grip on Marcus and turned to me.

"Then why did you follow him?"

I looked at Marcus; Marcus looked at me.

"You were seen," the duke said, "leaving the house after him."

I shrugged. "We lost him in the city."

"I'm going to ask you again. Why did you follow him?"

I drew in my breath, opened my mouth to ask him the questions only he could answer—and then I shut it again. He had plenty of his own secrets already. This one was ours. "For a test," I said. "I'm learning to be a swordsman. This is part of it."

"Did Master Drake assign you this test?"

"No." I stared him in the eyes, telling him where I had learned it, and from whom.

The duke looked away. "Well, then," he said. "If you lost him so easily, you'd better practice harder. Just not on my guests, that's all."

We started to turn away, but the duke's voice stopped us, hard and serious. "Understand this, both of you, about people who come to this house. Their business is my business. Their secrets are my secrets. Stalk whom you like, but not my guests. Like just about everyone in the city but you, it seems, that man is not supposed to be here. It would go very ill for him if anyone outside this house learned of his presence here. Do you understand?"

Marcus looked down at the floor. "We're sorry." I nodded in agreement, looking penitent as a good niece should.

"Where's the rest of that gingerbread?" my uncle asked.

We shared it out, and then went down to the kitchen together looking for more cake. The pastry cook was creating little icing flowers to decorate something. The duke appropriated the flowers and bore them and us off to the library, where we saw the sun down playing a complicated gambling game using them as tokens, joined by a couple of resident scholars. Winners got to eat their own sweets; Marcus occasionally was sent down for more plates of flowers to keep the game going. No one wanted any supper—instead, the scholars started quizzing each other on points so obscure that the joking guesses Marcus and I threw out were sometimes right. Candles were lit. The duke scrambled up and down ladders fetching volumes to adjudicate between them.

The night went on, the candles burned down and we sent for

more, and the kitchen started sending up jellies and syllabubs, along with cakes decorated with the little flowers. The duke's homely friend Flavia came in, looking for a book, but she refused to play. She picked a few flowers off the cakes, listened for a bit, and then said, "I didn't know it was possible to get drunk on sugar, but I think you've managed it," and went off grumbling. She may have been right, though. One moment I was screaming with laughter, and the next it was all I could do to keep from falling asleep on the window seat.

"The untroubled dreams of youth," one scholar said, and the duke asked me, "Where did you learn so much about the Battle of Pommerey?" and Marcus said, "Bedtime, Katie."

I felt faintly sick, and altogether happy. Before he shut the library door behind me, I got the chance to whisper to Marcus, "There's something going on! He doesn't want us to know. I'm going to find out—are you with me?"

"I'm with you," he said softly, and shut the door.

chapter IV

ARTEMISIA FITZ-LEVI HAD NOT YET BEEN ALONE
with her betrothed. She did not mind; it made everything they did together seem like a play, performed for
an appreciative audience of ever-changing watchers. She was always well dressed and the sets were beautiful. Lord Ferris also was
well dressed and knew his part to perfection. The Crescent
Chancellor gallantly handed her into her carriage under the eyes
of dinner or ball guests; he courteously escorted her and her
mother to shops, and even to the theater, while other girls looked
on in envy; he monopolized her at balls, and said very nice things
about her where everyone could hear. She appeared at parties
decked out in jewels that he had sent her, and he was always
sure to tell her how well they became her. They were to be married in the spring, before people left town for their country estates. Sometimes Artemisia wished this engagement could go on
forever.

More of her other friends had now been spoken for. They
drank chocolate together, a very worldly-wise group of young
ladies, casting knowing glances at the less fortunate and freely

dispensing advice. Whatever their fortunes, though, Lady Artemisia knew, as did they all, that she had taken the prize. Ferris was rich and he was powerful; he was still fairly handsome, and clearly he adored her to distraction. When she was with him, she felt witty and beautiful, drunk on the same fevered wine she had known the night of the Halliday ball.

Tonight, though, she was conscious of a vague unease. Oh, the room glittered, the people glittered, and the jewels round her neck and on her fingers, all gifts of her betrothed or lent her by her mother against her inheritance. Nothing pleased her, though, not the rare sweets and drinks or the swirling patterns of costumed dancers.... It seemed to her that the envious looks were fewer, that the handsome young men looked only once at her, saw her as taken and did not look again, no matter how rich her jewels or how low-cut her gown. Lord Ferris had arrived late, pressed by business of the Council, and though he apologized handsomely and thenceforth never left her side, she found herself wishing he had never come at all.

She made him fetch and carry for her, changed her mind a dozen times about her shawl, her drinks, whether she would dance or no. It gave her less pleasure than she'd expected, knowing she could command one of the chief nobles of the city, the head of the Council of Lords. It changed nothing, really: they were still the same drinks, the same dances.

Lord Ferris kept his temper admirably. She knew he was doing it, and even that made her cross. For his part, he tried flirting with her, praising her, until finally he realized that only direct address would work. And so he took her aside and said, "My dear. Tell me what's wrong. Has someone insulted you? Or injured you in any way?"

To her own amazement, Artemisia burst into tears.

"Dear me," Ferris sighed. "It's not your mother again, is it?"

She giggled through her tears. Her handkerchief was soaked; not surprising, since it was a tiny piece of paper-thin fabric surrounded by waves of useless lace. Lord Ferris handed her his: a reasonable linen square, lightly scented with something agreeable, some fine, expensive scent twined with something else she could not name. She held it to her nose, praying it was not getting too red. He reached a hand up to hers, as if he would take the kerchief from her, then he touched the tip of her nose, instead. The tip of her nose, and then her ear.

"It's the waiting, isn't it?" he murmured. "It's hard on your nerves. I had thought best to give you time to enjoy your Season and enjoy lording it over the other girls . . . but there is too much of a good thing. Perhaps we might move up the date?"

His breath was warm on her face. The other scent on the handkerchief was Lord Ferris himself. He was so close that she could see the pinpricks of beard that made up the shadow of his cheek.

"What say you, pretty lady? Shall we be married right away?"

"No!" she cried, but it came out a whimper. "No, I cannot—"

"Nerves," he breathed, "that's all. All this fuss . . ."

She drew a deep breath and exclaimed passionately, "I wish I were not getting married at all!"

Her father would have laughed, her mother *tut-tutted*, but her intended did neither of those things. She felt the chill as he backed away. "No? Be careful what you say, my dear. It is certainly within your power to break off the engagement if you choose."

"I—" The wet handkerchief was tight in her hand.

"But if you so choose, you must give good reasons. Neither of us wants to look like a fool."

"I don't—I didn't—"

He smiled at her, the fond lover once again. "Of course you didn't. Nerves. It will all be over soon."

She sniffled into the kerchief. Of course he was right. She didn't know where she was these days, with everything changing so.

"I'll find a maid to help you wash your face."

"Don't let Mama know—"

"Certainly not. This is between the two of us." But secretly he resolved to give her fewer gifts and more attention.

⌒

THE DUKE NEVER CAME TO WATCH ME PRACTICE, and as a rule, Marcus didn't either. He wasn't interested in swordsmen. When he showed up in the middle of one of my lessons, I knew it had to be important. Master Drake and I were running through a complicated sequence of attacks and counters that had defeated me twice already—like the worst kind of patterned country dance, where if you fall out of step you have everyone piled up on top of you—and I hated to stop just when I felt I was getting the flow of it set in my bones. Besides, I wanted my friend to see me carry off something really hard, so I just edged my back closer to Marcus and asked, "What?"

"Our man's back," he muttered. "Headed out the West door."

"Go follow him!"

"Can't. I'm waiting on Tremontaine. Just came to tell you—"

"Can't, now! Dammit, Marcus, you made me miss my stroke!"

My swordmaster laughed. "Avoid distracting onlookers. Very important, Lady K. First rule of dueling. No, no, keep going, don't stop. That's it, come at me in four, from the passe, and...*now!* Good, very good...."

I picked up the rhythm again, and moved across the room after Phillip Drake, my concentration suddenly perfect with Marcus watching. I wasn't even counting under my breath. It was as if I had become the sword and knew just what to do without thinking. I finished triumphantly, my point at Master Drake's chest. Both of us were breathing heavily. I heard Marcus give a low *whew!* of approval. He said, "I didn't know you could do that."

I felt very much like Fabian at that moment. "There's a lot," I said, just for the pleasure of saying it, "you don't know about me."

Master Drake rapped on my blade. "Enough," he said. "Remember the rule: in any given fight, the weaker sword can win through luck or sheer accident. Let's do it once more, to prove it wasn't accident."

It certainly wasn't that, but it took me three more trials before I fell back into the unthinking rhythms of the match. By the time I emerged from practice, dripping and happy, I had forgotten all about the mysterious nobleman, and he was long gone.

A YOUNG GIRL ABOUT TO MAKE A GOOD MARRIAGE is at the center of her world, and may perhaps be forgiven for thinking she is more important than she actually is, or wiser.

Since crossing her often leads to a spasm of pre-bridal nerves, older relatives may choose to indulge her until the wedding. Relatives closer to her own age, however, are less inclined to make allowances. Already Artemisia's brother Robert had thrown a shoe at her. Her cousin Lucius Perry, who had dropped by to find Robert gone, soon wished he hadn't.

"Lucius, where *were* you last night? I particularly wanted you for my little supper party, to sit next to Lydia's cousin Harriett who is just in from the country and knows no one yet."

"How delightful for me." Lucius yawned. "I sent a note; something came up."

"I don't believe you. You're always late these days, or tired, or missing. Are you up to something?"

"If I were," he said, "do you think I'd tell you?"

There was an edge to his voice she wasn't accustomed to. "Now, now." She cocked her head to one side in a charming and feminine fashion. "I think I know what the problem is. You need to settle down, that's all. Find a nice young lady who will care for you and all will be well."

He snorted rudely. "Someone like Lady Lydia's country cousin? You must not think much of her, to want to fob her off on the younger son of a younger son with no money and no prospects."

"My dear," she said gravely, "do you think that is all that marriage is about?"

"And it's not as if the Perrys are depending on me to carry on the name. Both sides of my family breed like rabbits already—a fact surely not lost on your prospective bridegroom."

"Lucius Perry! How can you say such things? Rabbits, indeed. Marriage is a sacred bond of two loving hearts."

He looked hard at her. "Oh, it is, is it? And do you love Lord Ferris?"

"I—well, I don't know yet. I hardly know him, do I? But he admires me to distraction. I admire him, too, of course."

"You hardly know him."

"That will change. I feel sure we will be blissful together. Oh, Lucius, you must not be hard on yourself. I feel certain that the right woman—"

He gritted his teeth. "Artemisia. Come back in a year and lecture me on the joys of the married state. Right now, stop preaching about things you know nothing about."

"And what is that supposed to mean, pray?"

"Nothing, nothing at all."

"No, Lucius, I want to know what you mean."

"Nothing. I'm sure your parents have taken every precaution to ensure that your bridegroom is all he should be. Your dowry's substantial, everyone knows it, and the lawyers will have drawn up an excellent contract. As long as you produce a son for him quickly, Lord Ferris should never give you a moment's unease."

Artemisia gasped in shock. "That is vulgar talk, Lucius Perry," she managed to say. "If you mean to imply that Lord Ferris is—is *buying* me, somehow—"

He shook his head and turned away. "Nothing. I'm not implying anything. I'm sorry, Mia; I—I lost a bet earlier; something I can't afford to lose, and I'm out of sorts, that's all. I'll try to be more enthusiastic."

Lucius Perry never spoke about himself if he could help it. Even a month ago she would have accepted the peace offering for what it was. But he had unnerved her, and she attacked. "You have no right to walk in here and criticize Lord Ferris!" she shrilled. "He is the Crescent Chancellor. Everyone approves of him! He's an important man! Who are you, anyway? A nobody— you said so yourself."

"Right." He stood up. "Fine. I'm nobody, he's everything, and it's nothing to me whether you go into this marriage with your eyes open or squinnied tight shut."

Artemisia lifted her chin. "What are you babbling about, Lucius?"

"You don't know him very well, that's all. Ask him, sometime, about the balls and parties you're not invited to."

She raised her chin even higher. "There are no balls I'm not invited to."

"Yes, there are. Ask him."

"All right, then, I will."

He saw the haughty terror on her face, and thought of another woman he knew who had been this young, once, and faced the same choices with even less to go on. "No, don't," he said gently. "Look, I spoke out of turn, and I'm sorry. I should not have said anything."

"No, you should not."

"But, coz—" He took her hand in his; not the light touch of the ballroom, but tight and earnest. "Artemisia. You do understand, don't you? The difference between a man's world and a woman's world?"

Tears trembled in her eyes. "What do you mean?"

"You know what I mean. There are parts of a man's life—any man's life—that you're expected to ignore. Men have secrets, and it's best to let them keep them."

"Do you have secrets, Lucius?"

"Oh, many," he said. "If you were my wife, it would be particularly important that you knew nothing about them, or pretended, anyway. But we get along, don't we? I'm sure Lord Ferris is no better or worse than any other man you could have chosen. I'm sure he'll make a fine husband."

"I know he will." She dabbed her eye before a tear could fall. "Lucius," she said in a small voice, "you mustn't bet or gamble again if losing makes you so unkind. Promise me you won't."

He kissed her hand, and patted her head, but promised nothing.

chapter V

ONE DAY MY UNCLE SAID TO ME, "SABINA IS planning a Rogues' Ball. I think you should come. It will be instructive."

Wouldn't you know it? My first real city ball, and it was something roguish. Still, "Shall I wear a ballgown?" I asked.

"Not for this."

The last thing on earth I wanted was to make my city debut dressed like a boy. "Can I go masked?"

"You won't need to go masked. No one you know will be there. No one, that is, that you could admit to knowing to the sort of people you would go masked against. It is, after all, a Rogues' Ball." He flicked the invitation's stiff paper between his long fingers, then glanced at it again more closely: "Or, *Rouges'* Ball, as she's put it. If the woman can't spell—and believe me, she can't—she should get someone else to do her writing for her. She's invited half of Riverside, and everyone on the Hill who still finds her amusing. I wouldn't miss it for anything. We have a bet on how long it will take a fight to start. Dress for action, and don't carry a purse with any money: I can

guarantee those will be the first to go, with all the cutpurses in attendance."

I knew who Sabina was by now: a professional mistress. She
seemed to know my uncle well. She sent him chatty letters from
her house in the Old City, which he sometimes read aloud to me
and Marcus.

Sabina claimed always to be bored, bored, bored—bored by
the lovers, bored by the duels, bored by the gold and the silk.
But she kept at it nonetheless; the letters were full of her conquests and extravagances. I confess I was shocked by them:
what she paid for a bracelet would have put a new roof on my
mother's house; what she paid for bed-hangings would have
bought the woman a small farm. It seemed to me that if only
Sabina could be bothered to put some aside, she could retire
very nicely from the conquests and find something that did not
bore her.

Now she was hiring a guildhall to have room for all her invit-
eds, along with the inevitable drop-ins. The duke said to me,
"Come armed."

There was no question in my mind but that I would take my
master's sword. For form's sake I consulted with Phillip Drake,
and to my surprise he was against it. "Old-fashioned," he said.
"Look at the hilt."

"It's perfectly balanced."

"I'm not saying it's not a good sword; nice, flexible steel and
all, but plain, lady, plain." He smiled. "I think we could persuade
the duke to part with some funds to make a good showing at your
first ball."

I shook my head, though I was tempted for a moment.
"There's my New Year's knife for pretty. Although...a new scabbard would be nice. I don't think anyone would notice the hilt," I
wheedled, "if it were tucked in a green leather scabbard worked
with gold and scarlet, do you?"

Phillip Drake said, "I'll tell you what: you break my guard
three times with the new double-pass I taught you, and I'll see to
it you get any scabbard you like."

In any given fight, the weaker sword can prevail
through sheer accident. But not in a drill, not three times in

a row. I did it, though, and got my scabbard. So that was all right.

⌒

THE NEXT TIME THEY MET, AT A CARD PARTY, LORD Ferris was determined to let Lady Artemisia feel her consequence.

"You will be pleased to know," he said, "that half the young men of the town aren't speaking to me, because I have carried off the jewel that might have been in one of their caps."

Knowing her friends were looking, Artemisia could not resist tapping the Chancellor's arm with her fan.

"Really, sir?" she said frostily. "Then how is it that you find yourself invited to so many *fascinating* parties without me?"

He said, "No party is fascinating without you, sweet. And, as you well know, no one would dare to invite me anywhere without my intended."

Artemisia felt herself blushing. At first she was inclined to mind, but then she remembered that to see a blushing woman in a courting couple was expected. She raised her fan to her face to be sure that it was seen.

"I hear," she murmured behind it, "there is a ball to which I have not been invited."

"Really?" the Crescent Chancellor drawled. "Then I expect that I have not been, either."

"Oh, but I think you have, sir. Or what is that letter in your pocket, which you were not eager to let me see?"

And, indeed, the Crescent Chancellor's ringed hand flew to his inner pocket, but only for a moment. "Oh, that. Do you think it is from some woman?" he said loudly. "God love the puss, she's jealous already." He looked around the table for confirmation; the men guffawed, and Artemisia blushed in truth.

But she got it out of him in the end, when they were nearly alone, with her maid a discreet distance away. It was a ball, a ball comprised of rogues, the invitation said, but a ball nonetheless, and was she not an ornament at any ball? Her star shone too brightly for such low company—very well, then, she would cover it with a mask. She'd heard of married ladies who went to such places for a lark, suitably disguised, and were she and my lord not to be married so soon as made no never mind? As for rough company, well, it was soon to be his life's job to protect her, and what better place to test it than at a roguish ball? Ferris laughed at that, and allowed that if he could not protect her, no one could. But this would require more discretion than he feared she was mistress of, to quit the house without even her maid's knowledge. And what would her parents think of him if they found out?

Pooh, she said, her parents thought he'd hung the moon. If he wouldn't take her, she'd find another who would. There's Terence Monteith, quite mad for her, everyone knew he'd been drooping like a willow ever since she'd put on Ferris's engagement jewel ... or her cousin Lucius Perry, he'd do anything for her.

Well, said His Lordship, we can't have you imposing on discarded lovers or worse yet, relatives. I see it is my duty to escort you safely there and back, for one last little girlish adventure.... If she could contrive to be at her own garden gate when the clock struck nine that night, he would be waiting, cloak in hand.

When he left, Artemisia was breathless with excitement. Such a victory, to bend such a man to her will! She would not mind being married to him at all, if this was a taste of things to come.

⁓

ON THE NIGHT OF THE ROGUES' BALL, BETTY LAID out my nicest suit, the blue shot with crimson, and a new shirt with ruffles and a little gold edging, and low boots neatly cuffed. Just because I had no ballgown, I need not go looking like the dog's offal! I was going to the ball, and I was going as the Mad Duke's niece who studied the swordsman's art and wore a swordsman's clothes. What was the point of trying to hide it? Sooner or later it would all come out. It might as well be now. And if I found a mask to wear, he would only tear it off. I did have my new scabbard, though.

Marcus was delighted. He had retired to his room with a book of essays and a bowl of apples, with instructions to me to enjoy myself because he hated these things and not to let the duke do anything really stupid.

I waited in the front hall for some time, trying not to fidget with my sword. Nothing looks stupider than a swordsman who can't keep his hand off his tool, the master had said, and although Phillip Drake had laughed uproariously when I repeated that to him, I planned to stand by it. Finally I gave up and went and knocked on the door of the duke's chamber. Although the sun was nearly setting, the world bathed in its last colors, my uncle's rooms were shadowy and candlelit, the heavy curtains drawn. He still sat before the glass, his long hair falling all about him, sleek and new-brushed. His eyes looked very large, their color bright, gazing into the glass in which he saw me behind him. There was something about him of the enchanted prince, in the pallor of his skin or the brightness of his eyes, the surprising fineness of his hair and the etched bones of his face. He wore only plain black linen, over a very white shirt whose edges reported crisply at neck and wrists.

"Nothing too gaudy," he said to me in the mirror, "for a Rogues' Ball." But his right hand dazzled with rings. His valet combed the hair back from the duke's face and bound it with a velvet ribbon.

My uncle rose, and looked down at my head, and further down to my toes. He nodded; I was all right. "Stay close to me," he said. He wore not even a dagger. The gold rings, I supposed, were his weapon. And the plain black linen was exquisitely tailored; when he turned, I saw all the tiny folds and tucks stitched up and down the front.

He stumbled into a stool, and flung his hand out to the bedpost for support, and steadied himself there. "Stay close to me," he said again. "Things aren't quite where they should be."

"My lord," said his valet, "do you wish a draught of something steadying?"

"No," said the duke; "what for?"

I followed him down the stairs, where he was wrapped in a heavy cloak. At the door, a palanquin was waiting. He got through the curtains and into his seat very slowly, and lay back with his eyes closed. "Is it summer?" he said. "It's very warm."

I didn't answer; he wasn't listening to me anyway. When we were over the old bridge, a carriage attended. It took us slowly along the river. Now I could see all the other people going our way, mostly on foot—Riversiders, all decked out in their tasteless best, like painted poles at a Spring fair. Some impudent rascal rapped at the side of our door, demanding a lift—our footman beat him off, but the duke put a restraining hand on my arm, although I hadn't moved but to look. "Easy," he said. "Not yet."

The guildhall was so brightly lit inside that from the outside its tall windows shone like beaten gold. I was not the duke's only guard; other of our men had ridden outside the carriage, and it took the entire escort to clear a path to the guildhall steps. But they left us at the door. The duke put a hand on my shoulder, balancing. A huge footman in a livery all of ribbons came forward. He looked at my uncle. My uncle looked at him. Clearly something was supposed to be happening but wasn't. I wondered just how awful things would get if the footman tried to throw us out.

"We were invited," I said nervously, but nobody even looked at me.

My uncle spoke, finally, to the footman. "What a getup. You look," he said slowly but clearly, "like a booth at a fair."

"Ah," said the footman. "You've got that right. Shall I announce you, sir?"

"Why bother? Everyone knows who I am."

And so we entered the Rogues' Ball.

I recognized Sabina only because I didn't think our hostess would allow any other woman at her ball to be reclining in a nest of red velvet at the heart of a huge golden shell. Anyone, I suppose, was free to wear pink gauze and a necklace of the biggest pearls I'd ever seen. The shell was on a platform at the center of the room; all the activity swirled around her. The duke was staring hard at it and blinking. She caught sight of us and called "Alec!" and waved a napkin in our direction. As we drew nearer she shrieked, "Black! You wore *black* to my party!"

"Get me a drink," my uncle muttered, but he wouldn't let go of my shoulder.

By now, of course, everyone was staring at us. "Is *this* your new *boyfriend?*" Sabina demanded. We were now at the foot of the shell. It was raised above the throng, supported by carved horses with fishes' tails rising from the waves. It reminded me a lot of a serving platter for a banquet table, and I'm not sure she didn't mean it to.

"No, dear," he replied; "this is one you'd find very hard to steal from me. Unless you *like* unnatural blondes?" he asked me; but, not waiting for an answer, told her, "This one *guards* my body, instead of trying to rob it of my vital fluids."

Sabina threw back her head. She did have a glorious neck. "Brilliant. We all wondered when you were going to think of that. Well, then, I won't worry about your getting snuffed at my party. You're so considerate, you plan for everything."

"Shove over," he told her; "I want to sit down."

The pink gauze shifted in our direction. "No. You'll ruin my effect."

"Shove over, I said; you've got the best view."

"I will not."

She was getting mad, and I wasn't Marcus. But I tried. "My lord duke," I said, "don't you want to go see who's here?"

"Oh, good god," said Sabina. "This isn't a boy at all. It's the baby chick poor Ginnie was telling me about. Send her home, Alec, what's wrong with you?"

"I can fight," I said staunchly, to my surprise.

"Well," she replied, "keep your uncle out of trouble, or you're going to have to."

"I am staying out of trouble." He arranged himself on the steps to the shell. "How's that? And don't say you won't get a huge bang out of having the Duke Tremontaine sitting tamely at your feet. People will talk for days."

"No, no, no!" She smacked him with her fan. "Not only are you ruining the effect, but people always *want* things from you. I am not having my lovely seashell turned into a queuing for petitions for better drains on Tulliver Street."

"I'll stand guard," I said. It seemed like the safest place to be.

"I'm sure you will, angel," she purred, "but I want you to have a good time. Both of you. Alec, dearest darling, do go enjoy yourself and pick up some pretty man, and then you can tell me all about it tomorrow. I'll let you be the very first one to call on me, I promise, and we'll thrash the whole thing out together first thing. Will you do that for me? Please? Oh my goodness, who's this dashing blade?" This last was addressed, not to us, but to a masked young man in very tight breeches and an open collar. He was awfully good-looking, and he was leaning over us to kiss her hand.

"Oh god," my uncle groaned, "dinner is served. Get me out of here."

I took his cold hand, and led him into the throng.

⁓

Lady Artemisia Fitz-Levi was afraid that her mask was slipping. Nervously she tugged at the ribbons that held it in back. If only she hadn't had to sneak out without her maid's help; Dorrie would have been able to pin it more tightly into her hair. Unlike every other party she'd ever been to, here there was no room to retire to with ladies' maids standing by to mend tears and turn up stray locks of hair. She was on her own.

"Don't worry," her escort breathed in her ear, "they'll all think you are my ladybird, isn't that the point? Put your head up, dearest, and laugh. Look like you're having a good time, or they'll know you're not."

"But I'm afraid it will come loose—"

"My dear." Her intended ran his finger carefully along the place where the bottom of the mask ended and her cheek began. She felt a chill at the base of her spine: excitement, or fear, or that thing the older girls talked about? "If I see any sign of it coming loose, I will be the first to help you hide your face. Do you think I want the world to know my wife was at this affair? No, my little madcap puss," and his arm was around her back now, holding her to him, his hand cradling her hip through the heavy layers of her skirt, "this will just be our little secret, our first adventure together. Isn't that what you wanted?" and she had to say, "Yes, of course it is."

The room was aswirl with people. It was like being in a pool of water, in a river that moved against her. Someone knocked into her and Artemisia gasped reflexively, "Oh! Excuse me!"

But her escort squeezed her waist and chuckled, "That's no

way to go about it. Not here, not with these types. The next time that happens, you jab out with your elbow and say, 'Watch it, jackass!'"

She giggled nervously. "I can't!"

"Yes you can...try it." Without warning, he swung her around so she ran into a short man whose hands were full of pie. "Watch it, sister!" the man sputtered through a mouthful of pie, and she said, "Watch it, yourself," and though she spoiled the effect by giggling, he told her she had done well.

A BAND STRUCK UP IN ONE CORNER OF THE ROOM. It was the kind of music you could hear in any Riverside tavern, fiddles and ratchety pipes and drums, and everyone loved it. The Riversiders and University students knew the tunes and the steps that went with them and threw themselves into the dance, right at home. The nobles, some dressed in rags and some in ball regalia, but all easily distinguished by their cleanliness, started casting about for likely looking girls to dance with. I was glad my clothes ensured that no one could take me for one. I passed behind, the dark duke's bright shadow, as he drifted looking for amusement.

His eye was caught by a group of men dressed in brightly fluttering tatters. They had braided ribbons into their hair, twined them through the careful rents in their shirts and sleeves and breeches. Some had tied in little bells; you couldn't hear them above the noise, but they looked nice.

"What ho!" one of them cried, roguishly, I guess, to the crowd. "We are the Companions of the King! Come join us in our devilish revelry!" They seemed to be trying to arrange people into a pyramid against the wall behind them. A red-haired man had a food-stained tablecloth laid out on the floor and was drawing on it with a burnt stick.

The duke moved towards them as if their colors were flame on a cold night. One spotted us and shouted, "Oh, joy! It's darkest Night—"

"Or Nightmare," said the redhead, "allied with Temptation.

Just what we need to complete the tableau. Do join us, please, and we'll make you immortal."

"I am already immortal," the duke said, a little thickly. "Have you discovered a new method?"

"Art, sir, art is the medium! As it ever was. Art renders immortality through the medium of allegory. Twin art with morality, and there is nothing to offend anyone, yet something for all tastes."

We looked up at the artists' tableau. It was a complicated twist of people arranged reaching for fruit, for wine, or for each other. "It doesn't look very moral to me," my uncle said.

"Exactly."

"What my friend means, severe and beautiful one, is that in the interest of revealing virtue, we mask it in vice."

"Didn't Placid say that?" asked the other.

"No, I said it," snapped the red-haired artist. "It is a grand concept. A masked ball of virtue, the obverse of roguery, disguised as the very thing it seeks to cast down."

The duke actually smiled. "Very apt." He gestured to the pyramid. "And this represents . . . ?"

"Man's heedless quest for Pleasure, of appetites temporal and carnal. See how in their striving each man treads upon the other? And how the Pleasures reach out mindlessly to tempt us?"

I certainly did. One of the Pleasures, a man all tucked up behind another one, untwisted his arm, encased in peacock blue silk, to wave it languidly at the duke. I had seen his sleek head before, and this time I knew where.

It was Artemisia's friend, and the Mad Duke's as well. I was dying to say something clever to my uncle about that particular beauty being one of the pleasures he'd already enjoyed—but if I hoped to find out more about the mysterious young man who visited nice young girls on the Hill and also worked at Glinley's, I would have to be chary. I would discover his name tonight; that would be my quest, and if I was very lucky, my uncle would not know of it.

"So in the interest of illuminating virtue," the artist was saying, "it is possible, indeed necessary, to show vice in all its manifestations. It will be a tremendous crowd-pleaser."

"Right," said the duke. "Well then, get out your sketchbooks and get started, because I want to be at the top, and I probably won't last long."

As he handed me his empty glass, I recalled my duty. "Oh, no. I really don't think you should—"

"You are my swordsman, not my governess," the duke said sternly. "If someone attacks me with anything sharp and pointed, you kill them. Otherwise, leave me alone."

There was no use arguing with him. If he broke his leg, someone could probably set it.

The duke set one finely shod foot on the thigh of a crouching earth spirit and began his ascent. I'd climbed some trees in my time, and clearly so had he. But the trees didn't usually shudder and giggle underfoot. The red-haired artist wasn't really helping, rushing in and patting people who were falling out of pose back into place. He nearly got kicked in the teeth by a ticklish Temperance. A couple of the others began sketching madly. It looked like roiling clouds of form all over their paper, not like people at all, but I saw they were drawing a sort of map of the scene. I'd never seen anything like it, and I was so fascinated that I missed the downfall of the allegory. I heard my uncle shout, "*You!* You—" and then the voices became indecipherable, and it was all a mess of arms and legs and skirts and hair and ribbons and shrieks and laughter.

The duke crawled out from underneath the heaving throng. He pointed into it. "Kill him," he said. "He bit me."

"I don't think I—"

"My lord, I beg your pardon." A bright head with rosy cheeks emerged from the sprawl. "I mistook you for a most delicious fruit."

"An easy mistake for anyone to make," the duke said smoothly. "Do I know you?"

I knew him. It was the horrible Alcuin.

⌢

ARTEMISIA HAD A STITCH IN HER SIDE. SHE REACHED across the dancers for Lord Ferris, but his hand seemed to slip away from hers as if pulled by the awful music, the straining strings. A stranger with garlic breath had his arm around her waist, and she was close to tears. The dance was not one she knew. There were no steps, it was just leaping back and forth in time to the music, with your partner swinging you this way and that and handing you off to someone else at a signal, but she did not know what it was. All sorts of men had had their hands all over her, and it was too much, really too much, but every time Lord Ferris came in view he smiled brightly at her and said, "Enjoying yourself, sweetheart?" It was all that kept her from tearing herself out of the crowds and running for home.... The garlic went away and she smelt a familiar scent, looked up and re-alized it was Lord Ferris with his arms around her, and she leaned into his chest and whimpered up at him, "I'm thirsty."

"Poor kitten," he said. "Of course you are. What a treat you were there, a jewel ornamenting the arms of some of the roughest men in town." He was holding her as close as some of them had, closer than he had ever held her before. But at least they were off the dance floor, headed for a quiet corner away from the worst of the brawl. "What shall I feed you now, my sweet pet, wine? Or maybe beer, in the spirit of the evening."

"Water," she said, "or a fruit coolant."

But he went on as if she had not spoken, "I'm not sure she's serving wine tonight; they'd guzzle it like rough ale, these types, and there would be chaos. But don't worry; I've brought this." He drew a flask from his jacket, and raised it to his lips. When he lowered it, a little moisture clung to them. "Taste?" he whispered.

"What?" Artemisia was baffled.

He leaned his face down to hers, so that his wet lips were nearly touching hers. "Put out your tongue," he said, "and taste."

No one knew where she was. No one here would care what he asked her to do. They were in a corner where no one could see them. Closing her eyes, she slowly put out her tongue and tasted burning brandy and the skin of his lips.

"Ah!" His sudden hot breath shot right into her lungs; she gasped and tried to pull back, but his arms were tight around her.

"Ah," he said again, and his mouth was all over her, her lips, her chin, her ears, her neck, her chest where the gown was cut as low as she had dared.

"My wicked girl," he said, "how I adore you." Artemisia knew she should be pleased, but she was frightened. His hands were everywhere, too, rumpling her skirts, pushing at her bodice, pinning back her hands while he kissed her.

"Please," she breathed, "I—"

"Oh, do you?" he growled. "Do you? Of course you do, of course you do, so do I—"

"No!"

She said it, she heard herself say it, but he did not seem to. He did not seem to hear anything except his own hot breath, which was terribly loud in her ear while he did things to her skirts until there was nothing at all between him and her, really nothing whatsoever, and although she wailed in distress it only seemed to make him hotter and he forced her up against the wall and rammed himself into her over and over and she had to stop thinking because there was nothing else to do until he let out a revolting noise and draped himself over her all sweaty and said, "Couldn't wait, could you?"

She was shivering as if her whole body would shake to pieces.

"My dearest love," he said, and pulled a lock of hair back from her cheek, "are you cold?"

"Please," she said, "I want to go home."

"Come home with me," he murmured. "We've the whole night ahead of us."

He wrapped his arms tight round her, and she tasted sick in the back of her throat. She swallowed hard and tried to match his tone, but her voice came out all squeaky. "How can you say that? How can you say that to me?"

"But why not, sweetheart?" Lord Ferris murmured in her hair.

"How dare you suggest that I—that I—"

"That you are the sort of young lady who would go off un-chaperoned with a man to a strange place with no protection? That you'd allow him liberties with you there?" Something caught in her throat and she made a kind of barking noise. "Now, now," he said, "don't cry. Can't you see I love you all the better for it, you wanton little sweet sweet slut?"

She was sobbing so hard she could scarcely breathe, and she heard herself making awful retching noises. She reached out blindly for someone, for something, but only his hands were there to catch hers, and "Oh, come on," he said; "it's not that bad. Stop howling like a kitchen maid. Maybe I was a little quick for your first time, but can you blame me? Overcome as I was by the rapture of your beauty—I've been overcome for weeks, now, and you damn well know it, you hot little piece. You lead me on, and then expect me to control myself? There, there, stop crying; I promise I'll be good and slow and patient when we're married. You'll like it fine, you'll see."

"Married?" she gasped. "Married? To *you?*"

As she spoke the words, she realized what it meant. Married to Lord Ferris. There would be all the gowns and the jewels, the wedding ceremony and the guests and the banquet, and then she would go home with him to his house, and she would belong to him forever and he could do this to her whenever he liked, without asking. That was what it meant.

"Well, yes, married to me," he said reasonably, and chuckled. "Were you thinking of doing this, and then marrying someone else? That's not how it works, you sweet little slut, and you know it."

Artemisia tried to catch her breath—once, twice, and she found the air she needed to say, "Never. I will never marry you."

"Oh, yes, you will," he said comfortably. "Think of it this way: at least we know now we'll suit between the sheets. Not bad, that. Now pull yourself together; you're a bit of a mess. I'll find you something nice to drink, and when I come back we'll have a little dance, shall we?" She shook her head in protest. "Don't worry," he said, "I won't make you dance with any of those buffoons. I admit I enjoyed seeing them holding you there—but you're mine now, and I won't let you out of my hands ever again."

⌒

M Y UNCLE LOOKED ALCUIN UP AND DOWN. "OH. You. I thought I got rid of you ages ago. What were you doing lurking in allegories biting me?"

"Old habits die hard?" suggested the beautiful Alcuin.

"It is a habit," the duke said, "that I would endeavor to cor-rect if I were you."

"Oh, really?" Alcuin lowered his eyelids and looked up through long lashes. "And are you going to help correct me?"

As if entranced, the duke slowly moved one hand toward the handsome man's face—but at the last moment, Alcuin turned his face away. "Leave me alone," he said sharply. "You had your chance."

I didn't like this. Other people were getting interested. I looked around for the sleek man from Glinley's, but he had slipped away from the crowd. The artists may not have known who my uncle was, but various Riversiders did, and I heard the whispering behind us: *Tremontaine* . . .

My uncle looked his former lover in the eye. "You shoe-scraping," he said. "You worthless piece of trash."

Alcuin's face turned pale, and then dark. "Not so worthless," he said. "I've got something you don't have. Something I happen to know you want."

He raised his chin and made a little moue with his rosy lips. A well-built dark-haired man came to his side, a sword slung low at his hips.

"Is someone," the swordsman said to his friend, "offering you trouble?"

The duke's face stiffened with distaste. Ignoring the swords-man, he said to Alcuin, "You can't challenge me, you monkey's turd. Only a noble can do that, and you're not exactly noble; the Court of Honor would never hear your case. A civil court would sentence you to death, even if you won."

"No one would dream of challenging you, sir." Alcuin did not budge. "But my swordsman has every right to challenge your . . . your *thing*."

My hand was on my sword. I heard the duke say, "It appears, Lady Katherine, that my old sweetheart here would like some of our blood."

I didn't care. I was more than ready for him.

And I did not like being called a *thing*.

Alcuin's swordsman was much bigger than I was, and much

stronger, too. He looked me up and down. "Do you really think this is even worth it?"

"Just do it," Alcuin told him through gritted teeth.

"But—no offense, dear—but it's a *girl*, right?" Like Alcuin, he wasn't very bright.

"I don't care if it's a spotted baboon! She's got a sword, and she offends me. So if you want to get any tonight, or ever again for that matter, you'll draw your steel right now and teach her some respect!"

"She is a noble," the duke drawled, "and you are not. The privilege of the sword extends only to—"

"I accept the challenge," I said quickly. "On my own behalf, sword to sword, I accept."

"Well, then," my uncle said.

I looked around at the considerable crowd. "Where do we—"

"Fall back." The duke and some others started clearing people back to form a circle. I had the sudden fierce wish that Marcus could be there, not to help me, but to see me doing it for real at last.

"Five on the girl." The betting had begun. "Twenty on Rippington." So that was his name. What a stupid name. Rippington.

Rippington and I faced each other across the circle. "Oh, lord," he said, and sighed. As the challenger, he had the right to begin the match, but as the challenged, I could call the terms.

"First blood," I said. My hand was closed around the pommel of the master's sword. I was glad I had not let Phillip Drake talk me out of bringing it tonight. I thought, Well, at least *you've* done this before. I breathed deep, felt the balance in my feet. Balance is everything.

"Ready?" he asked formally.

I nodded. He drew, and I drew, and we stood at guard. Then Rippington advanced and tapped my blade gently. I didn't move. Don't waste your moves, and don't show your strengths until you have to. Make them wait, and make them guess, and make them show you theirs.

Rippington fought like a training lesson. He pulled back and executed a perfect lunge, hoping to get it over with quickly, I guess, but I saw it coming a mile away and stepped gently aside to let him pass, which he did, nearly falling on his face.

"Dammit!" he said, and I heard, "Twenty on the girl."

I turned around and attacked him in a high line to see if he'd go for it, and of course he did, opening his entire front for just long enough for me to have killed him if I had wanted to. He parried this time, and I replied a bit show-offishly with a fancy riposte, just to see if he'd follow the move. God, he was slow! I realized later he must have been drinking to be so slow and precise; he fenced as if he was doing lessons, as if he was always trying to be sure his feet were in exactly the right position. Wine is enemy to sword. But at the time, I thought that he was making fun of me, refusing to take me seriously, so I got a little flashy and began speeding things up.

Mistake. Drunk or not, his sword was still perfectly long and deathly sharp, and when we closed at close quarters I realized that he could wrench the blade from my hand simply by applying enough force. Spooked, I backed off, nearly crashing into the ring of onlookers. There were jeers; I tried not to hear them, but I knew what they meant. I looked like a fool, and I felt like one. This was not a lesson. Rippington's blade was not tipped, and he would not pull back if he came too close. When he lunged, I felt the steel sweep past my face, and knew it *was* steel. He hadn't been making an effort because he thought I wasn't worth it. Now he wasn't so nice. Now he was working harder, testing me, trying to draw me out. I kept my moves small, trying to give little away, but it was hard not to bring out my fiercest defensive moves. Save them, a voice inside me said. Save them for when you need them. Watch him and see what he does.

I watched, and I responded. The crowd was quieter now. This was the way it was supposed to be, a conversation between equals, an argument of steel. I wasn't going to die. The worst that I could do was lose the bout, but I wasn't going to lose if I could help it. Because at last I found the move that my opponent loved best: a nice, flashy double-riposte. I found it, and I found that I could make him do it every time. High parry, low parry, wherever I came in didn't matter, I could count on him coming back with that double-riposte. Like making a cat jump to a piece of string. It probably worked better with a taller opponent; with me he didn't have to reach quite so far as he was used to. He kept doing it out of habit, and because he looked good in the pose, but the difference between us made it just a little off-balance for him. That's the problem with having one favorite move. I enticed him into it one more time, and then I came in right where I was supposed to, in a clean line straight to the—

Straight to the heart, it would have been, and I don't know whether he could have defended himself in time, but at the last minute I realized what I was doing, and turned my wrist just a fraction so that instead the point slashed messily across his arm, tearing his shirt and the skin under it.

"Blood!" The cry went up. I fell back, gasping; I hadn't realized I was working so hard. "First blood to—what's your name, dearie?"

"Uh, Katherine," I said. "Katherine Talbert."

My uncle was gazing delightedly at me. "This," he began, "is my—"

"Shut up!" I told him. "Just shut up, don't say it, all right? Just for once."

So then he was laughing so hard the red-haired artist had to hold him up. I had a feeling the red-haired artist who loved allegory was in for an interesting night.

"Alec!" Sabina had arrived; I guess it took her a long time to get down from the seashell. "Alec, *when* did I tell you there would be *fighting* at my party?"

I looked for Rippington. Alcuin was binding up his wounds surrounded by a coterie of friends. They shot me some truly dirty looks. It had never occurred to me that not everyone loved you after you'd won a fight. It wasn't in the books. Even Richard St Vier hadn't mentioned it.

Not that people weren't all around me saying some very nice things, trying to get my attention. But I had no stomach for answering questions just then. I was thirsty, and I just wanted to be alone for a bit.

"Here, you." Someone put a cup in my hands. It was the woman I'd met my first day out in Riverside, the colorful Ginnie

Vandall. I drank. Water had never tasted so good. She put her arm around my waist, and I let her lead me out of the crowd. But she wanted something from me, too. "Where is he?" she murmured low and urgent in my ear. "I know those moves. Where is he?"

I broke away from her, and ran.

I ran to the furthest corner I could find, but it was already occupied, by a dark-haired woman in a truly beautiful lavender gown, a color I cannot wear. Her back was to me, but then she turned around and I recognized Artemisia Fitz-Levi, of all people.

"Oh!" she said brightly. "It's you! Are you here, too? Are you having a good time?"

It was perfectly obvious that she'd been crying her eyes out. And her hair was a mess.

"What happened?" I asked because clearly something had, and it was not good, whatever it was.

"Oh, nothing. I'm just fine. How are you?"

Her hands were shaking. I took them in mine. They were icy cold. I said, "I'm fine. I just almost killed someone. I'm here as the duke's bodyguard, but I think you need one more."

She looked at me with terror. "Is my hair really awful?"

"A rat's nest."

Her face melted and crumpled, and she started to cry. She put her hands up over her face, as if she could hide it, and she shook her head when I tried to touch her, but I did for her what I sometimes did for my mother, and just put my arms around her until she naturally laid her head on my shoulder and clung to me, and she sobbed there for a good long while. When she got a little quieter, I disengaged enough to dig out my handkerchief and offer it to her.

"Look," I said, "can you tell me what happened? Maybe I can do something."

"You can't do anything," she sniffled. "No one can. It's all my fault and there's nothing I can do, but I'll never marry him, never!"

"Marry who?"

"Lord F-Ferris. My intended. I made him bring me here, and then he—he—"

I stepped back a pace. "A nobleman brought you here? To this? What is he, an idiot?"

"He's the Crescent Chancellor, you dolt!" Well, she was up-set. "I'm supposed to marry him, but I can't, now. I can't marry anyone, never, ever. I'm ruined!" she wailed.

"Ruined how?"

She hiccupped and looked me in the eye. "Ruined. Exactly like in the books. That kind of ruined."

"And your Lord Ferris stood by and let someone—"

"No. He did it himself." I seized her sticky hand, and she gripped mine, hard. "He says I'll learn to enjoy it. But I won't. I won't. I won't marry him. I'll never let him touch me again."

I said, "Certainly not. Look, you'd better go home."

"Will you take me?" she asked piteously.

"I—I'll have to ask my uncle."

"No! You mustn't tell anyone! Above all, not him!"

"I won't tell him, I'll just…" Just what? Then I thought of something. "Look," I said, "do you remember that day I came to see you? And you were visiting with that pretty young man?"

"Pretty enough, I suppose," she sniffed. "That's my cousin Lucius. Lucius Perry."

"Your cousin! Perfect. Because he's here, Artemisia, I saw him not long ago. I'm going to go find him, and he will take you home."

She clutched my sleeve. "Oh, no! Don't leave me! Lord Ferris might come back at any moment."

"Then you must hide. Hurry, the time is short." We found her a niche outside the main hall and she huddled into it, pale in the moonlight and the shadows from the hall.

"Be strong," I said to her; "be brave, Artemisia. I'll find this Lucius, and all may yet be well."

Her eyes got a little wide, and then I watched her face change subtly. Some of the pain went out of it, to be replaced by a soft determination. "All will be well," she said, and I knew she was thinking of the same chapter I was, "with you at my side."

I turned back to the ballroom then, which was good because I was blushing. Although I'd thought about it a lot on my own, no one had ever compared me to Fabian before.

The place was a madhouse, with people dancing and kissing and who knows what. I was never going to find her cousin Lucius without some kind of a plan. *Lucius Perry, Lucius Perry* . . . He was a nobleman, and a Perry at that. Even I had heard of the Perrys, a large and prosperous family. No wonder the duke didn't want us to know who his visitor really was. The duke was encouraging Artemisia's cousin Lucius in a life of vice, and taking his share out of the profits, too. Maybe the duke was blackmailing young Perry. Did Tremontaine blackmail people, or did he draw the line at that? He had some strange notions about honor, did my uncle the Mad Duke.

"Out of my way, boy!" A big man in red brocade bumped into me, and I jumped about a foot. Was this Artemisia's betrothed, that evil man? I didn't know what the Crescent Chancellor looked like, but I wanted to be sure he didn't find her again tonight. Now I really wished Marcus were here. But he wasn't. That might be for the best, though. I would definitely tell him about Lucius Perry; Perry was ours. But what had happened to Artemisia Fitz-Levi, that was something I must keep to myself.

If you were a nobleman leading a double life who had decided to attend a Rogues' Ball where half the people knew you as one sort of person, and the other as another, where would you be? Masked, I thought, if you had any sense. But had he? He had been in the allegory bare-faced. My master said that there were swordsmen who courted the dangerous opponent and the sudden move. He must be like that, her cousin Lucius.

"I'm writing a song." The voice was so close I thought it was directed at me, but the speakers were off to one side, above my head. "'The Maid with the Blade.' It will sell like mad on the street."

"Dirty or clean?"

"Oh, romantic, I think. With lots of verses; maybe I'll even run to two sides. . . ."

It was about me, and it wasn't, but I couldn't worry about that now. I moved slowly onwards, looking.

Lucius Perry was masked, so it's a good thing I recognized his smooth dark hair, that and his sleeve, which was of an unusual cut in that glorious peacock blue. When you've mended as many clothes as I have, you sort of memorize fabrics without realizing it. He stood off to one side, leaning against the wall with a drink in his hand, watching everyone.

"Come quickly!" I said, without wasting time. "Artemisia is here, and she needs you!"

He lifted the soft velvet mask off his eyes. "Who—oh, you're the— Wait a minute. What's happened?"

I grabbed his wrist. "Just come!"

I had thought she would fall into his arms weeping, but when she saw her cousin, Artemisia simply held out her trembling hands. "Lucius," she whispered, "take me home."

"I will." But first he took off his mask, and tied it securely over her face. "Come," he said; "come with me, and don't speak a word."

He put an arm around her waist, and she leaned on him, very shaky. "Don't worry," I said encouragingly, and tried to think of something better to say. "Tonight's deed will not go unpunished."

She turned and smiled at me, and then she and Lucius Perry disappeared into the crowd.

Pinking Alcuin's bullyblade Rippington had been nothing, just swordplay and acrobatics. But at least now I knew that I could win a fight against a full-grown man. What Lord Ferris had done to my friend was unspeakable, disgusting. When she told her family, they would probably kill him. But if they didn't, I would.

chapter VI

I WOKE UP WITH KITTENS ALL OVER MY FACE. I RAISED
a hand to brush them off, but they turned out not to have
any legs or tails. My uncle the mad duke was sweeping
swathes of velvet over me, cheerfully urging, "Get up, get up—
have some tea and tell me which one you like best."

I pulled the blankets up around my neck. The swathes were
attached to several large bolts of fabric, which a nervous shop assistant was holding while the duke tried them against my face. I
looked around for Marcus, but he, thank god, was not there to
see; only Betty stood by, patiently holding a cup of tea. I seized it
from her and drank, and said, "My sword!" I had put it away dirty
last night. Blick, blick, blick, as Venturus would say. I'd be ages
getting the rust out.

"Never mind that," my uncle said. "Just tell me which one
you like best."

"I like them all," I said, playing for time while I tried to wake
up. There was a fire in the hearth, and the sun coming through
the thick old windows was mid-afternoonish. I remembered coming home in the thin light of dawn, my uncle a dead weight in

the sedan chair beside me. He'd had his fill of the red-haired artist and a number of other stimulants, besides. There'd been no moving him without two hefty footmen. I'd tumbled into bed without a thought for anything other than how soft it was.

"Well, you're not having them all, just one."

"One what? You shouldn't be here," I groused. "I'm not even dressed."

"Don't be prudish. You can defend yourself perfectly well. You proved that last night. I am very, very pleased. Also relieved. I'm making you a present: a lovely velvet cloak. Made to your measure, with room to grow. Now, which do you like best?"

I clutched at the nearest velvet, and to my shame I started to cry. It was unbelievable. I had almost killed a man last night, and now I was going to have the cloak of my dreams. And my friend Artemisia had been forced in a crowded ballroom, in her beautiful lavender gown.

~

I T'S NOT TO BE BORNE." LADY FITZ-LEVI PUT HER HANDS on her breast. "Really, Fitz, it is intolerable."

"Agreed." Her husband shifted his chair closer to the fire, and picked a spot of egg off his vest.

"Something must be done."

"Indeed."

"I can hardly bear it."

"Terrible." Her husband shook his head in annoyance. "What on earth was she thinking of, running off like that? A young lady betrothed, and to such a place. It's a wonder she wasn't set upon by rogues of the vilest kind." His lady nodded. "Of course, Ferris had no business taking her there. A grown man like that, helping her in a schoolgirl prank. I thought he had more sense."

"It was she, my dear, who lacked sense. I'm sure she just twisted Ferris round her little finger, as she always does. She got in over her head, and now she's sorry and wants to call off the wedding. Well, I'm not having it. She'll take the consequences of her folly and make us proud in the end, and that is that."

"I saw those flowers he sent this morning; man's besotted."

"He surely must be. She's a lucky girl and doesn't even know it. Refusing her food like that. I've tried all morning, but I cannot talk sense into her."

"Well, girls have their humors. We cannot *force* her to eat."

"Do you think so?" Nervously his wife twisted her lace fichu in her ringed fingers. "They always forced *me* to eat. Boiled carrots. I hated them."

"I think she's a bit old for boiled carrots," said her husband. "But you're welcome to try."

"She's a bit old to be carrying on like a baby! Maybe boiled carrots is what she deserves."

"Why don't you make her something she particularly likes? A nice cake, or something."

"She refused her toast and chocolate; am I to treat her like an invalid? No, indeed. She must know that I am very displeased. All she will say is that she wants you to challenge Lord Ferris."

Lord Fitz-Levi snorted. "Why would I want to do that? Ruin the wedding and ruin her name at the same time? And ruin our highest ally in the Council of Lords? I'm counting on him to help Robbie to a good post this year. What a lot of fuss over nothing."

"That's what I told her. Do you know, I think we should move the wedding up? They'll have to work harder on the gown, but it will be worth it. Oh, she'll make a lovely bride!"

⌒

THE DUKE TREMONTAINE PERSONALLY SIGNED THE order for his niece's new garment, all three yards of it, silk lining and tassels and all. He signed it with a flourish, and picked up his next piece of business, ignoring the opening of the study door, since he knew perfectly well who it was.

"Are you happy now?" the Ugly Girl said. "Your niece is the talk of the town."

"How would you know?" the duke asked, amused. "You don't get out much."

She held up a cheap sheet of paper, as cheaply printed. It was a rude cartoon of a tall, thin, unhappy-looking man and a bosomy girl with a sword pointed upwards; the words underneath were: *"Oh, no! My Tool is useless, I must find a Girl to do the Work for me!"*

He took the page from her, and held it up to a candle. "Don't let her see it. And if she does, don't explain it to her."

"What about you? Don't you mind?"

The duke singed the edges of the page so that they were evenly crisped all round. "About this one more than any of the others? Why should I? I'm a popular figure. They like doing my nose." He turned it around again; the lowest letters, which named the printer and engraver, blackened away. "Alcuin's not the first of my discards to try something like this: nasty drawings, imprecations on my manhood. Horrible, isn't it?" he said cheerfully. "Do you think I should have him killed, or what?"

"You've already subjected your pretty friend to a fate worse than death, haven't you?" she said peevishly. "Let's leave it at that. What I want to know is, are you through with the girl, or just beginning?"

"I didn't know you were so fond of her," the duke said.

"I'm not. It's a theoretical question. I'm interested in the way your mind works—or doesn't work, depending."

"Do you mean: she's done her trick, now I should find some nice nobleman and marry her off? In that case, no, I'm not done with her. Besides, she's company for Marcus. He needs more friends his own age."

⁓

T HE FIRST LETTER REACHED ME THE NEXT MORNING. It was addressed to the Lady Katherine at Tremontaine House, and had clearly passed through several hands, not all of them clean. The sealing wax was scented, and the loopy handwriting was in violet ink. But there were spots on the paper where tears had made the ink run, and the letters sloped downward across the page.

Dearest Friend, it read. *I am beset. I am without hope. My parents Know All, but my woe means nothing to them. They*

*are monsters and tyrants. They want me to marry him, still. I
will die, first. You understand. You are the only one who does. I
will never forget your kindness to me. Do not try to visit me. I
am a prisoner here. But if you can contrive to send a line or two
of simple hope to me in my wretched misery, it will speak more
than volumes of insincere verse from less noble souls
than yours. I hope this letter finds you well. I will bribe the
underhousemaid with my last year's silk stockings to bring it to
you from your own—*

Stella

I stuffed it in my pocket when Marcus came in. Of course he
noticed.

"From your mother?" he said.

"No. You know that's not allowed."

"I don't care." He studied his nails. "I'm your friend. I'll help
you, if you like."

"I don't need help, thanks."

My friend took a step backwards. "I guess not. After that
swordfight, and all. The duke's pleased, anyway. Do whatever you
want; you could fill your room with apes and parrots, and he'd
only ask if you wanted to feed them oranges."

"I don't want parrots," I said. He did not look happy. "Do you
want to play shesh?" I asked, partly to make him feel better, and
partly to distract him from the letter.

"Not really."

"Well, then...do you want to hear about my swordfight?"

"Dying to tell me, are you?"

"Well, who else am I going to tell?" I was dying to tell someone, after all. It was my first real fight, and I had won! I almost
wished that Venturus were still around, so I could tell him.
Marcus lacked expertise and enthusiasm, but at least he would
listen. I decided to ignore his mood and continued ruefully,
"Betty will only start going on about how I should have seen St
Vier in his heyday or something; besides, I want to get it all clear
in my head before I have to run through it for Phillip Drake so he
can tell me everything I did wrong."

Marcus wasn't interested in the subtleties of my swordplay, but he was very enthusiastic about the results. He'd disliked Alcuin more than most, and utterly approved of his public humiliation at the Rogues' Ball. "You've got a real future, Katie," he concluded approvingly, "in hitting irritating people where it hurts. No wonder the duke is pleased with you."

He didn't ask again about my letter, but then, it wasn't the only one I got. Sabina actually wrote to thank me for providing such wonderful entertainment at her party, and did I want to do it again for a private event? Two people offered me jobs as a guard, and a theatre asked if I would be interested in entertaining crowds between shows. The duke's private secretary, Arthur Ghent, offered to open all my letters and take care of the crazy ones for me. But I didn't want him to see what was coming to me, because I was expecting another one soon from Artemisia.

I had written her back saying:

Stella—
To live is to hope, and while we breathe, we hope and live.
(That was from the book.) *Though I serve another, I am yours to command.* (So was that; it was a line of Tyrian's, but I liked him sometimes better than Fabian. He had sense.) *Be brave, be strong, and know that you are ever in the thoughts of your faithful—*

KT

Getting it delivered to the Hill without any of my friends on the duke's staff knowing about it would be tricky. In the end, I went out on the streets of Riverside and picked the hungriest kid I could find.

"Watch it, pal," he said, and I said, "You!" because it was the one who had tried to rob me that first day in the snow. He had nerve, even if he didn't have much sense. His name was Kevin, and I gave him two coppers to carry my letter to Artemisia's maid, with the promise of five more if he came back with a ribbon to prove it had gotten there.

It was a lavender ribbon. I tied it around my wrist under my shirt, as a token not to forget.

A FTER A FEW DAYS, ARTEMISIA'S PARENTS WERE AT their wits' end.

"I am at wits' end, Fitz," his lady said to him for the third time that hour. "She's showing no sense whatsoever."

"Seems simple enough," her husband repeated. "Easy for her, really. She's already agreed once to this marriage. She just has to do it again. Simple."

"It's not as if we forced her into it, is it? We let her choose for herself, and she chose Lord F."

"Certainly she did." Lord Fitz-Levi examined his neckcloth in the mirror. It had held up remarkably well under the morning's stresses. "All this fuss over a little cuddle in the dark."

"They were, after all, betrothed."

He gave a final tug to put it in place. "She'll settle down once she's married, god love her."

But their daughter seemed to have suffered a sea change. She spoke wildly, most unlike herself. She had no wish to go out, she said, lest she encounter *him*. She refused even the most tempting food, and would not try on her wedding dress, although it was magnificent. There was talk of a physician, or a trip to the country, and they put it about that she was down with the grippe. No one but her maid noticed the purple inkstain on her middle finger.

Gentle Friend,

Do not believe anything they say of me. Not even if you hear the wedding is going forward. If it does, it is without my consent. They say I am to blame. I do not understand how that could be. Men are supposed to protect women. And when they do insult them, their fathers and brothers are supposed to rush to their defense, not call them horrible names and laugh at their distress.

How I envy you. Your uncle may be mad, but at least he lets you fight back.

The anguished,

Stella

I replied to her at once:

Lady Stella,
I am not so gentle a friend that I am not filled with righteous wrath on your account. By no means hearken to the voices of those who say it was your fault, because it wasn't. Any more than it is my fault that I have to learn the sword and wear funny clothes. They are bigger than we are, and older and have more money and can make us do things we don't want to. Remember when we met at my uncle's ball? I thought you were so brave and elegant and daring, and you were, too. I wished I could be like you.
I have a new cloak now. It is moss green figured velvet with gold tassels and a silk lining called moth's wing. I wish you could see it.
Your family is wrong, that's all. Don't get married to him, whatever you do.

I looked at our two letters, sitting side by side. *He lets you fight back.* What would I do in her place? Well, that was the wrong question, because I would never be in her place. Thanks to the duke, no one like Lord Ferris was ever going to want to marry me. Did that mean my uncle was protecting me? If someone violated me, would he have them killed without question? I bet he would. But did that mean he cared, or just that he was crazy and bloody-minded? How could Artemisia's parents love her and not believe her now?

Oh, it was hopeless. I wasn't Artemisia, and she wasn't me.

I liked the way Artemisia saw me as a heroic swordsman. Was St Vier heroic? He was, in his way, as much a legend as *The Swordsman Whose Name Was Not Death*. What would he say about Artemisia? He'd probably say she shouldn't have been there in the first place without knowing how to defend herself, and he was probably right. But what did he know about it? He'd always been able to defend himself. He'd probably never been to a ball in his life, and if he had, he didn't know what it was like to hope you were pretty, and that people would like your dress and ask you to dance.... What did he know? What did any of them know?

Of course her father and brother were hopeless. They didn't know, either.

I did.

I picked up my pen again.

The insult is not to be borne, I wrote. *If neither father nor brother will rise to your defense, then the lot must fall to one who, however unworthy of the position, is eager to stand as your champion. Not only for your own sake, but for that of all ladies misprised. What, after all, am I doing here, anyway? To what end my skills, if not for this? I wear your ribbon, and will avenge your wrong. And woe to he who stands in my way!*

Your loving friend and staunch defender,

KT

But don't worry, I added in postscript. *I'm not telling anyone.*

I sealed it with candlewax and went looking for Kevin to deliver it. He was eager for the work. "So am I, like, your new guard or something?" he asked. "I'd make a good guard."

"You are my private messenger," I said. "It's very confidential."

"Huh?"

"Secret. Go and return within the hour, and I will have another task for you. Now, make it snappy!"

Then I went and found Arthur Ghent and asked the secretary a lot of intelligent questions about the Council of Lords and its officers: the Crescent Chancellor, the Raven and the Dragon, and all the rest. He was pleased that I was taking such an interest in government. "Would you like to visit the Council Hall someday?" he asked. "His Grace's attendance is, ah, spotty, but I usually know when he's going to take his seat. You could accompany him, and watch it all in action."

"Thanks," I said.

But I wasn't going to wait that long. It was a bright, clear day. I dressed warmly, and strapped on my good sword and dagger, and waited for Kevin to come and take me to where the Council of Lords met across the river.

I had never crossed to the East Bank before. It was in the oldest part of the city, the part built by the old kings and queens that had ruled before the Council of Lords deposed them. Kevin didn't know anything about that; his sense of the place was based entirely on where he had or had not gotten into food or into trouble. The docks and warehouses were especially fertile grounds for these reminiscences, but as we came up upon the Old Fort and finally to Justice Place, he ran out of narrative.

He wasn't stupid, he just didn't know about anything. I decided to instruct him, since it distracted me from being nervous and might do him some good. "These are very historic buildings," I told him. "The Council Hall was once the Hall of the Kings— see those heads carved all along it? They're carvings of the old kings."

"I hate kings. We always kill the king on Harvest Night— throw him in the fire, and he burns up like this—blam!! If I saw a king, I'd kill him dead. What are you doing here, anyway? You gonna kill someone?"

"Stick around and find out. But make yourself scarce for now, so nobody sees you. I'll pay you when we get back to Riverside."

Kevin faded back into the buildings' shadows, and I was alone watching the great doors of the Council Hall remain resolutely closed. My fingers were cold. I bought some hot chestnuts from one of the vendors that scattered the plaza, and that helped some, although they turned dusty in my dry mouth. At last a bell rang, as I knew it must. Servants and secretaries started coming out the door, and then carriages began pulling up along one side of the plaza, to carry their masters home.

And there he was on the steps. It wasn't hard to recognize Lord Ferris from the secretary's description. There might be more than one tall, handsome middle-aged man with black hair streaked with silver, but there was only one with an eyepatch. Arthur Ghent had neglected to mention that his mouth was cruel. At least, I thought so. He was talking to another noble, waiting for the carriages to come round. I took a deep breath, and walked boldly up to them.

"Lord Ferris?" I asked, and he nodded. "Um, Anthony Deverin, Lord Ferris, Crescent Chancellor of the Council of Lords of this city and this land, I challenge you."

He looked down his long nose at me. "Whatever for?"

"I'm not sure you want your friend to hear."

The other man blinked and laughed. "Good lord! It's that chit of Tremontaine's! My valet told me about it. Were you at that famous ball, too, Ferris?"

"Ask your valet," Ferris retorted.

"What can you have done to offend Tremontaine this time?"

"What can one do not to offend him?" Ferris drawled. His friend laughed, but the Crescent's look on me was fierce for a moment. "Come, young lady," he said with smooth civility, "let us discuss this matter out of the cold." I followed him back up the shallow steps of the Council Hall. At his nod, the guards drew aside. Lord Ferris led me into a small room, wood-paneled like the Riverside house, with a small fire just dying in the hearth. "Now then," he said, "what is this nonsense?"

"It's not nonsense. I challenge you."

"My dear." Lord Ferris unpeeled his gloves from his hands and held them to the fire. "Please tell your uncle that this descends well below the annoying to the merely pathetic. If Tremontaine has a quarrel with me, let him say so himself, and not send a girl to do his business for him."

"It's not his quarrel. It's on behalf of someone else." Ferris tilted his head inquiringly. I did not like looking at him, knowing what he'd done. I found it hard to speak the crime out loud or say her name. "A friend of mine. You forced her. Against her will."

"You know nothing about it." But he didn't sound so smooth now.

"I know that honor has been violated. I know you did it, and that it has gone unpunished. On behalf of Artemisia Fitz-Levi, I demand satisfaction. I challenge you to combat in the place and time of your choosing, with what champion you will, until honor is washed clean with blood."

Ferris laughed, and I hated him. "The girl is not without family. She has a father. She has a brother. If honor has been violated, as you so quaintly put it, it is their business, indeed their duty, to call challenge on me."

"But it isn't their honor, sir. It's hers."

He went on as if I hadn't spoken, "And have they come after me with swordsmen? They have not. Indeed, I hope to be married soon. So you just run along."

I was so angry I wanted to cry. I swallowed my tears. "It's hers. Her honor, not theirs."

"You don't seem to understand," Lord Ferris said. "It is not the duke's business to interfere in this. Whatever strange notions he holds about women—and if your situation is an example of them, I hope you will not take it as an insult when I say that they are very strange indeed—" He lifted a hand against my interruption. "Stop just a moment and think. You're an intelligent girl. I mean you no harm. Why should I? Your uncle, the Duke Tremontaine, is a dreamer and a lunatic. His treatment of you should tell you that, if nothing else. My dear, I know you're in a difficult situation. A poor relation, he's got you where he wants you, and no fault of yours...." I let the insults go by. A good swordsman doesn't pay attention to words in a fight. Lord Ferris turned his head to look me full in the face with his one good eye. "But I am here to tell you that if you persist in this, you'll only make fools of the lot of us."

"The challenge stands," I told him. "Artemisia's the only one who can call it off now, and I bet she won't. You could, I suppose, try going down on your knees and begging her forgiveness. I'm not sure it would work, but you could try. Otherwise, name the time and the place, and look to your honor and your sword."

He said, "How quaintly old-fashioned. No, my dear, it is you who will withdraw the challenge. There will be no time and no place, and we will not speak of this again." He did not wait for my answer, simply pulled on his gloves and opened the door to the little room, saying with the practiced heartiness of someone who is always telling people what to do, "Now, you are going to walk out of this building and back to Riverside and tell your uncle what I said. And there will be no more of this nonsense."

The sun was very bright. I walked stiffly across the expanse of Justice Place, not looking behind me. It was my guide who caught up to me.

"You didn't kill him," he accused. "I was sure you were gonna kill him."

I said, "I wish I had."

⸻

Lord Ferris strolled without haste to where a knot of noblemen awaited carriages to take them home to a hot dinner. "Trouble, Tony?" Philibert Davenant asked. "I heard there was something like a challenge."

"Something like." Ferris smiled. "Only a joke, that's all. Just more madness from poor Tremontaine."

His friends nodded. In recent years few of them had not been touched by some slight or folly of the duke's.

"Someone should do something," grumbled old Karleigh, and Ferris said, "Perhaps someone should."

⸻

I took Kevin down to the kitchens with me to see whether anyone would feed him or give him a real job. If he ever learned to shut up, I thought he'd make a good guard or footman or something.

"Bread and cheese," the undercook told me, "that's all you're getting at this hour, with a host of starving scholars coming tonight that always expect the best, with hardly any warning, and woe betide us if they don't get it, too! He's more particular about his scholars than about his ladies and gentlemen."

At the other end of the long kitchen table, behind a stack of cabbages, beets and half-plucked fowl, someone made a choking noise. It was Marcus, coughing on a crumb from a large meat pie, or possibly his bowl of soup. I grabbed his soup bowl and offered it to Kevin.

"Hey!" Marcus protested.

"You don't need it."

"I do need it. I'm growing. I need my strength. Arthur Ghent says so, and he's got five brothers, he should know."

He was growing, it was true. "Marcus," I asked, "what about you? Do you have any brothers?"

"All thinking men are my brothers," Marcus said loftily.

Kevin lowered the soup bowl from his face for a moment. "I ain't your brother, pal."

"You can say that again." Marcus examined him. "Where'd you pick this one up?"

"Same place as you," Kevin cheeked him, and called him a name.

Marcus shoved back his bench. He rose towering above the scrawny Kevin. "Give me my soup back."

"Make me."

It looked as if he would, too. I could not believe it. "We are not starting a brawl in this kitchen!" I hissed at them both.

Marcus shrugged and drew back. "Have you checked your pockets, Katie? I would if I were you."

Kevin put down his soup and raised his hands. "I never did! You think I'm stupid or what? Not with the duke's own, never, I swear."

"Oh, honestly!" I huffed. "He was helping me, Marcus, to keep me from getting lost, that's all." I didn't like lying to him, even indirectly. But I wasn't ready to tell anyone about the challenge to Lord Ferris, not even Marcus. It was Artemisia's secret.

"I'm sure he was. But what do you think he does for a living, when he's not helping you cross the street?"

I stared hard at my friend. He reminded me of a farm dog when someone's on his territory. "I can guess," I said. "But it's none of my business."

"You think he's only a pickpocket? Not likely. Guess again."

"It's none of my business," I repeated doggedly. "And it's not very polite to talk about him in front of him like that, as if he weren't really there."

"Yeah," Kevin jeered. "Where was you raised, fella, in a ditch?"

Marcus grabbed his collar. "Out," he said. "Now."

"You kids are *all* outta here, right now!" The senior cook descended on us like the wrath of the storm god. "You think this is a schoolyard, or what? Out—or do I need to call Master Osborne?" Master Osborne was the steward. He had a lot of time for Marcus, who made his life so much easier by explaining what the duke really wanted, but you wouldn't want to risk getting on his bad side. Master Osborne was the one who decided how often your sheets got changed and how much firewood was in your room. "There's work going on here; someone's gonna chop you up instead of an onion, you don't yield space this minute!"

While Marcus was busy placating the cooks and I was busy avoiding him, Kevin disappeared with the soup bowl and a handful of beets.

⌐

S O THAT WAS WHY MARCUS STILL WASN'T SPEAKING to me. I didn't have much to say to him, either. Around the duke and his people, Marcus was always very poised and subtle; I'd never seen him downright rude before. To be fair, he'd lived in this house a long time, and he wasn't going to learn manners from my uncle. But I saw no reason for him to be so mean to some poor starving Riverside kid. He'd been edgy ever since my fight at the Rogues' Ball. Had he guessed that I was keeping secrets from him? If he was my friend he would ask me himself, not take it out on a boy I was trying to help, wouldn't he?

I don't know how long this would have gone on if Lucius Perry hadn't made one of his regular visits to the Riverside house.

I got out of the way just in time. One of the servants was guiding him down the hall to my uncle's bedroom, and I was coming the other way, and I realized that meeting Perry here after the events of the Rogues' Ball would be more awkward than I could bear. So I grabbed the nearest doorknob and ducked inside, which was not very swordsmanly of me, but swordsmanship is not made for awkward social situations.

I turned, and there was Marcus, sitting at his shesh board, wrapped in a quilted silk robe. "You should knock first," he said snarkily. "Where were you raised, anyhow?"

"Look, I'm sorry," I babbled, "but it's him and I forgot to tell you but I know who he is now!"

He put the piece he was holding carefully down on the board. "How intriguing."

"I'm going to kill you," I snapped. "I know how, and all."

"One blow, straight to the heart...if I have to hear it one more time, I'm going to kill *myself*, don't bother. Who's in the hallway?"

I inclined my head toward the duke's bedroom.

"*Alcuin?*"

I couldn't resist a smile. "Lucius Perry."

"Who the hell is Lucius Perry?"

I told him.

Before I had even finished, Marcus was dressing to go out. "Rope," he said. "This time, we're going to get over that wall."

"What on earth for? We already know who he is."

"Maybe. Maybe not. I thought you were worried about your friend and him."

"It turns out he's her *cousin*, that's all, I already told you. What he does with his spare time is his own business."

"Or ours."

"Or the duke's," I said primly, remembering my uncle's admonitions.

"It's the duke's business only if we want it to be. But we don't. What do you bet His Lordship doesn't even know about that little house?"

"So what? It's just a regular house, Marcus. If we were going to follow Lucius Perry to Glinley's House of You-Know-What, that would be something."

"Next time," Marcus said, pulling on his boots, almost breathless with excitement. "Oh, Katie, can't you see it? Your Perry is a nobleman who lives all these different lives, and nobody knows about all of them, not even Tremontaine. We're the only ones; we'll be the only ones who'll have all the pieces."

"I don't want to hurt him," I cautioned. After what I'd witnessed in the kitchen, I wasn't sure I knew Marcus as well as I thought. "I mean, if you were thinking of extortion or something. . . ."

"Don't be silly." Marcus pulled his boots snug. "I just want to know. Don't you?"

W E WERE NEITHER OF US VERY BIG, BUT SOMEHOW these past weeks Marcus had gotten taller than I. He was walking so quickly that I had to break into an undignified trot to keep up. "What's the hurry?" I panted as we toiled up the sloping street across the river.

"Are you sure you remember the house? I want to get there before him. I want to see him come in, see what he does."

We had a brief dispute about which alley it was, and then we recognized the cherry tree limb sticking out over the back wall of the house—it was definitely cherry, I could tell, now that it was showing signs of budding—so we knew we were in the right place. We did clever things with the rope and the branches, and then it was really pretty easy for us to skimble up and over the wall with hardly any whitewash on our legs.

It was a smallish garden, nicely laid out with little stone paths running between bushes and herbs that had been cut back for the winter, and patches covered with straw that would probably be flowers or strawberries. The back room of the house had tall windows that looked onto the garden. The tall bushes against the wall gave us a perfect spot for hiding, and a perfect view of the room and its occupant.

It was a woman close to my mother's age, with a strong face and auburn hair that looked like it had been carefully dressed in braided coils and a chignon that morning, but turned into a bird's nest by the succession of pens and paintbrushes she was pushing in and out of it. Her eyes were very wide set, and her lower lip was so full that it looked as though someone had taken a dessert spoon and scooped a little out from under it. She was not plump, but she was large, somehow, like a heroic stone sculpture. And even under the loose smock she wore, I could see she had quite a bosom.

The woman sat at a long table, staring intently at a bowl of fruit. Then she pulled a paintbrush out of her hair, licked the tip, dipped it into some paint and drew a few lines on the outside of a white bowl.

"What on earth is she doing?" Marcus hissed in my frozen ear.

"Painting china."

"Is she a painter, then? Is that all he's doing here, getting his portrait done?"

"This is different. It's very stylish; everyone wants painted china. Even ladies do it sometimes."

We watched her work on the bowl. It was turning into the petals of a flower.

"Is she a lady, then? She doesn't look like one. She's got paint on her smock, and her hands are dirty."

"Maybe it's his sister. Let's go," I whispered to Marcus; "I'm cold."

"Put your hood up," he murmured. "Wait 'til he comes."

I shifted uncomfortably. The shrub was scratching my neck. The woman looked up, and I was sure she'd heard me, but it was the maid coming into the room, and after her came Lucius Perry.

As soon as the maid had left with his cloak, Lucius Perry leaned over the woman and kissed her. He drew the pens and brushes out of her hair one by one, and he put his fingers into it and pulled it way out over her shoulders. It was very thick and lush, the woman's hair. You could tell from the way he was holding it that it weighed a lot. He kissed her again, and started to draw her toward the couch by the window.

"That's enough," I said, trying not to sound nervous. "I'm going."

"Shh!" said Marcus. "Do you think we can get closer? I want to hear what they're saying."

"They're not saying *anything*, Marcus. Just *Ooh, ahh, my darling* or something like that."

"They're talking," he said. "She's annoyed with him."

"Maybe she's just found out about Glinley's."

"Not that annoyed."

"So what is she saying?"

⌒

S HE WAS SAYING, "I'VE GOT TO GET THAT LAYER DONE before it dries, Lucius. Really."

"Paint it over." Lucius Perry was untying her smock with one hand, and feeling underneath it for her bodice with the other. "Later. I'll help you."

"Goodness. Such enthusiasm." Pulling herself up on one elbow (and pulling her chemise back over her shoulder), she ran a finger along his lips. She felt his hands loosen, his mouth part a little, and she smiled. "What have you been up to, to be so inspired?"

"Paying the duke his fee."

"I should have known. You always like that."

He lay back in blissful reflective surrender, and in a flash she'd leapt off the couch and over to her work table.

"Teresa!" Lucius Perry leaned precariously off the edge of the daybed, reaching across the studio to her. "Don't leave me like this!"

"Go to bed, Lucius," she said, and picked up a brush. "I mean, to real bed. I'll come to you there when I'm done."

"When?" he asked plaintively, lying back and staring at the ceiling.

"What does it matter, when? You'll go right to sleep, I know you. You've been up all night at the one place and half the day at the duke's already." She saw him arranging himself in an attractive position, left arm flung carelessly over his head, right-hand fingers curled against his thigh. He stretched like a cat in the weak winter sun, so that everything he had to offer was clearly defined.

Teresa took a sip of tisane that had gotten good and cold. "Now, listen," she said. "This afternoon Helena Montague is coming to take chocolate. She's one of the few still speaking to me; I

cannot disappoint her. And she's asked me for six matching bowls."
She curled her brush around the rim of this one, making an azure
border. "I showed her my work last time she came, and very admiring of it she was. Claimed it was quite the prettiest she'd ever seen,
and wanted a complete set, if I wasn't too busy." Teresa smiled
dryly. "I assured her I was not. I can't imagine what she'll do with
them; give them to her hatmaker or something, I suppose, but she's
going to pay me good money, and that's what matters."

"Good money?" Lucius said dreamily. His body had gone
slack, as if he were talking in his sleep, which he practically was.
"I've got money."

"I'm sure you've got plenty. Buy yourself a new hat."

He closed his eyes at last. His face was suddenly as still and
holy as a king's on a tomb. "Marry me."

"Not this year," she said. "Maybe next. Come on, wake up,"
she said without looking at him, still working on her bowl. "Don't
you want to be able to marry a respectable woman? If Helena
Montague finds you lolling on my daybed looking like a model for
the Oak God's lover, whatever is left of my name will go up in
smoke like bonfire wishes."

"Marry..."

"Mmm-hmm. Well, at least they dry quickly. Though I suppose I'll just have to keep giving her more cakes until they do, so
she can see. I should have started these last week, but I got a new
idea for my first act. I do wish writing paid as reliably as painted
china; it's so much more entertaining. But the public is fickle,
and the theatre such a quagmire. . . . I'm sure Sterling is cheating
me on the gate. I wish I could do something original. I wish I
could do comedy, but I'm just not—*Lucius!*" She said it so loudly
that the two listening in the garden heard her voice bounce off
the walls. "Wake up and go to bed. And send Nancy in to do my
hair; it's come all undone."

⌒

WE WATCHED LUCIUS PERRY GET UP AND DRAG HIM-
self out of the room. "It's sooo exhausting," Marcus whispered, "working for the duke."

I giggled. "Now what?" I said.

"Back over the wall, Katie, quick! We have to see if he goes out the front."

"If he does, we'll follow him, right? Maybe he's got another girl somewhere else."

"Two girls! And don't forget the pony...."

We barely made it over the wall, and when we had watched the front of the house for long enough (in a not-very-good hiding place next to a house down the street—"Bring knucklebones next time," said Marcus; "we'll need to look like we're playing, like we belong here."), we went back and wrestled the rope out of the tree. No one set any dogs or guards on us, so we must have been quiet and stealthy enough, though we were so charged up with the thrill of our triumph, I was sure we'd be caught.

Flushed and sweaty and grinning, we stowed the rope away. "And so?"

"Gingerbread," said Marcus. "It's traditional."

chapter VII

THEY TRIED FORCING HER TO EAT, AND THEY TRIED denying her food. It made no difference; Artemisia remained obdurate. They tried promising her treats, offering to buy her pets and jewels, even a trip to the races, for which she'd been agitating for months, but to no effect. Her mother considered threatening to cut off her hair—that had worked once—but it would spoil the wedding. Lord Ferris sent flowers, and daily notes inquiring after her health, which, after what she did to the first one they showed her, they kept to themselves.

When her good friend Lydia Godwin came to inquire after her, they very nearly turned her away. But Lydia was glowing with joy at her recent engagement to Armand Lindley, and perhaps, thought Lady Fitz, the girl could talk some sense into her.

When she saw Lydia's sweet face come through the door to her room, Artemisia melted altogether. She flung herself into her friend's arms, and wept there without a word. Strongly moved, Lydia wept, too. It was not until they both stopped to look for handkerchiefs that Lydia asked, "My dearest Mi, whatever is the matter?"

Artemisia seized her friend's hand. "Your father," she said tremulously, "Lord Godwin, he knows the law, does he not? Might you—might you ask him for me whether a girl is compelled to marry if her parents wish it, even if she does not? Even if she has given her word in betrothal—but now, she does not wish to?"

"Of course I will ask him, sweetest one. But surely your parents will not force you against your will? Even they cannot be so hopelessly old-fashioned."

"They will, I know they will—they are at me every day, and no one understands!"

"Dearest Mi, whatever has happened to you? What has Lord Ferris done, for you to take him so violently in dislike?"

For a moment, Artemisia considered telling her friend everything. But she knew that her dearest Lydia was a very conduit of news about all their friends' doings. And so she knew that, despite their great love, it would be next to impossible for Lydia to keep the sensational news of her ruin to herself. Artemisia wisely contented herself with crying out, "I cannot marry him! I would rather die!"

Lydia did her best to explain that, from her experience, true love and mutual understanding, such as she shared with her gentle Armand, were enough to conquer all impediments. But her words had little effect. Artemisia pressed her hands to her mouth and would not look at her.

Lydia sat and gently stroked her friend's hair. It was worse than she had thought. She'd seen Artemisia in a passion before, especially when she was trying to scare her parents. But never before had she refused to open her heart to her dearest friend—and never before had her eyes been quite so red, her face so taut, her breath so ragged. Lydia thought best how to divert her, that she might regain some comfort and composure.

"Mi," she said, "do you remember when we went to the theatre to see *The Empress*, and you had nightmares after?"

Artemisia shuddered. "That terrible woman, putting all those men to death. Why, is it playing again? I declare I would love to see it now, indeed I would. I understand her perfectly, now."

"It's not playing again, no; but the same splendid actress who was so proud and fierce in the role of the Empress, the actress they call the Black Rose...what will you think when I tell you that her company has commissioned a new play, for her to play the part of Stella!"

"You mean—" Artemisia caught her breath at the thought. "They are going to perform *The Swordsman Whose Name Was Not Death*—in a *theatre?*"

"It's already been played! Lavinia Perry and Jane Hetley both have seen it, for Jane's birthday."

"And?"

"Lavinia says that Henry Sterling as Fabian is a pale and feeble joke, though Jane says she'd marry him in an instant. But Lavinia has hardly a good word to say for the piece; she's vexed that they've left out the entire bit about the hunting cats, though I can hardly see how they'd play that onstage. Jane says it doesn't matter, because Mangrove's repentance at the end is even more affecting than it is in the book. But Lavinia thinks it is not true to the spirit of the novel."

"I never thought he was truly penitent. It's all a ruse, to confuse Stella to the last."

"That's what Jane says, too. She says you want to kill him yourself, he is so very wicked. Deliciously, she says."

"What about Tyrian? Is he handsome?"

"Oh, as for that, it hardly signifies. They've got a girl playing Tyrian."

"A girl? The same one who played the hero's friend in *The King's Wizard?* I bet it is. My brother Robbie was greatly taken with her. Still, a girl playing Tyrian..."

"They say her swordplay is very dashing."

"Does she kiss Stella, though?"

"They didn't say."

"What, after all that time we all spent practicing kissing with Lavinia, she didn't say? Rubbish."

"Well, we must go, then," Lydia said cheerfully, "and see it together and find out for ourselves."

Artemisia drew back. "I cannot."

"You cannot stay locked up in here forever!"

"I won't go out; I can't go out until I am free of this marriage."

"I'll tell you what, then!" Lydie tended to bounce when pleased, and she did so now. "We can sneak you out in secret. You can go masked—"

"No! No! No!" Artemisia's hands were over her ears. Lydie drew back in alarm, but then she chided herself for a false friend. She approached Artemisia cautiously. "Dearest darling, can't you tell me what is wrong?"

"I cannot marry him," Artemisia repeated. "I shall never marry anyone. It is too horrible to contemplate."

"Mi," Lydia said delicately, "has your mama perhaps said something to you about the married state that, perhaps, might frighten you or strike you as distasteful?"

Artemisia looked wonderingly at her. Was this the same Lydia who had helped her hide *The Couch of Eros* under her last year's hats? But she only said, "Mama speaks much of gowns and jewels and houses in the country. And," she added meanly, "of how marrying Lord Ferris means I should take precedence over you, no matter who you marry."

Lydia drew back. "Does she?"

"I hate her!" Artemisia exploded. "I hate her, I hate you all!"

To her eternal credit, Lydia Godwin weathered the storm. Indeed, she brought her friend nearly all the handkerchiefs in her box, one by one, saying cheerfully, "I shall have to speak to Dorrie about keeping your box well filled."

"Robbie says I am a watering-pot. I hate him, too."

"Robbie is often hateful. But I hope you know I would never do anything to injure you, my darling."

More tears, then, and vows of eternal friendship. And in that sweet moment, Artemisia thought of something. "Lydia," she said, "do you remember when Stella is in the country and Mangrove's minions are all around her and she doesn't know who to trust? And she needs to get a message to Fabian that would kill him if it goes awry? Well, there is a letter I need you to carry for me—just carry it out of the house, no more, and give it to someone to deliver."

Lydia's eyes opened wide. "Artemisia Fitz-Levi," she said, "do you have a *lover*?"

"Don't be disgusting, Lydia. What would I do with a lover?

No, it's just a friend. But don't you understand? I'm a prisoner here. They guard me from all visitors but you, my darling, and of course they read my mail. I'm running out of things to bribe Dorrie with—I need you to do this!"

"I see...." Lydia twisted the handkerchief in her hands. "Give me the letter."

"Here." Artemisia lifted up one corner of her pink-flowered rug. "The maids only sweep under it once a week, lazy things."

It was addressed to *KT, Riverside House*. Lydia tucked it in her apron pocket, and Artemisia gripped both her hands, staring into her face with a desperate fury not unlike that of the Empress when ordering her favorite to the sword. "Now swear!" she said. "Swear by your precious love for Lindley that you will tell no one. Not your mama, not your papa, not even him who your soul adores. No one. If you will do this for me, Lydia, then someday I will dance at your wedding, though I can never hope myself for such joy as you possess."

⁓

SOMETIMES AT BREAKFAST, IF SHE KEPT QUIET ENOUGH, Lydia's parents would forget that she was there. It was one reason she did not often breakfast in her room. She ate her toast very slowly, and listened to her mother telling her father, "Tremontaine is at it again. Dora Nevilleson told me her husband told her his valet saw him at the Rogues' Ball. Of course you know Nevilleson was there himself and just won't own up to it. The number of valets who were there, it must have been a convocation of nothing but gentlemen with clothes brushes, to hear the husbands tell of it."

"Funny." Lydia's father, Michael, Lord Godwin, buttered a piece of toast and sat watching the butter melt into the crispy bread. He was very particular about his toast. "My own valet did not attend. Or if he did, he's not saying."

"Good," said his wife. "Then you know nothing about this putative niece? The girl with the sword, who fought Todd Rippington there?"

"Of course I've heard about the niece, Rosamund, what do you take me for? I'm the Raven Chancellor. If the Duke Tremontaine has trained up some girl with a sword, and she's a relative, and she's begun to fight duels, it's going to come up before the Council of Honor sooner or later. It's our business to know. We don't want to look too alarmed when it does."

"Why should that alarm you?"

"The privilege of the sword is one of the rights of the nobility. The privilege only, and not the sword itself. That, we leave to professionals."

She touched his hand. "I know one noble who did things differently, once."

From the way Godwin returned his lady's look, Lydia was afraid her parents were going to head right upstairs for one of their little talks, leaving breakfast unfinished and her curiosity unsatisfied. But Michael Godwin just said, "That man took up both blade and privilege only once, and for a very worthy prize."

Was this the notorious duel her father had fought over her mother? She held her breath, waiting for details. But even her silence was too loud. Her mother returned to the debate.

"So," Rosamund persisted, "a young noblewoman with a blade who could fight for herself if she chose is very different from that young man?"

"Possibly." Lord Godwin sighed. "You have no idea what a muddle the rules and traditions of the Court of Honor is. Does the privilege even extend to women, or does it merely derive from their male relatives? There are precedents for one, and for the other, case by case and year by year, as the members change by fate and election. The dukes and Arlen have the only permanent seats, which is supposed to give it all some stability—and you'll know what that means when I remind you that the Duke Tremontaine is one of them!" His lady nodded wryly. "'Honor' appears to be a maze of unwritten rules and fiercely defended traditions. In the end, what is this girl? What's her legal status, and even her social one? Does she pass back and forth from noble to sword at a whim? And if so, whose whim?"

"Her uncle's, I imagine. Unless she kills him first."

"She can't kill him. Not in honorable challenge, anyway; the

Court permits no one to profit from challenge within their own family. If she kills, she does it on his behalf."

"Or her own."

"It's all pretty alarming."

"I see. And what will you noble lords do about it now?"

"We watch and wait."

"I cannot like it, Michael. If this truly is his sister Talbert's child, then it's disgraceful for the duke to be encouraging her to run wild like that. A noble's daughter should be gently raised and properly cared for. Someone should do something."

"Tremontaine is the head of the family, and the family has not complained—not in Council, anyway, where it might do some good. I hear Greg Talbert's locked himself up with a serious head cold rather than answer any questions."

"She's only a girl, they say, no older than Lydia here."

"Well, sometimes I do wonder," Michael Godwin said, "if I should not have taught Lydia the sword. I won't always be around, you know, and if that goatish Lindley tries anything once they're wed..."

"Oh, Papa!" It hadn't been funny the first time, and had grown less so with every repetition since.

Her mother rushed in to the rescue, asking "How is your friend Artemisia, Lydie? I heard she was ill. Did you visit her yesterday?"

Her mother was so sensible and kind, not at all like Lady Fitz-Levi. It wouldn't be breaking her word to her friend to tell her mother how unhappy Mia was. "She's not so much ill as heartsick, Mama. She does not want to marry Lord Ferris at all, and they are going to *force* her. She weeps and weeps and will not eat, and is truly pitiful. Oh, is there nothing we can do?"

Her mother, who had ample experience of young Lady Artemisia's temperament, said cautiously, "Do you know what made her change her mind about her intended, dearest?"

"She will not say. But she is wretched, Mama. I've never seen her so distraught—well, almost never. Not for so long, anyway."

Her father gave her mother a look across the table. "My word on it," he said, "she's found out about the Black Rose."

"Michael," Lady Godwin warned, "perhaps this is not the time...."

"Rosamund, I think it is very much the time, with Lydie about to be married herself and launched into the world. I've been meaning to speak to her about it, in fact." He turned to his only daughter. "Lydia, dearest, what do you know about women who...Lydia. Let me begin again." Lady Godwin sighed audibly, but did not offer her husband assistance. "Men, as you know, have certain interests in life, and these interests sometimes lead them to do foolish things. Things their wives would not approve of. And I hope that if you see your husband doing anything foolish, you will not stand by without calling him to account for it."

Lydia tried to look very adult and trustworthy. "You need have no fears on that account, Papa. Armand and I have vowed always to tell each other everything."

"Just so," said Lord Godwin. "Of course, unmarried men are allowed to be a little foolish sometimes. It gives them something to improve upon, and their wives as well. So I hope you will not be altogether surprised if you learn, someday, that one of your friends' young husbands before his marriage was, ah, friendly with certain women of the town, hostesses and actresses and such, and became their protector. Most men, in fact, have such a past."

"But never their wives?"

"Oh, never the wives." Eyes downcast, her mother smiled. "Women have no past, just a grand and glorious future."

Lydia kept her face schooled to look as if all this was news to her. "The Black Rose is an actress," she said helpfully. "Is Lord Ferris her protector?"

"Was," said Michael Godwin. "She's a magnificent piece, just the sort of high-ticket, high-profile item Ferris goes for, and he went for her. It wasn't easy, either. The Rose is very picky. Easily bored, she says, and considering how many 'protectors' she's turned away, it must be true. But he likes a bit of a challenge, does our Crescent."

"Michael." His wife's voice carried a hint of steel.

"Just common knowledge," he added doucely. "It didn't last long, though. They had a bit of a row."

"A bit?" her mother said with relish. "I heard he had her

thrown out of his house in the middle of the night like a common thing, with only the shift on her back."

Lydia gasped. "If Artemisia did something he disliked, would he have her thrown out in the snow, too? No wonder she doesn't want to marry him!"

"Certainly not, darling. No nobleman would dare to treat his wife that way. It would get back to her parents and her brother, and he would pay dearly for it. No, don't worry, it's surely not anything like that."

"Think about it, Lydie," her father said. "Your friend has a great deal of pride. She heard about the affair, and she wants to make him sorry. You must admit, she always does like to have the upper hand."

Lydia knit her brow in thought. It was true that Mia had been most interested when the Black Rose's name came up. And, to be fair, Mia had never liked being upstaged by anyone. "But if Lord Ferris has already left his mistress, then why should Mia mind so?"

"Because," her mother explained crisply, "it all happened around MidWinter. He was courting them both at the same time, that's why." Lydia let out a low whistle. "There!" Lady Godwin accused her husband. "That's what all this vulgar talk leads to. Lydia, no whistling in public, you know better."

"If you knew about Lord Ferris and the Black Rose, then surely her parents did as well. Why didn't anyone say anything?"

Lord Godwin said, "Artemisia's father is, ah, a man of the town. Even if he did know about Lord Ferris's affair with an actress, he surely knew it would blow over. He wouldn't let it interfere with a good marriage contract."

Lydia sat slowly digesting all this knowledge. Artemisia had never really loved Lord Ferris, she knew that. Maybe she was right not to marry him. Her parents could not force her, surely. This matter would prove to be just another long contest of wills, such as were not unknown in the Fitz-Levi family. She vowed to visit Mia again soon with a box of her favorite chocolates and some diversion.

"The Black Rose is in a new play," Lydia said, "and all my friends have seen it. May I go?"

"Oh, dear," sighed her mother, "it's that awful piece of trash about the swordsman lover, isn't it? My friends were mad for that book when we were young."

"It's not trash," her daughter said. "It is full of great and noble truths of the heart. And swordfights."

"I'll have to read it," her father said brightly, but no one paid him any attention.

"I so want Mia to see the play," Lydia said. "If I can assure her that Lord Ferris will not be there—"

"He won't," her mother chuckled. "The Black Rose denied him entry to the theatre the morning after, and he hasn't been back since."

"Well, there you have it," Michael Godwin said to his daughter. "Actresses are spiteful creatures. You be sure you tell your Armand that he should be very cautious when he chooses a mistress."

A year ago, Lydia might still have giggled when he talked like that. But love had turned her serious, at least where love was concerned. "Oh, Papa," she said. "You know Armand never would."

"Of course not," her father said. "He knows I've got my eye on him."

chapter VIII

J UST KNOWING ABOUT LUCIUS PERRY AND HIS LADYLOVE
made life more enjoyable. Whenever the duke got highhanded
with us, implying that we were young and what did we know?
we had to bite the inside of our cheeks to keep from laughing over
the things we knew now that he did not.

Marcus and I speculated endlessly on what we had witnessed.
I thought the lady was very wise, knowing Perry's proclivities, to
refuse to yield to his advances, since clearly he'd lose interest the
moment she did. Marcus, though, claimed she must be ignorant
of his other lives, or she'd never let him in the door. His colorful
theories included the possibility that the woman was really
Perry's sister, so a little kissing was all she would allow. "He's
steeped in vice," he said; "why shouldn't it run in the family?"

I pointed out stiffly that these things did not always run in
families.

We should have been trying to find out who owned her
house. It would have been fairly easy to go up to the door with a
misdelivered message and use that as an excuse to grill the maid,
or the neighbors' maids. . . . We talked about it, but we never did

anything. That wasn't the game, really. It was more of a challenge to try and catch both Lucius and his lady out together, see what they would betray to our inquisitiveness. What did they mean to each other? What were they hiding, and why? We wanted the secrets of their hearts, something no one else had, something they would be reluctant to yield to anyone else. We would hold it for them, and keep it safe, our treasure, whole and unique. Besides, the maid had a walleye.

It is possible, though, that lurking in late winter gardens was bad for the health. A few days later, Marcus caught a serious cold. While Marcus was in bed, my uncle sent for me. The duke was in his study with his friend Flavia, the unmercifully homely woman he kept around so they could make fun of people and do mathematical puzzles or something—at least, that's what they always seemed to be doing when I saw them together. Today they were constructing some kind of model—a tower, or maybe a clock, I couldn't quite tell, and I didn't want to ask and be lectured. I was wearing my splendid new cloak, because the day was finally warm enough that I could sling it back by the tassel and not have to worry about puddles.

Flavia looked up at me when I came in and said, "I've got it: You could have a career on the stage."

"As what?" my uncle asked. "She can't memorize anything, none of us can. Dates of crowns and battles leave her hapless."

"I know poetry," I said, but they ignored me.

"Well," Flavia told him, "in case you haven't noticed, the demand for female swordfighters is pretty much limited to Tremontaine House and the theatre, where they are enjoying a certain vogue."

"They can't really fight," he said crossly. "They just know a few moves, and they leap about showing their legs. Whereas Katherine is an excellent duelist—and always very modestly dressed," he added primly.

"Three yards of silk velvet isn't what I'd call modest," she said, but I knew he meant I didn't flash my legs around.

"Look," said my uncle, "speaking of theatre, how would you like to see a play?"

"Me?" I squeaked.

"Why not? I've got a box at the Hart, you may as well use it. They're playing this afternoon. You should go. Enjoy yourself." I waited. As a benevolent uncle, he wasn't very convincing. "And when it's done, you might like to go backstage and meet one of the actresses."

"The swordfighter?" Did he want me to give her a few tips? I'd die.

"No, the romantic lead. She's called the Black Rose. I've got something I'd like you to give her." He handed me a brocade pouch with something heavy slinking inside it. "It's a gold chain," he said, "and I'm trusting you not to run off with it. Just give it to her. She'll know who it's from, and what it means. But if anyone asks, it's a tribute from you to her, in admiration of her fine performance."

"Is she really that good?"

My uncle smiled creamily. "The best."

"Dear one, cease the salacious thoughts and hand me that piece—no, the little one. Butterfingers."

"Butterfingers, yourself."

S O THAT WAS HOW I WENT TO THE THEATRE FOR THE first time. I would have thought it was a temple, with its painted columns and bright facade, but the banners proclaimed it the LEAPING HART THEATRE, HENRY STERLING, ACTOR/MANAGER. At the last minute the duke had realized that if the chain was not to be seen coming from him, I shouldn't sit in his box. So he gave me money for a good seat in the stalls across from the stage, and money to tip the seatman, and more for snacks and incidentals. A girl in a lowcut bodice was selling nuts; I bought some but forgot to eat them, I was so excited to be there.

I felt a bit like an actress myself, in my gorgeous cloak and a new hat with a plume that Betty had produced at the last minute. The ticket-taker called me "sir," and I didn't bother to correct him; why not pass for a boy and enjoy the freedom of one? All things were permitted here, it seemed. I couldn't wait to see the actress with the sword.

Candles were lit on the stage, although it was still broad daylight. There was a bed on it, a big one with curtains. There were also curtains at the windows at the back of the stage, which were very tall, and a dressing table and a carpet. It looked like a lady's bedroom.

To the side of the stage, a consort started to play, and the audience quieted. Then a woman entered. There was a little sigh, because she was so very beautiful, deep bosomed and dark haired, gorgeously dressed in a rose-colored gown with many flounces, but her white throat was decked with simple pearls.

"No, thank you," she said to someone we couldn't see offstage, her maid, I guess. "I will put myself to bed." Somebody chuckled and was shushed. The woman unclasped her cloak and laid it on a chair. She did it with such an air of sweet weariness that you somehow knew that she had been out late, and enjoyed herself, too, but was more than ready for the day to be over. Languidly she reached up to her hair, and pulled two pins out. A fall of dark tresses released itself down her back, like an animal let loose. She reached for the clasp at her throat. It was then, when we were admiring her private moment of grace and release, thinking it was only for us, that a man stepped out from behind one of her long bedroom curtains. He was devastatingly handsome and carried a sword. His voice, when he spoke, was warm and rich like poured chocolate—but it was not that which made me catch my breath.

"Lady Stella," he said. "Allow me."

I had to dig my nails into my palms to keep from squeaking out loud. As it was, I began moving my lips along with the lines. I knew them all, from the opening chapter of my favorite book.

Fabian snuffed the candles, one by one. On the dusky stage he drew Stella to him, and they disappeared together within the bedcurtains. A woman behind me squeaked happily. The curtains didn't stir, but the consort began to play a slow and lovely air. When it was done, her maid came in and pulled back the draperies, first the high ones at the window, and then the bedcurtains.

Stella was revealed alone in the bed, her dark hair falling over her white ruffled nightdress. She rose and went to the window, and we saw that it was open a little, as though someone had left without quite closing it behind him. She turned and looked out over the audience, one hand stroking her hair.

"I was a girl before tonight. I am a woman now."

It was the oddest feeling in the world, seeing something that had belonged so utterly to me alone being made to happen up on the stage with living people doing it, and others watching it. (I'd lent Marcus the book once. When I finally asked for it back he never said anything, so either he hadn't liked it or he hadn't bothered to read it.)

When they got to the fight in the clocktower between Mangrove and Fabian, the swords finally came out in earnest. Henry Sterling's swordplay was not bad—he certainly had the flair and the spirit of Fabian—but whoever played Mangrove really knew what he was doing with his wrist. It was almost a surprise when he dropped his sword and fled in confusion.

Mangrove was all wrong, of course—too short, for one thing, because he's supposed to be much taller than Fabian, and Henry Sterling was a truly magnificent Fabian, especially when he tells Stella (wrongly) that he's glad it's Tyrian's child because Mangrove is right and his own seed is cursed—but it must have been hard to find an actor taller than Sterling. And Mangrove should have had a mustache, because in the scene where he kisses Stella, she is repelled by it, but of course they left that out. The gorgeous actress playing Stella, who was surely the Black Rose, did a wonderful job of looking repelled just the same: she did a little thing with curling her fingers behind her back that meant she was filled with disgust, you could tell.

Tyrian. I wasn't sure how I felt about Tyrian. You could tell it was a woman, if you looked hard and thought about it. But everyone onstage referred to her as "he" and treated her like a man, so you sort of had to go along with it. She did take big swaggering steps like a man, and held her head a certain way, and she had cut all her hair right off, so that it stood in fair little curls all over her head. Even in the book there is a certain softness to Tyrian, a gentleness that makes you like him and think it would not be so bad if Stella chose him over his friend. The actress was very good at that, the way she looked at Stella when Stella wasn't looking, and the way she stepped back when Stella was thinking and all. Maybe they just couldn't find a man to play Tyrian that well. She did look very dashing with her sword at her side; I could hardly wait to see her use it later.

Tyrian made his vow to Fabian, and the two of them left, and everyone applauded. I waited eagerly, but nothing happened. The stage was empty, the consort was playing, and the audience started talking and getting up. I worried that something had gone wrong, but no one else seemed concerned. Vendors came back selling bags of nuts and bunches of flowers. Some had little black silk rosettes and tiny silver swords for people to pin in their hats or on their sleeves as tokens of the two lead actresses to show which they liked best. The actress playing Tyrian was called Viola Fine. Her little sword appealed to me, but I thought I should buy a rose if I was going to see the Black Rose. In the end I did neither, but I did get a printed picture of the actor Henry Sterling in the role of Fabian, his arm raised to his brow in an attitude of anguish. They had colored ones, too, for more money, but I thought I could color it myself when I got home. I would ask my uncle to give me watercolors.

Then they blew trumpets, and we all found our seats again.

The second half wasn't as good as the first, because they had to cut too much out, like Stella's horse race and the terror of the hunting cats. Instead the actors made long speeches about love which were never in the book, and weren't as good. I watched Tyrian more closely. Viola Fine was supposed to be an actual man, not a woman swordsman, but if you thought about it realistically, that's what she was. Like me. Only not for real: my uncle was right, her swordplay was just for show. That huge disengage of hers would get her killed in a real fight. I wondered if she liked playing a man. When Viola Fine first went on the stage, had she *chosen* roles where she could stride about, her cloak swirling around her, or had she really been hoping to play Stella or someone with gorgeous gowns and luxurious curls and jewels that couldn't have been real but glittered fantastically, and men saying they would die for her?

I was not the only person in the audience holding her breath when Tyrian approached Stella for the kiss. "You have done tonight," she said, "what ten thousand men could not."

"Now," the Black Rose murmured low, but we could all hear it, somehow, "let me show you what one woman alone can do."

She leaned towards Viola. Viola's eyes closed languidly. The Black Rose came closer—and then her eyes opened wide, following the entrance of Mangrove's minions on the roof (instead of the hunting cats).

It might be nice to be an actress, after all. I was a better swordsman than Viola Fine already, wasn't I? Maybe someone would write a play just for me, one where a real woman could fight with her sword, and had many fine adventures and changes of costume. Maybe Henry Sterling would play a man who loves me madly but thinks I love only the sword, while really I am smoldering with passion for him. Or maybe Viola could play the hero, and I could play a woman who disguises herself as a man in order to get close to her and—what? We could have a terrific fight at the end, maybe, and kill each other, and the audience would be sobbing, the way they do at the end of the play when Tyrian cradles Stella's head in his arms, rocking her and letting her think he's Fabian, who's already taken the potion, but Stella doesn't know it.

I can make myself cry just thinking of it. And the way Viola rose to her feet, looking for someone to fight but there is no one left—there was such a look of desolation there. I wondered if she was lonely, too.

All around me, people were jumping to their feet and clapping and yelling and throwing things—flowers, nuts, handkerchiefs stained with kisses—and wiping their eyes, as well. A girl behind me said to her friend, "I've seen it eleven times now, and I always say I won't cry, and then I do."

"I know," her friend said. "I keep wanting it to end differently, but it never does. Oh, there she is!"

The Black Rose swept back onstage, glowing with a tragic dignity. Her magnificent bosom swelled as she took a deep breath and bowed low to the crowd. The girl behind me started gasping, "I'll die, I'll die...Oh, just hold me! Isn't she *fine*? I've written her a dozen letters, but she never answers."

I thought smugly of the chain in my pocket that would gain me access to her dressing room.

But it turned out not to be that simple. There was a porter guarding the back door to the stage, and quite a few other people who were trying to get in, as well. Most of them had brought bunches of flowers, some very nice indeed. A couple of the biggest were carried by liveried servants, whose masters waited behind in their carriages, watching through the doors to see what transpired.

It was too late to go back for flowers, I thought; best get this over with. I shoved myself to the front of the crowd, right up against a woman with a necklace of silver swords strung around a turban on her head. She pulled away as though I had bitten her. "How dare you, fellow!"

"I'm sorry," I stammered, horribly flustered, for if I had been a man it would of course have been unspeakable for me to brush up against a woman like that. "I'm not— It's all right, really it is. I'm a lady—like Tyrian, I mean Viola."

"Rea-ally?" She looked me up and down. "Is it a new fad?"

"I wish I had the legs for it," said the well-dressed older woman next to her, who wore a black velvet neck ribbon with a silver sword depending from it. "What's your name, sweetheart?"

"Katherine."

"Is that a real sword you've got?"

"Do you like swords, Katherine?"

The people behind us were pushing forward, so that the ladies were very nearly on top of me. They smelled of powder and expensive perfume. Their only blades may have been finger-length, but I fell back before them as if they carried real ones, and I defenseless.

I stepped on the porter's toe. "Oi!" he said. "None of that here. What do you think you're doing?"

I turned around and looked up into his solid face. "My name is Katherine Talbert. I'm here to see the Black Rose."

"You and half the city," he grumbled. "Listen, kiddo, nice try, but the part of Tyrian is already booked. You want to act, you come back another time. Master Sterling don't see new actresses but on Tuesday mornings."

"Oh, please," I said. "I'll only be a moment. I've just got to give her this—" and I held up the chain in its sack, letting him hear the chink of metal.

"Nice for her," he said gruffly. An aggressive servant shoved a huge hothouse bouquet in his face—as the porter tried to defend against it, I reached for his hand, stuck a coin in it, and, with the slippery little sideways wriggle that always worked when I needed to grab something from the kitchen table when the cooks were all busy, slipped past him and through the back door of the theatre.

It was a different world: quiet and frantic, real and imaginary, all at once. It smelt of oil and wax and sweat and fresh wood shavings. There were raw beams and intricately painted canvases, yards of dusty air overhead and people appearing and disappearing below.

"I'm sick to death of it!" One of Fabian's friends strode past me with another, still wearing the top half of his costume. "He does it every time, on purpose, just to make me look cheap."

"Of course he does, my dear; you threaten him."

Against the wall I recognized props from scenes in the play: Stella's bedroom candelabra, Mangrove's velvet chair, the trunk from the sea voyage and halberds from the guards. A workman held one in his hand, shouting, "You're mad if you think I can make another horse before tomorrow! What do I look like, a brood mare? Just nail the damned thing back together, and tell him I'm working on it!"

"Excuse me." I tugged at his sleeve. "I've come to see the Black Rose."

He nodded at a door across the way. "In there." He raised the halberd again. "And tell them to be *careful* next time! It's *not a real horse!*"

The door was not fully closed. I stood for a moment, trying to breathe normally, to get the feel for where I was and what I was doing.

I heard a woman's voice inside. "God, you are the biggest tease in the world. I'll have that kiss now, Rose, if you please."

There was a low, throaty chuckle. I recognized it from Stella's ball scene. "Why not? You worked hard for it."

Stiff cloth rustled. Someone hummed. Then the voice that was not Rose's spoke a line from the play, mockingly, romantically: "*I was a girl before tonight.*"

I put my head very carefully inside the door. A black head and a fair one with short, close-cropped curls were pressed together.

It was the missing kiss from *The Swordsman Whose Name Was Not Death*, the kiss Tyrian wanted but never got. Stella was giving it to Tyrian now, at last, as I watched them. I lifted my fingers to my own mouth, barely breathing. Viola was still wearing her costume; the Black Rose had changed into a loose gown over her chemise. Viola's fingers were pressed into the Rose's hair, pulling her head even closer. She moaned softly, and I think I did, too.

I felt a strange glowing in my body, right at the fork of my breeches. It was like nothing on earth I'd ever felt before, and it was right there where a man keeps his tool. Oh, dear god. Heat and cold touched me all at once. Was all this dressing up and swordfighting turning me into a man? Had it happened to the actress already, with her sword and her breeches and her cropped hair? No one had warned me. What could I do? I would die, I would die if I was growing one. Slowly, cautiously, I put my hand down there to see. I didn't feel anything through my breeches that hadn't been there before. I squeezed a little harder to be sure, and caught my breath at the sense that shot through me. It was indescribably, undeniably good. Suddenly it didn't seem to matter what was down there. So what if I was growing one? Men never complained of it, did they? In fact, if this was the pleasure they were always crowing about, I wasn't sure I didn't want one after all. I thought of Marcus. He had one, too, didn't he? He could show me how to use it. I wouldn't mind if he did. I squeezed a little harder.

My eyes were closed. I saw Tyrian kissing the Black Rose, and Viola kissing Stella. I thought about curling up in bed with my curtains drawn and reading the book again, but this time seeing the two of them kissing, kissing, kissing after the play was over and the real story began.

I squeezed harder still, and then I didn't think anything at all except how I wished what was happening wouldn't stop, only it did, rather suddenly, and I had to put my hand on the doorpost. The kiss had finished; they were looking into each other's eyes.

"You're a girl still," the Black Rose told her. "Don't let that sword deceive you."

Viola laughed huskily. "Thanks for nothing. I know exactly what it's good for."

"Be careful," Rose said. "Don't let it go to your head. They come on strong, but they can leave you with nothing."

"Speak for yourself, sweetness." Viola straightened her jacket. "I know how to handle them."

Rose shook her head. "You really don't mind, do you?"

"Mind what?"

"The way they want you to be *him* for them."

"Why not? I love acting. Don't you?"

"In a well-crafted play, of course. But I don't do private theatricals."

"You don't know what you're missing." As she turned to the door, I gathered myself together and knocked. "Adoring Public, Rose!" Viola cried jauntily as she passed me.

My face was still flushed, my breathing shallow. "Come in!" the Black Rose sang out melodiously, but when she saw me in my boy's clothes she said, "Oh, dear."

"It's not what you think," I said. "I'm real."

She said, "Oh," and then she said, "Oh," again, in a different tone. "I know. You're the duke's girl."

"He sent you this." I fumbled the brocade pouch out of my pocket with my sweaty hand, and held it out to her. I couldn't meet her eyes.

The Black Rose was very tall. She looked at me, and then she went and closed the door, and came back and sat down. She took the chain out. It was heavy, made of several links braided together, and very long.

"That's worth a lot," she said. She bent her neck and pulled her hair up out of the way. "Would you like to put it on me?"

She must have known my face would be in her hair. She smelled like nothing else on earth. I kissed her hair, and put my hand on her white hand that held it above her neck. She turned, and tilted her head up to me, and I kissed her on the lips.

Her lips were very soft and warm and full. I felt them curve in a smile under mine. I couldn't help smiling back.

"I see," she said. She lowered her hair and turned around, and reached up and kissed me again, a mother's kiss. "What's your name, sweetness?"

"Katherine. Katherine Talbert."

"Well, Katherine Talbert, thank you for the gift."

"It's from my—"

"That wasn't what I meant."

"Oh." I felt my face color up, but I stood my ground. She must have liked the kiss, after all. I was sure I'd done it all wrong.

She weighed a length of chain in her hand. "He's a kind man, your uncle. Thoughtful. Please tell him—since we are alone here—please tell him that I will have something for him soon."

I said, "He likes other men, you know."

"So do I." The Black Rose smiled. She reached up her hand again and pushed back my hair. "You're a pretty girl, Katherine. Did you like the play?"

"Yes. Very much."

"Come again, then. I'll do better next time on the 'I am a woman' speech. I don't think I quite nailed it tonight. Though the bit with Mangrove on the stairs went rather well, I thought...." There was a sharp knock on the door. "My dresser," she told me. "You'd better go before the hordes descend."

I went out the door. I felt as if I had no body, I was so light. It was not an entirely pleasant feeling; I had gotten used to knowing exactly where I was. I leaned against the wall and watched as the dresser opened the door to some well-dressed men with flowers. I heard the actress crowing, "My dear! It's been ages! What hole have you been hiding in?"

I left the theatre. I walked for a long time, and not home to Riverside. When I stopped, I was standing in front of the house of the china painter, Lucius Perry's mistress. The last time we were there, I had wanted to leave when they started kissing on the couch. But now I wished that I could see it, very much. I wanted to bang on her door until she came out with brushes in her hair, and make her invite me in for tea so I could ask her whether she really liked it, and if she'd done it with anyone besides Lucius

Perry, if she even had, and why? But I didn't dare. I was wearing my best clothes; I could not go up over the wall, either. And if I did, all I'd probably see was her painting china, anyway.

⌐

TERESA LAY ON THE COUCH IN HER STUDIO, AND CRIED and cried. She was pretty much done when Lucius came in, pink and disheveled from a quick nap in her room and a long night before that. He blinked at her and said, "I have to go. I'm expected at my cousins' for a card party, and I've cried off too many times before."

"Off you go, then," Teresa said, but her voice sounded strange, even to her. She jammed the letter into her pocket.

"What's that?" he asked.

"Oh, nothing. Another bill, that's all."

"You've been crying."

"Rubbing my eyes, that's all. I got paint in them or something."

"Do you need money?" He sat on the couch, on a shawl still damp and wrinkled from her weeping, and held out his hand to her, asking, "What is it, what's the matter?"

She stared at the hand as if it might bite her. But she answered him. "It's Roddy—my husband's family, I mean. They send me these horrible letters. I shouldn't read them, really, they're always the same. It all comes down to the same stupid thing: they won't return my dowry, what remains of it, anyway, because I left him. That's all."

There was a table between them, cluttered with art supplies. Still, he went down on his knees, self-consciously theatrical, and held out his arms to her.

"Marry me," he said. "I know I'm not much of a prize, but I can offer you the protection of my name, and all the true devotion you can stand."

She stared at him. "Oh, Lucius." She was laughing, but the tears refused to stop. "Oh, Lucius, no. I can't."

"Am I too loose for you? I could reform, you know."

"I don't want you to reform. You're even worse than I am. I like that."

"Then marry me, and we'll be bad together all the time."

"I can't." He looked so silly down there. She was laughing; the tears were just left over, that's all.

"Come on, Teresa, please?"

"I just can't, that's all. Even if I wanted to, I couldn't marry you."

"Why not?"

"Because my husband's still alive."

He dropped his arms. From his knees, he looked up at her. "Your husband is dead."

"No, he isn't. I wish he were, but he is not."

"You told me he was dead."

"I never said so. I just let you think it."

"And you think I didn't inquire elsewhere? No one's seen Roderick Trevelyn for years."

She jammed her hand in her pocket. "Then how is he writing me letters?"

Her lover took the paper from her. She let him unfold it and watched him scan the words, his face wrinkling in disgust. "This is insane," Lucius said. "It's revolting. He doesn't—this is insane."

"Yes. They've got him nicely locked away, but he still writes."

"Who lets him send them?"

"His family, of course. They won't give me a divorce. They want me back."

"For landsake, *why?*"

She wiped her eyes, took a breath. "To punish me, I suppose. I didn't give them what they wanted. It got worse, after I left, they tell me. They say if I came back, he would get better."

"No one who writes like this is going to get better. Why didn't you try to divorce him before you left? There would have been witnesses, you could have—"

She seized the paper back from him. "Do you think I wanted witnesses?" she flared. "Do you think I wanted the world to know what he was doing to me? I had no family, no money of my own—do you think anyone would even have believed me if I'd taken my stories to court against my husband and all his family?"

He watched her blaze across the room, back and forth like a comet in its course.

"I'm sorry," he said. She flew at him as if she would attack him, but he stood his ground, arms at his side, and she flung hers around him and clung to Lucius Perry for dear life.

~

IT WAS COLD IN THE SHADOW OF THE HOUSES. I FELT lightheaded; it was hours since I'd eaten anything. I reached in my pocket for the nuts I'd bought at the theatre, and ate them, and felt a little better. I unfolded the paper they came in. It was a playbill from the theatre.

THE SWORDSMAN WHOSE NAME WAS NOT DEATH,
A NEW DRAMA
BY A LADY OF QUALITY
NOW PLAYING
AT THE LEAPING HART THEATRE ON WEST BANK,
HENRY STERLING, ACTOR & MANAGER
WITH THE ADDITIONAL TALENTS OF
THE INCOMPARABLE BLACK ROSE,
THE FIERCE MASTER PINCUS FURY,
AND INTRODUCING
THE BOLD & DASHING YOUNG MISTRESS VIOLA FINE AND
DIVERSE OTHER TALENTS
CERTAIN TO ENRAPTURE & ENTERTAIN
A NEW DRAMA NEVER BEFORE PLAYED BEFORE THE PUBLIC!
UNLIMITED ENGAGEMENT OPEN TO THE VAGARIES OF PUBLIC TASTE.
IF YOU APPEAR, WE WILL PLAY!

"By a Lady of Quality." Was it the same one who had written the novel? Maybe it was someone younger, someone who had read the book as a girl and loved it and wanted to see it on the stage. "A Lady of Quality"—that meant a noblewoman. Could it be someone I knew? Someone who had been to one of the duke's parties? The duke's ugly friend Flavia had been speaking of the theatre. She was clever, but I didn't think she was noble. I tried to see her as the mysterious author, but I could barely imagine her reading the book, much less writing about it.

Did the Lady of Quality ever come to see her own play onstage? What did she think of the way the actors played their roles? And did she ever go backstage to visit them after?

⌒

TERESA DREW A HARSH BREATH, AND THEN ANOTHER. HE let her try to find control in the safety of his arms.

"I understand," he said. "It's all right. It's not your fault. You couldn't know."

"I didn't know," she whimpered like a child. "I really didn't know. How could I? No one told me."

She didn't realize how tightly she held the letter in her hand. "Oh, Lucius, he was so beautiful once. He was like a young forest god, all dappled golden. It made it harder to believe what he was capable of. Even when I was all bloody and aching, I'd look at that face, that perfect face, and wonder if I could be mistaken, if somehow I really had done something so terrible that he was per-fectly justified in what he did.

"But he never said he was sorry. That's how I knew. The other girls—I knew women married to men who merely drank, or had bad tempers. They never tell you before the wedding—maybe your mother is supposed to know—but theirs must not have, and of course I didn't have one. Afterwards, though, it all comes out. We'd sit together over our sewing and our chocolate, and one would flinch or try to hide a bruise . . . and so we knew. And sometimes, though not often, one or the other would say, *It's all my fault, I know it is. I should try harder. I make him angry. He cries, you know, he cries and tells me how sorry he is, and begs me not to make him so angry. . . .* And she'd show us the jewel he'd bought her, to prove how much he really loved her after all.

"Roderick never said he was sorry. He would just look at me as if I weren't really there, as if my weeping were some pointless annoyance. So maybe I was lucky; at least I knew the truth." She laughed, an old, brittle echo of the drawing room. "I tried to kill him once."

"Why didn't you do it?" Lucius Perry asked harshly.

"I'm not sure." Teresa walked away from him, across the

room. If she was going to speak of these things, she did not want to be held or touched by anyone. "I stood over him with the poker while he slept in a chair by the fire. We'd both been reading there, very quiet and companionable, and Roddy fell asleep. I didn't know, when he woke up, whether he would be—agreeable, or the other way. You never knew with him. I stood there with the poker, knowing I had only a few minutes and that I would have to beat his brains out. And it wasn't that I didn't want to spoil his beauty, although I didn't, really. It was just a—a ridiculous moment of clarity, when I realized that putting an end to his life would ruin mine; that it would be simple now and simple afterwards because it would all be over, but that wasn't what I really wanted. I realized I had another choice, which was much less simple but much more attractive."

She put her hand up against the windowpane, looking out at the empty winter garden. "I knew in that moment that I would leave, that it was only a matter of time. It made the waiting bearable as things got worse. I had it all thought out—what I would take, how I would get out—not where I would go, though; there didn't seem to be anything more important than getting out the door, and I was afraid to tell anyone beforehand. So one day I went upstairs, put some things in a bag, and walked out the door and into a great many complications. But at least I had something I wanted. And I have it still."

He stood waiting, listening.

"They never forgave me, the ones who stayed." Her breath misted the glass. "Ladies who'd wept on my bosom, as I wept on theirs—girls I shared secrets with of how to layer powder so the bruises wouldn't show. They are not the ones who buy my work, or send me flowers left over from their parties. They are the ones who castigate me loudly in public for leaving my poor husband when he needed me most. They are the women who won't receive me in their houses, and turn their heads away when they see me on the street."

"I won't let them hurt you anymore."

She shook her head, smiling mirthlessly. "Now you sound like one of my heroes. Maybe that's why I like you so much."

"Love me," he insisted.

"I may. I probably do. But I've tried that word before, and those feelings, and look where it got me."

"Abjuring love? Real people don't do that. Now you're the one who sounds like someone on a stage. That's not the real world. Real people follow their hearts, wherever it takes them. Real people refuse to be put into a little tiny box. You can say you love me or you don't love me, it doesn't matter; I know you have forsworn nothing except an existence you found intolerable."

She really did smile this time. "Now you're making me sound like a heroine. Be honest, Lucius. For all that you go on about the real world with its real people, you don't really want to live in it, either."

"I like," he said in a nobleman's lazy drawl, "to have some choice of which world I inhabit, that's all."

"Yes. And so do I. Which is why I am perfectly content where I am, and as I am." She went to the table, straightened some brushes there. "Really, I don't know why I made such a scene. I must be spending too much time with the theatre. China is so much more restful. All those nice patterns. I'd better get back to it."

"Well, then," he said.

"Well, then." She kissed him, long and hard. "And you have business of your own to attend to." Teresa buttoned up his jacket. "Go to your card party. Come back when you can."

I SAW HIM COME OUT THE DOOR IN A HOODED CLOAK, old-fashioned and concealing. But I knew who it was. Lord Lucius Perry walked off up the street, and I followed him. He was headed up toward the Hill, and never looked behind him.

The house he stopped at was one of the grand ones, guarded, with a wall. The gates were open, and the house was brightly lit. Not one of his secret visits, then. A party in a noble's house. I thought about following him through the gates, trying to pass as a guest, and then I thought, What for? They wouldn't want me. Nobody did. Alcuin had been right: I was a *thing*, a sword for folk to bet on, a toy for actresses to play with. Even the mysterious Lucius Perry, the duke's pet, the Riverside prostitute, the painter's secret visitor, even Lucius Perry had places he could go, where he could sit and talk and eat and drink like a normal person, but I was nothing.

I stood outside the gate, my velvet cloak drawn tight around me against the cold. It was getting dark. How was I going to get safely back to Riverside? I'd need to hire a torch. It was a long way, through a bad part of town, and I was tired.

"Out of the way, damn you!"

A chaise carried by two burly men nearly ran me down as they turned into the gate. My heart was pounding with shock and rage, now that they were gone by. But as they came out, I saw they bore no crest and might be for hire.

"Stop," I said hoarsely. "Will you carry me to Riverside?"

"'S a long way. You want four men for that."

"To the Bridge, then, will you do that?"

"Maybe. Cost you. Two in silver—and we'll see your money, first."

I dug in my pocket for the theatre change. Eight coppers and five minnows was all I had left. I remembered the weight of the gold chain I'd just carried, and suddenly I felt hot and angry. I wasn't the duke's messenger boy. If my uncle wanted me to do him favors, let him pay for them. The Duke Tremontaine didn't think about these things? Well then, I would.

"To the duke's house in Riverside," I said. "The steward there will pay you—three silver." He could afford it. "And if you won't take it, I'll find others who will."

They were good chair men; it wasn't too bumpy a ride. But even if it had been, I was too tired to mind much. I closed my eyes and saw the stage, the brightly costumed actors trying so hard to be Mangrove and Fabian, Tyrian and Stella for us all, and the men and women crowding around afterwards, with their little swords and roses. I didn't want to think about the crop-haired, trousered Viola, but she was like a sore tooth I just had to poke at. Was I like her? Did I want to be?

The Black Rose had kissed her, and then kissed me. I thought of the way the actress's hair had smelt, how soft it was

under my hands, and I felt that warmth again at the cleft of my
legs. It wasn't quite as fierce this time, and I remembered that I
had, in fact, felt something like it before.

When I was very small, my nurse had caught me sleeping
with my blanket ruched up between my legs because it felt nice,
the way swinging on a tree branch sometimes did. She said,
"Don't you be rubbing yourself there. Do you want to start growing a birdie, like your brothers'?"

When I asked her if she had rubbed their birdies to make
them grow, she'd laughed so hard she could barely talk, and then
she said, "Indeed I did; and when you're married, you'll rub your
husband's to make it grow, oh yes you will."

When I was a little older, the cook's daughter took me to
help her feed the fowl in the yard and explained what the rooster
was doing to the hens, and how I was to think nothing of it, for
every creature on earth did the same. My mother said that wasn't
quite true, for men and women weren't like the brute beasts; we
had to be married first for it to work.

I'd never thought of all these things at once, never connected each story to the others, and as the chair bumped along, I
unraveled and interwove them.

Of course I wasn't growing a birdie now. I shook my head and
snorted at my panic in the theatre. I wasn't a baby. Women had
pleasure down there. I just hadn't known it could take you so suddenly like that, for no reason.

My grandmother—my mother's mother, and the duke's—had
a special chapel in her house. It was because she was Reform,
which seemed to mean she believed that everything wrong with
the world was because the old kings had been especially evil and
done things to displease the gods, and the nobles who overthrew
them had been cleansing the land of impurities. She was very pi-
ous and always lit candles on the Feast of the Last King's Fall, and
told me about our heroic ancestor, who had killed him in a duel.
She tried to get me to be Reform, too, but I was very young when
she died, and I hadn't met anyone Reform since then. I thought
about the things she'd said that had not quite made sense, and realized that what she'd meant about the kings being so awful was

not so much that the kings had not always been married, but that they had gone with other men.

No wonder my uncle wasn't speaking to her when she died.

Was I really like him? Did it run in families, after all?

No. There was no way on earth I would ever take up with someone like the horrible Alcuin, let alone start getting drunk and inviting fifteen naked people into my bedroom. Not on this earth. I was not like that, and never would be. I pulled my cloak tight around me—and shivered at the memory that assailed me, the thing I'd almost managed to forget. Last Night, and the fire-light at Highcombe, and the sense that my uncle belonged there, in that small room with me and the master. He belonged there as much as I did, because St Vier loved him the way the old kings were not supposed to love people, and whatever my uncle did with the others, he loved the man at Highcombe almost too much to bear.

Well, if I ever loved anyone that much, man or woman, I would never do what he did. I'd been happy at Highcombe; I knew where I was and what I was doing there. And the duke had come and ruined everything, and dragged me back here where I didn't belong. He couldn't stay at Highcombe with the person he loved best in the world, so I couldn't either. He was a selfish crazy pig and I hated him utterly.

I cried then, because it was all so hopeless and I was so lonely and nothing and no one made any sense at all. This city was a terrible place. Look what had happened to Artemisia. When I first came to the city and met her, she had everything I thought I'd wanted, and look where she was now.

I wondered if she had seen the play, and what she would think of it, and what she would think of the Black Rose, and what she would think of me if she knew that Rose had kissed me. In her letters to me, Artemisia signed herself *Lady Stella*. Did she really think of me as Fabian, the peerless and righteous master swordsman? I was glad I had a sword to defend her; I liked being her champion. But what about the kiss that came after?

Would Artemisia kiss me, too, if I wanted her to? What if I killed Mangrove, and then stood over her and said, "Lady Stella, though your enemies sought your destruction, I have made them my own, and made them pay the price for it," what then?

I would definitely kiss Lady Stella. I wasn't sure about Artemisia, though. She was inclined to be a little silly, and not always reliable.

The chaise set down with a bump. I pulled back the curtain and found we were already at the Riverside house. I hadn't even known we'd crossed the Bridge. The house's torches were burning, and my friend Ralph was one of the guards at the door. I got out of the chaise as grandly as I could (considering my feet were so cold I could no longer feel them), gathering my cloak and my sword about me, and, "Ralph," I said, "please see to it that these men are paid. Three silver, not a minnow more. Oh, and make sure they get something hot to drink. It was a long trip."

I went inside the house. I felt as if I had been gone a hundred years, but it was just past dinnertime (the duke dined early and sometimes, when he got hungry, he dined twice). Betty was in the servants' hall. I went and rousted her, and she took my hat and cloak up to my room with me.

"Feather's ruined," she said. "Good show, then, eh, my lady?"

"It was all right."

"Never mind, we'll get you another. Dinner's past; I'll bring you up a tray."

"Take it to Marcus's room, then; I want to go see how he is."

"Sick is how he is," Betty said firmly, "and Cora is nursing him. But I've been wanting to talk about that," she continued ominously. My heart skipped a beat. Was Marcus sicker than we'd thought? Had his throat turned septic?

I grabbed Betty's hand. "What? What is it?"

"Sit down," she said, and I sat. "Don't be in such a twitter, my lady. You know I've got some experience of the world..."

"What's that to do with Marcus?"

"I've made some mistakes, we all have, and I don't want to see you making the same ones." She shook out my cloak, and started unbuttoning my jacket. "There, do you see?"

Not Marcus, then; only her usual rambling about her past. "I'm hungry, Betty; just get my dinner, will you?"

"You're growing," she said. "I'm going to have to start corseting you tighter. It's a pity; I could push them up just so to make the most of what you've got ... But it would ruin the line."

"I don't care about the line. Can I have my dressing gown? I want to go see Marcus."

"Now that," she said, "is what I'm talking about. You haven't got a mother, and your uncle doesn't care, but I'm here to tell you that you shouldn't be visiting that boy alone in his room, let alone half-dressed."

"Don't be ridiculous. Anyhow, Cora's there."

"Cora's there and he's too sick to move. But what about after-wards, I ask you?"

"Afterwards what?"

My maid stood over me, shaking her head. "*You* may be the little innocent, but that boy never was—and he's plenty old now to play the fool with you, my lady."

For a moment I wanted to hit her. But then I looked at her red round little pudding face and remembered it was only Betty, after all.

"Don't worry," I said. "Marcus is not like that, and neither am I. We talk, and we play shesh, and anyhow the duke keeps us too busy to get up to anything." I felt a rush of warmth toward her. She might not be much, but she did care about me, in her way. And so did Marcus, of course. It was funny that, when I'd been so miserable in the chaise, I had forgotten all about him.

chapter IX

T HE NEXT TIME IT PLEASED THE DUKE TREMONTAINE
to attend a meeting of the Council of Lords, he seemed to
be the subject of more than usual interest. Whenever
there was a lull in the proceedings, people would turn to look at
him—pretending to be talking to a neighbor, or checking the pro-
cession of the sun out the window, but their heads turned in his direction.

What have I done now? he thought. It couldn't be Galing
or Davenant, that was old business. Were they only just getting wind of the events of the Rogues' Ball? Surely not. But it
was something to do with Katherine. When they met in the
hallway outside, Lord Ferris himself remarked pleasantly, "A
spirited girl, your young niece. The next time you have business
for her in Council, you should bring her with you, though. She's
a bit rough around the edges, particularly for a Tremontaine
lady."

"Like the former duchess," Alec replied, "my niece professes
no interest in politics." He said it automatically, because it was an
easy dig at the man who had once been the duchess's lover and

political mouthpiece; the rest of his mind was busy wondering what the Crescent was talking about.

"Teach her, then," said Ferris. "It will keep her off the streets, and out of other people's business."

"My niece is quite safe on the streets," the duke said frostily. "I've seen to that."

YOUR NIECE IS PERFECTLY CHARMING," THE BLACK Rose told him when she visited him that night in Riverside, in the red velvet chamber. "Is she really your niece?"

"She's really my niece. My sister gave birth to her, a few years back."

"Then you should be more kind to her."

"*What?*" The duke dropped her leg back on the bed.

"She's very young. The young are hungry, very hungry for all sorts of things, and half the time they don't even know what they are. Do *you* know?"

"I'm perfectly kind to her," he said. "I sent her to the theatre, didn't I?"

"Do you even remember when you were her age?" The actress stroked his back with her foot. "You must have been a perfect horror. All arms and legs and rage and nameless lusts."

"That," he purred, "is precisely my point. I'm not having her go through what I went through, or what my sister did, either."

"You're a funny man." Her foot moved down his body. "You don't get this close to many women, but it would never occur to you to ask me what it is a young girl wants."

"I don't care what she wants. I know what's good for her."

"Heavens." She lay back, arms stretched over her head in the enormous bed. "Is that your mother's or your father's voice I'm hearing?" He reared up, startled. "Are you going to throw me out of bed?" she asked languidly.

"Possibly."

"I may be an actress, my lord, but I'm not stupid." He closed his fingers around her wrists, and she let him stretch his length upon her; allowing him the upper hand, she felt more secure in digging deeper. "What about the boy," she asked, "the shadowy one who follows you? He's not a relative, too, is he?"

"Leave the boy alone," he said sharply. "Nobody touches Marcus."

"Not even you?"

His fingers dug into her wrists. But he made his voice light. "I would be very much surprised if he ever asked me to. Meanwhile, you are not to bother him. Do you understand?"

She said, "When we quarreled, Lord Ferris said that I had played too many Empresses. What he meant was that I thought I was his equal. You would never say that, but you might be under the illusion that I am a creature of huge uncontrollable lusts for everything that moves, including awkward young boys."

"I never—"

"It's all right. I'm just telling you how annoying it is for me when people confuse me with my roles, that's all."

"Believe me, I have no desire to sleep with the Empress."

"Good. Do you know, I don't think you're mad at all."

"Stick around."

"I will."

"And tell me more," he said, "about Lord Ferris."

⌢

Sweetest Katherine, my One True Friend—

How long it seems since we were girls together, innocently comparing beaux at the Tr—— Ball! How I treasure our time together! I still have the feather I wore in my hair that night— some might call it a plume—but its lustre is sadly faded—or perhaps 'tis the dullness of mine eye that makes it seem so. I am sure that if you saw me now, you would not look twice—for my eyes are red with perpetual weeping—and yet, such is the virtue of your eyes that I know you would see into my heart as you have always done, and view with kindness the crushed flower hiding there. Oh, when I think of him I feel vile and disgusting! But then I picture your dear face, flushed with righteous wrath, and it is as if your angry tears can wash away my stain.

Like Stella at the races, I see much but say little—and I
believe that, like Fabian, you keep faith with me despite
appearances. Oh, do let me hear from you! If only to tell me
that you are well, and remember your loving—

A F-L

The handwriting was large and loopy and violet, and it just
about broke my heart. But what could I do? I'd challenged Lord
Ferris, and he'd refused me. Poor Artemisia! I'd hoped at least the
challenge would frighten the Crescent into crying off, but it
hadn't done even that. Nevertheless, she must be answered. I
dashed off a reply.

Lady S—
Know that you and your grievance, though little talked on,
are far from forgotten. I watch and wait, and will prevail.
Have you seen the play yet?
Your assured friend,

KT

I sealed it with candlewax and stuffed it in my jacket, and set
out to find my delivery boy. But in the hallway I met Marcus,
capped and booted and mufflered, a handkerchief in his fist.
"It's the chairs," he snuffled. "He wants to go see the chairs."
"What are you doing out of bed?"
"I'm bored. I want to see them, too."
"What chairs?"
"New ones." He coughed. "New design. It's a fine day. Like
spring. We're walking. Want to come?"
"Love to."
So the fine springlike day found the three of us sloshing
through the fine Riverside mud on our way to a shop that would
have been more than happy to bring the chairs to us if we'd been
content to stay indoors. Ever since my trip to the theatre, I'd
been taking more care to dress well when I went out; if people
saw me, I wanted them to see someone who mattered. Today I
wore my green suit, though not my velvet cloak, with an embroidered scabbard and a shirt whose cuffs were trimmed with lace.

My uncle noticed. "Pretty," he said, "but hardly practical. You're my swordsman, not my maid of honor. Steel catches on lace; Richard would never wear it. If it comes to a fight, now, you'll tuck your cuffs under. I know you're a young girl full of nameless lusts involving fashion, but you don't want to die of vanity your next fight. Whenever that may be." He looked around and shrugged. "It's a wonder you've gone unchallenged, after your triumph at Sabina's ball. In the old days, they would have been lined up around the block to try you, the bright new blade in town. No one has any ambition anymore—they just want to sit on their nicely muscled asses drawing nobles' pay to defend the indefensible."

"I'm in your household," I pointed out before he could say any more about swordsmen's anatomy. "They might be afraid a challenge to me is an insult to you."

"Riverside." He sighed gustily, and stepped around an indescribable pile of something that had emerged from the melted snow. "It's not what it was."

"Whose fault is that?" Marcus muttered. We crossed the Bridge, and picked up a couple more guards at the Tremontaine postern.

I had a thought. "But," I asked, "if I *were* to maybe challenge someone, challenge him on my own, I mean, without your authority—would I be able to do that?"

The duke stopped in the middle of the street. Marcus and the guards and I stopped with him and narrowly missed being run over by a carriage that was barreling up behind us. Our retainers and the carriage lackeys had it out while His Grace of Tremontaine regarded me fixedly from above.

"Such as?" he asked. "What sort of hypothetical person were you hypothetically thinking of maybe challenging?" I couldn't say anything. "Not some bravo," the duke hypothesized, "in a tavern brawl or street fight . . . not your style. Those are boys' games."

"Do you think," I asked, momentarily distracted, "they don't even want to fight me? They think, because I'm a girl, I'm not even worth bothering with? Or is it just because I'm related?"

"I don't know," the duke said. Behind us the two factions were close to blows. "Tremontaine makes place for no one!"

shouted Ralph, our man. That was certainly true. The duke was placidly ignoring the whole fracas. "But I would very much prefer that you not spill your blood for anything trivial."

"It's not trivial!" I blurted out.

"My Lord of Tremontaine!" a well-bred voice called from the carriage. "If you please! I have a very sick rabbit in here!"

"A rabbit?" said Marcus. "May I see?"

"Bloody Furnival and his stupid pets," the duke growled. "It bites. And he said it's diseased. What are you all doing, standing in the middle of the street—you're supposed to be protecting me, not encouraging nobles with unnatural tastes to run me down!"

But he did not forget.

We went and saw the chairs, and he ordered a dozen, all curvy and strange—very modern, he said approvingly—and we were going to stop at White's for chocolate when he suddenly said, "No, let's go on to Tremontaine House. I want to see the room they'll go in, while it's fresh in my mind. Do you know," he said cheerfully as we trudged on up the Hill, "maybe I should have the whole room redone to match them? Soften the angles of the walls, with molding, maybe, so it's all nothing but curves? That would help take the curse off the place."

We were passing the street that Lucius Perry's sweetheart lived on. I glanced over at Marcus to see if he'd catch my eye, and I didn't like what I saw. My friend's face was pale, his eyes were bleary and his forehead looked damp. I sidled over to him. "Go home," I said.

Marcus coughed. "We're almost there."

"All right, but when we get to Tremontaine House, you're going straight to bed." He didn't have the strength to do anything but nod, and when we hit a steep part, he actually took my arm.

Astonishingly, Tremontaine House was ready to receive us. Marcus went upstairs to collapse on clean sheets. The staff set a table in the pretty room overlooking the garden, and the duke and I sat down there to a small collation of chocolate and biscuits, dried fruit and nuts. Outside the tall windows, the blooming witch hazel and forsythia made streaks of bright color against the general gloom.

"Almost spring," my uncle remarked. "Riverside is turning into a swamp already. We'll bring the household back up here soon."

Just when I'd gotten used to Riverside, he wanted to move me again. It figured. "It's so quiet up here," I said. "Kind of boring, don't you think?"

"I do my best," he drawled, "to enliven it. Tell me, Katherine: does this hypothetical challenge of yours involve one of the neighbors up here?"

I sloshed chocolate all over my saucer. "What challenge?"

"The one everybody in the city appears to know about but me."

"That isn't so! No one knows about it except Lord—" I felt myself flush with the embarrassment of having walked right into his trap. "I was very discreet," I added lamely.

"Discreet is good," my uncle said encouragingly. He was leaning across the table toward me, like a tutor trying to help me with my arithmetic. "Now, then, where does he live?"

"I don't know, exactly."

"You can't fight him if you can't find him, Katherine."

"I can find him."

"I can help—discreetly, of course. This is, as you say, your fight. What's the cause?"

"It's—personal."

His whole body tightened like a string that had been pulled. "How personal? Has someone offered you insult?"

He was so like a father in a book, I couldn't help smiling. "Please," I said as airily as possible, "I can manage."

"Of course you can, I've seen to that. But if anyone has done anything, anything *bad* to you, rest assured that I—"

It was his usual polished hauteur, all drawly and annoying, but I paid attention and saw that his green eyes were glittering and very fierce. I actually reached across the table and touched his hand. "Nothing like that. I'm fine. It's for someone else, a friend."

He looked, if anything, fiercer. "Not your friend Marcus?"

"Marcus? Of course not. Someone else. I can't tell you, though. It's a secret."

The duke nearly choked on his chocolate. "My dear! I've got

more secrets than you've got teeth in your mouth. Believe me, I can keep a secret." I didn't say anything. "Never mind," he said, "I can find out. Will you tell me who it is you're challenging, or do I have to lock you in your room and feed you on bread and wa-ter 'til I starve it out of you?"

"It doesn't matter," I said glumly. "He refused me."

My uncle put down his cup. "Hold on. You issued a public challenge to a noble of this city, and he turned you down?"

"It wasn't very public. Just one or two other men there, and then he took me aside and told me not to be silly. I could kill him just for that. He wasn't taking me seriously at all. He kept thinking I'd come from you, even though I told him I hadn't."

My uncle raised his eyebrows, and then his face broke into a slow, delighted grin. "It's Ferris," he said. "You've challenged the Crescent Chancellor. No wonder he never comes to see me any-more."

"He's not—is he a friend of yours?" I hadn't thought of that. I'd never seen Lord Ferris at any of Tremontaine's gatherings, but clearly he didn't have much self-control when it came to the kinds of things the duke didn't either, so maybe...

"The ways in which Ferris is no friend to me are beyond counting. That goes for Tremontaine in general: he's got a grudge against the lot of us; he'll kill you if he thinks he can. Fortunately I know some of his secrets, so he's chary of us. Old ones, and new ones, too. What's the latest? What has he done to this friend of yours?"

"I can't tell you," I said miserably. "It's too shameful. And it isn't my secret. It's a question of honor."

My uncle took a deep breath. "Look. Did you tell Ferris what the challenge was about?"

"Of course I did. He did it!—the thing. The thing I'm chal-lenging him about."

"La, la." My uncle shook his head sadly. "She'll tell Lord Ferris what she won't tell me." His eyes met mine. He looked seri-ous all of a sudden. "There are quite a few things Ferris has to be ashamed about. One of them concerns money. One of them con-cerns the Black Rose." The mention of the actress startled me.

My uncle watched me for a moment, and then, satisfied that the challenge did not concern her, went on, "Now, Ferris doesn't know I know about either of those things, not yet. He won't be pleased when he finds out, assuming he ever does. But I can take care of myself; indeed, knowing things about him can be very useful to me. For you, though...for you, it's different. If you know something bad about him that no one else knows, he isn't going to feel entirely safe around you. And a worried Ferris can turn very nasty."

My uncle leaned back in his chair; I thought of a tutor again, as he raised his chin to the ceiling. "Think of secrets," he told me, "as being like money. The more you have—of other people's, I mean—the richer you are, and the more likely to be able to afford something you want when you really need it. Now, I'm the head of the family, which means I hold most of the family fortune: houses, land...and secrets. You are a junior member, and you hold—one. Give it to me, and you add to the family fortunes. Keep it, and I'm going to set a guard on you. Just in case the Crescent Chancellor decides he'd rather you didn't tell anyone after all."

I stared down at my knuckles. I didn't think he was bluffing. He was really worried.

"If I tell you," I said, "do you promise not to tell anyone else?"

My uncle nodded.

"And if you think it's stupid, you won't lock me in my room and refuse to let me fight?"

He looked at the ceiling. "Good question. Will I? Let's say I won't, this time."

"What you were saying before," I muttered, "when you thought it might be me? It wasn't me; it was someone else."

"Forgive my bluntness, but I need to get this straight: Anthony Deverin, Lord Ferris, raped a girl, and now you want to kill him for it?"

"I'm not sure I'm going to kill him. He has to admit it was wrong, and beg her forgiveness."

"Are you in love with her yourself?"

I could feel myself turning an interesting color. But I wasn't going to give way to him now. I said, "Is that all you can think about?"

"Not all. I just wanted to make sure."

"Well, it's not the point. The point is, he did this awful thing against her will, and he doesn't care, and her family doesn't care—they all want her to get married to him anyway, and she doesn't want to, and nobody's going to do anything about it if I don't!"

"Ahhh." The duke nodded in satisfaction. "The little Fitz-Levi." He shook his head mournfully. "Oh, Ferris. Those years in Arkenvelt have coarsened you, I fear, and given you a trader's soul: tasting the wares before the final sale." He said to me, "You are quite right to call him out. That's no way to behave, with him thinking he can have whatever he wants whenever he wants it. Let him learn some humility first. It's a lesson he's got long a-coming; he's always treated women badly, and only the one time did we make him pay for it." Lost inside a memory, the duke cut a long spiral of apple peel; then he looked up and said, "He's not young, you know. He can't go on like this forever. Tell your little friend to do her utmost, and maybe he'll drop dead on his wedding night."

I said, "That's disgusting. Aren't you listening? She doesn't want to marry him."

"You're not thinking it through," he said at his most supercil-iously annoying. "She's damaged goods. Now that she's ruined, marriage to Ferris is the only safe course open to her."

"How can you say that," I hissed, "you of all people? How can you say it's *safe* for her? To live for the rest of her life with some-one who could do something like that?" I found that I had risen to my feet and was leaning over the table glaring at him. "Someone *you* don't even like?"

"Oh, thank you," he said dryly. "Sit down, please. I only meant, safe in the eyes of the world. I didn't say I approved. You should know that—you, of all people."

But I did not sit down. "Then *do* something," I said. "Why don't you *do* something, if it matters to you so much? The truth is, you don't care about her. You don't care about any of us, and you're not going to do anything. But I do, and I will."

His knuckles were very white against the table's rim. I was afraid I'd gone too far. But his voice, when he spoke, was measured and calm. "Let me understand you clearly," he said, as though testing a mathematical proof. "You are going to cry challenge against Lord Ferris, not merely to avenge a wrong, but so that this girl need not marry against her will?"

"I'm going to challenge him because you can't treat people that way. No one seems to realize it; no one seems to care. *He* certainly doesn't. He thinks he owns her already, and her parents do, too—and even you. It makes me sick."

My uncle was looking up at me with the strangest expression, as if he were going to cry, if such a thing were possible. What he said next was even more confusing: "Katherine?" There was a curious smile on his face, as if he were telling himself a story that he liked very much. "What do you want for your birthday?"

What did I want? He was the Duke Tremontaine. There was a lot he could give me. There was a lot he had taken from me, too. Why was he asking me this now, all of a sudden? I didn't know what to say. "I'll think about it."

"Good enough. Now sit down. You're right. I'm not going to do anything. I'm going to let you do it." I sat. "So." He was all business now. "You challenged Ferris once, but he did not accept. Neither did you revoke the challenge. So as far as he knows, you could appear any day with a skewer to his gut. He won't like that."

"I told him he could apologize to her."

The duke smiled. "Oh, *that* will definitely happen. When the river boils over. But that's not the point anymore."

"Why not? He's insulted her honor. It isn't as if girls don't have any."

"Have you asked yourself why he doesn't want a fight? And why he's so insistent that the marriage go forward despite your friend's objections?" He held up a hand. "Don't start. I'm not that coarse; I'm sure he had a lovely time wherever he did it with her, but it's not like Ferris to think with his—ah, his privates. He did it to secure the wedding. He did it to secure the funds."

"Isn't he rich already?"

The duke bisected an apple with the paring knife. "Nope. That's his little secret—the one I have, the one he must be afraid is going to come out."

"How do you know?"

"I know it because...people tell me things they shouldn't." He took a bite from the apple and grinned. "Sometimes I pay them to. Terrible. Trust no one; or if you do, try not to have any secrets."

"I don't understand."

"Ferris always liked being twisty. Overcomplication has been his downfall in the past. Before you were born, he tried to double-cross your great-grandmother—that's her, there on the wall." He pointed to the glorious lady in grey silk, the portrait with the flamingo mallet I had so admired. "It was my pleasure to ruin him the first time, and get him sent to Arkenvelt. From which he returned about ten years ago, laden with furs which he turned into cash, and so was able to buy his way back into society, a good marriage and back up the rungs of the Council of Lords to his present glorious position. But he never had much land, what he's got is mortgaged to the hilt, and now he's nearly out of cash. He has nothing left to fall back on except what he can create for himself. It's perfectly obvious: every bill he supports, every vote he casts is designed to feather his own nest—taxing the landowners, encouraging trade...It makes him look progressive—Karleigh's cronies just hate him, but for all the wrong reasons.

"Politics. I'm boring you. I should start sending you to Council meetings—then you'd know what boredom is. But listen: Ferris needs this marriage. And he needs you not to mess it up. You're lucky he's not taking you too seriously, or he would have had you knifed on the street."

I felt cold. "But that's dishonorable!"

"Ferris has no more real sense of honor than that doorknob. Honor is a tool he uses to manipulate others. Challenge him soon. Do it right; do it in public with everyone watching. Then he can't weasel out. Do you want to rid us all of him forever, or give him time to find a swordsman to take the challenge for him?"

"I don't think I should kill him."

"Probably not. Killing a noble in challenge means it goes to the Court of Honor, and then everything would come out. Either that, or I'd have to step forward and claim the challenge myself, and I'm not really interested in the eternal gratitude of the Fitz-Levis. No, you just fight his champion, and refuse to answer any questions after. Say it was a private affair of honor. People will draw their own conclusions, but with any luck they'll get it wrong, and you'll keep your friend's name out of it. But do it by the book, and do it soon."

"How soon?"

"Because I am your uncle and I have many employees, I will make it my business to learn Lord Ferris's schedule for tomorrow and the next day. That soon."

I nodded.

The duke rose. "Oh, and Katherine . . ."

"Yes, uncle?"

"Where's Marcus?"

"In bed. He's sick again."

"Well, never mind; I'll just write a letter and send it down to Riverside, and then you can ask Marcus where—oh, never mind; I can find the stuff myself."

It was the last time I saw him sober that night.

I went up to make sure Marcus was all right. He was dozing in bed. His room here was smaller than the one in the Riverside house, but it was cozy, with a fire lit and rain beginning to patter against the windows. He opened his eyes when I came in, and I sent for some broth for him and watched him drink it.

It was comforting just to sit with him in silence. There was so much I couldn't tell him now, about Lord Ferris and Artemisia and what the duke had said to me. But Marcus and I had secrets of our own.

"We can't just keep calling her 'Lucius Perry's friend,'" I said aloud.

"Ah." Marcus smiled. "We don't have to. I found out her name."

"How did you . . . ?"

"I do get out occasionally, you know." He sounded like the duke, only with such a bad cough I didn't have the heart to deny him his triumph.

"All right, tell me."

"Her name is Teresa Grey."

"Who told you?"

"No one. I read it on a letter she left lying on a table."

"You went into her studio?!"

"Don't be an idiot. I went over the wall again. She wasn't there, so I went right up to the window and saw it."

"I can't believe you went without me."

"I would have taken you if I'd been able to find you. But you've been hard to find these days. Anyway, it wasn't for long."

I did not tell him that I had gone there without him, too, the day of the theatre. What was there to tell, really? I hadn't seen any letters, just lurked on the street and followed Lucius Perry up the Hill to a gate I'd been scared to go through. I hadn't told Marcus about the theatre, either, or the Black Rose, or anything. I owed him. And so I said, "All right. You are remarkable. Teresa Grey. I like that name."

Marcus lay back and closed his eyes. "Isn't it lovely, Katie?"

"What?"

"Knowing something *he* doesn't know."

"What if he does know?"

"He doesn't. I'd bet on it."

I giggled. "Maybe we should offer to sell him the information. He likes secrets."

"Not this one. This one's ours."

"Ours and Teresa Grey's." My friend's eyes were shut; he looked as if he were dreaming already. Softly I said, "He'd be furious if he knew we were doing this."

"He doesn't own us. He's the Duke Tremontaine, he's not the king of the entire world."

"What if he finds out?"

"He won't."

"And we won't tell him, will we?"

When Marcus opened his eyes, they were brown and disarming and utterly frank. "I see no reason to. Do you?"

I tucked his blanket back in. "None whatsoever. Good night."

I passed the duke's study. The hall smelt of a peculiar, sweet smoke; I went past quickly. I could hear him crashing around in there, calling for Marcus. I went downstairs and found a footman who could take care of him, and the staff gave me some hot soup and tried to pump me for gossip from the Riverside house, so I went back upstairs through the dark and empty house, and found myself standing in front of the doors with the wet rabbits on them. Funny to think about the first time I'd seen them, with Betty nervous beside me, and me nervous clutching my short cloak to hide my legs. And Master Venturus waiting behind the door, to teach me how not hold sword. And me maybe having already met Marcus, but not knowing really who he was, and still dreaming of sweeping down staircases in a ballgown . . . It was the same day I ran away to see Artemisia. I had not yet picked up a sword. I had not met Richard St Vier.

I went into the dark room; the mirrors gave it what glow there was, but I didn't need to see much. I thought of Highcombe, of the man practicing there with no opponent, who might be practicing now. I ran through the opening moves of a fight, any fight, and then I started thinking about what he would do next, and moved to counter him.

⌒

IN THE MORNING, WHEN I WENT TO PUT MY JACKET back on, I found my note to Artemisia still tucked up inside it. I opened it up and sat down and added these words:

Sweetest Lady Stella,

A challenge has been issued, and awaits but the turning of the tide to bear a bitter fruit—bitter for some, but sweet, I hope, to your tongue, and a balm to your sad eyes. I told you he'd regret it, and I wasn't joking. Be of good courage—hold fast,

and keep faith, for I will meet his champion on the field of
battle, and blot out your stain with his blood.
      Not Fabian, but True and Faithful

                                              TYRIAN

I signed it with a flourish, and sealed it with several blobs of
the duke's best wax.

Part IV

CHALLENGE

chapter I

MARCUS WAS BETTER THE NEXT DAY, BUT THE duke was badly hung over and didn't want anyone near him whom he could hear breathing. I felt jittery about the challenge, jittery about the letter I'd written to Artemisia (which I'd sent by the simple expedient of charging one of the Tremontaine House servants to safely deliver it to her maid). I didn't want Marcus to ask why. To distract us both, I proposed a little stroll down to what I jauntily referred to as "Lucius Perry's Love Nest."

To our silent delight, Perry was there, too. He was sitting on the sofa in a loose dressing gown, drinking chocolate and watching Teresa paint. He must have spent the night: the gown was a flowered print of yellow-gold on a dusky green that looked wonderful with her auburn hair, but didn't do a thing for his complexion. Knowing he was wrapped up in one of her gowns, and that he was slight enough to fit in it, made me feel tremendously tender toward them both.

It was a very domestic scene. We watched as Perry reached for more chocolate, and then he felt in the pocket of the gown and pulled out a folded paper, its seal broken, and looked hard at it.

Teresa Grey had gotten a letter, too.

⁓

Another one?"

"Don't open it," she said swiftly. "It's just more nonsense: ravings and accusations, pleading and boasting. . . . I shouldn't even break the seals anymore. I should just throw them in the fire." Her fingers closed on his, forbidding him the paper.

"Why do they let him?"

"They don't *let* him, Lucius, they force him to write. He doesn't really want me. They egg him on, they keep him in drink until he's all fired up and turns out his pages. I doubt he remembers a day later what he's done."

"But why? Why won't they let you go?"

"Cruelty, I suppose. And oddly enough, I'm still their last best hope for an heir. If the marriage is dissolved, they'd never find anyone else to take him as he is now."

Perry's face contorted with revulsion. "An heir."

"Well, we tried," she said. "Before I left, we tried."

"All right, that's it." He got up from the couch, hitching up his robe. "I'm an idiot. I don't know why I didn't think of this sooner. It's so much simpler, really."

"What is?"

"I'm going to kill him."

"You can't kill Roderick!"

"Yes, I can. It's simple." He put one foot up on the windowsill, looking back over his shoulder. "I know exactly how it's done. Find a swordsman, pay him to challenge poor Roderick to the death without warning, and *poof!* No more letters. No more husband. And you are free to choose. . ." he opened his robe ". . . another." She giggled, and came to his arms. He closed the robe around them both. "Choose me," he murmured, feeling her settle against him.

"No," she murmured. He felt her smile against his neck.

"Or not," he added agreeably. "You'll be free, at any rate."

"But really, Lucius, you mustn't do it. You mustn't think of it."

"Oh?" He drew back, wrapping the robe around himself. "Do you harbor still some tenderness for this forest god of yours?"

"Don't be disgusting. I harbor some desire to keep my privacy intact, and to keep you out of prison."

"Prison? For what?"

"For *this*, Lucius!" she said angrily. "For playing with their property! I married their son; in the eyes of the law, I'm their property yet. Don't you understand that?"

"The laws of challenge—"

"Yes, yes, I know. Your swordsman will slay him and then you'll stand up in the Court of Honor and proudly tell everyone why you killed their son. And the Lords Justiciar will say, 'Well, that's all right, then, never mind; just take her and be happy.' Is that what you're thinking?"

"I'll keep it private. If I must, I'll pay the swordsman to lie."

"And Roddy's family will swoop in with the truth. For all I know they've got spies on me already, and are just saving the juicy facts until they need them—which is to say, in case I ever try anything."

"But—"

"This isn't a game to me: the hiding, the being secret. I'm not doing it for fun, like you. If our liaison became public—and I assure you, if you challenge Roderick and kill him, it will be—then all that still makes my life tolerable will be taken from me in the wake of the ensuing scandal."

"You're a scandal already. You left your husband, you write trash for a living—"

"It isn't trash. And that's a secret. All everyone knows is that I live on the kindness of others, in a house provided by a sympathetic cousin. I make my pin money from friends who buy my china painting. That's the life I live, and the world will put up with it as long as they don't know any other."

"*I* know it," he said quietly.

"Yes. You do know. And I know yours."

He smiled. "Do you think that's why we get along so well?"

"You love your secrets. I merely require mine. It is why I trust you, though."

"You can trust me with anything."

"Can I trust you to be careful? You love danger, you love the sense that you could be caught at any time." In answer, he kissed her hand, bowing low. She touched his hair. "You are my only luxury, Lucius. So far, the cost hasn't been too high. Which is why there will be no challenge. Not from you."

He straightened. "I am a noble of the House of Perry. I have the right to call challenge where honor has been offended."

"Stop playing," she said irritably. "If you won't respect my secrets, have a thought to yours. Challenge him, and they will surely come out. You would hate it, you know you would. But if self-sacrifice is your current dangerous passion, spare a thought for how I'd feel watching them spend my dowry on their petty persecution of us both."

"At least you'd get your dowry back in the end."

"You think so? You've never hired lawyers, have you? And how would the rest of the noble House of Perry feel? Your family would cast you off, Lucius, they'd have to. Even if you're enjoying the image of yourself as my noble champion, this is one role I won't let you try out."

"It doesn't matter," he said softly. "It's not as if I can't support us both."

"Oh, lovely," she said, choking back angry tears. "You'll pay for our room and board by selling your body in Riverside. I'd like that. And when you can't work, I'll support you painting flowers on china and writing drama for whatever theatre will take it as long as they can pretend they don't know who it came from...."

"Intolerable," he growled, "the lot of them. I'll start with him, and then I'll pick them off, one by one, see if I don't."

"You might kill my husband with some justice," she said gently, "for his offenses against me. You cannot kill them all, my Lucius. And you would have to kill them all, to make the world a safe place for the likes of us."

"*He* talks like that, sometimes," Lucius Perry said thoughtfully. "When he talks to me at all."

"*No.*" She seized his wrist in her strong fingers. "Stop think-ing what you're thinking. I'm not having it."

"He likes me. He says I'm not a hypocrite. I think he'd like you."

"Lucius, no."

"What's the point of having the Duke Tremontaine as a pa-tron, if he can't do me any real good when I need him?"

"You haven't thought it through," she said, but she didn't sound annoyed. Amused, maybe, and a little sad. "He's not your patron, and he doesn't mean you any good. He has you for the same reason I do; because you're such a lovely secret."

"I'm serious," Lucius Perry said. "I would take on the world for you."

"I believe you." She kissed him. "And I'm not going to let you."

⌒

Marcus sneezed.
"Let's go home," I said. "I have to practice."

chapter II

A CHALLENGE HAS BEEN ISSUED." ROBERT FITZ-Levi flicked at the paper with a well-manicured hand. "My dear sister, what does this mean?"

Artemisia glared at her brother across her room, not even rising from the chair she was sunk in, her tangled embroidery on her lap. "It means, my dear brother, that you have been reading my private correspondence without asking."

"Mother read it. She asked me to come and speak with you."

Artemisia sat up straight, her arms on the chair. "What have you to say, then, Robert?"

Robert drew a deep breath, went to the window, and then let it out and turned to her. "Do you know what I really want to say? I want to say that I wish you'd grow up and stop behaving like the queen in some tragedy. You made a stupid error, and now you refuse to admit it and face the consequences. Listen, Artie, do you have any idea how lucky you are?"

"*Lucky?* Lucky to be forced against my will?"

"By your intended, just a few weeks before your wedding night. What's the difference?"

She said, "You make me sick. I thought you'd understand, but you're on *their* side now."

He shouted, "I'm on *your* side, but you're just too stupid to see it!"

"If you really cared for me, you'd fight for me! You'd be out there defending my honor, instead of sucking up to Father so he'll raise your allowance so you and your stupid friends can hire swordsmen to fight over women you—you aren't even related to."

"If you weren't such a romantic bubble-headed idiot, you'd know that your honor isn't compromised unless this gets out."

"Robert," she said. "My honor was compromised the moment that monster laid a hand on me. If you don't see that, there's others who do."

"Enough!" he said, brandishing the letter heavy with blobs of sealing wax. "Who is this *Tyrian?*"

"A friend. A true friend, and willing to fight for me."

"My god," he groaned. "How many of them are there? It's not enough that you drag Ferris off to some sleazy ball for your fun, but now you've got some punk swordsman on your string as well?"

His sister threw the nearest thing to hand, a small table. "How dare you? I'll have her kill you next, see if I don't!"

"You've hired a *woman* to kill Lord Ferris?"

"She's a girl, a girl like me. She's brave and bold and true, and no one could ever make her do a thing that she despises, or harm the innocent. She's not one of your swaggering bullies who fight for money; she's a *real* swordsman. Like Fabian."

"Oh, lord." Her brother looked pale. He put his hand against the wall, oblivious that it covered a frolicking nymph. "Who's Fab—"

"Never mind about Fabian." A tight-lipped Lady Fitz-Levi had entered the room. "That's quite enough nonsense. I don't know where you managed to meet this heroic young lady, but unless you're planning to marry *her*, you'd better tell her to keep her heroics to herself, and leave us all alone. Here, put this on." She held up a gown of soft pink silk, ruffled to perfection.

"I *hate* pink."

"It will give you color, which you sadly lack. Dorrie—" Artemisia's maid appeared. "The hair, please."

"What—"

"Sit still, you'll knot it."

"I don't—"

"Daughter, be still. You will be made presentable, and you will go out. Whether or not you enjoy yourself is entirely up to you, but I urge you to try. (Robert, turn your back.) All the city knows is that you've been ill and fretful, and that Lord Ferris is pining for you. (No, Dorrie, the pearls.) Before we leave, you will write to your heroic friend, telling her she is on no account to make a fuss of any kind."

"It's not a 'fuss,' Mama," Artemisia protested, even as she felt the cool weight of the pearls settle around her neck. "It's a challenge, for my honor."

"Your 'honor' is no one's business but ours, child. More particularly, honor is the business of men."

"But men are supposed to fight for a woman's honor. If Papa and Robert—"

"If your father and brother feel insulted, of course they will fight for you; isn't that so, Robbie?"

"Naturally, Mama. How could I do otherwise?"

"There, you see? (The curls a little higher—where is the butterfly pin?) Your honor is tarnished only if theirs is. And we have all made very sure that there is no breath of scandal, so no tarnish. (Don't tight-lace, Dorrie, she's thin enough as is.) Do you understand, now, dear?"

"Do try, Artie," her brother added encouragingly. "You've always been game. I'm sorry what I said about your champion before—you see, I do take your honor most seriously, on my word I do. I'm your brother, I'm supposed to protect you. I know it's been tough on you, old girl, but you must realize we care a lot for you. While you've been up here soaking your handkerchiefs, we've been making sure there's nothing to fight about. Do you see?"

"I think so."

"Of course she does. She knows how much we love her and want what's best for her." Lady Fitz-Levi pinched her daughter's cheeks evenly, to bring out the glow. "Oh, look at her; doesn't she look pretty?"

"A picture, madam."

"Just so. We can all be proud of our little girl, and I know you will never do anything to make us feel otherwise. Now, which slippers do you like, the rosettes with the little heels, or the satin grey?"

"I wore those last year."

"The rose, then. Stand up. Yes, you're quite right about the heels, dear. The line is better so. Turn around. Robert, isn't she a picture? Oh, Dorrie, look at that ruffle, it's uneven—get your sewing kit, quickly. Yes, Kirk, what is it?"

"The carriage, my lady."

"Dear me, already? I'll just go change my gown—no one minds what I look like—and you sit and write that note."

"But Mama—"

Covered in a muslin robe to protect her toilette, Artemisia wrote:

Dearest Fabian,
All is lost. My ruin is complete. My kind parents and brother have explained it all to me. There is no hope. Consider me as one dead and lost to the world. I will always remember you fondly, and will never forget what you were willing to do to save your—

Artemisia

"Hmph." Lady Fitz-Levi read it over. "That will do. To whom is it addressed? Come, tell me—do not make me pump the servants for information, for I know they have delivered others."

"To—to Lady Katherine Talbert. At Tremontaine House."

"Oh . . . my . . . god," her brother said feelingly.

⁓

LITTLE WAS SAID IN THE CARRIAGE, BUT WHEN Artemisia's mother was looking out the window, her brother passed her a flask and Lady Fitz-Levi pretended not to notice.

"A little afternoon musicale," said her mother soothingly, "at your friends the Godwins. Your dear Lydia will be there, that will be nice for you. She has written you almost every day, you know."

"I know."

"And there will be no need to say much; just listen to the music, nod and smile, very simple."

"Will—will *he* be there?"

"Oh, lord, child, how do I know? He doesn't send me his comings and goings."

"Don't worry, sis." Her brother squeezed her hand. "If he offends you in public in any way, I'll fight him for sure."

"Will you, Robbie?" she whispered. "Promise? If he's there and he tries to get me alone, you won't let me out of your sight, promise?"

"'Course I do. You're safe as Nanny's Hedgehog."

She smiled at the childhood memory, and allowed herself to settle back a little.

E VERYONE AT THE GODWIN PARTY WAS CAREFULLY pleased to see her. Lydia practically crushed all her ruffles in a fierce embrace, and whispered, "You look divine! All pale and interesting. I mustn't let Armand catch sight of you; he'll think me a pig by comparison."

Her cousin Lucius was there, too, impeccably dressed as always. He took her hand and bowed and said, "It's good to see you well," but that was all. She saw her old beau Gregory, Lord Talbert, across the room flirting with an older woman, and wondered for a moment what would have happened if she had betrothed herself to him, and wished him well.

She sat on a velvet-covered love seat, wedged between her mother and her brother, and listened to two women playing flute and harp. The sun was coming in the tall windows overlooking the gardens. Lydia and Armand sat between them, a curtain half-pulled across them to disguise the fact that they were holding hands.

When *he* came in, she knew it.

She felt it on the back of her neck, a disturbance of the air, the disturbance of his gaze. The music didn't stop. She gripped the edge of Robert's jacket. She thought she could smell him, over the other people and the hothouse flowers. She found her handkerchief and a vial of geranium scent and applied some and took deep breaths through the linen, although it smelt far too sweet.

She prayed for the music never to end, but then it did. People applauded; she balled her handkerchief in her palm and did so, too. Her mother poked her; she sat up straight, and prepared to greet her promised bridegroom.

Lord Ferris was exactly as she had first met him: well dressed, well groomed, well spoken. He greeted her and her family with just the right degree of civility and warmth. Her mother was flirting like a fool; Robert was trying to be smooth and adult, and sounding prissy instead. Only Lord Ferris was acting normal: charming and considerate, just this side of conspiratorial where she was concerned, as though he shared her opinion of her family, and wanted her to know that he was being good.

"Are you feeling faint?" he asked Artemisia, all intimate concern. He leaned in so close to her that she could see the pores of his face. "Let me get you a glass of something."

Artemisia felt like some actress in a play, and in a sense she was: anyone in the room could be watching her. Whatever she might feel about her family, she would not disgrace *herself*. But her hand was shaking, she couldn't help it. The only way she was going to get through this was to be Stella—Stella at the country house when Mangrove comes to visit... Stella, carrying Fabian's child, but to let Mangrove know could mean both their deaths, and so she dances and laughs and flirts with a surprised young cousin, to the disgust of Tyrian, who she doesn't know is there to guard her... and in a feat of bravado, she goes to the races and rides her cousin's horse to victory.... Fortunately, no dancing would be expected here, or racing either, and Robert made a poor excuse for loyal Tyrian—but she drew in a deep breath, and another, and her hand stopped shaking.

Lord Ferris returned with lemon water. "Are you enjoying the music?" he asked. For once, her mother's tendency to answer for her was a blessing. But then he proposed to sit down next to her, and her mother's skirts rustled as she shifted aside to let him. Artemisia was looking at the floor, thinking, It won't be so bad if I can't see him....

And then the most marvelous thing in the world happened:

a pair of shoes appeared. Small shoes, on a girl's small feet, but cut in a boy's pattern, and above them were fine ankles in heavy stockings that met with breeches just below the knee, and the point of a sword hanging by them, surrounded by green velvet with a gold tassel.

"I came as soon as I could," said Katherine Talbert.

"Oh!" Artemisia gasped in admiration. "Don't you look wonderful!"

"Armed, and with a challenge." Lord Ferris sighed. "Lady Godwin may not thank you for interrupting her musicale."

"I am to convey my regrets to Lady Godwin."

"By all means do so," Lord Ferris said. He was still standing. He looked down at her with his good eye. "She is over by the window, the lady in blue."

"I will," Katherine replied, "when we have finished our business, Lord Ferris. Would you like to step outside?"

The girl with her long hair tied back, dressed in a man's suit and carrying a sword, had not joined the Godwins' guests unnoticed. Artemisia could feel the tension in Ferris's stance as the ring of interested onlookers tightened around them. And she watched him make utterly the wrong choice when he replied to Katherine Talbert, "I have no business with you."

"That isn't true," Katherine said clearly. "I challenged you weeks ago, and as far as I know, you have not withdrawn the offense."

On either side of her, Artemisia's mother clutched her hand, and her brother sat poised to do something. Artemisia admired the way Katherine wasn't looking at her, and she enjoyed the preposterous sight the girl made in the music room. If Artemisia had known that she was grinning, she would have hidden it—but it had been so long since she had smiled with all her heart that Artemisia Fitz-Levi only knew that she was happy.

"Oh. So you did. Some time ago." Ferris chuckled. "I imagined, my dear, that *you* had withdrawn, having taken my advice and thought better of it."

"Well, I haven't. So now I must ask you: will you take the fight yourself, or do you have a champion?"

The crowd had been silent. Now Michael, Lord Godwin, resplendent in blue and gold, stepped forward saying, "Ferris, my house swordsman is of course at your disposal."

"You're very kind, Godwin, but I have a man with me, if someone will but send for him."

Lord Godwin looked at the newcomer, and then he looked again. "You are Tremontaine's niece?"

"I'm afraid so. But he's not the challenger, you're not to think he is. I'm—I'm fighting on another's behalf. Someone Lord Ferris has deeply offended."

"I understand," said Michael Godwin gravely.

Lady Godwin put her hand on her husband's arm. "There's to be no fighting in the music room. Out in the courtyard, I think, and people can watch from the steps."

"What about the garden?"

"Too muddy, still, I think, don't you?"

Artemisia's mother tried to hold her back, but she thrust her way to the very front, where the balustrade overlooked the stone courtyard of the Godwin townhouse. Her heart was throbbing not unpleasantly in her chest, and in her throat. She wished Lydia were by her side, but Lydia was back against a pillar with Armand Lindley's protective arm around her.

Ferris's house swordsman was a handsome man, long-limbed and graceful. He bowed to his patron, to the assembled company, and to his opponent. Katherine bowed once to them all, but Artemisia felt the extra flourish of her sword was all for her.

The man standing behind her said, "Good god. Kitty."

"Talbert," his companion drawled, "don't tell me you know the chit. Who is she?"

"It's my sister," said Gregory Talbert. "Or was. I really don't know."

Artemisia wanted to make sharp retort, but the business was going forward. "To the Death," Lord Godwin asked, "or First Blood?"

Ferris was standing in the yard, next to a hitching ring. "Oh, hardly to the Death; it's not that kind of matter. First Blood will more than suffice."

Artemisia hated him all over again. But Katherine nodded

assent and saluted her opponent, and then all her care was for her friend. Katherine Talbert was so small and compact next to Ferris's lanky swordsman. How would she even be able to reach him with her blade?

Clearly her opponent thought the same. He circled her lazily, eyeing her stance with a mocking eye, then started twirling the tip of his blade in her direction like a tease, a provocation. She ignored it, though; she followed his movement, but her blade was still. He made a couple of half-passes at her, and her wrist shifted only slightly.

Katherine's face was taut with concentration; his showed disdain. He stamped and thrust, trying to spook her. Someone laughed. She didn't move.

"Five royals on that girl," a man said, but another muttered, "Not here."

Ferris's swordsman made a beautiful move, a twist and turn, darting like a hawk's flight straight to the heart of the stocky little figure. Her frown deepened. She shifted her weight, shifted her blade, and ran a deep gash up her opponent's arm. She looked extremely surprised.

The swordsman yelped inelegantly. His blade flew from his hand. "Blood!" shouted Lord Godwin, and servants ran forward to help the wounded man.

If it had been Katherine's blood, Artemisia thought, I would have bound her wound with my own handkerchief. As it was, she was balling it in her fist, thinking, I've won. I've won.

"Lord Ferris?" Michael Godwin nodded to his guest. "Will you withdraw?"

"From this gathering, most certainly, by your leave," the Crescent answered. "But from the city, no."

"Are you sure?"

"The matter was of no great importance. I will take my seat in Council tomorrow, as always."

"Are you sure, my lord? If it is more convenient for you to be elsewhere at this time, we can make other arrangements."

The Crescent Chancellor drew himself up. "Godwin, do you seek to convene the Court of Honor in your stableyard? I said this matter was not such as would dictate my absence. I will be there tomorrow."

"Forgive me." Michael Godwin bowed slightly, and led his lady back indoors.

Although they would have liked to stay, the other guests followed Lord Godwin's example, leaving Katherine Talbert quite alone in the courtyard, cleaning the blood off her sword.

Gregory Talbert lingered for a moment on the stairs, watching his sister as she busied herself with her terrible weapon. Had she seen him? She did not look up. Should he speak to her? It was against the rules. And what would he say? *Well done, Kitty; we are so proud of you?* He should never have said she was his sister. He hurried away.

Artemisia's mother seized her wrist in an iron grip. She made her go through the motions of thanking their hosts and bidding them good-bye, pleading a headache and far too much excitement for a young girl's first day out after a long illness. But when they got in the carriage, she slapped her daughter hard.

"You slut! You fool!" Lady Fitz-Levi burst into tears. "Oh, who's going to marry you now?"

And indeed, the next day Lord Ferris's offer was quietly withdrawn, and the contract dissolved.

chapter III

I RETURNED TO TREMONTAINE HOUSE TO FIND MY
uncle the Mad Duke sitting in the library, shredding things.
There was a huge pile of ripped-up pages in front of him,
and he was fiercely attacking more with a paper knife.

He looked up when I came in. "Old books," he said, "worm-
eaten. Theo said it needed doing; I decided to help." The brandy
decanter beside him was nearly empty. "How did it go?"

"Well," I told him. I tried to be nonchalant, but it was hard.
All the energy from the fight was still with me, converted by my
triumph to cheerful bounciness. "Better than I expected. He
didn't take me seriously, so he didn't have a chance. It was just
like St—just like he taught me: when someone tries a flashy
move, look for what they're covering up and take it as an invitation. I got First Blood in about five moves."

"Well, don't get too smug. The next one might take you seriously, and then where will you be?" I lunged at a wall. "Don't you
dare hurt my books."

"I'm hungry."

"Didn't they have food, the Godwin musicale?"

"I didn't ask. Nobody offered. I left. Why don't *you* ever have a musicale?"

"I did, once. She bit me."

I laughed.

"And Lord Ferris?"

"He left. I think the wedding is off."

"Good work," he said, and drained the decanter. "Marcus!" My friend appeared. "Get this champion a sandwich."

I started to follow Marcus down to the kitchens, but he turned to me and said, "Don't come down; I'll bring you something. Do you want me to tell Betty you're back? She can draw you a bath."

"Not now," I said, "she'll only fuss. Let's go out to the gardens. It's a lovely day. I want to tell you all about my fight."

"I don't want to hear all about your fight. You hit someone with your sword, and he didn't hit you, that's all I need to know. Fish pond?"

"Meet me there."

Carp flitted amongst the weeds. I took a big bite of the bread and cheese he'd brought. "I like it up here," I said. "The Hill is much nicer than Riverside." Marcus's cold was better, but he still wasn't eating much. He rolled bits of my bread into pellets to chuck at the carp. "The air is healthier, too." I took off my stocking so I could stick one foot in the fish pond. "Why don't you want to hear about my fight?"

"I just don't, that's all. In case you hadn't noticed, I'm not really interested in swordplay."

"I am. Do you think I'm boring, then?"

"Hardly." Marcus rolled onto his stomach so I couldn't see his face.

I flicked my foot at the carp to keep them from the bread. I wondered if I could move without triggering their perfect flight. A swordsman, I thought, should be as quick to sense as a fish. "Who do you think is more interesting, the duke or me?"

"Now that," he drawled languidly, "is just the sort of question *he* would ask."

I nearly pushed him into the fish pond. "And that," I said, "is just the sort of tone of voice he uses when he's trying to get out of answering something."

"Oh re-eally? And what do you suppose I might possibly be avoiding?"

He was doing it on purpose, but I went after him anyway. With one wet foot I flipped him over like a fish on a grill, and pinned his shoulders with my knees. "You tell me," I said. "I don't know what's got into you, but if you think acting like my uncle is going to sweeten me up, you're insane."

"You're the one who's like him, not me."

I gaped at him. "How can you say that?"

"Isn't it obvious?"

I searched his face to see if he was teasing. I didn't know how to read what I saw there. "You're being ridiculous, Marcus."

He pushed against my knees. "You're hurting me."

"I don't care. You're insulting me."

"See what I mean? You don't care about anyone else. You don't even notice what they're feeling, ever. You just care about getting what you want, and how you're feeling. How much more like him do you want to be?"

"You rotten little—" I grabbed a fistful of earth and rubbed it on his face. "You take that back."

Marcus spat dirt out of his mouth. "You're not Tremontaine," he said; "make me." All that training, and I was so mad I just slapped him, hard, across the face.

With a sharp twist he was out from under me, eyes blazing. "You never, ever strike me again, do you hear me?"

"What do you want, then, a sword in the gut?"

He punched me. In the stomach. I doubled over, retching and wheezing in the new grass.

When I looked up, Marcus was sitting in a tree, well out of arm's reach, looking down at me and swinging his legs. "You all right?"

I coughed and wiped my eyes. "You fight like guttertrash."

"There's a reason for that. You fight like a girl."

"There's a reason for that, too."

Marcus stopped swinging his legs. "Peace. Can I come down?"

I looked up at him, successfully treed. My stomach still hurt, and there was a wretched taste in my mouth. "No," I said meanly, lifting my chin. "I don't think so. Not just yet."

"You look like him."

"You act like him," I snapped. "You've got a nerve telling me *I* do, when you're the one who says mean things like that. I never do; I'm always careful. I don't know what's gotten into you. You can be a total pig, Marcus, and you have been off and on for weeks, now. If I've done something to deserve it, I'll say I'm sorry—but I won't apologize if you won't tell me what it is."

"Don't be silly," he drawled affectedly. "What could you possibly have done? It is I who am to blame, I who annoyed you so much you quite rightly slapped me like a kitchenmaid, and I who consequently punched you most foully in the gut. You should report me to the duke. I should be punished, sacked, turned out of my place—"

"Stop being stupid." Why was he refusing to be serious, all of a sudden? "He doesn't care. You're more like family to him than I am—" I caught my breath. Why hadn't I seen it before? "You're his son, aren't you?"

Marcus hooted. "Oh, not you, too! No, of course I'm not his son. He bought me off the street, fair and square. You don't pay money for your own flesh and blood, do you? Oh, wait a minute." Marcus paused to consider. "Maybe he does. He bought you, after all." He meant it to hurt, and it did. It felt like I was being stabbed. "You think I don't know all about it? I was there for the meetings with the lawyers. I was there when he came up with the idea for your contract," he taunted mercilessly. "I'm always there, so I hear everything. I heard him dictate all those letters to your mother. I heard how much she needed the money..." I picked up a smallish rock, and clutched it hard. "I probably knew the whole deal way before anyone told you about it. The whole household knew; Arthur Ghent was the one who wrote those letters, after all. We all knew about you before you ever came here."

I clenched the rock's edges sharp in my hand, but didn't throw it. "He didn't buy me," I said. "It's not like that."

"Why not? You think because you're his blood he cares more about you? He paid good money for us both, but at least I do useful work around here. You're just a toy to him."

"You're not my friend." The pain was real; I felt it in my throat, and in my chest, so I could barely get the words out. "I thought you were, but I was wrong." I threw the rock in the fish pond. "I don't know what you are, Marcus." I started up the long path back to the house.

"No, wait!" He was out of the tree so fast his jacket tore. "Oh, lord...Kit, wait—" He caught up with me, started to touch my shoulder and pulled away as though it burned his hand. I kept on walking. "Will you at least turn around and look at me?"

I ignored him.

"Katie, please listen. I have a temper. It's bad, it's really bad, and I never lose it, but when I do, I just say things. I say things I don't mean—I don't even know what I'm doing, it just comes out, none of it's true—oh, god, Kit, I wish I could cut my tongue out, I really do—please don't walk away from me. Please!"

There was something in his voice—not just pleading, but panic, as though if I didn't turn around he wasn't going to be able to breathe much longer. I stopped walking and turned around and looked at him. He was pulling at his own fingers as if he wanted to tear them off, babbling apologies. "I didn't mean any of it, it was just lies, I swear. I'm all wrong, I know I am. I'm barely a civilized human being. I've read a lot of books, I know a lot of words, but in the end I'm nothing, nothing—I'm nothing but a minnow-a-toss street punk with good clothes and fancy manners."

His desperation cut the knot of shocked rage in me, and I started to sob.

"Don't cry, Katie, please don't cry because of me."

I knuckled tears out of my eyes. "How could you say those things to me?"

"I didn't mean them, please don't hate me—"

"I thought you understood," I whimpered miserably. "I thought we were together here...."

"We are, we are. Look, don't we watch each other's backs? And don't we have secrets together?"

"It doesn't mean anything if you can't be good to me." I sniffled. "How can I trust you?"

"And I let you have your secrets, too, don't I? I'm a good friend, I don't pry. Like, I know you set up that duel without me, and I know you snuck back to Perry's without me, and I didn't say anything because I knew you didn't want me to—"

"Yes, but—"

"And what about Highcombe? Do I ever ask you about who-ever it is at Highcombe you still won't tell me about, even though you know I'm dying to and you just love to torment me with it . . ."

Something in his voice made me laugh. He was doing it on purpose; the look on his face was silly and hopeful. "I'll tell you about it someday."

"It's someone you miss. You both do. Is it someone you love more than me?"

"Marcus—are you jealous?"

"You're all I have," he said softly; "you and him." Slowly he unfolded a pristine handkerchief. He reached with it, very care-fully, towards the tears on my face, and I stood quite still and let him wipe them away, tender and methodical.

I said, "You know I love you best."

"You do?"

"Better than any of them."

He handed me the white linen. "Blow your nose."

"Especially the duke. You love him, too, don't you? I don't know how you stand him all the time."

"He's interesting."

"So's a bat, or a thunderstorm. I wouldn't choose to live with one."

"He's clever, and he can be kind if he likes you. When he re-members."

I sniffed. "He's not reliable."

Marcus looked at me with steady brown eyes. "I am reliable."

I felt it then, that curious warmth below. It had something to do with wanting to touch his curving mouth and knowing that he wanted me to. He was watching me very carefully. If anything was going to happen, I would have to do it first. I felt the edges of his lips with my fingers, and his breath on them. He was standing very still, his hands at his sides. What would have happened then is hard to say, because it didn't; instead we heard someone run-ning down the path towards us, and it was Betty's voice, calling, "Lady Katherine!"

We broke apart, and just in time, for she took one look at me and started to carry on. "Look at the state you're in! All over mud, and no time to clean your hair; I'll just have to put it up, that's all. And you the duke's own champion, too, I hear, but when we're going to celebrate I do not know, for such a to-do with her coming here I cannot possibly get you all cleaned up in time. Such a fine lady, what will she think of the care that I've been giving you? But if you will go fighting and playing in the garden—"

"Who is it?" I asked. "Who's here?"

"It's your mother."

I felt the whole world shift and drop out from under me.

"My mother?"

What was she doing here? Why had no one told me?

"Don't worry about your hands, we'll just put some cream on them..."

But it wasn't my hands I was worried about. "Marcus, I can't!" I gasped. "I can't see her now. I am—I look—I don't have any dresses! Oh, tell her to go away, tell her I'll write to her, I can't, I can't—"

"Katie, stop." He took my clenched hands in his. "Don't be a fool. You can do this. Just go wash up, and put on a clean shirt, and go welcome your mother to Tremontaine House. I'll tell her you're coming."

I held on to his arm. "No! No, I don't want her to see you—"

"She won't." He smiled a funny little smile, and let me watch him transform into a sedate, well-trained servant, perfectly composed. "There, see? Nobody here."

"Don't tell her..." I whispered.

He smiled into my eyes. "Don't worry, Lady Katherine. I'm very good at not telling people things. And I'm very reliable."

He bowed, and kissed my hand. He didn't do it very well, but it was adorable. I squared my shoulders, and went off to get cleaned up.

⌢

I HAD FORGOTTEN HOW BEAUTIFUL SHE WAS, AND HOW much she looked like the duke. The skin at her temples was thin, and her hair was plainly dressed. She sat in a velvet chair by the window in the mirrored drawing room, looking out over the garden and the river beyond it. I entered very quietly, so that I could look at her first. It was strange how well she fit the room; she didn't look countrified at all, just plain and elegant. She had a book on her lap, but she wasn't reading it; she was turning the pages while staring out the window.

"Hello, Mother," I said.

I saw the shock on her face.

"It's true," she said. "Oh, my god, Katherine, what's he done to you?" She didn't wait for an answer. I felt my swordsman's poise deserting me; suddenly I didn't know what to do with my hands, and I was horribly aware of my legs. "I came as soon as I could. Gregory told me you were just in some kind of fight, and I meant to wait a day, but I came rushing up yesterday because it's been six months, my darling, six long months and I could not wait a moment longer. I wanted to surprise you—"

"I'm surprised," I said. "Truly."

She rushed to me, and took my face in her hands. "Oh, my darling, are you all right?"

I tried not to let her feel me stiffen and draw back. "Of course I'm all right, Mother. It was a short fight. I won."

"Oh, Katherine." Her voice was full of sorrow. "My sweet, brave, good darling. I can only imagine what you have been through. . . ."

I squirmed. "It's all right, Mother, really."

"You don't have to be brave any longer," she said softly. "You've done it, my darling; you've saved us."

I looked down and felt myself flush with pleasure. This was more like it. When she held out her arms this time, I went to her and let her embrace me, and breathed in the scent of lavender from our gardens at home. She guided me back to her chair and I nestled down in the corner of her skirt, my special spot where I always felt safe. "Your hair's gotten thicker," she said, stroking it.

"My maid washes it with special stuff."

"You've got your own maid? Oh, Kitty!"

"And a big room over the river, and a velvet cloak with gold tassels, and—oh, Mother! Are you staying with Gregory? I want you to see my room. You can stay with me, if you like; the bed is huge."

"Now, now, Kitty, we'll talk about all that later. We've got more important things to talk about right now."

"What things?"

She laughed, and patted my back like a puppy's: "Just run up-stairs and tell your maid to put you into one of your nice dresses, and you can order us some refreshment, if you like."

"I—shall I order us something now?"

"What's the matter, darling?"

"Nothing, I just—I don't feel like changing right now, that's all."

"I just thought you'd like to show me one of your new dresses."

"Maybe later." I wanted to put the moment off as long as pos-sible, when she would find out what my life in the duke's house was really like. She would not be happy, I knew that. I so wanted her to be happy, now. "Tell me all about you, first. Is your tooth all better? How are the boys? Has Annie married her sailor yet? Did the Oldest Oak survive another winter? What did Seb sow in the south reach this year?"

"You'll see, won't you?" she said mischievously.

"Will I?"

"Well, of course you will, my pet. Not right away, of course: I thought I'd stay in town and do a little shopping—you don't want to be seen with your silly old mother looking like some country frump, do you? And I can still have my own 'Season,' even if it's a little late!" She laughed. "You won't mind that, will you my dar-ling, if we stay a few weeks?"

"Of course not, Mother," I said automatically.

She squeezed my shoulder. "I knew you'd understand, Katherine, you always do. After all, there's no hurry, is there?"

"I don't think so. I mean, if Sebastian's all right at home without you—and you haven't seen Gregory in ages—is he com-ing to visit me, too?"

"I don't think so, darling; he and your uncle don't really see eye to eye."

"Oh." That didn't surprise me.

"Anyway, it doesn't matter—Greg will put up with me awhile longer, and then, when the town empties out for the sum-mer, we can all go home together."

There was a clutch in my stomach. "Home?"

"Yes, my love."

"But my uncle—the contract—don't I have to stay?"

She flicked her hands in the air, very like the duke. "He's not as clever as he thinks he is, for all his money. I've got new lawyers, much better ones than before. They say there's absolutely nothing to keep you here. We promised him six months, and he's had them."

I had never seen the contract, but I had watched my mother go through lawyers like kindling before, trying to get out of other unwise bargains she had made. I wondered what the truth was this time. I wondered why it had never occurred to me until now simply to ask Arthur Ghent to take it out and read it with me, so I could understand it myself.

"Just think—you'll see all the dear little ducklings, and the lambs. You always love to give them names and help Fergus with them."

"Of course, Mama." I'd forgotten all about the lambs—the lambs and the linen and the liniments and all that. It seemed like a hundred years ago, or something I'd read in a book. Did I like lambs? I did, of course I did. Lambs were sweet. Then why was my heart pounding as if I were in a fight? I took a deep breath. "Just not quite yet, as you say. You want to see the city, first."

"That's my darling." She hugged me. I had dreamed of her arms, but now I was finding them a little too tight. "I know I can always depend on you." She smiled tenderly at me. "You have no idea how lovely it will all be, now that we've got our money back again. All the funds that were tied up while he picked quarrels about them, returned to me with interest; it's quite a lot, much more than I thought it would be, and I mean to spend it now. I'm going to have a carriage, and I've ordered new hangings for the bedrooms, and all sorts of lovely fabrics and china—"

She was always forgetting the practical things. "What about the roof?"

"Oh, a new roof, of course, and books for poor Sebastian, and more kitchenmaids, so Cook has agreed to stay on after all— It will be lovely, much nicer than before, you'll see! I'd no idea there was so much there. All thanks to you, of course, my brave heroic daughter, who walked right into the ogre's den without a thought for herself, and captured his treasure for us." She hugged me. "I mean to get you the best of everything: pretty clothes, and fine furnishings, and an extra sewing maid so you don't ever have to do that nasty mending again— You can even have a real Season someday, if you want one, with balls and gowns and flowers and everything."

I thought of the Godwins' musicale, the girls in their bright dresses, and me with my sword and breeches standing before Artemisia to challenge Lord Ferris. "Oh, that's all right," I said. "I don't think I'll bother with that after all."

"But don't you want to be like all the other girls here?" she asked anxiously.

"Not really."

"Oh, Katherine." She breathed a sigh of admiration—or maybe it was just relief. "I couldn't do without you."

I took the end of her hair ribbon and twisted it gently, teasing her, but anxious for the answer. "But you've managed a *little* without me, haven't you? Just a little bit, on your own, for six months?"

"Just a *little*. Of course Sebastian has been a great help with the house, once he stopped moping. I think he wished the Mad Duke had sent for *him* instead of you—the duke is a patron of the University, and you know how Seb loves his books."

"Maybe he can come to classes, when we've got everything settled."

The little frown appeared between my mother's brows. "Oh, no. No one else understands farming the way Seb does. I wouldn't know what to plant, or how to tell if the tenants were cheating us."

Sebastian was by far my favorite brother. I wondered if the duke would like him. Perhaps he would be willing to help him find a farm manager and send him to University. "I'm longing to see Seb again. Maybe he can come back with me in the fall, for a visit."

My mother's frown increased. "But why would you want to come back so soon?"

"Back here?" I looked at her blankly. "I—well, I've got things to do here."

"What things, Katherine?"

"Well—friends and things. And my lessons, of course. And, well—things."

"Katherine Samantha," she sighed. "You have not been listening to what I've been telling you. You're coming home with me, so we can put this all behind you."

"What? No. I mean, that's not possible."

"My poor heroic darling. Of course it looks that way to you, locked up here with this madman for so long, and no one to turn to for good counsel. But listen to me." My mother leaned forward. "You can still have a normal life. Nobody blames you. They know my brother is a lunatic; Gregory says no one decent will even visit him anymore, or have him in their homes. It's not your fault if he's sent you out in public like this—" she indicated my jacket and breeches "—And now this awful fight at Lord Godwin's..." At least Greg hadn't told her about the Rogues' Ball—maybe he didn't know himself. "Well, they'll forget in time, if we let them. The best thing to do," she explained with elaborate patience, "is to get you settled back home, do you see? Just long enough that people can forget all about it. A year or so should be enough."

"And then?"

"And then...well," she said archly, "if you decide someday that you can do without me—for I surely will never be able to do without you—well then, perhaps we can find a nice man for you to marry, and you can have—"

I couldn't say it. Not to her face, not with my heart pounding and my breath catching in my chest. I stood up, crossed the room so I stood under the portrait of the lady in grey, and clutched the marble behind me.

"I can't," I said. "I can't do any of that. I'm sorry, Mother. It's too late."

"But that's just what I'm saying! It isn't too late. We can still save you—"

"I don't need to be saved."

My mother twisted the ends of her hair. I'd seen her do it a hundred times. It used to look sweet, but now it just looked silly to me. "Katherine. Stop it. You're not being very adult. There's a whole world out there you know nothing about. Gregory has been out in Society, and he understands these things far better than you. He agrees with me that the best thing to do is to get you out of this madhouse as quickly as possible. I've got it all worked out. You'll have a quiet summer at home, and then you can start over, as if it had never been."

"But it has b—" I began, but stopped myself. You didn't tell my mother things like that.

"You can't stay in your uncle's house playing at swordfights forever, all dressed up like some booth at a fair." You couldn't argue with her when she got like this. If only she would be quiet and let me think. But her voice rattled on, more and more shrill. "You may be having fun now, but my brother is utterly mad. When he gets tired of you, you'll be out on the street, and then you'll come running home but the damage will have been done. And then what will you do? Answer me that." What kind of damage did she think there was that hadn't been done already? I remembered Marcus saying, "He bought you, too." If my uncle had bought me, my mother had sold me to him. "We must think of your future, Katherine. You know I only want what's best for you."

"You should have thought of that before you sent me here." The words were out of my mouth before I could stop them.

I opened my mouth to apologize, to take them back before I could do any more harm. But my mother was quite still. She stood looking at me as if she were looking at a stranger, at someone she did not love or even like at all.

"You'll do as I say," she told me. "Go get your things. We're leaving."

"No, Mother, please. If you could just—"

"Katherine," she said, her voice musical with suppressed rage. "Don't make a scene." She picked up a silk pillow, thick with embroidery of exotic birds with long tail feathers, and began picking at the threads with her nails. "This nonsense has to stop. We must think of your future."

"I can't," I said miserably, watching the bright threads of silk flying out of her hands, clinging to her skirt, falling to the floor. "I would if I could, honestly, Mother, but I just can't do it now."

Her fingers dug into the cloth of the cushion. "It isn't like you to be so selfish. Do you want to bring disgrace on our entire family? What am I going to do without you? I can't manage alone!"

There was a noise as the door opened. The Duke Tremontaine stood in the doorway, dressed to go out, and only slightly more sober than when I'd seen him last. He looked at me, and looked at his sister, and blinked.

"Hello, Janine," he said. "Welcome to Tremontaine House."

My mother looked her brother in the eyes. He was taller than she was, but her gaze was fierce. "My daughter," she said to him. "You have ruined my daughter."

My uncle looked startled. "Ruined her? I never touched her."

"You didn't have to. Look what you've done to her!"

"She seems all right to me. Are you all right, Katherine?" I pressed my back against the wall, as if I could melt right into it, and didn't answer. I knew what was coming, even if he didn't. He took a step toward my mother. "There's nothing wrong with your daughter. My cushion, on the other hand, you are certainly ruining."

"What do you care?" she said, tearing it further. "You've got plenty more. You've got everything in the world here, haven't you? Look at this house! Look at your suit, for that matter—I can't imagine what that costs."

"Neither can I; that's why they send me the bill."

"Are you trying to make me laugh? You have everything, everything, everything—money, jewels, land, heaven knows what, and it isn't enough for you—you have everything you want and more—and now you try to take my child from me."

I wondered if it was worth darting in and trying to clear things from her path. But that would only make it worse. And she was right; he could buy plenty more.

"That's ridiculous," the duke said weakly.

"Is it?" my mother hissed. "Is that what it is?"

"Janine, stop carrying on like some sort of mad stage witch." She picked up an etched glass bud vase, clutching it in her hand like a dagger. "Janine, listen to me and be reasonable and put that down."

"Why should I be reasonable? Were you reasonable? You didn't think much about being reasonable when you ran away and ruined our chances with Grandmama and left us thinking you were dead, did you? You left me all alone to deal with Mother and you know what she was like—"

"I left you? *I* left you?" Something changed in him, like a fighter who thinks he's playing in a practice bout and suddenly realizes the swords are not tipped. His face was very white, and his hands were no longer elegant. He opened them and closed them on nothing. "You're the one who left, Janine. I was there waiting for you. Don't you remember? You said you would run away before you'd marry that old fool. And I said, Right, then, we'll do it. I said, No one is going to take my sister away like that. I said, Meet me in the orchard—in the *orchard*, Janine, *not in the goddamned chapel!*"

I had never heard him roar like that before. She was staring at him, mesmerized, as white as he was and whiter, down to her lips, as though his story were draining all the blood from her. He stepped toward her, and she didn't move. "What on earth was I doing freezing in the orchard all night with a bag of food and a pair of cloaks, while you were being laced into your wedding dress?"

My mother shook her head, mute. I had my hands pressed to my mouth, listening, listening. The trouble was, I could see it. I could see it all perfectly clearly.

"I missed the main event," he said dryly, a bit more like himself. "I got in trouble for that, for missing my sister's wedding. Mother locked me in the—" for a moment he lost the word, lost his smooth and cruel habit of speech—then he gasped and regained it— "She had them lock me in the storage cell, you remember? Well, of course you do, you'd been there, too, not long before. I wasn't whipped; I was just locked in, to teach me manners. It was very cramped in there, I was getting big for it. But it didn't matter. Nothing did, because you weren't coming back."

She held out a hand to him. "I didn't know. I thought you were angry with me, that's why you weren't there. I wanted to come. But I was so afraid of them."

"I would have helped you!"

"You couldn't." When she said that, he actually flinched as if he had been struck. "You couldn't help me. You couldn't do anything. You couldn't stop them marrying me off any more than you could stop them locking you up, Davey. I knew that then."

She tried to touch him, but he turned away. "It was a long time ago," she said. "But I did the right thing."

"You did what they told you to do. And what did it gain you?"

"I had a husband," she said. "I have my children. I did my duty."

"You should have fought," he growled. "You should have stood and fought."

Oh, stop, I wanted to tell him. *Mother never fights, not the way you mean. Stop before something happens.* But I was afraid to come between them.

"You're being unfair. Our parents meant well. They wanted the best for us."

He looked at her in real surprise. "No, they didn't. We were raised by servants. Don't you remember? All Father cared about was his maps. Mother cared about chapel and about getting back at her own mother, the dread Duchess Tremontaine, who was, let me tell you, a real piece of work."

"I wouldn't know. I never met her. She had no interest in me, Mother said."

"Mother didn't wait to find out, did she? She was in too much of a hurry to marry you off to the highest-bidding country bumpkin. I would have brought you to the city with me—"

"No, Davey. She did try. When Charles first offered for me, Mother wrote to the duchess, to ask if she would bring me out properly and make a better match. But the duchess wrote back to say, no, she wasn't interested. So Mother accepted Charles's suit."

My uncle stared at her. "To *spite* her? She married you off to that idiot just to spite her mother?"

"Charles wasn't an idiot. He was a prosperous landowner, from a fine old family. I was very lucky, really. So were Father and Mother, because I lived nearby so I could look after them—"

"Stop it!" he raged. "Stop *lying!* How can you be saying all these things? You, you who were—oh, god. You, Janine. You were so pure of heart. You saved my life, you held me in your arms and told me stories when things were really bad—you made up whole countries for us to hide in, horses for us to ride there . . . don't you remember Storm Cloud and Flame of the Sea?"

My mother clutched the folds of her skirt, saying nothing. He turned his back to her, poured himself a brandy. "You were strong and true. I wanted to be like you." He knocked back the drink. "I know you fought them. You've forgotten, that's all. I wasn't there. I was in the orchard. But you tried, I know. I re-member, if you don't. And afterwards—everything I did, I did to avenge what they did to you. Everything."

"Including trying to ruin me and my family?"

He turned slowly to look at her, his head low. "You could have come to me. You could have written, or you could have come."

She turned to him with that same strange gesture he had made before, hands outstretched, opening and closing on noth-ing. "You know why I couldn't come."

"I know now," he said harshly. "It's because you've forgotten everything. You've turned it all into comfortable lies. You're just like the rest of them now. Go away. I don't want you in my house."

"No!" I heard my own voice shatter the awful stillness of the room. But I wasn't fast enough this time. I should have been. Had I forgotten? I should have seen her looking back at the glass bud vase. I should have been by her side, I should have taken it out of her hand before she smashed it against the table and held a shard so tightly the blood started seeping between her fingers.

"Oh!" I heard the duke draw in his breath, not shocked, but as if he'd suddenly remembered something.

She dropped the glass to the carpet, showed him her open hand, bleeding. "This is truth," she said. "I know that this is truth, don't you?"

"Oh, yes," he said. "I used to do that, too." He took her palm and examined it. "It's all right." She let him wrap his large white handkerchief lightly around her hand to catch the blood. "But I've got something better, now. Here, I'll show you. Want to see?" She stared at him, spellbound. He crossed the room to a locked cabinet and took out the key.

I knew what he kept in there. "You can't give my mother that!"

"Watch me," he said calmly, taking out the little vials of precious stuff. "Or better yet, don't."

I shouted, "You put that down!"

"Don't speak to your uncle like that," my mother said. "He'll think you weren't brought up properly."

"Run along, Katherine," my uncle said. "Your mother and I have a lot to talk about."

I took the stairs to my room two at a time, and slammed the door and locked it behind me. Maybe Marcus could stop him, but he'd never stopped the duke before, and I didn't want him to see my mother like this. I didn't want to ask Marcus for anything, either, not after what had nearly happened in the garden between us. I got into bed and snapped the curtains on their rings closed around me, and pulled the covers over my head.

I had wanted to know family secrets. Well, now I knew them. My uncle didn't hate my mother after all. And he had always been angry at everyone, not just us. He didn't know that she still told wonderful stories, and snuck off to the orchard to eat apples when she should be counting spoons. He didn't know that my father and mother had planned a garden together, and stayed up all night when I was sick. Maybe she was telling him now. If she was even there. If they could even talk.

The night was coming on. I unwrapped myself, and lay stiffly staring up at the dusky canopy above me.

Today I had wounded a man, and hit my best friend and almost kissed him. I had seen my mother for the first time in half a year and defied her. Three fights in one day, and only one I knew that I had won for certain, the one with rules.

Just that morning, I had been polishing my sword for the duel. I had to remember that whatever else happened, today I had avenged the honor of my friend Artemisia. I had challenged a real swordsman, who was neither stupid nor drunk, and I had bested him. Maybe my family didn't want to hear about my fight, but half the nobility of the city had witnessed it. People would talk about me, and know my name. I had spoken it loudly and clearly, for all to hear. Maybe I would become fashionable; maybe people would invite me to dinner and demand to hear the details. In my head, I played over again all the moves of the duel. It was harder than I thought to remember each one in order, but I wanted to get it right, for when someone finally asked me.

I T WAS DARK WHEN I WOKE UP. BETTY HAD UNLOCKED my door. I heard the clatter as she warmed milk for me at the hearth.

"Where's the duke?" I asked, and she said, "Out."

"Where is my mother?"

"Gone with him, gone . . . Never you mind all that, my hero, it doesn't matter. You be easy, now."

She poured whiskey into my milk, and stirred, and gave it to me and I drank it. She poured cans of warm water into my tub, and bathed me, and washed and dried and plaited my hair, and crooned, "My champion, my great sword, you are, you are . . ." I smelt the whiskey on her breath, and I didn't care. I just sat in the tub and cried, and let her dry me off and put me back to bed.

I WOKE UP EARLY THE NEXT MORNING. THE HOUSEHOLD was barely stirring. The duke would not be up for hours yet. Marcus might be awake, but I wasn't ready to face him. I had to see my uncle, first.

I put on some loose clothes and went to the wet-rabbit room and practiced furiously for a long time. When I heard the commotion that meant the duke was awake and asking for things, I went to change out of my practice clothes, because it would be another hour before he was fit to be spoken to.

At noon I found the Duke Tremontaine eating breakfast in the morning room.

"Where's my mother?" I demanded.

He looked quizzically at me. "Are you going to accuse me of

ruining her? Please don't. And don't speak to me in that tone; I'll think you weren't brought up properly."

I didn't laugh. "Where is she?"

"How should I know? She cried a lot. We talked. We devoured eight whole tablets of raw chocolate and the rest of the brandy. We talked until midnight, when it was time for me to be at Blackwoods'. She lost money at cards. She plays very badly, your mother."

I ground my teeth. "Has she gone back home?"

"To your brother's. The respectable one on Lower Patrick Street. I don't know where she's going next; I suspect she doesn't, either. You can write her and ask," he said. "You're free to correspond with anyone you like, now, you know. As she reminded me more than once. The woman has no head for drink, none at all. If I understood her, she will be writing you frequently. I'm sure you'll hear all about it."

He was in that kind of mood.

"And get your things together. We're going back to Riverside until this place is truly habitable."

"I'm staying," I said.

"Here? On the Hill? By yourself?"

"I mean, I'm staying with you."

"Well, of course you are. Pass the jam."

I wanted to throw the toast in his face. "What about me? Were you so busy debauching my mother you lost track of why she came here in the first place? Did you get her drunk just so you wouldn't have to talk about my—my *future*?"

"Your future is entirely up to you." The jam was perfectly within his reach when he bothered to lean up and over for it.

"Well, who is going to provide for me?"

"Please don't shout."

"I'm not shouting. My mother thinks you're going to toss me back out when you're sick of me, you know. She thinks you've made me into an unmarriageable freak." He didn't interrupt; he just kept crunching on his toast. I'd had enough. "Do you even think of me as your kin at all, or am I just some—some minnow-a-toss street kid to you, with good clothes and a sword?"

It got his attention—but not the way I wanted. He put down

his toast half-eaten, and gazed at me icily. "Where did you hear that phrase, pray?"

It's what Marcus had called himself yesterday, but I was certainly not going to tell him that. "I dunno."

"Do you know what it means?" he asked.

Cowed, I answered, like a schoolgirl with a lesson: "A minnow's what they call a brass coin in Riverside. A toss—some kind of ball game, I guess."

"Keep guessing," he said dryly. "And don't let me hear you use that phrase again."

I glowered at him. "You're not my mother."

"She doesn't know what it means either. But if you say it around someone who does, they will either slap your face or laugh at you. There—you are warned." He slathered more jam on his half a piece of cold toast. "I suppose, if Janine is going to be unreasonable, that I'm going to have to offer you something or you'll pester me to death. A salary, or a gift of land, or something. You figure it out; it will be good for you, teach you the value of money and how things work. Come to me when you have some idea, and we'll negotiate. You'll learn a lot."

"I'll ask a lot," I said, and he said, "Fine."

"And by the way," I added, "I think I know all your names now."

"What?" he asked, through a mouthful of toast.

"The first day I came here—you don't even remember, do you?"

"Of course I remember the first day you came. Ring for more toast. Have you eaten? Well, in that case, have you seen Marcus yet today? He seemed a little odd."

I had not seen Marcus; I'd wanted to confront my uncle before anything else happened. Now I went upstairs to find him and bring him up to date.

Marcus was extremely odd. He was in his room packing for Riverside already. He folded each of his own shirts very carefully, lining up all the seams like folds on a map.

"Your mother's pretty," he said, folding.

"What did she say to you?"

"Nothing. I make a very convincing servant."

"Well... well, thank you." It was utterly maddening, the way he fussed over that shirt and wouldn't look at me. "Marcus," I asked, "are you still angry with me?"

"No."

"Then tell me what's wrong or I'm going to rip that shirt right out of your hands!"

He put it down and looked straight at me.

"Are you leaving?" he said. His face was very white—I could see some stubble against his skin. I didn't know he shaved.

"No. She wanted me to, but I said not."

"Oh." He picked up the shirt, and put it down again. "Oh."

"Why are you doing that? I bet Fleming would pack for you, if you asked him."

"I don't like other people touching my things."

"How about me?" I offered. "I bet we could get it done in no time, if you let me help."

Marcus smiled slowly. "Katie. You're up to something."

"I was just thinking..." And I was. I needed my friend now; I needed to put yesterday behind us, and take us back to where we were together, bonded in mischief and common cause. "The duke's still in his dressing gown, eating toast," I said. "He'll be hours, yet. If we hurry, we can still nip down the Hill to Teresa Grey's together before we leave for Riverside. That is, if you're still interested in what she might be up to."

"Hand me those brushes," Marcus said.

We left the duke being shaved by his valet and changing his mind about his clothes again, and went off down the hill to the house of Lucius Perry's mysterious lady, together.

chapter IV

LUCIUS PERRY'S LOVER APPEARED TO HAVE GONE mad. We stared, fascinated, from the bushes, as Teresa Grey paced up and down the length of her studio, waving her hands in the air and shouting. We couldn't hear what she was saying, but it was clearly pretty awful. She lunged into space, twisted, fell down, and then jumped up again and dashed to the table where she dipped a pen in ink and started scribbling furiously.

Marcus poked me with his elbow and grinned. Her hair was a mess, and there was an inkblot on her nose where she'd rubbed it without thinking.

"Love letter?" I mouthed, but he shook his head: "Watch."

I watched. She got up and did it all over again, and then went back to her pen, and then she rose and turned her back to us and shouted something.

She must have been calling for Lucius Perry, because he came in then, looking fresh as a daisy and very glad to be summoned. She moved him into place, and did the same movements again, only this time he was talking and gesturing back at her so she didn't look so crazy, and then it all started making sense. They were acting out a scene together, a fight of some kind: first an argument, and then a struggle that ended with Teresa Grey falling to the floor. Lucius helped her up, and then he hung over her shoulder while she wrote. He pointed at the paper, and she changed something and laughed. Our Lucius looked very young; he wasn't trying to be anything, he was just enjoying himself.

Then she shook sand onto the wet ink, and blew it off and lifted up her page and read. She pitched her voice loud enough that we could hear just the sound of it, but not any of the words. In the bushes, we writhed quietly in frustration—if only we could get close enough to the window to hear! Seeing them through the long double windows, with curtains on either side...it was like being at the theatre with wax stuffed in our ears.

"A novel?" Marcus murmured. "One of those things girls like to read?"

Teresa Grey bowed, and Lucius Perry applauded. But I already knew. "It's a play," I said. "She writes plays."

Lucius put his arms around her, and the paper dropped to the ground. This time, she returned his embrace eagerly, warmly. Oh, the way he held her, the way he touched her hair! The way she smiled and stretched out her throat for his kiss....I dug my nails into my palms. The way her fingers clenched in the small of his back, the way he moved to be closer to her.

I snuck a look at Marcus. Did he see what I saw? A way for two people to be together, to touch each other and be happy and be friends without fear? What if he laughed at them, or was disgusted? What if he saw something entirely different?

He was watching them with enormous concentration, as if he were trying to figure something out for the first time: a math problem, maybe, or a series of moves in shesh, and not at all sure he'd got it right.

"If it's a play," he said, "I hope it has a happy ending."

I'd moved a little closer to him without realizing it, but now I moved away. "Come on," I said, "we'd better not be late."

We didn't even bother to be quiet going over the wall; they weren't going to hear us.

⌒

ARTEMISIA FITZ-LEVI WAS NOW FREE TO MARRY ANYone who would have her. She was not, however, free to leave the house.

She had taken up fancywork. It gave her something to do with her hands, so that she didn't tear her mother's eyes out, or better yet, her tongue. She plied her tiny hook with a vengeance, creating yards of tatted lace of varying sizes.

"At least Lord Ferris is behaving like a gentleman," Lady Fitz-Levi said again.

Artemisia jabbed the shuttle through another hole. It made a change from yesterday's refrain of *There, miss, are you satisfied?* or the day before, with its shrieks of *Ruined, ruined, this friend of yours has ruined you!*

"A real gentleman would have permitted me to break the engagement myself."

"And make you look like a jilt? Oh, no. Lord Ferris is behaving as he should—though I could wish he had waited just a little longer after that odious challenge so people would not be tempted to connect the two. As long as he continues to comport himself with discretion and not let anyone suggest the fault was yours..."

"But Mother, I won the duel! That proves it wasn't my fault!"

"Shh, darling. We know that, but you understand that no one else must, now must they? Or they could find out about that—*other* thing, and we don't want that, now, do we? Oh, Artemisia, we must do what we can to get you back on your feet! Perhaps a companion, someone sedate... My cousin Lettice married a drunkard, she never had any sense, and now that she's widowed she's short of funds; perhaps she'd be willing to come chaperone you."

"I don't care."

Her mother considered her. "No, Lettice could never handle you. There's only one thing for it. You need a new lover, and quickly."

"What?"

"Yes, indeed, my darling. It's the only way to allay suspicion: to make it look as though you fell for someone else and Ferris kindly released you. Now, who among all your beaux did you like second-best?"

"No one." Artemisia twisted her shuttle with a sure hand. "I will never marry."

"Is that what you want to be, a disgraced old maid? It's not a life for you, my dear, indeed it's not." Now her mother softened and seemed to look at her directly. Even sulky and resentful, Artemisia was a pretty picture in the low chair by the window, her dark curls gleaming, her slender neck bent over her work. "You like lively people and nice things. You love Society—and Society will love you once again, once we have you settled. The question is, who is still available who's worth having? Someone nearer your own age, I think, dearest, so you can enjoy a long life together." Artemisia shuddered. "It's a pity Terence Monteith is taken—he was just mad about you, wasn't he?"

"He was a bore."

"Yes, a bit. Still, he is such a *safe* young man. So unexceptionable."

"He wouldn't want me now."

"Do you think so?" Her mother looked archly at her. "I happen to know he'd snap you up in an instant. But he would have to break with Lady Eugenia first, and that would cause scandal, and I think we've had enough of that for one season. What about Gregory Talbert, then?"

"You said he was unsuitable."

"His mother has come to town. She is spending a great deal on clothes for herself and furnishings for their country house. He is not as unsuitable as he once was. And he is still free."

"Dream on, Mama. The fact is, I'm damaged goods."

"Don't be a fool, girl. Nobody knows about that unfortunate incident, and as long as Lord Ferris keeps on being a gentleman, nobody has to, since fortunately there was no... untoward result. It is simply a matter of discretion. Discretion, breeding, and... well, a reasonable offer on our part, which of course we will make. Your marriage portion will be the same as it was for Lord Ferris; better, even. He can see that and regret it 'til his dying day."

"May it be soon," Artemisia muttered.

Her mother ignored her. "Many of the finest families are overburdened with second, third, even fourth sons whose inheritance is nothing to speak of. Any one of them would be delighted with the match. In fact— Oh!" Her mother smiled. "Why did I not think of this before? It seems so obvious, and you've been such good friends for years, now."

"I can't marry my brother," Artemisia said waspishly.

"No! I was thinking of your cousin Lucius."

"Lucius Perry," Artemisia said softly. Well, of course. He already knew of her condition; he'd brought her home from the Rogues' Ball, after all, and never told a soul. "I thought he'd disgraced himself, somehow."

"Well, dear..." Her mother weighed the situation and decided it was time to be frank. "The truth is, when dear Lucius first came to town he was very young, and he fell in with the wrong crowd. He made a bit of a spectacle of himself, and your aunt and uncle were very upset."

Artemisia remembered Lucius sitting in her window seat saying, "It's the old story: boy comes to city, boy disobliges family, family hears about it, ructions ensue." Is this what he'd meant?

"But he's a good boy, you see. As soon as he learned how much harm he might be doing his family and himself, he promised them he'd stop. And I think you'll agree he's behaved admirably ever since. There's not a breath of scandal anyone can attach to Lucius Perry."

"No," Artemisia said thoughtfully, "he's never around for people to notice. He's sleepy, and quiet, and he's always late for things."

"But there's no harm in that. He's a handsome boy with nice manners, very fond of you. I really think I shall write to my sister and see what we can arrange."

"*Then* may I go to the play?" She said it just to annoy, knowing the answer already.

Predictably, her mother launched into: "And don't think I don't know what kind of nonsense That Book's put into your head. 'Fabian,' indeed. When we read it, my friends and I knew that he was a monster, a seducer and a cheat—we all agreed Tyrian was worth two of him—Helena Nevilleson was even planning to name her firstborn Tyrian, but her husband wouldn't permit it. To put such a thing on the stage, and with the Black Rose, of all people..."

"All the girls have seen it," she wheedled.

"Well, now," her mother said. "Maybe you should go, at that. We don't want you to disappear, do we? Why don't we all go next week, and invite your cousin Lucius to join us?"

⌒

THE DUKE TREMONTAINE HAD RETURNED TO RIVERSIDE. The Black Rose did not like visiting him there as well as she liked his house on the Hill, but now that she had accepted a substantial gift from him and severed her ties with her last protector, she hardly felt that she could be too choosy about where to consummate their new arrangement.

"Points to you," she said; "points to you and your little niece."

"What in hell are you talking about?" He sucked a deep breath in on his pipe. "You must forgive me, but I've been enmeshed in family matters. I'm not up on the talk of the town."

"The talk of the town, as you very well know, is that Katherine challenged and defeated Anthony Deverin, though it didn't faze Ferris one little bit. No one is claiming the challenge, so it's anyone's guess what the offense was, and to whom—but all the safe money's on you, of course, on behalf of someone he'd insulted....Oh, Alec," she wrapped herself sinuously around him, "dare I think that it was on my behalf?"

"Think what you like," he said; "it wasn't."

She laughed. "If you weren't so completely useless, I'd be in love with you already. You're the only one who tells me the truth."

"It was Katherine's idea, really. Ask her, if you like. She's around. I thought it best to keep her in Riverside for a while. The Hill is such a...busy place right now."

"Yes, you're right. Much safer for her here, if dear Tony tries anything. He's not a forgiving sort, as I know." He offered her the pipe, but she shook her head. "I don't. You shouldn't, either."

"Why not? It relaxes me."

"You want to be on your guard," she said. "You've made a real enemy of Lord Ferris."

"I did that before you were born." He laid a warm hand on her thigh, and she did not contradict his arithmetic. "Kiss me," he drawled, "I can't feel my knees."

chapter V

ANTHONY DEVERIN, LORD FERRIS, WAS PREPARED
to put up with a great deal of inconvenience, even of af-
front. But he did not readily forgive. In the matter of his
stymied marriage, he put the blame where it truly lay: not with the
gormless Fitz-Levi clan and their bubble-headed daughter, but with
his ancient and annoying enemy, the Duke Tremontaine. Ferris
needed to know: had the duel been a mere whim, an opportunity to
discomfit him and show off the duke's latest family eccentric, or was
it more, the opening salvo in a plan to bring Ferris down altogether?
It would not do to wait to find out. He would strike first, to make
sure Tremontaine knew he was not without resources.

Ferris made certain inquiries and was not disappointed; if
anything, he was a bit surprised at just how many fronts young
Campion had left himself exposed on. Going after him would be
like shooting arrows at a popinjay tied to a pole. Only the question of St Vier remained open. But it was early days, yet.

It began, innocently enough, with a bit of doggerel and a little artwork, nothing out of the ordinary in a city where printers
regularly catered to the tastes of a population that simultaneously

gloried in the glamour of its resident nobility and loved seeing them taken down a notch.

On this particular broadsheet, it was His Lordship of Tremontaine being taken down. But instead of the usual willing boy or overendowed swordsman, the duke's partner was a grossly fat woman, dressed like a cross between a peasant and a shop-keeper from what one could see, for her skirts were up over her head with His Lordship crawling under them exclaiming: *Behold the motions of the stars!* while she pointed upward, responding: *No, you fool! They're up there still!*

The duke's Riverside household staff, from scullions to secretaries, were far from pleased. What went on between their walls was private business, family business. Those snooty Hill servants might be given to passing on gossip up and down town, but in Riverside things were different. For the duke's ugly Mathematical Girl to be the butt of city jokes was dead wrong. Someone had been talking, and the wrong person had been listening.

"I'll have them put out on the street," the duke told Flavia, "whoever it is."

"You're an idiot," she said mechanically. The Ugly Girl herself was unaware of the rush of sympathy the household felt on her behalf. She'd received little of it in her life, and did not look for it now. "It could be anyone—one of your scholars, drinking in a tavern, making a quip where some apprentice would overhear him, that's all it would take."

"I'll find someone to whip the printer, then. If it distresses you so."

"Don't be an idiot."

The second broadsheet was even more offensive: calculations on a slate being made by a piglike woman with the duke's own tool engulfed in her hammy hand—

"And they're not even *right!*" she wailed, waving the sheet.

He chuckled. "Would you expect them to be?"

She said, "Yes, dammit. They owe me that, at least."

Again he said, "I'll make them stop, if you mind so much."

She looked bleakly at her friend. "*How* will you make them stop? Will you really set bullies on the printer? the artist?"

"Why not?" he said airily; but he knew he was in the wrong.

He answered her unspoken accusation himself: "It's not unheard of. Karleigh did it when they targeted his mother. Davenant is known as a man not to mock. In a city where most of the wealth is controlled by a small few, certain things are overlooked, particularly when it comes to the assertion of privilege."

"Don't you dare." She stood rigid, clutching the latest broadsheet in her two hands in front of her.

"Well, it's not as if I can cry challenge on tradesmen, more's the pity."

"You damnable hypocrite, don't you dare."

The duke paced his study once, twice. His back to her, he stopped and said, "Flavia. I'm the Duke of Riverside. I build things here and pretty much keep the peace, and discourage certain behaviors. If you think all that has been achieved through entirely civil and lawful means, you've had your head in a bucket."

"I've enjoyed having my head in a bucket. It's a very nice bucket. I've enjoyed the books and the fire and food and conversation. But you're right to call me on it. You're right." She picked up a couple of books, examined the spines. "These are mine, aren't they? You really did give them to me?"

"Put those down," he said. "Don't be an idiot. Our theories stand. We both see clearly; we know what's right. Even if it's not always possible to act on it, don't you think it matters to be able to call things by their true names?"

"It's not your fault," she said. "I'm not a total idiot. I know you do your best. I was just stupid to think you could—I could—" She shrugged and swiped at her nose with one wrist, her hands being full of books. "I thought I would be safe here."

"You are." For the first time, he touched her, touched her hand. "Safe from everything but paper and ink. Please. Put those down."

"Paper and ink." She clutched the books to her ample chest. "They're not nothing, Alec. They're pretty much everything to me: the embodiment of ideas, of thought—of free and open thought. Of inquiry and supposition. All of it."

"I know," he said. "But—"

"You've got all your other things—your poetry, your drugs, your pretty men and fancy clothes. You don't need just this. I do."

He said with unusual patience, "Do you think, if you leave my house, everything will suddenly slip back into place?" And when she didn't answer right away, he said more heatedly, "And you're going back where? To an unheated room at University and one cooked meal a week, tutoring students too stupid and lazy to attend lectures given by masters with half your brains? You'd leave my house for that?"

"Your patronage," the Ugly Girl said. "I'm leaving your patronage. Don't you understand? I don't like being looked at. I don't like being talked about. I don't really like compromise."

He said, "And I don't like you letting them chase you away. It seems, well, cowardly."

"It is. I have my limits. Clever of them to find them. Who are 'they,' by the way?"

"I don't know," the duke said. "I wonder who I've offended lately?"

"Everyone. You offend everyone."

"Don't leave," he said. "It will give them so much pleasure."

"Almost, for that," she conceded, "but no. I'd better."

"Come to dinner next week," he urged. "Ridley and his gang are going to argue about circulation. Maybe he'll demonstrate on a roast chicken again."

"No," she said. "I'm going to disappear for a while—as much as I can, anyway; nobody really cares about the University. And I never liked those dinners. Didn't you notice? It was always best when you told me about them after."

"Breakfast next morning, then?"

"Don't wait up," she said.

She left the crumpled broadsheets on the floor. And she left an enormous space in the duke's library, in his study, in his days and nights.

But in the end he got back at her, even if he never got her back. Before the year was out, the stuffy old University at the heart of the City boasted the first ever Women's Fellowship in Mathematics, which was taken by the only suitable available candidate, a large and ugly woman of indeterminate age who always wore a voluminous black scholar's robe over her shapeless gowns and lectured with a combination of rigor and dry wit that made her classes, in time, immensely popular.

⁓

ARTEMISIA FITZ-LEVI WITNESSED LORD FERRIS'S second strike against the duke herself.

She witnessed it from a box at the theatre in the company of her mother, her brother, and her cousin Lucius. Lucius Perry had not yet declared himself a formal suitor, despite his parents' indication that they would view the match with favor, but Lady Fitz-Levi still wanted him seen with her daughter, and Artemisia was simply grateful for his company.

The truth was, it took courage for her to go out in public. Despite her friends' assurances that it was nothing, she knew people were still talking about her ruptured betrothal and its possible causes. Although no one who knew them well could seriously entertain the notion that the Fitz-Levi family had hired Tremontaine's wild niece, the proximity of the challenge to Lord Ferris's break with Artemisia was hard to ignore. There was talk of a romance between the two girls, though no one had ever seen them together. Those who believed the challenge lay between Ferris and the Mad Duke were still free to wonder what had caused the Crescent to release Lady Artemisia from her betrothal. If she had not been the wronged party, then perhaps something else about her had put Lord Ferris off, and her deficiencies were lovingly enumerated, even by her friends.

Thus the Fitz-Levi party arrived early at the theatre, so as to be settled in their box before the crowds started in. Artemisia sat towards the back of the box where she would not easily be seen, wishing she didn't have to. All thought of her own situation vanished, though, when the play began. Candles were lit, and there was Stella's bedroom, with its tall window and canopied bed, exactly as in the book. In walked a beautiful woman—a little old for girlish Stella to Artemisia's critical eye, but she carried herself well. "No, thank you," the actress said, her head turned a little offstage. "I will put myself to bed."

"Let the duke do it!"

A man's voice, crude, from the cheap back seats. There was general *shushing,* and the scene went on. The Black Rose won Artemisia over with her portrayal of Stella's gentle innocence. When Fabian appeared in her chamber, armed and ready to kill her as he was sworn to do, Artemisia clutched her fan so hard she nearly broke it. Stella did not plead for her life; she let her youth and beauty of spirit plead for her. And the swordsman succumbed, as he must. "Lady Stella," he said, "your girlhood ends tonight. Whether by my sword or in my arms, I leave the choice to you."

"It is no choice," she said, trembling. "Either way, my will is forced."

"Is it?" Though the length of his sword was still between them, he looked deep into her eyes. "Know this, then: that you choose for us both. For in taking your life tonight, I end mine as well. The sun cannot rise on the face of a man who has destroyed such a jewel."

"What is your name?"

"If you will it, it is Death. Death for us both."

"And if I will otherwise?"

"Then I will give you joy." He fell on his knees before her, his sword at his side, the distance still between them. "And I am your servant, now, until the moment I draw my final breath."

Artemisia found that she was weeping—not the slow pleasant tears that theatre usually called forth, but wrenching sobs she felt her body could barely contain. She tried to stifle them, to hear what came next, although she knew the words by heart:

"Then rise," bright Stella said. "I choose freely, and I choose you." She held out her hand.

"Save it for Tremontaine!" A different voice, from a different corner of the theatre.

"Shut your face!" a woman shouted back, and others chorused agreement. This was Stella's moment, and no man would take it from them. The theatre was silent as the Black Rose parted the curtains of the huge bed, and silent as the couple embraced within them.

Silent, too, as Viola appeared on the stage above, jacketed

and breeched as Tyrian, wondering what had happened to keep Fabian so late.

The two friends met (while the bedroom was made to disappear), and Fabian explained his desperate case and even more desperate remedy. To save Stella's life he must betray a patron, and in so doing betray his honor, a swordsman's most cherished possession, and next to his sword, his most valuable. But one bright, fated woman had turned the world inside out, changed honor to disgrace and death to life. He would leave the city now and send word to his patron that he had found the mark too easy, that his blade rebelled and sought a worthier foe.

"Think you," said Tyrian, "they'll let it go at that? Dream on, my friend. I will watch your beauty, and if she be not worthy of your love, I'll challenge her myself."

Mangrove appeared next. In the book this happened later, but Artemisia could see that it was time to present the villain, who was Stella's evil cousin's swordsman and second in command. Mangrove waited for Stella in a temple, where he knew she was coming to pray, which was not in the book but allowed them to drop some impressive columns from the flies above. He leaned arrogantly against one and said, "Here comes the lady now."

The Black Rose entered, veiled head to toe in midnight blue.

"Is it raining?" Lady Fitz-Levi inquired. It wasn't rain: all around the theatre, people were hissing. The sounds of *shh!* mixed with the hissing, making it worse. The Black Rose said something, but no one could hear her. She stood very still, and so did Mangrove, frozen in his sneer.

Someone began a rhythmic clapping, making it impossible for the actors to be heard. People in the audience started shouting, and the language wasn't pretty.

At last the noise subsided. Stella lifted a hand to her veil, and Mangrove stepped forward. "Gentle lady," he said, a terrible mockery of Fabian's opening lines, "allow me."

But she kept her hands on her veil. "Sir, you are not known to me. My face—" The rest of the speech was lost in a volley of hisses. Every time the Black Rose opened her mouth, it was the same.

"Let's go," said Lucius Perry. "They'll never get through the play."

Her mother was outraged. "Can't they make them stop?"

"You can't control such an audience, Aunt."

"But what's wrong?" Artemisia asked. "I think she's very good."

"Goose," her brother said fondly. "It's a setup. Someone's paid to have her booed. A rival, perhaps—for the part, or for her affections..."

"Well, whoever did it, I'd like to slap them," his sister said. "Oh, look, Robert, people are throwing flowers! Quick, rush out and buy me some, I want to throw them, too."

The stage was slowly carpeted in blossoms. When they grew deep enough, the Black Rose scooped up a great armful, and swept offstage.

⁓

WORD REACHED RIVERSIDE QUICKLY. THE DUKE Tremontaine sent his carriage for her, and it carried the Black Rose unimpeded to the Bridge, where a closed chair waited to bring her to him.

"They *booed* me." Her eyes flashed regally, and she would not sit down, although she accepted a goblet of brandy. "I have never been hissed in a theatre before. Never."

He said, "How lucky for you. Whom have you managed to offend?"

She stopped her pacing long enough to fix him with her startling eyes. She was not a small woman, and the duke was sitting down, teasing at a flower that had fallen from her hair. "Don't you know?" she said. "I heard it clearly, and so did everyone else, I'll be bound. Your name, dear, not mine. I am very popular. You, it seems, are not."

"What a surprise." He dropped petals on the floor. "And what a good thing I don't care."

"How nice for you that you don't have to."

"Meaning," he drawled, "that you do."

"Just so." She leaned down and kissed him long and hard, 'til she felt his breath quicken and his hands grow restless, then she pulled away and said complacently, "It's a good thing you're not stuck on screwing actresses, dearie, or you'd have a very dry time ahead of you."

The duke straightened his jacket. "You weren't by any chance brought up in Riverside, were you?"

She knelt before him in a rustle of skirts, so that her eyes were level with his. "You don't remember me, do you?" He looked dubious. "Well, why should you? I was just a scrawny girl, wiping down the tables and clearing away the beer mugs at Rosalie's."

"Rosalie's?" It was a name he hadn't heard in years: the tavern where he used to drink and wait with his lover, the swordsman St Vier, for a challenge or a fight.

"I thought you were a prince back then," Rose said. "I made up stories about you. You and him, you was—you were like magic, something no one could touch. I wanted people to look at me like that. And the way you talked—oh, lord...Rosalie let me bring you a drink, once. You were dicing—"

"Probably losing."

"Oh, yes, losing." She smiled. "When I brought it, you said, *Look, a glass of fresh luck!*" She imitated him perfectly. "You took the drink, but the swordsman paid for it, because you were broke. I remember, he said—"

"No." The duke held up his hand. "That's enough."

"It's all right," Rose said. "I never could do him the way I could do you. I used to make the other girls laugh with it...."

"What a good thing I didn't know! I might have had him kill you."

"Never." The Black Rose smiled. "He didn't do women, everyone knew that."

The duke said, "Last year. I sent you my ring, with that note.... When you came here and saw me, you must have been surprised."

"Oh, no, Alec. Not at all." Her arms twined around his neck. "Why do you think I came?"

He ran his lips along her cheek. "Revenge on a crooked lover, I thought. Not that I wasn't grateful. I put what you brought me to good use, I assure you. And I'm grateful yet. I won't let Ferris chase you from the theatre."

"No," she said, "you won't."

Through pride and perversity he strove to keep her with him as long as he could, but in the end she rose from the tangle of clothes and said, "Farewell, my prince. Act heartbroken if you can; curse me if you must. I'd rather one curse from your lips than a hundred *boos* from an annoyéd crowd."

He looked critically at her. "Someone else wrote that."

"Of course. I changed it a little to fit the circumstances, that's all." She busied herself with the hooks of her bodice, and he did not offer to help. "I'll do what I can to let them know we've quarreled. You do the same."

On the stairway she found the duke's niece, that peculiar girl with the sword. Rose straightened herself just a little more and adjusted her glow to become once again the Black Rose. "Katherine," she said brightly. "How wonderful to see you again."

"Oh." The girl looked startled. "Hello, there."

"I salute you," said Rose. "You are the hero of the hour."

"Am I?"

"The duke is very proud of you, and so he should be. Remind him of it, when you can. He's sad," Rose said. "I am a little, too." She put her hand on the girl's soft cheek, and Katherine blushed. "I know," the Black Rose said. "It's all so very difficult, until you get the hang of it." She kissed the girl on her brow, and left the Riverside house.

⁓

I T WAS NOT FAIR. THE DUKE ALWAYS GOT WHATEVER he wanted. What did he need the Black Rose for? He had the whole city to choose from. She liked me, I knew she did. Hadn't she kissed me in the theatre?

It probably wasn't her fault at all that she'd ended up with him. She was just an actress, and he had money and influence that she probably needed, while I had nothing to offer but my true heart and my sword. Girls were dying all over the city for her. And there she was, patting me on the head and telling me to cheer up my uncle and look after him. Why didn't she tell any-one to look after *me*?

I didn't go down to dinner; I did not want to see the Duke Tremontaine that night. I found some old biscuits in my emer-gency hunger tin and ate those. But it turned out I'd missed a meal for nothing; the duke, too, was taking his meals in his rooms.

Or so Marcus told me, when he banged on my door to see what had happened to me.

I opened the door a crack. "Go away," I said. "You're not sup-posed to be in here alone with me. Betty doesn't approve."

Marcus laughed. "Betty," he said, "is making up to Master Osborne, who knew her back in the old days when he wasn't good enough for her. You don't have to worry about Betty for a while. He's got the keys to the wine cellar, after all."

"Well, anyway, I'm busy. I'm thinking."

"So am I," Marcus said insinuatingly. "I've been planning amusements and diversions. Want to know?"

"Tell me," I said.

"I'll tell you when I've got all the bits worked out. Maybe to-morrow, if all goes well. Meanwhile, I'll have a tray sent up. You must keep up your strength. Then you can practice killing some-one. It'll do you the world of good."

He was the most provoking boy.

⌒

DAVID ALEXANDER TIELMAN CAMPION, DUKE Tremontaine, knew that he had annoyed a lot of people. It wasn't fair to blame everything on Lord Ferris. He set his net-work to make inquiries, first through the usual channels: the University and Riverside. Riversiders got around. Some were vir-tuoso housebreakers and pickpockets, still others had climbed up the social ladder to become house staff of various kinds. Servants, all but the most disciplined, talked. So did scholars—outrageous gossips all, even those who now worked as tutors and secretaries to the nobility, many of whom Tremontaine had helped out in their starving student days. Spread his nets wide enough and something would turn up that he could use—and, as usual, a number of things he hadn't been looking for that could be useful later would come to light as well.

The question was, how serious were these strikes against his friends? Did his enemy wish only to annoy, or was this the prelude to something worse? It was not the first time Tremontaine had been under attack. When he'd inherited the duchy quite a few disgruntled contenders had tried to alter the succession through means foul and fair. And there had been others since then. He was well defended, now, with swordsmen and lawyers and everything in between. But what was he to defend against?

He made a list of possible serious foes. Heading it was Anthony Deverin, Lord Ferris. It wasn't just that Ferris currently had legitimate grudges against both Tremontaine's lover for spying on him (if he'd found out) and his niece for challenging him. It was also a matter of style. The petty cruelty, particularly directed toward vulnerable women, smelt very familiar.

In the old tales, things always came in threes. So who was next? The duke made his best guess and doubled the guard on certain people who, with luck, need never know that it was there at all. And he sent once last time for the Black Rose, to come in secret and speak to him in his Riverside house, and he asked her to go as his messenger to Highcombe.

ARTEMISIA BEGAN GOING OUT AGAIN TO SElected parties. She held her head high, even when she had to sit out dances without a partner. She refused to flirt with any of her old beaux. If the ones who had once clustered around her begging for a smile now thought themselves too good for her, so much the worse for them. She had won her challenge. She was free and in the right. Lydia Godwin's father always made a point of dancing with her, gracefully and superbly, and so did Armand Lindley. Lydia would take Artemisia's arm and walk around the ballroom with her in open declaration of affection. Jane Hetley often joined them, though Lavinia Perry, now betrothed to Petrus Davenant, was making herself scarce. It was going to be that way,

Artemisia realized: they would be friends in future only if their husbands got along.

She found herself hoping more and more to see Lucius Perry at these events. Lucius would always talk with her, easy and amusing. He made her feel like herself. He was a good dancer, too, and he never failed to claim her for a dance and bow deeply when it was over. Even when he was on his way elsewhere, he seemed to make the effort to drop in where he knew she would be. He would stay long enough to dance with her twice—but the third dance, the one that declared him a serious suitor, that Lucius Perry never gave her.

Once, just once, it almost happened. The music being over, Artemisia held on to his hand that little bit longer, and as the next tune started up they nearly merged back into the dance. She saw him pause, and look at her, and realize. He kept her hand, though, as he guided her back in the direction of her seat, and so doing, he slipped his arm around her waist, drew her a little closer to him— She didn't mean to flinch and pull back, she just did it.

"What a clumsy dolt I am!" Lucius said smoothly. "Always stepping on people's toes..."

She felt a rush of great warmth for him then. Lucius understood. As she watched his back disappear across the ballroom floor, off to whatever his next engagement was that night, Artemisia realized that she would marry him if he asked her. She would take good care of him. She'd make a beautiful home, and invite his friends to dinner, and she would see to it that there were always plates of his favorite biscuits, the brown crispy cinnamon ones. They would attend the theatre together, and give musical afternoons, and on quiet evenings she would sew and he would read to her. And he would never, never do anything to her if she asked him not to. Surely he never would.

R OSE HAD NEVER KNOWN A CARRIAGE RIDE TO be so exhausting. It was ridiculous, really; here she was in the lap of luxury—the duke hated traveling, he said, so tried to make his carriages as comfortable as possible, and as far as she was concerned, he'd succeeded. His footmen, in plain dress (as was the carriage, with the duke's escutcheon covered), were attentive but not presumptuous, and the basket of provisions abundant. It was the opposite of what she usually had to put up with on tour, and she should have been luxuriating in it. But all she wanted to do was sleep.

It was especially annoying because she had lines to learn. Henry had decided to mount a new production of an old romance, *Lord Ruthven's Lady*. It was a difficult play, seldom performed, being neither wholly tragedy nor comedy; but based on the success of *The Swordsman Whose Name Was Not Death*, Henry felt *Lord Ruthven's Lady* would draw crowds.

Lord Ruthven is a courtier who offends the king's young sister Helena by his callous and predatory conduct toward women. Helena persuades the court wizard to turn Ruthven into a woman, cursed to remain so until he can gain a woman's love. As a woman, Ruthven realizes he loves Helena and must bend all his skills and powers toward seducing her in his woman's form, or perish of terrible, unslakeable desire unlike anything he has ever known. Rose would play Ruthven once he was transformed. She had seen the play done entirely for laughs, but she had no intention of letting that happen here. While there were certainly comic moments to work with, her Ruthven would be troubled and passionate, vulnerable and confused, and ultimately tragic. By the time Helena finally returned Ruthven's love, she wanted all the ladies in the audience to be moaning with need. Her dear friend Jessica Bell was cast as Helena. Jess would give the princess just the right mix of fragility and backbone, and her slender pallor would play well against Rose's robust stature. Never one to leave a profitable thing unexploited, Henry had insisted on writing in a part for Viola Fine: Helena now had a pageboy with a crush on Ruthven-the-woman, which was gilding the lily with a vengeance, in Rose's opinion. But Rose did not doubt that once the show opened, she would have her pick of noble lovers, passionate adoring women who would make a very nice change from the tortuous intrigues of Lord Ferris and the Mad Duke Tremontaine.

She would, at least, if she could ever learn her lines. Rose had begun studying the part and was finding it almost impossible. Long speeches usually gave her no trouble; she loved the rhythm of the words, but these refused to stick in her head. There was a lot of repartee and wordplay, as well, and she kept jumbling phrases. She had to be word-perfect or the comedy would be lost, and you needed the play's wit to balance the poignancy. *From the top, dear,* she told herself, and put her hand over her playbook and began the transformation scene:

> *What is this heaviness about my chest?*
> *My arms feel lighter, without strength or power.*
> *Have I been sleeping? Ill? I cannot tell.*
> *What, boy! Attend me here!—What is that*
> *   sound?*
> *That is not mine—my voice! My voice! My*
> *   voice!*

Oh, she was going to have a good time with this. Triple repeats gave you so much to do. The next line was—was— God, she'd lost it already. She'd lost it, and she was going to puke. She should know better than to read in a moving carriage. But it had never given her trouble in the past. She opened the basket, looking for the wine. There was something in there—something that smelt like—quinces. Quince tart. She loved quince tart, and the duke had remembered, how sweet. But not this quince tart. This one was overwhelming. It was as if she was choking on the very smell of quinces. It sat in her hand, all crispy and golden. She threw it out the window.

The air made her feel better. She took a sip of wine and lay back. Her corsets were too tight. She'd told her dresser to tie them looser, but Emily must not have been paying attention. Her breasts were popping right out of her bodice. Rose lay back and closed her eyes.

She was asleep when the carriage pulled into Highcombe and came to a halt on the sweeping drive before the house's front door, where torches were already lit, expecting her arrival. The duke had insisted that she travel alone, but he had sent an outrider on ahead, and the household's small staff miraculously included women who could take care of her. Muzzy with fatigue, she let them usher her up to a quiet bedroom and unlace her shoes and coo over her elegant dress and petticoats, hang them up and bring her water to wash away the journey. "Put your feet up, my lady," they said in their thick country accents, and she did not correct their assumption—she'd played great ladies often enough, and could certainly do so now—"that'll help they swelling to go down." She had never enjoyed the unlacing of her corsets quite so much. This was the country, and there was no "adoring public" here, no audience except for the mysterious personage she was to meet, for whom the duke had hired her to read the letter she carried. With that duty discharged, she could go with her laces loose for a couple of days; maybe it would ease the ache in her breasts.

Sitting upright in her chair with her feet on a stool, waiting for a soothing tisane, Rose fell asleep again, and was roused by an elderly maid who, unsure of the etiquette for waking nobility, was holding the steaming mug under her nose. The acrid smell of herbs made her flinch. "Take it away," she said; "I don't want it."

The sharpness in her own voice surprised her. These people were trying to be kind. Rose shook her head and laughed. "I'm sorry! I don't know what's wrong with me!"

"That's all right, my lady," the servant said. "It just takes some women that way, is all."

"Oh, no," Rose laughed, "I'm usually quite a hardy traveler."

The older woman chuckled. "Most every woman finds this journey hard, ma'am," and Rose said, "Oh, no," in quite a different tone.

chapter VI

A YEAR AGO, ALEC CAMPION WOULD HAVE TOSSED
Lord Ferris's brief note of invitation on the fire.

Let us sit and discuss together, it read, *like reasonable men,
matters to our mutual advantage.*

Now the duke's secretary drafted a reply saying that His
Lordship of Tremontaine would call upon Lord Ferris at a particular day and time. Ferris replied that the day would be perfectly
convenient, and as to the time, he hoped that His Lordship
would not be much delayed.

The duke arrived early. Conceding the gesture, Ferris did not
make him wait but had him shown directly into his study and insisted on sending for refreshments. With his good eye, he surveyed the younger man. Tremontaine had taken trouble to dress
up for the visit: his lace was very white and there was plenty of it.
Instead of his accustomed black he wore the green of the House
of Tremontaine, which also matched his disturbing eyes. The
duke did not lack for jewels: prominent among them was the

oblong ring of the Tremontaine ruby, set with diamonds. Ferris knew it well; his own abuse of the jewel had helped bring about his humiliation at Tremontaine's hands almost twenty years back. For the boy to choose to wear it to this meeting was either provocation or poor judgment—or possibly both.

The duke refused brandy. "Keeping a clear head?" asked Ferris, delicately sipping his. "Good. This needn't take long, and I want you to remember what was said."

"Stop enjoying yourself, Ferris. I'm here and I'm sober, and I want to know what you think you're doing."

"Consider it an invitation," Ferris said cordially. "This is, after all, the first time you have ever bothered to call on me. If it took making a little trouble for some of your friends to get you here, I suppose it was worth it."

"You admit it? All of it?"

"Why not? An invitation, as I said. To come sit down and discuss our situation together, like noble and reasonable men."

"Which involves threatening my friends?"

"I was afraid you wouldn't take me seriously."

"I did. But I am preparing," the duke said, "to revise that opinion. Stop playing and tell me what you want."

"And you'll give it to me?"

"What do you think? If it's reasonable, I'll consider it. If it's not, I have the resources to annoy you very much as you've been annoying me. It's true I have more scruples—but I'm willing to suspend them. I also have more money, you see—lots more money. I wasn't planning to waste any of it on you, but I could be convinced to change my mind."

"Ah." Ferris rolled his glass between his fingertips. "That answers that question. The interference with my wedding plans was just one of your little pot shots, not the launch of a new campaign."

"I never—" The duke began to say something, but then thought better of it. He settled back in his chair—which Ferris was meanly gratified to note was just a bit too small for the duke's long body—and said simply, "No campaign. Your fiancée wanted out, and it was an easy fix."

"Well, that's all right, then," said Ferris smoothly. It was all coming together, in one of the several patterns he'd laid out against this meeting. He felt the almost sexual thrill of being the one in the room with all the power. The words seemed already written for him to speak. "I have now, as you say, an easy fix for both our troubles. You don't really trust me to stop attacking you where you're vulnerable—or you shouldn't, anyway—and I certainly do not trust you not to make such attacks necessary to me. Even with your great supply of scruples, not even you can always be quite sure what you'll do next, can you?"

The duke glared at him, but said nothing. "So," Lord Ferris went on, "you are going to provide me with a very fine token of your goodwill, which will also recompense me for the trouble you've caused already."

"And that is?"

"You are going to contract with me to marry your niece."

The duke turned very pale, right down to his lips. Then his cheeks flushed, making his green eyes appear to glitter.

"Oh, come, Campion, what else were you planning to do with her? It's a generous offer. In one sweep she is reinstated in Society with a position higher than any she might otherwise hope for. Even your crimes against her delicate girlhood—" Tremontaine started to rise; Lord Ferris lifted a manicured hand "—I mean, of course, only the silly masquerade of sword and breeches—are forgotten in the general haze of romance. We'll say I fell in love with her at the Godwin swordfight. It'll delight the entire city, just like a play—like that swordsman one the Rose is doing now, in fact. Lady Katherine likes the theatre, I hear."

The duke said nothing.

"You will provide her with a suitable dowry, of course. I know you are very fond of her. And should the two of us be blessed with issue—well, I would never presume to interfere with the ducal succession (that's not my place, is it?)—but I know you would take them into consideration, being so fond of the Lady Katherine and wanting the best for all of your family."

The duke sat very still, as if he were afraid to move. He wet his lips. "Are you sure," he said, "there isn't some ruling in the books somewhere stating that once you have slept with a woman it's a crime to marry her great-granddaughter?"

"None that I know of."

"Pity. I'll have to put a motion up before the Council to have one passed."

"Oh, no you won't," said the Crescent comfortably. "There's a fine now for frivolous suits."

"I'll pay it," the duke said. "But it might be cheaper for me just to hire a swordsman to settle the matter and put you out of your premarital miseries."

"Well, now." Ferris leaned back, brimming with his own particular kind of happiness. He'd always known he was ten times smarter than this man, but seldom did he get such a good opportunity to display it. "You might want to think that one through. You see, if it turns out that we are not to be wed, I might want to challenge your niece, instead. Having now seen her fight, I admit I misjudged her ability as well as her persistence this last time; but I don't make the same mistake twice. I can find a swordsman with enough superior skill to mop up the floor with her. There are some serious ones left, you know—they can easily skewer a young blade, even one who somehow learned a few of St Vier's tricks."

The duke said, "I could send her away. Back to her mother's house."

"Oh? Do you think the mother would refuse my suit? I don't. There's some bad blood between you, isn't there? Just what did your noble sister do, exactly?"

"She married," the duke said dryly. "Against my will."

"I am sure you have given her ample opportunity to regret it." Lord Ferris rose, and stretched, and pulled on the bell by the hearth. "You act quickly," he told his visitor, "but you don't always think very quickly. So I'll give you a little time to think over my offer and its ramifications."

"How little?"

Ferris cocked his head. "One day should be sufficient. After that, I will expect your answer, or I may well extend another of my invitations. I will go well guarded until then." A footman answered his summons. "His Grace of Tremontaine requires his carriage. Will you pass the word and see him out? I've Council business to attend to. Good night, my lord."

It was a dismissal, and not a very civil one, from one great lord to another. Lord Ferris's footman was therefore very surprised when the Mad Duke not only tipped him handsomely but gave him a schoolboy's wink before getting up into his splendid carriage. He wasn't called the Mad Duke for nothing, then. The footman couldn't see anything to wink about. Neither could the duke, if truth be told, but he was damned if he'd let Ferris know it.

⌒

THE BLACK ROSE COUNTED ON HER FINGERS, AND DID not like the results. The thing was possible, and it certainly explained a lot. She could play Ruthven to the hilt, now, understanding what it was to feel sudden changes in one's body—transformation unwelcome, undesired, imposed from outside her by another person. . . . But could she get through the rest of the Season before she started to show? Could she keep awake? Could she remember her lines? Her breasts felt huge, now that she knew; they were like someone else's, darker and bigger than her own. *What is this heaviness about my chest,* indeed?

The Rose composed herself for her morning meeting with Highcombe's mysterious resident. She was a professional, after all, and Tremontaine was paying her well just to read a letter to some person here, an aged relative, perhaps, and to answer any questions he might have. Whatever her own situation, she could execute this not particularly demanding role with grace, dignity and ease.

When Richard St Vier walked into the room, she let out something between a squawk and a full-blown shriek.

He was unarmed, but she saw him start to make a move to defend himself, and then to realize, and stop, and smile. "He didn't tell you," he said.

"No." Her hands were shaking. She fumbled in her bodice. "Oh, god—I have a letter—I had no idea—"

"Sit down," he said. "It's all right. He's just being cautious, or theatrical, or something."

Rose grimaced. "Well, why not?"

"Or maybe he's annoyed with you."

"He is, a little." Rose sank into the chair by the window,

looking up at the swordsman anxiously. "But he told me he trusted my absolute discretion." She laughed shakily. "He must be desperate."

"Do you think he is?" Richard St Vier asked her.

"Annoyed, or desperate?" She tried to recapture her usual lightness. She was not a Riverside tavern girl anymore. She was the Black Rose, the toast of the city, the honor of the stage.

"They go together sometimes," St Vier said; "especially with him." He pulled up a chair. He sat so close that when he breathed deeply, his knee ruffled her skirts. "What does he want?"

She thought of the Mad Duke's plots, his vices and excesses, his quiet rages and his enemies. "You," she said.

"Ah," St Vier said. "What's in the letter?"

That morning, with defiant panache, she had folded it carefully so that it nestled in the cleft of her bosom, planning to whip it out with two fingers and present it to the mysterious resident. If she hadn't squawked before with so much force, it might not have slipped down that little extra way, causing her to have to fish for it with those same two fingers while her other hand kept her stays in place.

"You don't even know who I am," she said.

"Nor do I. You didn't introduce yourself, and I don't like to pry."

That sobered her up. "I'm an actress. I'm Rose." It reminded her, too, that even the neatest stage business sometimes misfired and costumes misbehaved, and then all it took was a quick hoist and a tug to bring the letter out into the light.

Rose broke the seal, and then she stopped. Shouldn't she just hand it to him? "I'm sorry," she explained; "he said to read it to you."

"Yes, please do."

She looked down at the page. "It's short," she said. "One line: *Will you come for Katherine, if not for me?*"

She cleared her throat. "That's all."

"That's discreet," St Vier said. He did not ask her anything else.

"Katherine's a nice girl," she said.

"Yes. I know." He stood very still in the middle of the room.

"He's made a lot of enemies. He doesn't mind it, but they do. I don't think he'd ask if—if it weren't..." Shut up, Rose, she thought.

He looked out the window for a while, and then he looked at her.

"Yes," he said. "I will go. He didn't say how soon?"

"He didn't say anything. But I would make it soon."

"I can be ready in a day or two."

"All right." Weariness washed over her, and the kind of sadness she had spent her life trying to keep at bay. She stood up. "Do you mind if I go lie down?" she asked. "The journey was very tiring."

She wanted to make a good exit, but her balance seemed to have deserted her. She staggered against Richard St Vier, and for the first time in her life she felt the swordsman's hand close around her, warm and firm on her elbow, holding her up. "Are you all right?" he asked. And she thought, *No, I'm not all right. I'm stuffed with your sweet Alec's child!*

She said, "I'm fine. Just tired, is all."

"What are you going to do?" he asked, and she thought somehow he knew, he knew with his supernaturally clever body that had kept him alive through so many fights, through his years in the streets and taverns, somehow it saw her and recognized her distress, her condition, and he knew—but then he went on, "Will you wait and ride back with me? or are you in a hurry to go home?"

Rose closed her eyes. "I don't know. I need to think about things. It's been a difficult season. I might stay here awhile; the rest would do me good. After that...we'll see. Life in the theatre is so unpredictable."

chapter VII

SERIOUS SWORD-PRACTICE MADE ME FORGET TO think in words, so that I didn't always understand when people spoke to me. I had been at it for some time, drilling first to a rhythm, and then tricking myself with changes, when Marcus came in and said something.

I shook sweat out of my eyes. "What?"

"I've got some time free. It's nearly dark, you'll have to stop soon anyway."

"Yes, all right." I stretched out around the room, carefully polished the sword and put it away.

"Good, Katie. Now that I have your attention, I thought I'd invite you out for a night on the town. What do you think?"

I'd just begun to get my breath back from practice, but now my heart started beating hard again. Something about his jaunty nonchalance, just a little too studied ... He was up to something, and he was mighty pleased with himself. "A night out in Riverside?" I did my best to match his tone. "How naughty. How daring. Why not? What's up?"

Marcus negligently kicked the stand so that all the swords rattled back in place. "I'm taking you to Glinley's."

That undid me; I barely managed not to squeak. I had to call on the duke for backup: "Oh, re-eally?" I said, in my best Tremontaine.

"Not just the two of us, of course. Your uncle would never permit it." The look on my face must have been enough. Marcus dropped the pose and grinned at me. "It's Perry. He's here right now, and I happen to know he's working tonight. Want to follow him?"

This was ground I knew; stalking Perry was just something we did. "Why not?" I said, but this time I meant it.

I toweled off in my room and changed into a clean shirt with dark clothes and soft boots, and buckled on a sword; it was, after all, night in Riverside. No one was in the kitchen; we helped ourselves to bread and cheese and our favorite ginger beer, and then went out the side kitchen door to wait for Lucius Perry.

He wasn't long in coming. He wore his old-fashioned hooded cloak, with the hood pulled over his head, and he moved quickly. It was a good time of day to be following someone. Although the sky was still pearly in patches between the roofs, down in the street it was dark. I pretended I was a moving shadow, and Marcus, breathing softly next to me, was another. Only Perry was real, as he passed by other shadows, shadows of women heading for clients, shadows of musicians heading for jobs, shadows of thieves heading for houses, shadows of cats heading for food. We were almost to the Bridge when Perry turned down a side street and stopped in front of a large and rambly house with a deep-roofed portico.

"So," I said softly, "that's Glinley's."

"That's Glinley's." Marcus was smug, as if he'd pulled it out of the air for me.

Like our house, Glinley's had once been many small town houses, now knit together into one. Lucius Perry hesitated at the front door and then turned round the side as people came out to set torches in the holders in front.

We drew back further into the shadows. "Now what?" I asked.

"He takes off his clothes and wallows in depravity, what do you think?"

"No, I mean—now what do we do? Shouldn't we follow him?"

I heard Marcus's clothes rustle as he pulled back sharply. "In *there*? You can't go in there!"

"Why not?" Even at Teresa Grey's we had tried to climb the wall.

"Because—because you're a lady!"

I stared at where I knew he was in the darkness. "Marcus," I said. "That is completely idiotic. The duke has just spent half a year making sure I'm not a lady."

"Katie—"

"I'm not going to *do* anything, Marcus, I just want to see what it looks like inside." I could sense his whole body taut with resistance. "Marcus, have you been in there already without me?"

"No, I haven't. But I know what goes on in places like that."

"Well, so do I. It's just like the duke and all his friends, isn't it?" He was being so protective, it made me want to do something rash just to show him. But I wasn't going in there alone. "You've said it yourself: it's just full of people copulating. It can't be any worse than home. What are you afraid of?"

"I'm not afraid of anything. It's just, you won't like it."

"If I don't like it, or you don't like it, we'll leave."

"Promise?"

"I promise. I only want to see, that's all. Like Teresa Grey's: we'll just look, we won't do anything."

"Good," he said, "because it costs money, and we don't have enough. You're right. It is just a house. A house, and some people doing what people do everywhere. Nothing to worry about. Let's go."

I followed him as he strode across the street into the circle of light and under the dark porch of Glinley's front door. "Now what?" I whispered. "Do we just knock, or what?"

"There's a bell." Marcus turned the plain brass door-pull. After a moment that was just long enough to belie the fact that people were always waiting for it to ring, the door opened. Light from inside nearly blinded us. A stocky, muscular man stood there, plainly dressed, quietly armed. I felt his eyes flicking up and down, sizing up our clothes and our purses.

"Well, hello there," he said to Marcus. "Fancy seeing you here after all this time. What's your pleasure, then?"

Marcus drew himself up. "We're here to see Mistress Glinley," he said haughtily.

That worked. What we were going to tell her, I had no idea, but the man drew back and bowed, and let us in.

The halls were dark and shadowy, well suited to a house of vice. I'm sure brothels uptown are better lit. It was all part of what the duke liked to call the Riverside Flair. We followed the man to a small room hung in red, with a fainting couch prominently placed next to a little round table. He lit the candles. There was a decanter of wine and two glasses on the table. Marcus stood there watching while the man filled both glasses of wine for us. Where did he know Marcus from? Maybe the man had worked for the duke once.

"I'm sure you and your...friend will be comfortable here," the man told him, glancing at the couch. I wondered how many women with swords he saw each week. He looked back again at Marcus, and his face shifted in a sly way. He said, "Very comfortable for you, sir. Tremontaine business, is it, sir?"

Marcus turned his back, and took a glass of wine. "I thought," he said, "you were paid not to ask questions here."

"Oh, no, sir, of course, sir." The man bowed his way out of the room, leaving us in sole possession of couch, candles and wine.

"Well, I'm impressed." I plumped myself down, testing the couch. It appeared to be stuffed with goose down. "That was quick thinking, Marcus. You've got him on the run, cheeky villain. I don't know what we'll tell Mistress Glinley, but we'll think of something, won't we?"

"She'll think we're from the duke." Marcus drank. "I hope she doesn't tell him, that's all."

"What do you think this room is used for?" I bounced a few times, keeping my sword nicely out of the way. "Do you think people come here in pairs, or do they send someone in? Would we both fit on this couch?"

"Quit that." He held me still with both hands on my shoulders. "You're not five years old."

"I'll bounce if I want to. That's what it's there for."

He stood looking down at me, his two hands on my shoulders. "You know, Lady Katherine, if you screamed in here, no one would care."

"I know." I stopped bouncing and looked up into his eyes. "I could say the same to you."

"They'd just think we were having fun."

His eyes were dark, the pupils large in the candlelight. "Well, that's what it's here for, isn't it?" I said.

"Of course."

"Do you want to try anything, then?"

"Yes," he said, so suddenly I had only just heard him when his mouth was down on mine. It was hard and warm and exotic and very, very nice. I kept my arms at my sides. His fingers were still; everything was happening with our mouths, which changed shapes and textures to accommodate all sorts of feelings. My eyes were closed. I felt the velvet under my hand, and I wanted to sink down into it while his mouth and mine explored.

A gentle knock on the door made it necessary to stop. No one might care if we screamed, but one of us did have to say, "Come in."

Nan Glinley was everyone's vision of a perfect mother: small, round, placid and pleasant-faced. She was gowned in grey, and her hair was modestly coiffed in the manner of city women. I could tell from the way she looked at me only once that she knew who I was. But she spoke to both of us. "How can I help you?"

"Um," I said, and Marcus said, "We're investigating."

"My house," its mistress asked, "or yourselves?"

Was it that obvious? I guess it was. With the little sense left to me, I realized that if we stayed in there alone, Marcus and I could very well end up naked on the couch, and that was not what I had come to Glinley's for. "I want to see a man," I said imperiously. "A really, really handsome one. Dark haired, not too young—experienced, that is. Classy, though. Not trash."

"I see." She turned to Marcus. "And you?"

"Me, too," he said swiftly, having caught my plan. "We're together."

"Shall I show you what's available?"

I nodded. We would find Lucius Perry in here, actually see him in place in the halls of Glinley's House of You-Know-What. Why waste the chance? After that, we could go.

"You may select a partner first, if you like, and then we can all discuss what sort of setting you'd prefer, and what combination. Or we can sit down together now and decide in advance—"

"Oh, lord!" I exclaimed gauchely as I caught her drift. "I mean—we just want to look—to see—"

"Ah." Nan Glinley nodded. "Hidden observation? We can accommodate that."

I let out a breath of relief, and only hoped she didn't hear. No way on earth was I ending up on a couch with Lucius Perry, and neither was Marcus.

"Discretion, I think, is key here," she said, "given your tender years. We'll let you go masked while you search. Excuse me just a moment."

Nan Glinley left the room. Marcus and I looked at each other and burst out laughing.

"Hidden observation!" That's what we'd been doing all along.

"We'll never get away with this," Marcus chortled nervously.

"What if they throw us out?" I put my hands over my mouth to keep in the laughter.

"Get a grip on yourself and they won't. Start thinking up a story—"

Nan Glinley came back, carrying a bundle. "You might like to disarm," she said. "Your weapon will be safe here. Unless that's part of your personal preference . . . ?"

She knew perfectly well it wasn't. But she was treating us like real clients. I was impressed. If I ever really did want a little experience, this would be the place to get it, with a nice woman like that taking care of me. I took off my sword with a rueful smile to say of course we wouldn't be needing it in this lovely woman's house.

Nothing was forbidden at Glinley's, but privacy was respected. We were encased in silk capes from neck to toe, surmounted by masks with animal faces. I was a cat, and Marcus was

an owl. He cut a caper in the corridor, so that his shadow danced
wingéd on the wall. "Come," said Mistress Glinley, and we followed her through the halls.

We started by looking through peep holes into bedrooms
decorated in various styles. They were also decorated with young
men sitting or lying around trying to keep themselves amused. It
was too early for them to be busy, but clearly they were expecting
to be very busy soon. One was painting his nails, one practicing
the guitar. Another was smoothing oil all over his body; I was
tempted to stay and see what happened with him next—but it
wasn't Perry, after all.

"No?" Nan Glinley asked us at the end of the corridor.

We shook our heads.

"Then let us try the Flower Garden."

The Flower Garden was amazing: an indoor room with a pool
surrounded by plants, strewn with a variety of bodies scantily clad.
We picked our way amongst them, feeling almost indecently over-
dressed, and moving strangely because we had to turn our heads to
see anything through the eyeholes of the masks. Cloaked as we
were, we had no gender. Bodies of both men and women did what
they could to entice us: a languid glance, a flutter of fingers, a roll
of the hips. Suddenly it all seemed possible—not seemed, but
was—to take one by the hand, go off and learn to minister to desire in perfect safety. I licked my lips. That one . . . or that one . . .
the golden hair just edging above the trouser line, but how swiftly
they'd slip off to reveal the whole . . . the soft breasts floating un-
confined beneath the gauze, to be nuzzled, stroked, explored. . . .

"Come on!" hissed Marcus.

"Are you made of stone?" I whispered back.

He said, "They're only whores," as though their very avail-
ability rendered them worthless.

We nearly missed Lucius Perry altogether. He was dressed
like some nobleman wandered down from the Hill, in black brocade and silver lace. But his face was painted like a mask, skin
powdered to white, and his eyes, with blue and gold on the
lids, were lined with black, so that they seemed immense. His lips
were stained red as old blood. He was sitting solitary by a fountain, staring at the water. He looked very helpless, fragile and

alone. It wasn't only his painted face that made him unrecogniz-
able—I'd never seen those qualities in him before. I wondered if
he was doing it on purpose, if it was a mask he liked to wear. He
did have a choice, after all.

Marcus raised his arm and pointed. Perry's eyes flicked our
way, and he rose in one graceful movement. But Nan Glinley
came forward and put her hand on his arm and murmured something low to him. He nodded and walked out of the room.

"You like him, do you?" She smiled. "You've made a good
choice. And you're in luck; he's got some clients arranged, and he
doesn't mind being watched tonight."

Now was the time to tell her, *No, that's all right, we don't want
to see any of that, thanks; sorry to bother you, we're just leaving. . . .*
Nobody's ever really died from embarrassment, have they? I
turned to catch Marcus's gaze so I could pick up his thoughts, but
of course the stupid costumes made it impossible. My friend was
an owl. And I was amazed to hear his muffled voice saying,
"Good," from behind the mask. "I'd like that. I want to see what
he does. I want to see how he does it."

Well, if he did, so did I. This was better than anything we'd see
at Teresa Grey's—or anything we wanted to see there—wasn't it?
The final piece to Perry's puzzle, and practically with his consent.

She led us to a little cupboard of a room. We took off our
capes and masks and gave them to her. "I'll be back in an hour,"
Nan Glinley said. "That should be enough." Well, it should. I
could always close my eyes if it got to be too much. I turned my
attention to the room.

There was a long slit in the wall, a sort of narrow window covered in mesh through which we could look into a luxurious bed
chamber, dimly lit and gloriously appointed. It wasn't very tasteful;
it practically screamed wealth and power—or at least, wealth.
There wasn't a thing, from firetools to candlesticks to bedposts,
that wasn't gilded or carved or ornamented in some way.

In his lace and brocade, Lucius Perry looked like yet another
ornament, and not a very tasteful one, either. He sat in a chair
next to the bed, as still as he had sat by the fountain in the
Flower Garden. Gold candlelight on rich hangings made it look
like a scene in a painting.

I wondered what he was thinking. Did he know we were there yet? Probably not, or he'd be doing something more enticing, wouldn't he? Why didn't he have a book to read? When would something happen? Marcus shifted in his seat and I moved away from him; there wasn't much room in there, but we were careful not to touch each other.

We both jumped when a knock on the door to the room broke the stillness. Perry turned slowly. A man came in and threw his coat on a chair.

"Well, hello." Lucius Perry smiled.

I peered at his customer. The man was short and a bit stout; he could have been anyone you'd pass on the street without a second thought. He stood staring at Perry as if he couldn't believe his eyes. "Yes," he said. "Yes. God, you're gorgeous. They were right."

"I'm here for you. Name your desire—or better yet, don't name it, just show me." Perry began advancing on him, but the man held up his hand.

"No, wait. I want to look at you." Perry stopped, obedient. "You are . . . exquisite. But the paint—the eyes, and whatnot—it's a little much. I wonder if you'd mind wiping it off?"

"That," Lucius said, "I cannot do." As the man drew breath to object, he added swiftly, "But why confine yourself to looking, when you can touch?"

"Yes," the man said again. "Yes. Come here, then." He put his hands to either side of Perry's face, and pulled his mouth down, kissing him. He pulled Perry's head back, and traced his eyes, his cheeks . . . the paint was smeared all over his face, making the mask all the more effective, but the way he held his body—I watched Lucius Perry melting, melting in a fluid surrender, as though sinking into a water of anonymity. . . . The man's hands were all over him now, opening his jacket, plunging under his shirt, squeezing and pulling on his body, and Lucius Perry flowed with it all, his head thrown back, his eyes closed. He loved being touched. He loved being admired. Glinley's was made for him.

But the client wasn't really interested in Lucius Perry's pleasure. He was undoing his own breeches now, and guiding Perry's hands down to where his tool sprang out. I shut my eyes for a moment, and heard moaning. I peeked through my lashes. Lucius was kneeling before him, obscuring the worst of the view. It was perfectly obvious what they were doing.

"Hmph," Marcus muttered beside me. "He could have had that on the corner for a whole lot less than he's paying here."

"Hush," I hissed. The man dug his fingers into Lucius's hair, and arced his back, and shouted so loud I thought the whole house would come running. But nothing happened. The man subsided onto the bed, and Lucius handed him a towel. The man wiped himself off and started to get up, though you could tell he didn't really want to move.

"There's no hurry," Perry said. "Can I get you something to drink?"

The man drank a glass of wine. From his face, I guessed it was better wine than he was used to.

"Thank you," he said. He began putting his clothing together. "I wish that I could stay, but…" He shrugged. Glinley's was expensive.

Perry nodded. "Come back," he said. "Come back and see me, when you can."

The man smiled. "Don't tempt me. I'll dream of you, first, for a good long time."

He closed the door softly behind him.

So that was it, was it? Did they all do that? A solid hour of this would be the end of me. Our hiding room wasn't very big, and it was dark. I couldn't see Marcus, but I could hear his breathing next to me, shallow and a bit uneven.

"Are you all right?" I whispered. I wondered if we really should have come.

"Fine. Don't fuss."

Lucius Perry was carefully putting himself back together again. Like an actor, he cleaned off his face—and for a moment, I saw the man we knew, his skin pale in the candlelight, his eyes bright. He was staring into the mirror over his dressing table. He turned his face from side to side, examining it as if trying to see what it was that other people saw. He touched his lips, ran his finger down the straight line of his nose, smoothed his eyebrows, stuck out his tongue and laughed. He took out little pots from a drawer and began layering the paint back over his eyes. The colors made him look magical, like a creature in a dream. The last thing he did was his lips, drawing his crimsoned finger across them slowly, savoring the sensation. He rubbed them over and over, until they were saturated with color. If you didn't know about the paint, it was as if he had flushed them with stroking. He picked up a comb and drew it down through his tangled hair, again and again until it lay sleek on his head. Then he peered critically into the mirror and ran a hand through his hair, and looked up.

I had missed the knock. Another man came in. Lucius Perry stood, and bowed to him. The new client was dressed like a merchant, a shopkeeper, perhaps. He looked around the room at the canopied bed, the hearthfire, the tapestry; at one point he even looked straight at us, which gave me a scare, but our peephole must have been part of something like a picture or a hanging, and I suppose he was admiring it. "Well," he said. "A nobleman's bedroom. I've never been in one of these before."

Lucius Perry drawled, "You'll find it's much like any man's." He sounded quite a lot like the duke, actually.

The client's hands were clenching and unclenching. "And are you much like any man?"

Lucius preened. "I'm better. Look at me. Don't you think so?"

"A better man than I? I do not think so."

"Don't you? Maybe you need a better look."

"Anyone looks good with thirty royals' worth of clothing on his back. Take it off."

"How dare you?" Perry said arrogantly. Oh, he was enjoying himself, even I could tell, being just as horrible as the man expected him to be. This was different from the last one. There was a contest here, and a sort of drama. "This coat alone cost fifty."

"I deal in cloth, you slut. I know exactly what that getup's worth. You've probably passed my shop a hundred times and never looked at me. But you'll look at me now. You'll look at me, and like it." He was breathing so hard, I was afraid he was going to hit poor Lucius. But the younger man showed no alarm.

"I'm looking," Perry said.

"Keep looking," the man growled.

"I'm looking." They were both starting to breathe hard.

"What do you see?"

"I see you. I see you, and I like it. You make me want things I shouldn't want."

"Such as?"

"I want to take my clothing off for you. I want you to strip me naked. I want you to see me the way no one's ever seen me before."

"Your noble friends would not approve."

"My noble friends cannot imagine the pleasure. Strip me. Reveal me."

"Strip yourself," the man said thickly. "I want to watch."

Perry lifted a hand to the buttons of his coat and slowly undid them, and his breeches as well, 'til he stood there in his shirt, lovely as ivory, with the silver lace framing his shoulders.

The man watched, entranced. It was like wizardry: Lord Lucius Perry, who wasn't himself but someone else who looked just like him, taking off layers of disguise until he stood revealed as a painted whore, less himself now than when he started fully clothed in noble's garb. That's what I thought, anyway. He wanted to see how far from himself he could go, and this was how he did it. I hoped someday he didn't lose himself entirely.

The cloth merchant lifted Perry's shirt behind, and stroked him. "Lie down," he said. "You're mine, now."

"I'm yours," Perry sighed, and laid himself facedown on the tasteless, gilded bed.

What they did didn't really seem so terrible, because I couldn't see much, just a back and some legs. The noise was the worst of it, especially at the end.

Beside me, I felt Marcus turn to the wall. I reached for his hand in the dark, but caught only the edge of his cloak. He was shaking.

The man was already up and buttoning his clothes. "Get dressed," he said curtly. "I'll see you next week. Wear something different, though."

"As you wish."

When he'd left, and Perry was washing himself, Marcus murmured to me, "Well. Now I know how it looks from the outside."

"Outside what?" I whispered.

He pulled away suddenly. "Sorry," he said, and flung the little door open. I tumbled into the hallway after him, and found him kneeling over a convenient basin, puking his guts into it. There were, I saw, many such basins, large and ornamental, placed strategically along the hall. I guessed they were used fairly often, for one thing and another, at Glinley's.

I tried to hold his shoulders, but he waved me away. Of course he had brought his own clean handkerchief. "You need water," I said. "It'll wash the taste out. Was it the wine, Marcus? Did it make you sick?"

He sat all scrunched up with his arms tight around his knees. "No. I'd like more of it, actually." His teeth were chattering. "C-can you find me some?"

I looked wildly up and down the candlelit corridor. "Not a prayer. But—" There was a bellpull. I pulled it. The man who came was the same one who had first let us into the house.

"My friend is ill," I said. "We need to get our things and go. I'm sorry about the mess—"

"That's normal," he said. "A little too rich for your blood, sir?"

"Stuff it," Marcus growled.

"Quit being so uppity," the man said. "You may be the duke's own bumboy now, but I'm an old friend of Red Jack's, and I know what you was."

Marcus seized the sides of the basin again.

"You lay off him," I said to Red Jack's friend. "He can be uppity if he wants to." I heard Marcus laugh—it was an awful sound, in the midst of his retching, but it gave me heart. "Now show us to our room," I said, "and make yourself scarce."

The man glowered at me, but when Marcus could stand, he led us back to the room with the couch.

"You won't get much good of him here, my lady," the man said rudely. "Too bad—he used to be the sweetest little tosser on the streets."

"*Out*," I said, looking for my sword. He left before I could find it—and without a tip, I need hardly add.

My friend sat shivering on the couch. I put my cloak around him and made him drink some wine. "Never mind," I said. I needed to pace, since Marcus wouldn't let me touch him. "He's just a filthy stupid whoremongering idiot. We'll tell my uncle, and he'll have him thrown out on the street."

"No! Katie, no, you can't ever tell Tremontaine about this, *please*, Katie, swear!"

"Well, all right," I said. "You're right. I guess it was a bad idea. But it's over now, Marcus; you'll feel better soon. I'm sorry it made you sick. You couldn't know."

"Yes, I could," he said fiercely. "I knew exactly. Don't you understand?" He was shaking so hard he could barely hold the wineglass, so he knocked it back in one gulp. "You heard the man. And I told you that day, in the garden, but you still don't really understand, do you?"

I was beginning to; I just wished I didn't have to. "It's not your fault," I said. "You were just a kid. It was in Riverside, and you were just a little kid and you needed the money, right?"

"I didn't get any money. My mother's man sold me to Jack when she died. Jack gave me food and a place to sleep, and I worked for him. When I stopped being little and cute, he didn't have any use for me. Someone told him the Mad Duke liked them older. So he took me to the duke and sold me to him."

It was true, then, about him and my uncle, what people said and what I'd refused to believe. I swallowed bile. I didn't know how I could stand it, but I was going to have to. Fear is enemy to sword. I listened, and I kept very still, but I couldn't look my friend in the face.

"Tremontaine saved my life. He gave me a room, and a door that locked."

I let out breath I hadn't known I'd been holding, and drank some of the wine. "Oh, Marcus." I wanted to put my arms around him, but I saw from the way he was gripping my cloak around himself that he didn't want to be touched; he wasn't done saying things.

"He gave me teachers, and books, and—well, you know, everything. I owe him like nobody's business. He's been protecting me all this time; nobody touches me, and oh god god god, after all that—" Marcus was twisting his fingers together— "If Tremontaine finds out I came here after all that, he'll fucking kill me, Katherine. He will. You mustn't tell him!"

"I won't," I promised.

"I mean, it's been all right for so long, I thought I could do this—I didn't think it mattered, it was all about someone else, like I could test myself—just watching Perry—I don't know how he does it, honestly I don't—"

"He's testing himself," I said. "Like a swordsman. It's some kind of challenge for him."

"Well, he can have it. He's crazier than I thought."

"Is there any wine left?" I poured us each another glass, and drank. It made me feel warmer and braver at once. "Let's just go," I said. "I think I can find the main door." I buckled my sword on, a little unsteadily.

"Right." He was still shaking. He turned his dark eyes wide on me. "Do you hate me now?"

"Hate you? How could I hate you?" I put my arm around him, and this time he let me. "Come on," I said; "we're going home."

Glinley's smelt of sandalwood and beeswax and smoke and drugs and bodies. We wound our way down infinite identical corridors, trying not to be noticed. Once we actually stood like statues in empty niches as customers passed by. The halls started looking familiar. "Have we been here already?" I whispered. A door opened, and since there was no niche, we flattened ourselves against a wall. It was Lucius Perry, leaving the room where he worked. He was brushed and cloaked, on his way out. We followed him through the house, dropping back far enough not to be obvious. Once he looked behind him, so we quickly seized one another in embrace. I buried my head in my friend's shoulder, and Marcus put his face in my hair until we heard his footsteps fade away.

When we got outside, even the Riverside air smelled fresh.

I began to turn toward home, but Marcus held my wrist. He nodded in the direction of Perry's departing back and raised his eyebrows. I shook my head: enough was enough for one night. Besides, Perry was nearly out of the radius of the house's torchlight—he'd be stopping for a linkboy or his own torch soon, and I didn't fancy trailing behind him in the dark. We stood in the shadows of Glinley's, and watched Lucius Perry walk away into the night.

And we watched two men walk after him, faster and faster, and then we heard a loud thump and an even louder shout.

We ran toward the sound, Marcus with his knife and I with

my sword. It was one of those little Riverside streets where the houses nearly touch across. We could barely see the shapes of the two men and one more, whaling on one crouching figure who was not quiet as they laid into him.

"Stop!" I shouted, and to my horror I heard one say, "Is that the girl? That's her!"

"Run, Katie!"

With my sword in my hand, I could not run. I just couldn't do it. I knew I could take them on—they didn't have swords, and I did.

"Katie, *please!*"

"Get help," I said to Marcus as they came at me, leaving poor Lucius Perry gasping on the ground—but help was already there.

Men from my uncle's house—a footman and a swordsman, not wearing livery, but I knew them well and had never been so glad to see them. They laid into the three bullies, and they were much better trained and well-armed, besides. I'd like to say I helped, but I didn't—everyone was much bigger than me, and it was street-fighting without any rules—I hung back, and it was over so fast, with two of the bullies running away and the third one kept for questions, hands bound behind him. The swordsman took charge of him and the footman picked up Lucius Perry, because he couldn't walk. We went slowly. I felt much better when the Tremontaine swordsman, Twohey was his name, who was having trouble with his prisoner, said, "Lady Katherine, if you could just give him a good jab in the ribs—with your pommel? Good and hard—that's it, thanks. Come on, you."

My uncle was wearing a bright yellow dressing gown that didn't suit him; I'm not sure it was even his. He stood blinking in the hall at the top of the main house stairs, having been alerted by what I was coming to see was an admirable network that something had happened.

"For once," he drawled, "I try to get to sleep at a reasonable hour, and you bring me—bodies."

"One for questioning and one for bed, my lord," said Twohey cheerfully.

"Not my bed, I hope," the duke said; "that one's a bloody mess—" He saw who it was. "Oh, god. Get him seen to. Now.

What the hell do you think you're doing, holding him in the hall like a package?"

"And this one?" My prisoner moaned, so I whacked him in the ribs again.

"Katherine, my dear! I want him for information, not for kickball. Take him down cellar—Finian can work on him. I'll be down later. Marcus, come help me find my—"

"I'd like to go to bed, now, please."

"Re-eally?" the duke drawled, then snapped, "Get up here."

Swaying gently, Marcus met his master on the stairs. I watched them anxiously. Was it all true? Had the duke saved my friend and never really touched him? If he hurt Marcus, I'd kill him.

As if he could hear my thoughts, the duke said coldly, "Katherine. I don't believe this. I leave you alone for one instant, and you debauch my personal attendant."

I felt utterly sick in the pit of my stomach. How did he know? What would he do?

"This boy is drunk," the duke said. "And I suppose that means you are, too. Go to bed, the pair of you. If you wake up in the morning with a bad head, ask Betty for some of that unspeakable green tisane. But don't disturb me; I'll be up all night torturing prisoners."

He stalked off in a blaze of mustard-colored glory. I suppose I was drunk enough to think that it would be a good idea to explain to him that I was not in the least bit drunk—I certainly didn't feel it. Marcus had had much more wine than I; but then, he'd needed it. I watched Marcus go on up the stairs alone. He had very nice shoulders.

"Good night," I said, though there was nobody left to hear me.

LUCIUS PERRY DREAMED HE WAS A TREE, AND that woodsmen were chopping at the bark that was his face. It hurt like anything. Well, now that he knew that trees felt pain, he'd tell his brother to stop cutting the ones on the estate. He was flying now, way above the forest where the trees were, but something was pulling on his leg, and he was all off balance. He fell into the trees, and branches exploded all over his body as he crashed to the forest floor, a wild goose shot full of arrows. They stung him when he tried to move.

Hold still, a deer said. *Drink this.*

It put him to sleep, the deer's drink. When he woke, he was in his own body, lying in a bed. The Duke Tremontaine was bent over his head. Lucius's mouth was all stuck together, and he could see out of only one eye. It hurt so much to move that all he could manage was a feeble moan of protest. The duke pulled away. "I'm not looking for your favors," Tremontaine said. Someone Lucius couldn't see put a spout between his lips—an invalid's beaker, filled with water that drizzled into his mouth.

He heard Tremontaine's voice. "Perry. I am sorry. I know the man responsible for this, and it is entirely my fault."

What happened? he wanted to ask, but his lips were too stiff to form the words.

"I had one day," the duke said. "I didn't know it ended at midnight. —Never mind. You may stay here while you recover. I promise you'll be safe. Or, when you are a little better, I can send you home." The duke went on, something about messages and assurances, but Lucius closed his eyes so he could see the walls of a little white house with the sun on them, and a bowl of roses, freshly blown, on a table reflected in a mirror.

⌐

YOUR UNCLE'S BEING A PIG," MARCUS SAID. WE'D BEEN playing shesh in his room all morning because we were not allowed to leave the house. Marcus wasn't really concentrating on his game, so for once I was winning. "He's not speaking to me, and he won't tell me what's going on."

"Because of Glinley's? You didn't—you didn't tell him, did you?"

"Are you joking? He'd have to torture it out of me, and he doesn't have time. But he knows we did something. He just won't say."

"Is he drunk?"

"No, then he'd talk. He just glares at me and says not to

bother him. No one in the kitchen knows anything, either—all he's eating is bread and cheese. And meeting with secretaries and lawyers and shady characters, and writing letters."

"It's Perry," I said wisely. "He's probably planning revenge on whoever did it. Do we know who yet?"

"How should I know? He won't talk to me."

"He's got to know. That man in the cellar . . ."

"He's gone; I've already checked."

"Check."

"I did."

"No, I'm *checking* you. Look to your other wizard."

Marcus took one of my peons. "I knew you'd do that." I ignored the gibe. "We're definitely still locked in," he said. "I think he thinks someone's after us, like Perry. After *you*, I should say."

"And you're just locked in with me to keep me company?" He took my queen. "Oh, dammit, Marcus, I didn't even *see* that!"

"I know." My hand was on the board; he put his own hand over it. His skin was warm, and a little damp.

"Marcus?" I asked. "Are you sorry you kissed me?"

"Not really. Unless you are."

"I'm not," I said. "I'd do it again." His hand tightened on mine, but he didn't do anything. "It's men that make you sick, right? Not me?"

"You don't at all."

"Just because I dress like one sometimes . . . If that puts you off, I can—well—"

"Take your clothes off?"

"Because I'm really not a man. I've got—well, developments."

"I'd noticed."

"So do you want to?"

"If you do."

I touched his mouth with my free hand. "I do."

This kissing was very different: more like eating, really, satisfying an appetite you hadn't even known was in you until you found yourself with a big mouthful of pleasure. It was as if the minds that had been playing shesh suddenly flew out through the roof. All I knew was what things felt good, and that I wanted more of them. I had never even imagined Marcus with his clothes off, and now here I was ripping them away to get at more of his skin. I didn't mind when his hands found my breasts—in fact, I encouraged him, and I pushed his head down so I could feel his face and his mouth on them.

We ended up on the rug because we were too embarrassed to get on the bed, and we rolled around on it and stroked each other and knocked over the shesh board (we never could find the black peon, after) and rolled all over each other. Marcus started groaning and saying, "Katie, stop," but I didn't see any reason to, and then he clutched me and cried out hard, and went very still. When he started to weep, I held him, and didn't even mind the mess he'd made all over us.

"Who cares about going out?" I whispered into his hair, and he laughed, then, and I licked his salty ear.

⌒

I N A COZY ARMCHAIR IN HIS STUDY, WHERE HE WAS reading a history of the rise of the Council of Lords after the fall of the decadent kings, Lord Ferris received word that David Alexander Tielman Campion, Duke Tremontaine, had arrived at his front door desiring to speak with him.

Lord Ferris smiled. "I am busy at the moment. He is welcome to wait, if he likes."

"Shall I offer him refreshment, my lord?"

"Of course. Nothing too sweet; I believe His Grace likes salty foods. And plenty of wine. He might want some diversion, as well. Why don't you give him this?" He handed the man his book, *The Triumph of the Crescent*. "It might prove instructive."

chapter VIII

THE HOUSEHOLD WAS SO TOPSY-TURVY, THERE WAS a chance no one would notice if we lay on the rug all day. But it was a chance we were not quite willing to take. And so we hunted down all our clothes and put them back on. There would be other mornings, when the duke did not rise early to torture prisoners. He never noticed anything in the morning.

Marcus went out to investigate, while I put my hair back into some kind of order. "He's gone out," he said when he came back. "And we're still not allowed to." He'd brought apple tart; we sat on the window seat feeding it to each other.

We wished we could be sure that what had happened to Lucius Perry had nothing to do with us, but we had to consider the possibility that it did. Maybe we'd led those bullies right to him. Maybe they'd been after us to begin with. One of them had recognized me—though, as Marcus pointed out, I was getting to be pretty well known. But why were we locked in the house now, if not for our own protection? If we hadn't followed Lucius Perry, maybe he never would have been attacked. Unless what happened to Perry had just scared the duke into worrying about us.

Then there was the question of those Tremontaine guards. They had been remarkably on the spot, coming to the rescue like that. Possibly the duke had set them to keep a protective eye on Lucius, or on Glinley's, which was part his, after all. He did have people watching all over Riverside... but maybe—horrible thought!—they'd been there to keep an eye on us. Maybe they'd been following us all along. In which case, the duke knew perfectly well where we'd been. When he got back from wherever he was, there would be ructions.

To take our minds off it, and because the last thing we wanted was for him to return and find us naked on the rug, we went to check on Perry's progress.

For reasons no one could entirely remember, Lucius Perry's nurse was named Gobber Slighcarp, or if they knew, they wouldn't tell us—I mean about his name. Gobber was a very competent nurse. It was perfectly reasonable for him to take care of Perry. He used to surgeon hurt swordsmen, having been thrown out of the College of Physic for unmentionable crimes that no one remembered either.

To make up for what had happened, we tried to make ourselves useful to Gobber Slighcarp. Marcus fetched things from the kitchens. I gave Betty money to go out and buy flowers and scented candles, which are nice when you're ill.

We weren't really eager to see Perry himself. But Gobber came out of the sickroom to say the nobleman wanted to speak to me, and before I could think of an excuse, I was by the hurt man's bedside.

After what I'd observed through the peephole at Glinley's, I couldn't imagine having a conversation with Lord Lucius. But that fled my mind as soon as I saw him now. He didn't look like the same man at all. His face was purple and green. One eye was swollen shut, and his nose was crooked and large and bandaged. And his mouth, his sensual, elegant mouth—

I said, "Oh! I'm so sorry—"

"Not to," Lucius Perry rasped. "You saved me."

"It's better than it looks," Gobber explained to both of us. "It won't heal pretty, but it'll heal all right. Ribs, too—I've seen worse. And if we're careful with that leg, it won't stiffen up too much."

"Come," said Lucius, gesturing with a scraped-up hand. I realized he couldn't see me unless I was near his good eye. "Cousin Artemi'a friend. You know. Mus' marry her."

"Why?"

"Family."

"The family want you to marry Artemisia?" This was awful. He was all wrong for her. And what about Teresa Grey? "But—does she want to? Have you asked her?"

"Ready now," he sighed. "Safe. All m'fault, w'happened. You write her. Ask her to. I'll sign."

Gobber looked at me and shrugged. He had no idea what this was about. But I did. And I wasn't having it.

"I'll write her," I said, and went to find Marcus. He didn't argue, much. And he liked showing how well he could sneak out of the Riverside house without being caught.

Once he left, I went and wrote a letter to Artemisia telling her she was on no account to agree to marriage with Lucius, whatever her family said. I didn't tell her that he was riddled with vice, or that he already loved someone else; I just reminded her that where there was no love there could be no lasting joy. I added that my heart was with her, and I hoped she'd find someone really nice to marry, but if she didn't, she should not marry at all.

Then I did what I should have done ages ago: I went to the duke's chief personal secretary, Arthur Ghent, and explained that Artemisia's family didn't want me writing to her, and might even be reading her letters, so could he please see to it that she got this one safely? Arthur smiled just short of a grin, and said he'd see to it.

Then, in utter penance, and to keep myself distracted, I went and offered to read aloud to Lucius Perry. He let me choose, and I was well into *The King's Hunt* when Marcus returned with the woman from the Hill, the one Lucius Perry truly loved.

She didn't handle it well. Marcus swore to me he really had told her just how bad Perry looked, and that he would get better, but it didn't seem to matter. When Teresa Grey saw Lucius Perry, she made an unhappy sound and clutched at the wall, and

Gobber had to make her sit and put her head down. "Oh, no," she moaned; "oh, no...."

I ran and got lavender water to chafe her wrists with. She had very strong and flexible hands; she could have learned to hold a sword if she'd wanted. "It's all my fault," she said. "Oh, what shall we do? What shall we do? Oh, Lucius..."

I held her hands tightly, and got her to look into my eyes. "It wasn't you," I told her. "Truly, it wasn't. I don't know if you know, but Lord Lucius has been working for Tremontaine."

"I know, all right, you curious child," she said to me, which at least was better than moaning.

"Well, then. It was all because of that. He has a lot of enemies, the duke."

"Does he?" she said in that annoying way adults have of humoring children who are telling them things they already know.

"Yes, well, if you know that already, you'll know this has nothing to do with you. It was someone trying to get at our house."

Teresa Grey stood up. Even with her hair all wild and her dress disordered, she managed to look astonishingly beautiful. "Where is the duke?" she said. "Let him see me, and tell me so himself."

Marcus said, "He doesn't know about you yet. We're the only ones who do."

She looked closely at him. "Is that so? And what do you know about me, pray?"

I said, "You are Lucius Perry's one true love. The rest mean nothing to him—especially not the duke. You are a painter, and a writer, and—well, a Lady of Quality."

She stared at me as though I'd lost my mind. "Oh, this is too much!" she cried. "You! You're a girl! Are you some kind of actress, some protégé of his? Am I supposed to be writing a vehicle for you, is that what this is about? Because I'll tell you right now, I'm not doing a thing for him or for anyone until I find out who's responsible for this. Right now, I—I wouldn't piss on the duke if he were on fire."

"Watch it," Marcus said with surprising heat. "Katie's a lady."

She swirled back to Marcus, and then to me, and back to him again. "You. You were the one who delivered those pigments."

He ducked his head.

"Marcus, you rat!" I said. "You did that without me!"

"Were you in on it, too?" she demanded.

There was a strangled noise from the bed. We all jumped and turned to attend to the hurt man. But there was no need. Lucius Perry was laughing.

"Go away," Teresa told us all, even Gobber Slighcarp.

We went. We left them alone together, and it did not even occur to us to try and look in through the keyhole until much later. They were both asleep, his head on her soft breast, and *The King's Hunt* lying open on the floor beside them.

⌒

THE DUKE TREMONTAINE WAITED IN A YELLOW-AND-black drawing room that was the height of fashion and reminded him of stinging wasps. He was prepared, he told Lord Ferris's man, to wait until tomorrow, if necessary, as long as they would bring him a pillow for the night. He ate only nuts from his pocket, and drank only water, but he opened the book Ferris had sent him and after a few pages took out a pencil nub and started scribbling comments in the margins.

The day was well advanced when Lord Ferris admitted the duke to his study.

He did not bother with preliminaries. "You come unarmed?"

"You know I can't fight."

"That, my lord duke, is becoming increasingly obvious. All the same, if you will empty your pockets, please?"

"You're joking."

"I am not joking. We are alone in this room. Let me see what you carry."

Tremontaine glared at him. "Do you want me to trade my marbles for your string collection and broken top?"

"Do you want me to have you searched? Please don't be offended—or rather, be as offended as you like. We both know you're not going anywhere."

The Duke Tremontaine put three nuts, two handkerchiefs, a penknife and his pencil stub on the table. He fished a little deeper and disgorged a button, two calling cards and half of the Knave of Cups with some calculations scribbled on it.

Ferris looked at them impassively. "And where is my contract?"

"Your what?"

"My marriage contract with your niece."

"She's just a girl," Tremontaine said bluntly. "What possible use can you have for her now? She's much too young."

"Early marriages are a tradition in your family," said Lord Ferris. "She's sixteen now— See? I cared enough to check— older, in fact, than your mother was when you were born, like her mother before her. But you don't respect your own traditions, do you? Your family's, or anyone else's. Do you think the Perrys will be pleased to know you've been employing their son as a Riverside whore? Or the Fitz-Levis, for that matter, who are even now trying to foist him on their not impenetrable daughter? Fussy people, the F-L's."

"You give me too much credit," the duke said. "I didn't find him his trade, I found him already at it."

"They might not believe that."

"They can ask him themselves. I've got him in my house— what's left of him."

Ferris laughed aloud. "If they ask him, he'll blame you, if he's got any sense."

"And say he does? What difference will it make? The Mad Duke debauches another beautiful nobleman—again. All yawn. The question is what they'll say when they learn what you've done to spoil his beauty."

"I?" Lord Ferris cocked his head. "What did *I* do?"

"Oh, come, my lord." The duke gave a pretty good imitation of the older man. "Hired bravos aren't that hard to bully information out of."

"Or to bribe. Of course you'd pay some Riverside tough to say I hired him. You've got plenty of money, we all know that." The duke glared at him. "Face it. You may have friends, I'm not saying you don't—all sorts of eccentric people adore you. But you've got no allies. No one who counts."

Lord Ferris picked up a paper-knife, a long silver tool

ornamented with a lascivious nymph. He rubbed his thumb along her while he talked. "You've brought this on yourself, you know. What do you think I've been doing for the past ten years? Building alliances, creating systems that will hold me. Yes, it's cost me, but I can get more funds, one way or another. People respect me—and they fear me—and well they should, as you now know. Do they fear you . . . Alec? I don't think so. They used to, back in your murderous Riverside days. But you've let that particular power go. You've gotten squeamish. Here I am, the elected leader of the land's most powerful governing council. And you are . . . what, now? An entertainment. A curiosity." He held the nymph up. "For your grandmother's sake, I did try to warn you. Now you're on your own."

"Ferris," said Alec Campion in a curious growl. "You are making me angry."

"Try to control it," Lord Ferris said agreeably, "or you'll never get anywhere in life."

"Very angry," the duke repeated in the same half-musical tone. "It makes me wonder what it would be like to take the battle you've begun to its next logical step. To hire people to attack your people on the streets on no provocation but that they support you. You'd retaliate in kind, of course. I'd need to arm my friends, or have them guarded well. But there are plenty of swords out there, looking for work."

Ferris turned his whole head like a bird, to look straight at the duke with his one good eye. "You would, too, wouldn't you? You'd plunge this city back a hundred years and more, to when liveried houses were fighting each other on the streets, when houses were fortresses, and nobles hired swords to keep from cutting each other down. You'd do all that, rather than capitulate or work out a reasoned, reasonable compromise. You would." Without warning, Ferris slammed his hand against his desk. "*What* was the woman thinking? Making something like you her heir! I admired her, I even loved her for a while, but in the end, she must have been mad."

"They say it runs in the family," the duke said doucely.

"I am hoping that isn't the case."

"Still planning on breeding my niece?"

"We'll merely skip a generation—write you off as a bad egg and then move on. The girl has neither your grandmother's looks nor her charm. Maybe she has brains, though. I trained with the duchess; she passed on to me what she knew of statecraft and the human heart—and believe me, she knew a lot. I've even forgiven her for throwing me over for Michael Godwin; I see now she chose well, he's a capable man." Lord Ferris's nostrils were white, distended. He was breathing rapidly through them. He had lost his temper, but didn't realize it yet. "Or maybe..." he went on cruelly, "maybe you had to sleep with her to get the benefits. I did wonder about you for a while, but now I'm quite sure you never did, or you wouldn't be such a fool."

"I'm crushed."

Eventually, people the duke disliked did lose their temper around him. It was a peculiar talent that he had, and he usually enjoyed it. He waited, now, to see what Ferris would say. The Crescent was working himself up to something unforgivable. The duke wondered what it would be.

"Did she think you'd change, I wonder? Or did she merely think St Vier would keep you in line?"

"We didn't discuss it. Her face was all frozen."

"She thought you'd keep him, though, I'll be bound. I would have bet on it myself. He seemed unreasonably attached to you. What on earth did you do to lose him?"

"How do you know he isn't dead?"

"I know," Ferris said. The ruby at the duke's throat jumped wildly against the lace it was pinned to. "Did he, too, come to find you unbearable? What would it take to drive him from your side? Not hissing, like your whore of an actress, or mockery, like your fat friend. St Vier was a reasonable man, and gifted. Not a man to be bought, as I found to my own sorrow. Perhaps, when his love soured on you, you trusted to all that nice money you have to keep him by you, only to find it wasn't enough. Really, you'd do better to give your niece to me, before she, too, finds you unbear—"

There was a bronze figurine in the duke's hand, and he swung it at Ferris's head—from the side with the eyepatch, of course. Ferris groaned, and went down.

It was a small statue of a god leaning on a pedestal. The pedestal had sharp edges; the back of Ferris's head was bleeding heavily. His eyes were closed, but his hands were moving.

The Duke Tremontaine considered the statue. It had little bits of skin and hair on it. Now that he'd relieved his feelings with one blow, he didn't really fancy bashing Ferris's skull in with it.

Nor did he like the idea of what Ferris would do if he survived now. His eye fell on the nymph, fallen from Ferris's hand. The long knife wasn't silver after all, just a strong alloy plated in silver. He could tell from the weight. He stuffed his neck stock into Ferris's mouth, to discourage breathing as well as noise.

"Listen, if you can hear me," said Alec Campion. "You were right about one thing. The duchess never named me her heir. She believed she was immune to death. Certainly she was very resistant; when it felled her, she stayed breathing for quite some time. They asked her whom she'd chosen, but by then she couldn't answer. They went through a list of names. Maybe yours was even on it; I don't know. But when they got to mine, she made a sign with her hand, and they took it for assent."

Lord Ferris groaned. The duke pulled open the man's jacket; no need to make this any harder than it had to be. Third and fourth ribs, right in between... He closed his eyes, pictured an anatomy text. Richard always made it look so easy. One blow, straight to the heart—if he liked you.

How many men had Alec driven onto St Vier's sword? His turn, now. Loser of knives, lover of steel... It took more force than he was master of. Ferris grunted and thrashed. I'm going to look like an idiot, he thought, if I don't do this right. He took a deep breath, and then struck home.

The duke did not ring for a servant, simply walked out the door, left the house and started walking back to Riverside. He washed his hands at a public fountain, and if a very tall man in very disheveled, very expensive clothing walking the length of the city was hard to miss, he was, if you knew the proclivities of the nobility, easy to ignore. And there had always been something about Alec Campion at his worst, some air of dangerous negligence, that made even the toughest element give him a wide berth.

chapter IX

A FTER DARK, A SMALL, NARROW CARRIAGE PULLED
into the courtyard of the duke's great Riverside house,
the horses sweating and dusty from the road. The footman knew better by now than to try to help his passenger out of
it; he merely opened the door and attended to the baggage, while
the man stiffly eased himself out. He stood for a moment in the
courtyard, waiting, or looking around. Many of the windows were
lit; in others, light passed from window to window as people hurried through the house.

One of the lights came toward him. "Finally," a young
man said. "You're here. He's been waiting for you. Please come
with—" He put his hand out, and jumped at the newcomer's re-
action.

"It's all right," the man said. "I'll follow you."

I N HIS STUDY, THE DUKE WAS BURNING PAPERS. WHEN
the pair came in he looked up but did not rise, just kept

feeding things to the fire. "Good," he said, "you're here. I was afraid the Bridge might be closed."

"Not yet. Will it be?"

"Soon, if they've got any sense."

"Alec, what on earth have you been doing?"

"You didn't get here in time, so I had to kill Ferris myself." The duke waited a moment for the full effect.

"Did you?" his friend asked curiously. "How?"

"Eclectically. But conclusively."

"You didn't poison him, did you?"

"Heavens, no. That would be dishonorable. No, I stabbed him with a nymph."

The other man laughed.

"I was in his house, and his whole staff knows it. I expect to be arrested any minute. So I'm leaving."

"Rather than face a Court of Honor? Look, it's not so bad, really. Did you challenge him first?"

"I forgot. There wasn't time. But I can always say I did. There was no one else there."

"You'll get off, then."

"Not necessarily. I had to whack him on the head first. Not very convincing as a challenge, even for a lenient Court, which this one won't be—did I tell you he was also the Crescent Chancellor?"

"Oh, Alec." St Vier shook his head. "Still, you are the Duke Tremontaine. Maybe you can bribe someone. You have support-ers, surely."

"The whole thing's too much trouble. And anyway, I'm sick of it here. You were right."

St Vier considered the fire. "I know."

For the first time, the young man spoke. "You mean we're leaving the city, my lord? Why didn't you tell me? I'd better pack—"

"I'm going," said the duke. "You're staying."

"No, I'm not. Not this time."

"Yes, you are, Marcus. Katherine's staying, so you're staying. It's all on the desk over there, signed and sealed. Make sure she opens it as soon as I've gone. That's important. Don't look right now—just find me my penknife—I know I put it down there somewhere, and it's gone."

"You're Marcus?" St Vier said. "Why didn't you say so? I thought you were younger."

"He was," said the duke. "They grow."

"So where are we going, anyway?"

"Somewhere nice. Somewhere with bees, and sun, and lots and lots of thyme."

⌒

HE SAT IN HER WINDOW SEAT, WATCHING THE SHADOWS shoot up against the walls of the courtyard as people with torches scurried about with horses and baggage. There was no light in her room. She sat with her knees hugged in her arms, her face pressed to the glass, just tilted so that her breath didn't mist it. It was a play, she thought; it was some kind of play, and when it was over someone would come and tell her what it meant, and what her part would be.

Then she saw him, or thought she did—the man who used to live here and said he'd never come back. He was standing in the courtyard, against a pillar near the well, just standing there looking at it all.

"Master!" Her breath fogged the glass. She struggled with the casement catch. "Master!" He didn't look up. "Master St Vier!" she shouted into the courtyard.

The man turned his head. She couldn't hear what he said. "Wait!" she cried. She bolted down the stairs, around the corridor, around another and out the door.

"It's you!" Katherine called. "Oh my god, it's really you!" She didn't think about whether or not he wanted to be touched; she just flung herself into his arms, and smelt the woodsmoke as he folded her in his cloak.

"Are you all right?" he asked.

"Yes," she gasped. "I'm different, but I'm all right."

"Good." Carefully he unwrapped her from the embrace, and set her before him. "I can't stay," he said. "Your uncle's finally killed someone."

"Oh, no!"

"Oh, yes."

"Are you going to—"

"No. Not this time. I can't stay."

"Please," she said; "I've got things to show you, things to tell you...."

"Let's go inside," he said. "I think that there are things to tell you, too."

I N THE HOUR BEFORE DAWN, THERE WAS A GREAT POUND-ing on the doors of Tremontaine's Riverside house. City guard, some adorned with moldy vegetables that had been flung by Riversiders who resented their incursion on their turf, escorted an officer of the Court of Honor of the Noble Council of Lords bear-ing a warrant heavy with seals that had taken most of the night to get fixed and approved, summoning the Duke Tremontaine before the Court.

A sleepy watchman opened the door. Like most of the house-hold, he'd only just gotten to bed.

"What in the Seven Hells do you want?" he asked.

"By order of the—"

"Do you know what *time* it is?"

"None of your cheek," the officer barked. "Just fetch Tremontaine, and be quick about it."

He wasn't invited in, but he stepped over the threshold any-way, as did as many of his guard as would fit in the tiny old hall-way. He wondered if he would find the Mad Duke wild and bloodstained, or in his cups, or draped with boys and unmention-ables.

A young girl appeared on the stairs above them. She had wrapped a velvet cloak of green and gold over her nightgown, and her long brown hair was plaited for the night.

"Yes?" she said.

"Young lady, I am here for Tremontaine. If you could just—"

"I am the Duchess Tremontaine," she said. "What is it you want?"

CODA

HAVING DEFEATED HER SWORDMASTER IN A SERIous bout that morning, and being in the process of acquiring a new dress that afternoon, the young Duchess Tremontaine was in excellent spirits. She stood in a sunny room overlooking the gardens of Tremontaine House encouraging her chief secretary, a balding young man named Arthur Ghent, to read her correspondence to her. The duchess's personal aide was ensconced in the window seat going over her farm books, eating oranges and lobbing bits of orange peel at her when he thought no one was looking, as she simultaneously tried to avoid them and to hold still for the modiste who was fitting the gown, while her maid begged her not to stand there making a half-naked spectacle of herself in front of everyone.

"I'm perfectly covered up, Betty," the duchess said, trying not to tug at the bodice, which pinched. "I've got yards of sarcenet over quite a lot of petticoat and corset, and a very modest fichu—ouch!"

"A thousand pardons, my lady," the modiste said, "but your

grace's waist has gotten smaller since our last fitting, and it must be taken in."

"It pinches," Katherine fretted. "And the sleeves—they're so tight, I can hardly move my arms. Can't you open up this seam here?"

"It is not the mode, madam."

"Well, *make* it the mode, why don't you? Attach some ribbons right across here—"

"Very seductive," the duchess's personal aide piped up from the window seat.

"Oh, honestly, Marcus. It's just my arm."

The modiste consulted with her assistant. "If my lady will permit us to remove the upper half of the garment, we will see what can be done."

The duchess sighed. "Close your eyes, Arthur. Betty, hand me my jacket. There, is everyone happy? Now, please! Lydia is coming to take chocolate soon, and then Lord Armand and the Godwins are joining us for dinner before we go to the concert—oh, hush, Marcus, it's very lofty and elevated music, not *tweedle tweedle*, Lydia says so—and then Mother's arriving tomorrow, but who knows when she'll really get here—oh, Betty, make sure they haven't forgotten the flowers for her room—and I promised Arthur I would get this business done before then, so now really is the only time. Go on, Arthur."

Arthur Ghent picked up a stack of colorful butterfly papers. "These are next month's invitations—but as time is short today, they can wait 'til last. Let's start with business." He unfolded a plain note from another pile. "The Duke of Hartsholt says you can have his daughter's mare at the price agreed, but only if you confirm it today."

"Tell him yes, then."

"You'll fall off," said Marcus dourly. "You'll fall and break your neck."

"I certainly won't. I grew up riding all over the countryside. This is nothing. But—it does seem a lot for a single horse. Can we honestly afford it?"

Marcus pretended to consult his calculations. "Hmm. Can we afford it? Only if you give up brandy."

"I don't drink brandy."

"Well, then. Get a horse. Get ten if you like—they don't eat much, do they?"

"Ahem," said Arthur Ghent, shuffling papers. "This should interest you. The Trevelyn divorce. Speaking of things you can afford. The lady has produced a written statement of cause for petition, and the lawyers have found an obscure law protecting it from any public scrutiny until the matter has been privately settled—that ought to give the family pause."

"Excellent. What about Perry's pension?"

Arthur extracted another letter. "Lord Lucius sends a note of thanks. He and Lady—Miss, ah, Grey are resident in Teverington. He writes that he is walking greater distances, and hopes soon to be rid of his cane."

"Oh, good! Put it on the stack for me to read later. What about my play?"

"Now as to that..." Arthur Ghent glanced at the door to the room. But the play, if he expected it to materialize, was not there.

"My lady?" The modiste and her assistant eased the duchess back into the top half of her new gown. Ribbons crisscrossed the seam below her upper arm. The duchess flexed her arm, trying a full extend and a riposte, while the modiste stifled a protest that gowns were not made to fight in and she truly hoped the duchess would not so tax her creation—

"This is such lovely fabric," the duchess said. "It moves very nicely, now. Do you think you could do me a pair of summer trousers in it, as well?"

"Oh. My. God." Artemisia Fitz-Levi stood in the doorway, a fat leather-bound tome in the crook of her arm. Her hair fell in perfect ringlets as always, but there was a smudge of dust on her forehead, and her apron, worn to protect a striped silk gown, was dusty, too. Nonetheless, Arthur Ghent straightened his jacket and ran his hand over what was left of his hair and bowed to her. "Katherine." She stared at the gown. "That is—that is beyond— Oh, Katherine, every girl in town is going to want those sleeves!"

The modiste permitted herself a smile of relief. In matters of fashion, Lady Artemisia was seldom mistaken.

"Do you think so?" Katherine said shyly. "I don't want to look silly."

"You won't." Her friend kissed her cheek.

"I'm doing papers with Arthur, and we're almost done." Artemisia stood back against the wall, the image of a useful person staying out of the way. "Go on, Arthur." The secretary handed the duchess two finished letters to approve, which she read standing. "Nothing from my uncle?"

"Nothing new. As far as we know, he and Master St Vier reached the sea and sailed as planned. The next letter may not reach us for some time."

"If he writes at all."

"He'll write," Marcus said. "When he runs out of money. Or books."

"Well, then. Is that it?"

"That's it for now, except for next month's invitations—"

"Invitations?" Artemisia butted in. "For next month? But my dear, no one will be in the city next month! No one who matters. Everyone goes to the country. Here, you'd better give me those." She held out her hand to Arthur Ghent, who delivered the invitations to her with a deep bow. "I'll just see if there's anything worthwhile, though I'm sure there's not." She shoved them in her apron pocket. "You won't want to stay here either, Duchess. Now, I've already gotten a list of your country houses, and I've noted the five most suitable for you to choose from. I can fetch my notes if you'd like."

"Not just yet." Katherine was still a prisoner of laces and pins. "Have you got *History of the Council, Book Four* there? I think we can get a bit more in while they finish my fitting."

Artemisia waved the book in the air, and a wad of paper fell out. "Oops! More invitations—"

But Katherine had seen the plain and heavy sheets. "It is not! It's my play, you wretch—it's the first act, isn't it? She's sent it!"

Artemisia and the secretary exchanged glances; hers was roguish, his helpless. "I was saving it," Artemisia said primly, "until we got to the end of the chapter on jurisdiction reform."

"Are you mad? My first commission? Read it. Now!"

"Yes, Your Grace." With a rustle of skirts, Artemisia seated herself in a sunny spot by the window, aware of all eyes upon her. She carefully unfolded the heavy sheets, thick with writing in a clear black hand, and began:

"*The Swordswoman's Triumph*. By a Lady of Quality.'"

ACKNOWLEDGMENTS

IT TOOK ME QUITE A FEW YEARS TO WRITE THIS BOOK, with starts and stops along the way. Many people encouraged me, and all deserve thanks. I hope I will not leave anyone out, but lest I hope in vain: *Thank you, all. You know who you are—even if I don't.*

Careful readers Holly Black, Gavin Grant, Kelly Link, Delia Sherman and Sarah Smith (the Massachusetts All-Stars) gave me the benefit of their whip-smart brains and nuance-sensitive souls this past year. Justine Larbalestier roused Katherine from her sleep in the file drawer and listened to me read for hours as I shuffled through dog-eared manuscript pages until I fell in love again. Eve Sweetser is one of Tremontaine's very oldest friends, and proved true once more with keen insights and wise suggestions. Paula Kate Marmor made me a promise and kept it. The *Rouges' Ball* was Skye Brainard's idea. eluki bes shahar drew pictures. Debbie Notkin championed the Ugly Girl. Christopher Schelling made me do it before the smoke was cleared and Julie Fallowfield undoubtedly wants to know what took us so long? Mimi Panitch is an invaluable Serpent Chancellor and always says the right thing. Patrick J. O'Connor is generous with both love and erudition. Other wise and patient readers included Beth Bernobich, Cassandra Claire, Theodora Goss, Deborah Manning, Helen Pilinovsky, Terri Windling and of course my editor, Anne Groell.

Many people on LiveJournal generously shared their knowledge of trees and ducks and pregnancy. Joshua Kronengold and Lisa Padol did the fact-checking for an imaginary country; any slips or omissions are mine, not theirs—they did try to warn me. Nancy Hanger is one copy editor in a million. Office Archaeologist Davey Snyder dug me out large blocks of uninterrupted time.

Gavin Grant and Kelly Link gave me a country retreat to write in when I needed it most, and so did Leigh and Eleanor Hoagland.

Finally, I owe a huge debt of gratitude to British writer Mary Gentle, who introduced me to Dean Wayland, who introduced me to the true world of the sword. If not for him, I would not really understand how sharp a sword is and how dangerous; how hard it is to get one to hang properly on your hip, and how easy it is to stand perfectly still while a man with no central vision takes a swing at you with one.

This book and the author owe much of their present delightful existence to Delia Sherman, the perfect editor, lover and friend.

ABOUT THE AUTHOR

Ellen Kushner is a novelist, performer, and public radio personality. Her work includes the weekly national public radio series *PRI's Sound & Spirit with Ellen Kushner*, the recording *The Golden Dreydl: a Klezmer 'Nutcracker' for Chanukah* (Rykodisc CD) and a live performance piece, *Esther: the Feast of Masks*. Her novels *Swordspoint* and (with Delia Sherman) *The Fall of the Kings* share a setting and quite a few characters with *The Privilege of the Sword*. She is a member of Terri Windling's Endicott Studio for Mythic Arts and co-founder of the Interstitial Arts Foundation. She lives in New York City and travels a lot, giving shows and readings, lecturing, and teaching. You can keep up with her whereabouts and learn more about Riverside and its denizens at *www.EllenKushner.com*.

HKENW KUSHN